THE COLOR OF CHARACTER

Glen Shuld

ISBN: 1508955158
ISBN 13: 9781508955153

Dedicated to The Bundtcake

PREFACE

I had a dream. I dreamed I stood slightly to the right and behind Dr. Martin Luther King, at the Lincoln Memorial, on that noteworthy August day in 1963 as he delivered his oft-quoted speech. I looked out over the sea of hopeful, well-intentioned, and earnest black faces that filled the Washington Mall.

I was proud to be there. I knew Mom, Dad, and Grandpa Leo could see me on the TV back home in Michigami, Illinois (a suburb of Chicago). Mom and especially Grandpa were the most socially just persons I knew. Grandpa was a warhorse for the civil rights movement. Grandma was watching too, but she was more concerned with who would clean up the mess left on the mall, "when all those colored people left."

When Dr. King got to the most familiar part of this nugget of American history, that his "four little children will one day live in a nation where they will not be judged by the color of their skin, but by the content of their character," I panicked. That was not how we rehearsed it. He left something out. Conscious of the vast, live audience, I subtly cleared my throat, and nudged him a bit, to no effect. He continued on. So I leaned in closer.

"Dr. King." I whispered with urgency. "You forgot something. You left something out—something important."

He stopped and slowly turned to look at me with eyes narrowed.

"Dr. King, you forgot to say: *and by their conduct,* remember? You want them not to be judged by the color of their skin, but by the content of their character, *and* by their conduct. Remember how we said it was good alliteration with another word beginning with a 'c'? Remember how I told you that a person's conduct is the first hint we have of a person's character. Sometimes that's all we have a chance to see. Their conduct is a manifestation of their character. You agreed. Remember, Dr. King? That was going to be part of the speech, and that's going to help out a lot of people— black and white—in the future if you include those words."

But I lost him. He stared past me, as if through a ghost, turned away, and continued where he left off. He said nothing about *conduct.*

"Get off the stage, honky." "Sit down and shut up, boy." An older, stern-faced, black woman in the audience, looking and sounding like the strict health teacher in my junior high school, opened a small milk carton, and tossed it at me. Just before the contents spilled on my head, I awoke.

CHAPTER ONE

Sunday, June 19, 2011

"I didn't take her phone, you white bitch."

I spun around towards the source of the slur, grabbing Mom's frail arm simultaneously. A middle-aged white woman in summer tourist garb sat on the sidewalk in front of Tiffany's on Michigan Avenue. In a daze, she attempted to examine her skinned left knee, exposed by her khaki shorts. It was her phone in question.

To her left, eight black teens, a mix of girls and boys, took turns smacking the head of a white teenage girl who boldly attempted to stop the alleged thief. A black girl was yanking on the white girl's long blond hair. Yet the white girl held tenaciously to the collar of the much larger black girl who called her a white bitch. She was thrown around like a rodeo rider trying to make eight seconds. The racial epithets continued—all anti-white slurs.

The white, gathering crowd hung back.

"They might have guns."

"Stay away. They don't care if they kill you."

"Animals."

"Where are the damned police?"

With a surge of adrenaline, I threw my gay, 54 year old ass into the mix, along with two young white men. We tried to break open the black circle that enveloped the white girl whose face and hair were red with blood.

"Racists. You're all racists. We didn't do nothing," one of the black girls screamed at no one in particular.

The accusation of racism ripped open memories, and pumped more adrenaline through my body.

With whistles blowing, the foot patrols rushed in from all sides. The cavalry had finally arrived. Squad cars with blue lights flashing and sirens screaming soon followed, blocking two lanes of southbound traffic along Michigan Avenue.

Chicago had been plagued during recent summers by gangs of black youth (the media reported them to be "urban youth," to avoid casting aspersions on their race) riding the L from their murderous neighborhoods to the tourist centers, fashionable shops, and popular Northside beaches and parks. Once arrived, they descend on stores en masse, looting and fleeing in the safety of numbers. They attack crowds of unwary pedestrians, knocking them aside, grabbing purses, and phones, and trampling the gardens along the parkway.

In the parks, they block pathways, and knock people off bikes, kicking them as they steal their cell phones, purses, or anything else of value. The same occurs at the beaches. Over the Memorial Day holiday, using the excuse that it was too hot and crowded, the mayor issued an unprecedented order to close one of the most popular beaches. The families who were ushered off the beach didn't have to be told that the heat was a politically correct excuse to shut down what had been a haven from the heat for the past century. The truth could not be comfortably told. The presence of a few hundred black youths victimizing the mostly white beach-goers, overwhelmed the surprised and understaffed police detail assigned to the normally peaceful lakefront.

The masses were sent through the tunnels under Lake Shore Drive, and deposited on the Magnificent Mile and the Gold Coast where the black youth went on a crime spree. They eventually forced the closure of Chicago Avenue where they had invaded a McDonalds on their way to the Red Line subway that would return them to their South Side turf.

As the police attempted to sort the parties involved in the melee in front of Tiffany's, I returned to Mom, and put my arms around her tiny shoulders. Tears streamed down her face. The matter of race in America had been breaking her heart for over forty years. She couldn't cope with the dissonance between the ideals she once held and a worsening reality.

She accompanied me to the police station to give my statement. The alleged muggers were minors, and released to their families, free to come back another day. When relatives showed up to claim their kids, the shouts of racism and police brutality echoed off the metal file cabinets lining the cinderblock walls.

"My boy's a good boy. He don't hurt nobody."

"Go ahead and blame the black kids when you know it's the white kids."

"The police are killing our children, and blaming it on gangs."

My insides knotted. I watched a policeman try to talk to an angry mother as she held out her hand in front of his face, and turned her head away. She was not going to listen to a bigoted, white police officer. The black police officers were called "plantation nig---s," (although I didn't say it, I'm not comfortable putting it in print).

I escorted Mom outside. We were tense. Violence threatened. Our ears rang with the slurs heaped on everyone by the youths and their families.

We cancelled our plans to walk to the Art Institute, attend the member's preview of the latest exhibit, and then take lunch at a nearby restaurant. We hailed a taxi, and went back to my place. From there, I drove Mom back to her house.

The event garnered no mention on the local evening news, and only a paragraph in the next day's newspapers. There was no mention of the race of the alleged perpetrators or the victims. The readers' comment section of the online version of the newspaper said what the paper didn't.

"We all know these gangsters are black. Who are you protecting?"

"Where are Al Sharpton, Jessie Jackson, Louis Farrakhan, and the rest of the town criers who would demand public apologies, and lead marches if the perpetrators were white—which they almost never are?"

And most to the point:

"How are we ever going to resolve black white issues if we can't talk about them honestly?"

Ironically timed, a lengthy op-ed piece in the paper opined that white racism did not disappear with the election of President Obama. Why, the author asked, did it remain so intractable? Why did so many whites hold prejudices against their black compatriots?

CHAPTER TWO

1965 - 1969

My first day of third grade was no big deal. It should've been memorable; since it was the day my elementary school was integrated. That morning, there were to be three black students in every classroom. My white classmates and I were indifferent to their color. Our parents had not instilled any fear or suspicion in us—only the usual curiosity about new kids. Were they nice? Smart? Bullies? Athletes? Where did they live? Would they be my friends?

They dressed in what we called birthday party clothes; the kind of clothes you wore to Sunday school. Our regular school clothes were less fancy.

That's the day I met Cleon, Roger, and Linette, nicknamed Etti. Their arrival had been carefully planned over the previous year by the progressive school board that oversaw our district, and by our approving parents.

I lived in Michigami. Our town was newer and more modest than Hampden, its older neighbor to the east. Hampden is the gateway to Chicago's elite north shore and was the home of my new black classmates. Michigami experienced explosive growth after World War II, when returning soldiers, with help from the GI Bill, completed college, and bought newly constructed, modest homes. All of Michigami's residents were white, with a slight Jewish majority. Many of our parents were the first or second generation of their families born in America. Our ancestors were part of Lady Liberty's wretched refuse who fled for their impoverished lives from the violent, anti-Semitic pogroms of the Poles, Lithuanians, Romanians, Hungarians, Russians, the Tsars and the churches.

In spite of American anti-Semitism, which thrived in the 1920s and 1930s of their childhoods, our parents believed America to be the greatest country in the world, and that they were the luckiest Jews since before the Romans conquered Israel. Their deeply rooted religious belief in social justice was in complete harmony with America's doctrines, at least as they were written.

I'm not sure of the historical reason why our corner of Michigami was assigned to the Hampden school district. This quirk of history created a unique, potentially volatile mix in the junior high school I would attend in a few years. That school comprised Michigami's white Jews, Hampden's minority blacks, and a small percentage of white Gentiles.

For one hundred years, the elegant town of Hampden had a small, segregated black population. They had been the servants who worked in the large homes to their east, and in the other towns that bordered Lake Michigan. These communities lined up along what became the commuter railroad to downtown Chicago as they evolved into the prestigious North Shore.

For nearly a century, Hampden's black community straddled the range of the middle class, and remained in the same neighborhood, confined to segregated schools until high school. There the blacks and whites of Hampden were educated in the massive school with a national reputation for excellence. Within its walls, they remained segregated for decades.

The blacks in my third grade class were the most polite kids I'd ever met. They called our teachers "ma'am," a strange word to our tongues. The boys dressed in white shirts, and Cleon wore a different color "dickey" under his shirt each day. I loved dickeys, (how prophetic). The girls wore frilly dresses, often with black patent leather shoes.

Whether instinctively, or from lessons learned at home, we knew the right thing to do was to approach the new kids, and include them in our playtime. After school, on a warm and windy September day, my best friend Ken and I went over to Cleon's house. It was a day of many firsts. Cleon's was the first home of a black person, a Christian, and a resident of Hampden that I visited.

Like many of the homes in his part of Hampden, Cleon's house was a white clapboard house that looked more like those found in small towns than in large suburbs. Inside, everything was subdued in color and material, with rugs on the hardwood floors instead of wall-to-wall carpeting—décor Mom would've called "Gentile." Today I would call it, "tasteful on a modest budget."

Cleon's mother was young and pretty. She wore a white sleeveless blouse and a tight brown skirt that stopped at her knees. She seemed pleased that Cleon brought us home as she sat us down around her kitchen table, and served us homemade cookies along with milk. I'm not sure what I expected to find, but nothing seemed out of the ordinary.

Cleon had a ping-pong table in his basement, and that's how we spent our afternoon, until Ken and I had to get home for dinner. After that, Cleon was often at my house, and we played with my slot car set. Grandma loved him. She said he was the sweetest little boy I ever brought home. When his mother came to pick him up, she always spent time chatting with Grandma and Mom, who, by that time of day, was usually home from the school where she worked.

During one of those talks, Cleon and I stood next to our respective mothers as Melva, our black housekeeper, passed through the foyer carrying cleaning supplies. Mom's eyes started to dart around betraying some discomfort. The notion of a black woman as a maid was transitioning from a norm to an offensive cliché. If Mrs. Jones only knew how much I loved Melva, and how integral to my family she was, surely she wouldn't see anything undignified about her position.

Trust grew with familiarity. Grandpa got three tickets, so he and I could take one of my friends to a Cubs' game. I asked Roger Parker, a black classmate. Dad honked his horn in front of Roger's house in Hampden that Saturday morning, on his way to drop us off at the L. Roger's mother peered out suspiciously, and then she opened the window.

"What do you want?"

I jumped out of the car, and started towards the front door. "Isn't Roger coming to the Cubs game with us?" It was Mrs. Parker who was confused. Roger had told her about the invitation earlier in the week, but she told Roger that the white boy was probably playing a joke on him.

"Why would some white boy take you to a Cubs game? I don't want you to be disappointed when nobody shows up here to take you." Roger explained this to me later as we rode the L to Wrigley Field.

After a moment, Mrs. Parker smiled from ear to ear, and waved towards the car holding up her index finger to indicate that Roger would be out in one minute. He soon came bounding out of the house with his Cubs hat on, and wearing his mitt. I saw delight in Mrs. Parker's face as she waved good-bye and closed the door.

Roger was a well-liked, friendly guy, and that's why none of us gave him a hard time for struggling whenever it was his turn to read aloud. We snickered at Bill Herman, a heavy, white kid who read below grade level, but we encouraged Roger by whispering the words to him. Could we be accused of patronizing Roger because he was black, or would it be more appropriate to say we were being cruel to Bill Herman because he was overweight?

Roger had a habit of sucking his thumb when he was uncomfortable, even refusing to speak. Still we overlooked this odd behavior, and reached out to him. He was just plain likable.

My appreciation for the unique senses of humor of black women was formed in the third grade as a result of my friendship with Etti. She was a plump girl with neat rows of braids. Etti was the funniest kid in class. She made jokes under her breath about teachers, especially our gym teacher. Etti's unique phrases such as "upside her head," "kick her booty," and "beaten with a switch," were new to us. She sang funny songs that she wrote in her head about various people, especially teachers.

After a game of *steal the bacon* in gym class, we changed from our gym shoes to our street shoes, and walked back to class. Etti spontaneously broke into song as she danced and twirled in her powder blue dress. "That lady sure is stanky, and she ain't got no butt, uh-uh. If she comes at me with a switch, she can kiss my booty." Etti danced along repeating these lyrics, until we were back in our seats.

Near the end of fourth grade, in May of 1967, the school board decided they would bus more blacks into Michigami's grade schools at the start of the next school year. We would all be together in junior high school in a few years anyway. To ease the transition for the new kids, in May of 1967 the school board instituted an orientation day at our school for the incoming black students. I was given one of the coveted buddy positions: to accompany a newcomer as he became acquainted with the school. I arrived that day anticipating the important role I would play by helping someone to feel at home. I suspected that my potential protégée would be nervous.

George Turner was tall, lanky, soft-spoken, and unflappable—characteristics that made him seem mature for a ten year old. Proud that I had such a cool black guy as my buddy, I acted protective—or perhaps possessive—of George. I explained to him how to get around the small school; pointed out the nice teachers, and other things that I thought were important. He listened politely, but didn't seem interested in anything I had to say. Ben Rubin, the most popular kid in school, was roughhousing with his black buddy, and they seemed to be having a lot more fun.

Then the games began, consisting mostly of track and field events that allowed George's physical prowess to explode into view. I was shoved aside as hordes of admiring white kids surrounded George hoping to become his friend. One of the competitions was a long jump. I drove my skinny body a respectable distance—far enough so that there was no derisive laughter. Then it was George's turn. His long legs looked like stilts under his black trousers. He took to the air for so great a distance that he appeared to fly. Kids rushed at him from all sides shouting words of wonder, and stretching to pat George on the back. Our gym teacher said he would have to check, but he guessed George broke our school long jump record.

As George's popularity kept him busy and away from me, I waved to him a few times. He'd found a kindred athletic spirit in Ben Rubin, the only one who came close to George's physical abilities.

The following September, on the first day of fifth grade, I ran up to George on the playground to say, "Hi." He looked down at me with absolutely no recognition in his eyes.

George was not in my class that year, so there was little chance for a friendship to develop, even if he had liked me. As the years went on I remembered how my excitement at being assigned to be George's buddy quickly turned to disappointment. George never spoke to me again. He went on to continued popularity, and earned a track scholarship to a leading university.

Years later, a white co-worker asked me if I knew a George Turner from grade school. Her "absolutely delightful" new next-door neighbor—she lived in a very exclusive neighborhood—went to junior high in Hampden during the same years that I did.

"I asked George if he remembered you, Glen, but he said he never heard of you. Do you remember him?"

"Nope. Never heard of him." I pursed my lips, and shook my head back and forth decisively, as if somehow George could feel slighted by my response.

Other blacks bussed to our school from across the canal with George included, Kevin McPherson, his sidekick Curtis, and the towering Serena. Kevin was square-faced and muscular; Curtis, lean and lithe. Light-skinned Serena kept her eyes fixed in angry slits. Their behavior was unfamiliar to us. This trio fought with teachers, and had no fear of being sent out to the hall where they pushed unsuspecting white kids into lockers. They weren't even fazed by a visit to the principal's office. To our surprise, Serena, a *girl*, was the most violent of the three.

They and others among the additional kids bussed to our school that year, came predisposed to dislike the rest of us. The other white kids and I attempted to befriend them, but we were rebuffed. We made an unconscious group decision to keep our distance, and to simply observe both them and the adults in authority who tried to figure out how to respond. We watched our black friends, like Cleon and Etti, navigate the increasingly choppy waters between the angry, sometimes violent new kids, and the rest of us.

One day I was acting the class clown, as I often did, and my teacher sent me out in the hall. This was considered punishment, and I took it seriously enough that I would never confess it at home. As I stood outside the door to the class, bored and waiting for the official wave from Mrs. Klein to re-enter, if I "were willing to exercise some self control," a lone figure slowly approached from the other end of the hall. He moved slowly, zigzagging from one side of the hall to the other, looking into classrooms. Then he noticed me. I looked like a lost seal pup to a hunting shark named Kevin McPherson. He approached with his usual saunter and sneer.

"Hey, Kev," I said, willing the tension away. "What're you doing out here? Did you get in trouble, like me?"

Without a word, he put his hands on my chest and pushed me up against the lockers.

"Gimme a quarter, boy."

I pushed back at him. "Why do you need a quarter?" I tried to buy some time as I looked quickly in both directions for a teacher to save me.

Kevin put me in a headlock. "You better give me a quarter, honky," he muttered, "or I'll kick your ass."

"Mr. McPherson! What do you think you're doing?" The librarian shouted from the stairwell door.

Kevin released me. "Glen, return to your classroom, and tell Mrs. Klein I sent you back. Kevin you come with me."

Kevin was suspended from school for three days, and I feared he would beat me up when he returned, but that didn't happen— at least not for another three years.

In the spring of fifth grade, in the wake of Martin Luther King's assassination, many of Chicago's blacks rioted through their own neighborhoods. Some of the fathers of my white classmates owned retail stores in those neighborhoods, employing blacks from the surrounding community. The businesses were burned down, their owners and the jobs they brought never returned. The vacant lots still remain. Being white in a black majority community had become life threatening.

Sixth grade meant it was time for the kids in Michigami to migrate over the canal to the junior high school located in the black neighborhood of Hampden.

To outsiders, Michigami was an undiversified, Jewish suburb that served as a postwar step from the city into America's growing middle class of homeowners. The incomes and postwar houses were modest by the standards of Chicago's north shore, but those of us residing within Michigami, attending the three elementary schools that funneled into the Hampden junior high school, were keenly aware of economic and other demographic differences that existed among our enclaves.

My school and our immediate neighborhood had originally been off-limit to Jews. Prosperous Irish-Catholics built their colonial style homes in the 1940s and '50s surrounding St. John's Church. The majority of property deeds had clauses restricting Jews and "Negroes" from purchasing the homes.

On June 13th of 1968, as we said good-bye to elementary school, Americans were on edge due to a paroxysm of violence that seemed to drag us inexorably to a dark place. Race riots after Dr. King's death in April were barely behind us; only one week had passed since Robert Kennedy's assassination. On the horizon: the Democratic National Convention, with its angry, youthful protesters, and violent police response; the killing of Fred Hampton; and the Manson murders. In spite of the national turmoil, my friends and I were only anxious about matriculating to junior high school.

With 270 fifth graders merging into one, sixth grade class, new pecking orders were established. Our pre-existing reputations were now put up for re-examination. Like-minded kids from each school gravitated to each other. The factors, both hard and nebulous, that made a kid cool or queer, or smart or dumb were universal.

Black kids had additional matters to contend with. They were absorbing increasingly loud and repetitive messages of black pride, black power, and black identity, with little direction accompanying these messages, and no guidance on how to apply them positively in school or elsewhere. Without guidance, many of my black classmates entered junior high believing they should be angry, and in battle mode against "honky." Some of the black kids absorbed the barrage of black power and pride messages, and cooked them into a sense of entitlement. No one in a leadership position at school diffused their anger, or gave an alternative way to channel it, other than to tell the black kids to feel some sort of free-floating pride in being black. I don't think the kids were sure of the origins of that pride, or how to manifest it for good, and no one was waiting for them at the school entrance with an award for showing up black. I don't know how I would've behaved with all that weight on my shoulders, and no one to guide me in the direction of personal accomplishment. The black kids groped for identities and status among themselves, in a parallel dimension that rarely overlapped the rest of us.

The predatory Kevins and Serenas replaced the friendly Cleons and Ettis as iconic black classmates. Few of the friendships with our black elementary school classmates survived the passage through junior high. No dramatic episode marked their devolution. By the end of sixth grade, our interactions dissolved into noncommittal nods and brief "heys," and our extracurricular playtimes came to an end. A new acquaintanceship formed between some of the black and white kids, but these rarely developed the intimacy shared in close friendships within the races. We became familiar strangers.

CHAPTER THREE

New Years Eve 1970

This was to be the year we'd refer to as the year Grandpa *died* and the year of my *incident*. Four decades later, when few of us are left to remember the year firsthand, we never say Grandpa was *murdered*, perhaps trying to avoid any residual pain. My *incident*, revolving as it did around race relations, is still a touchy subject we never mention.

The '60s would not go quietly into history. The revolutions they brought, although rooted in those ten years, continued unfinished, and branched continuously. That night, at age twelve, I stood at the entrance of the futuristic sounding decade of the 1970s, unable to imagine a more complex world. More precisely, I *sat* at the entrance of the new decade, in a worn velvet theater seat, in a neighborhood movie palace that wouldn't survive to see 1980. I leaned on my right arm to catch the scent of Mom's peppermint gum, thus diluting the odor of Grandma's Ben Gay emanating from my left. We watched Oliver Twist try to escape Bill Sykes, while Londoners sang catchy tunes. Outside of this isolation booth, the planet reeled. Our world had been knocked from its orbit of complacency during the decade that at the stroke of midnight would pass into history.

As midnight came and went unremarked, it was a malapropos passing of the tumultuous decade—the only one I really knew since the time of my birth, in 1957. I had no memory of the Eisenhower years. I was in first grade in 1963-64 when Lee Harvey Oswald and the Beatles blew open the doors to unrest. Or was it Pandora's Box? Now, in the darkened movie theater, there was no way to acknowledge that the '60s had given way to 1970. The audience for this second-run movie was older and probably immune to the thrill I felt at the fact that when I returned to school, I'd date my papers with a "7" instead of a "6."

Without missing a beat, at the turn of the decade my usual demons continued to scout out my mind for places to settle. On the screen I watched what I believed to be the safe, Victorian world where there was no room to doubt one's identity.

After the movie, my family's immediate concerns were modest. My internal struggles and those of humanity became a dim backdrop to the more pressing problem we faced as we entered the Gold Coin Delicatessen, ninety midnights into the New Year.

"Booth or table?" the beehive-haired, gum-chewing cliché of a diner waitress, whose name badge proclaimed her to be Lana, asked no one in particular. The difficulty Jews had in selecting seats at restaurants had not yet become fodder for Jackie Mason, and was a real concern to Mom and Grandma. Drafts, the proximity to doors (entrance, bathrooms, kitchen), who else was seated in the vicinity, lighting, heating or air conditioning vents, and the perceived cleanliness of the table or chairs or booths, all had to be weighed and ranked in a delicate balance. Based on past experience with my family, the chance of some hostess or maitre'd making all those calculations, and coming out with the correct location to seat us was nil.

Lana waited patiently, and we finally settled on a table in the center of the room, under a light fixture, away from any front entrance draft or germs traveling from a bathroom. There were no vents threatening to blow air on anyone. The dark, imitation walnut Formica table looked clean, and it was neatly set with mix and match silverware. Mom would inspect each utensil when she removed it from its napkin sheath. No one detected any objectionable material left on any of the imitation colonial wooden chairs that Grandma would eventually find too hard for her behind. No one sat at tables in our immediate vicinity.

The dark walls were made of sheet paneling that might have been left over from someone's basement remodeling project. Gold tinsel framed the wide window facing the street. A sign strung across a mirror behind the cash register spelled out Season's Greetings. For balance, there was a plastic Hanukkah menorah with all nine, low-voltage, orange candle tip bulbs glowing from the ledge beneath the mirror.

There were few New Years revelers in the restaurant, which sat on the southern border of Hampden along Evans Avenue, facing the northern border of Chicago across the street. It was a quiet commercial block of small family businesses. Nearby residents had probably gone to bed shortly after Guy Lombardo and his orchestra played *Auld Lang Syne*.

Within five minutes we had placed our orders. I hungered for my usual corned beef on rye with mustard, to be washed down with a chocolate phosphate.

Our conversation that night ranged from innocent chatter to analytical and self-critical musings, and finally, controversial topics—whispered in case someone was taking it all down on a tape recorder for Walter Cronkite to play back on the *CBS Evening News*. The world was in flux, and decades or even centuries-old social norms were crumbling. It was difficult to know what was still okay to talk about, or what was newly permitted that had previously been taboo.

Non-celebrities like us didn't make those decisions. We learned on our feet. The daily list of "in" and "out" came from sources of authority, such as television situation comedies.

"Did you notice how *shmutzadik* (*see the Glossary for Yiddish terms*) everything was back then? All that fish and food lying out in the open market, and all those people with dirty hands dancing around it? Feh." Grandma Mae weighed in with her review of the movie as she shifted the lox omelet around on her plate.

Grandpa Leo finished a gulp of his coffee with a drawn out "ah" sound that I always found annoying. "I'm glad you enjoyed the movie Mae. You took away the most important thing." He enjoyed gently chiding her, although Grandma, who couldn't laugh at herself, didn't appreciate it. Grandpa had the cerebral advantage, but Grandma spoke from the gut, frequently trumping Grandpa's humorous pokes. When there was no television handy, Grandma and Grandpa provided entertainment.

"Who bit you in the *tuches*, Leo? I'm just asking a question. I liked the picture. That little boy took a good part. I'm just saying I wouldn't eat that food." Grandma glanced at the rim of her coffee cup for any telltale lipstick marks from a previous user. Her weak blue eyes squinted, and she pursed her lips giving the cup a grudging approval.

"It looks like we are transitioning smoothly into the '70s. Nothing seems to have changed." Mom laughed at her own attempt at humor, looking to Dad and me, encouraging our laughter. Grandpa loved to see us laugh. Dad smiled and nodded knowingly as he reached over, and put a hand on my head, rubbing it affectionately, and leaning forward to see if I was smiling. I was. I felt loved and safe at that moment. As long as there were no peers to view this Rockwellian scene, I could soak it up.

"That *Sheyna* Wallis, the one who played Nancy," Grandma continued unperturbed, "she must be Jewish with a name like Sheyna. Like my Glen here, the *sheyna punim*." She reached over and pinched my cheek. I can remember every detail of Grandma's hands. She kept her nails short and rarely polished. It made her fingers appear stubbier and less elegant than Mom's. Grandpa had given Grandma some expensive jewelry over the years, but she kept it hidden in one of the dresser drawers that she lightly scented with lilac sachets. Lilacs were Grandma's favorite flower, and like me, she adored any shade of purple. I read somewhere that purple was the favorite color of immature people and homosexuals.

Grandma never removed her simple, silver wedding band that had tiny, linked hearts carved into it, but the rest of the jewelry remained in its flowery tomb. She never sought to impress with possessions—only with her housekeeping, and by the successes of her descendents.

I'm sure I was beaming after Grandma's reference to my "pretty face." As long as none of my friends were around to hear Grandma's unending ways of praising me, I actually enjoyed it, and found it reassuring. I had enough feedback in my short life to know I was a fairly cute boy, but I craved praise, particularly for my appearance and my intelligence. I didn't hold out for recognition of my athletic ability, so it helped to be smarter and at least as good looking as the jocks.

Mom rolled her eyes, and took a break from her Julian salad. "Ma, I think her name is ShayNEE, not Sheyna. And I guarantee you she isn't Jewish." I noticed a little of the usual impatience with Grandma in Mom's voice.

Not one to take correction lying down, Grandma shot back, although she looked at Dad for reassurance. "Oh? And do people know Dinah Shore, Shelly Winters, and Barbra Streisand are Jewish?" Grandma was almost indignant.

Mom's face showed her exasperation. "Ma, everybody knows Barbra Streisand is Jewish. She hardly tries to hide it. The Egyptians berated Omar Sharif for playing opposite her in *Funny Girl*, because she was Jewish. It was on the news."

I heard Grandpa sigh. I knew he wouldn't miss an opportunity to teach me some sort of lesson. Although he spoke to no one in particular, his eyes focused on me. He lowered his voice, and leaned into the table, a sure sign that controversy cometh.

"The knee-jerk hatred of all Jews by so many Arabs is immoral and disturbing."

"There's good and bad in all groups, Leo. Look at some of our Jews." That was the extent of Grandma's geopolitics. It aligned with her view of life in general: you had to take the good with the bad.

"This is different." Grandpa was still looking at me as he continued using his quieter voice. "There is a difference between randomly immoral people and an entire population that takes an immoral position. The anti-Jewish propaganda is dangerous and reminiscent of Nazism. How can it be so soon after the Holocaust?

"Okay, Dad. Let's not get into that now. Let's not get too serious." Mom worshipped Grandpa, but she wasn't in the mood for the direction the discussion was taking. Grandpa hadn't finished his lesson, and wasn't to be deterred, until I had something to think about. He gently rested his palm on Mom's hand.

"Just let me finish a moment Eileen. Glen, you remember this: sometimes, people who mean you no direct harm give free rein to those who do. Their reasons could be indifference, self-preservation, or a willingness to go along. After so much propaganda, they convince themselves the haters must be telling the truth. It reduces any internal conflict they might feel."

Now when I recall this scene in the diner, Grandpa was amazing. He could speak coherently and unscripted no matter the hour of the day, providing the subject matter was related to Jews or social justice or both. He continued, "In time, the besieged Jews will be written off as a scourge that was removed. History provides examples. You don't have to go back too far or too far away. It isn't the Indians who write our history books."

"Dad, that's actually quite profound, but it's New Year's Eve, and the start of a new decade..."

Grandpa was unstoppable, although he maintained an air of serenity that added heft to his words, in a way that a tirade could not.

"Can you imagine the global uproar if we dared say about any other people what they say about us? Of course we never would. Why? We are taught that God cares about all His children. Glen, what's the lesson at the Passover Seder surrounding the ten plagues? You know what I'm talking about. Tell us."

I was caught off guard. I expected to listen, and not to participate. Mom and Dad looked at me expectantly.

"He's tired, Dad. It's almost two o'clock in the morning." Mom pointed to her watch for emphasis. Her wrists were tiny, and the watch face was minuscule compared to the big round circle of Dad's timepiece.

In trying to shield me from the possibility of not knowing the answer to Grandpa's question, Mom had bought me some time.

"I know, Ma. Grandpa is talking about how we take a drop of wine out of our glasses for each plague to reduce our celebration, because we know God isn't happy about drowning the Egyptians in the Red Sea, because everyone is His child."

Grandpa beamed, and for the first time since we started this discussion of Arabs, he considered the food on his plate. "That's right, Glen. We have to treat everyone with dignity, because we're all made in God's image."

Now it was Dad's turn to take control.

"Dad, are you going to watch the Rose Bowl tomorrow with Glen and me?" Dad had jumped in to curry favor with Mom. I looked forward to spending that time with Dad and Grandpa. Neither Dad nor I followed sports closely, but he saw it as an opportunity to spend some man-to-man time with me. If we had talked more openly with each other back then, we might have chosen to do something else together. Mom found pleasure in seeing us sharing time. She often joined us, and became more involved in the action than either of "her men."

My older sister Nancy grudgingly accepted my time with Dad, only because she couldn't bear to sit and watch "anything so stupid." Grandma didn't understand subtleties, and if she saw Grandpa, Dad, and me seated together in front of the television, she took it as an opportunity to share random thoughts with a captive audience. If Grandma had something to say, the Bears' defensive line couldn't stop her.

"Of course I'll watch. But I'm more interested in seeing Penn State beat Missouri in the Orange Bowl, so I can call Uncle Irv in St. Louis, and gloat a bit." Grandpa and his older brother had a feigned rivalry. They used it as an excuse to talk to each other more often than they needed to.

"Speaking of all that, Eileen, we should call Aunt Agnes tomorrow to wish her and Faye a Happy New Year." We knew how Grandma's mind worked, and no one questioned her train of thought. The Orange Bowl represented Florida oranges to Grandma. Aunt Agnes spent the winters in Miami Beach, and her daughter Faye was visiting her. The connection couldn't be clearer.

With a swishing sound, the revolving door deposited two, black, teenage girls with four small children into the restaurant. Grandma began to cluck her tongue.

"Look at that," she said, and we were back down to a conspiratorial whisper. "Those girls with those little children. Those kids should be in bed, and those girls are barely out of high school. How are they going to raise those little children?" Then Grandma sat back, and nodded her head once, blinking her eyes for emphasis as she ran her hand down her ample bust, smoothing out any wrinkles on her purple wool dress.

"They may not be able to," Grandpa answered, shaking his head thoughtfully. "You and I and others might have to help them out."

"Let's stop right there," Mom hissed. "Let's not make any assumptions. How do you know if those are their children or younger sisters? Maybe they're babysitting. Dad, you know better than anyone how it could be with them."

Grandma raised an eyebrow at Mom's implication. I caught it, and knew she was thinking that this could be one of those rare, pleasurable examples of Mom doubting Grandpa's wisdom. Maybe this was a sign that 1970 would be a good year for Grandma; Mom would agree with her more than with Grandpa.

"Eileen, you know your old father better than that. I'm *not* judging, and I *am* speaking from my experience at the law center. Mother might be right, and if she is, the possible difficulties that lie ahead for those children sadden me."

"What decent babysitter has babies out at two in the morning? Who's kidding whom?" For Grandma the world was black and white, requiring little analysis beyond her instantaneous categorizations.

"Mom and Dad, I think we should enjoy each other's company, and celebrate another New Year that finds all of us healthy." Dad quietly drew a line in the sand. Mom's parents accommodated him. In Grandma's eyes, her beloved son-in-law was the one person who could do no wrong. She smiled at him.

Grandpa lifted his cup in a toast. "Here, here, Jerry. Good idea. Here's to 1970—a big year for us, when our Glen will become a *bar mitzvah*. We should all dance at his wedding someday, and find the world in peace." We toasted with coffee, water, and my phosphate. Grandpa made that extended "ah" sound again.

Grandma put her spin on Grandpa's toast. "I'll be happy to make it to Glen's *bar mitzvah* with this pain in my knee. I'm telling you, if that doctor got his license in this country, I'm Chinese."

"Mother, just toast with us please." Mom shook her head, and half smiled, half smirked. The year was off and running, and we would have to struggle to keep up with it.

I kept one eye on the black party seated in a booth by the window, and I looked for the behaviors I had come to expect after a year and a half of attending junior high school.

So much had changed from the first few years of integration at my elementary school. By some definitions, many of my friends and I had transitioned from innocent babes to closet racists.

CHAPTER FOUR

Wednesday, January 14, 1970

Winter vacation had been over for more than a week. Thank the Lord for the recently declared King holiday, since it meant no school the next day. Lincoln's birthday, always an important one in Illinois, was a cold month away. Today I faced the petty world of seventh grade where a daily minefield of threats to popularity threatened each of us. For boys, our perceived masculinity was our most valued and protected asset. For girls it was looks—in some cases as specific as breast size. For everyone, it was that elusive quality of coolness. None of our preoccupations had anything to do with formal education—an incidental of showing up to class.

I was still asleep enjoying my favorite, but rare dream of self-propelled flight. I wafted above the trees that stood at the street corner next to the grade school I used to attend. The bare winter trees allowed the kids and the crossing guard on the street below to notice me, and they began to point in amazement and envy. I was beyond the reach of the pettiness of the playground.

My status soared invincibly with the ability to fly, so I pretended to ignore the oohs and aahs below as they ascended to my privileged ears.

Something grabbed my leg. Had I gotten stuck in one of the upper branches of a tree?

"Come on, Glen. I want to make this bed. It's time for you to get up."

It was no tree. It was Grandma. I tried futilely to shut out the intrusion, but Grandma was persistent. I opened my eyes, and crashed mercilessly back to reality, sentenced to life on the ground with everyone else.

Grandma was in the housedress and no-nonsense shoes that she wore when she was tidying up, enforcing the message that she was locked and loaded for housework. Making my bed was next on her list.

"Alright, Grandma. Just a second." I tried not to sound annoyed, since it wasn't her fault that she had to yank me from my reverie. Dad, Mom, and Nancy already left for the day, so it fell to Grandma to see that I was ready for school. I closed my eyes for a second to see if I could conjure up the joyous feeling of floating, if only for a moment, but I failed.

I had taken the habit of wearing my briefs under my pajamas, in order to hide the fact that I woke up every morning with an erection. While some boys might take pride in their stiff penises, I was uncomfortable flaunting my maleness around anyone—especially, but not only, around family. The underwear also kept nocturnal emissions from leaving telltale signs on my sheets for Grandma or Melva, our housekeeper, to discover. I didn't think about the telltale signs in my underwear.

I took showers before going to bed. My showers were taking longer than they used to, because I used my alone time to masturbate. The thought of a shower in the cold morning was unappealing. I brushed my teeth, and washed my face, and then stuck my head under the faucet to get my dark brown hair to fall the way I wanted it to. I made a neat part on the left side, and brushed it to swoop down over my forehead, just above my eyes. When I was younger, I would hear Mom's friends marvel that my eye color changed from gray to blue to green depending on what I wore. They said I had "bedroom eyes," and that girls would fall for them. This pleased me.

I went back to my room, and took off my pajamas, leaving on my white Hanes briefs. I pulled a Hanes t-shirt from my top drawer. My dresser, in fact, everything in my room, was neat and orderly to please Grandma, Melva, and me. It was part of my pattern to try to maintain control over an uncooperative world. I also sought approval from everyone on the planet. The path I trod was a rough one.

I only wore Hanes underwear, because that was the brand Mom bought for me. She was as loyal to brands as she was to her beliefs, which were hard to unseat. It took extremely sound reasoning, tenacity, and evidence to get her to change a brand or an opinion. In the next months, some of the beliefs on which her life had been built would be put to the test, and found wanting.

In my closet, I easily located a blue, long-sleeve cotton shirt, my flared blue pants with broad grey stripes, and a blue v-neck sweater. Finally, I pulled on my heavy blue socks and the desert boots Mom had recently sprayed to keep the snow and street salt from penetrating.

As a final touch, I reached into the box made to look like a miniature pool table sitting on my dresser, and found the elastic choker of tiny black beads that I'd strung together during the previous "summer of love." My friends and I purchased the materials at a faux head shop at a strip mall in Michigami. You could also find incense burners, black light posters of rock bands, tie-dyed shirts, protest lapel pins, and any number of objects with the symbol for peace. There were all things salient to suburban, hippie-wannabe youth in revolt.

In the family room I stopped and turned on the TV to watch *Ray Raynor and Friends*, a staple of a baby boomer's childhood in Chicago. Though too juvenile for me, the show reminded me of the years before I attended school, when in "footie pajamas," I sat in front of the TV as everyone else rushed out of the house, and Grandma washed breakfast dishes. I didn't go to nursery school, as it was called, nor did anyone I knew.

At the kitchen table, Grandma immediately set a bowl of oatmeal in front of me, along with two pieces of rye bread toast spread with Fleischman's margarine and Welch's grape jelly. I drank a glass of orange juice, a glass of milk, and swallowed a vitamin tablet.

Matzah, our Miniature Schnauzer, was seated next to me in the chair he considered his own, and he pawed at my arm in anticipation of any food I'd hand over. Dad often said that Jews could pass a bar exam, sit for the CPA test or medical school boards, but never learn how to train a dog. In college, when I developed close friendships with non-Jews, I was amazed to see their dogs following them without a leash, and obeying the slightest click of the tongue. How ever did they do it?

The *Chicago Sun-Times* was open to where Grandma must've stopped reading when she heard me come downstairs. Her glasses rested on the newspaper. Grandma sat back down with her usual sigh as she reached over and pushed my plate closer to me.

"Don't forget to take your lunch. It's right there on the counter."

"Okay, Gram."

"I put your bus money next to the lunch. Don't forget it."

"Okay, Gram."

"Take your vitamin."

"I did, Gram."

"I tell you, my knee hurts me so in this weather."

Were there any meteorological conditions that didn't cause Grandma's knee or some other part of her body to ache?

"I'm going home after you leave to shop for Grandpa, but I'll be back when you get home from school. Be sure to come right home."

"Okay, Gram."

"I'm telling you, if I had stock in the CTA, I'd be rich with all this back and forth."

Before leaving, I glanced back enviously at Matzah stretched out and dozing in a patch of sunlight streaming through the family room window. I kissed Grandma's cheek as she warned me to watch for the machines—my 19th-century-born grandmother's word for cars—and headed out into the dazzling sunshine that reflected off the crusty layer of white snow. Brilliant days in January meant Arctic-like air, but no wind that day meant tolerable temperatures. I marched down the driveway that Dad and I had shoveled on Sunday, and walked the half block to the school bus stop on my way to the combination fun, misery, and theater that was our junior high school. I received many lessons in that building, although not always in the classroom, and not always what Mom and Dad planned for me to learn.

David and Mark, two friends from my block, were already at the bus stop. We knew each other since early childhood, but they weren't my very best friends. Neither one had older siblings, which I believed inclined them to be less cool. I theorized that older brothers and sisters exposed one to the latest fads sooner than anyone else could.

David was smarter than I was, but I found his humor to be immature by my 12-year-old standards. His family came from a small town, unusual for Jews, and they were blonds. In her frequent review of my friends, Grandma dismissed his family as Jews who had been turned into Gentiles by their time spent living in a small town.

That morning, we all looked the same in our parkas with our hoods up as we exhaled steam and stamped our feet for warmth. David and Mark wore parkas in a shade of green that reminded me of boogers, while mine was a rare chocolate brown that complemented my hair color. We nodded "hi" to each other, but didn't say much after that. Poor David was wearing Hush Puppies. You couldn't be cool in Hush Puppies. *Cool* and its opposite, *queer*, were the too most overworked words in our vocabularies.

The glare of the sun on the snow caused us to look down, and we collapsed within ourselves trying to stay warm thinking about the day's trials ahead. We didn't see the bus as it rounded the corner, until it stopped in front of us. By the time it arrived at our stop the bus was usually more than half-filled. I stepped up and paid my fifteen cents. I turned and faced the long aisle of insecurity that ran up the center of the bus. Each day there was a risk that someone would yell out a cutting remark, either in friendship or out of adolescent cruelty.

The only people who could vocalize loudly on the bus were cool kids, mostly the jocks who had the authority to do as they pleased, as did the few aberrant white kids whom I considered to meet the definition of juvenile delinquents. If someone cut you down on the bus in a friendly way, it was good for your reputation. It meant that a cool kid considered you worthy of a joke. If the remark was meant to sting and gain points for the assailant, you were doomed to sit in shame. Someone high up in the pecking order decreed you were not cool; therefore you were not.

For boys, the cruelest accusations, the ones that destroyed junior high careers, whether leveled boisterously by a white boy or softly by a white girl, were the ones that pilloried your masculinity: fem, sissy, fag, and faggot. A reputation had little chance of recovering from that sort of label.

Never having been the recipient of remarks on my daily walk down that aisle of insecurity, I only half braced myself as ᵣₚₐₐₐₕed the middle rows claimed by us seventh graders. I took the seat next to David, instantly recognizing the hot chocolate scent of his house that permeated his jacket. We pushed back our hoods, and held our lunch bags in our laps. The seats closest to the front of the bus were for the sixth graders. The eighth graders and one celebrity seventh grader owned the back rows.

"Have you seen *On Her Majesty's Secret Service?*" I asked David. I hoped to arrange an outing over the weekend with my friends. We often went to nearby PrairieVille mall to see movies or just hang out.

"I saw it already with Gary. He went with his parents last night, and they took me with." David had no idea how his words stung and threatened. Gary Kogan was one of my new best friends, since entering junior high. He was in my class, not David's. I would confront Gary when I saw him at school that morning. This was an attack on my status within my own group of friends. I couldn't let it go unchallenged.

Two stops later, Ben Rubin, our seventh grade celebrity, got on the bus and prepared to strut straight to the back to fall in with his eighth grade friends. Ben and I were best friends in elementary school, but his coolness and popularity now far surpassed mine. By the end of sixth grade, junior high school had reshuffled our elementary school hierarchy leaving Ben and me levels apart. His status as a jock had combined with his overall great looks to make an unbeatable combination. My slighter frame and the emerging traits that would come to be recognized as gay, worked against me. At the age of twelve, I was already regretting the lost glory of my youth. Bitterness found a home.

Ben and I hadn't spent time together since the end of sixth grade, but when the invitations, in fancy script, to my *bar mitzvah* went out in a few months his name would be on one of them. My decision to invite him was an effort to delay the inevitable. Ben would accept my invitation, but his presence was awkward among my real friends, and Ben and I never spoke much after my *bar mitzvah* party.

I look back with added regret that in fourth and fifth grades Ben seemed to be hinting at experimenting sexually with me, but I pretended not to notice and gave no encouragement. Though my instincts warned against it, I wanted to get naked with him so much that my stomach ached as I imagined being close to his exposed, beautiful body, and having the liberty to touch him. I never wanted to give anyone any ammunition to use against me in the future. By age ten I was fearful, while Ben had nothing to fear. He could always be secure in his reputation, as the epitome of masculinity.

On that bus, every girl (and I) watched Ben with desire, and every guy (me too) looked on with envy. Ben was so damned blessed with the things prized by adolescents. In addition to his good looks and superior athletic ability, his dimpled smile, cleft-ed chin, and teeth that wouldn't require braces were disarming to students and teachers alike. Living up to the lowered expectations of their highly assimilated parents, few of the Jewish girls cared that he was in the bottom half of the intelligence curve. Nor did they mind that he dropped out of Hebrew school, and wouldn't become a *bar mitzvah,* because he needed that time to hone his formidable athletic skills. Mom thought that those choices demonstrated poor parenting and a disregard for his heritage.

"They are stressing the wrong values in life. What message will he take from that choice? It's a *shanda.*" I was glad Mom thought that way, since I was ambivalent about sports. I hated standing in a hot, sunny field waiting for a ball that I didn't want to come my way; not when there was a cool, air-conditioned house, and a pitcher of lemonade waiting. Hebrew school was a good excuse to avoid intramurals or leagues that had after school practices. Either way, her message that our Jewish identity and the values that accompany it were important stuck with me.

As Ben stepped up on the bus, his biggest and probably most frustrated admirer, Nancy Lefko, shouted her daily greeting to him. Nancy never paid attention to me, though we'd been in classes together since kindergarten. Grandma always referred to "nice Jewish girls," but I didn't find Nancy or the girls in her clique to be very nice, nor were they very good students.

Nancy and her friends were the cool girls. I called them "mall girls" because they spent a lot of time at PrairieVille Mall where they bought outfits on the cutting edge of suburban fashion, made from natural fibers. They wore their hair parted in the center or on one side from where it descended straight down to below their cashmere-covered shoulders. They gossiped endlessly, and no one, including the girls in their own clique, was safe from their cruel judgments. During breaks from school they often went to Florida with their families. While almost every white student in our school would fall demographically into the middle to upper middle class, some were more *upper* than others.

If the cool kids were aware of the concerns of the larger world, they gave no sign of it. Pollution, Viet Nam, civil rights, the women's liberation movement, and the importance of a Jewish homeland— all topics around my family's dinner table and among me and my friends—never seemed to break through to their consciousness. I must confess: if given the choice back then, I think I could've given up those noble concerns to be accepted among the jocks and the mall girls, as one of their own.

While Ben and Nancy's crowd was not physically violent (that seemed to be the provenance of the black kids who went to our school, and the Catholic kids who did not), they were dangerous. There was an effeminate boy in school named Ed. The mall girls would whisper the dreaded *fem* to each other in front of Ed's face. The meanest among the guys would use the even more offensive "faggot." There but for a slightly stronger wrist went I. The pain in Ed's moist eyes was apparent to me, but there was nothing to be done for him. His lot had been cast, and neither he nor anyone of us could alter that fact. In 1970, there was no path of redress, no anti-bullying campaign, no counselors, and no acceptable alternatives to the cultural norms for masculine behavior. For us, the high school in the TV program *Glee* would've been science fiction.

I tried to stay beneath their radar. Once I heard that a mall girl found me cute. My gut reaction? I was flattered and reminded of the days in our little elementary school when Ben and I were twinned together at the pinnacle of popularity. I had seen another guy like me pulled up from the middle ranks by one of Nancy Lefko's friends, because she thought he was cute. Eventually, she threw him back, and he suffered a barrage of malicious comments from the pretty mall girls, until they lost interest, and moved on to another victim. I resisted the temptation to play out of my league.

My prediction for a girl like Nancy: she'll go to college to study elementary education, and then drop out when some Jewish jock, like Ben, asks her to marry. Quickly morphing into her mother, she'll devote herself to shopping, decorating, and redecorating her colonial style home, with a basketball hoop over its double garage for Ben Jr. She and her marital trophy and their offspring will spend winter breaks in Miami Beach. There she'll dictate the evening's dinner plans from poolside, under a sheen of baby oil, while the jock tunes her out as he follows some ballgame on a transistor radio, with an earplug. I was keenly aware that I envied Nancy and her friends this path that was closed to me by virtue of being a boy. This yearning to be a future Mrs. Rubin created an additional layer on the growing mass of guilt in my gut.

While my outer, cool indifference to the girls got no response from them, Ben's similar treatment of them only intensified their interest. I could feel the longing for the Adonis that was beyond the reach of mere mortals.

"Heeeey, Ben." Nancy called out, annoying me as Ben made his way up the aisle.

Ben ignored her, as usual. Suddenly, he yanked a sixth grader out of his seat by his jacket collar, and lifted the frozen window, out of which the younger boy had been staring only a moment earlier. Ben stuck his head out into the cold.

"Hey O'Malley. Suck my dick, you fuck," Ben shouted and then laughed. "Okay, Jerry. See you at practice."

There was silence throughout the bus except the pounding of my heart. The guys on the bus rolled their eyes, or pretended not to have heard what only Ben Rubin could've shouted out the bus window at eight o'clock in the morning as we rolled past Georgians, Tudors, colonials, and Greek revival houses. I replayed his words in my head maybe a thousand times in the fifteen seconds that had elapsed. I'd never actually heard that phrase vocalized. It had an effect on me, but I wasn't sure what it was. I was certain that later in the privacy of my room I'd examine the incident again, and imagine Ben speaking those words to me. All the girls shared smiles and blushes. I hoped I revealed nothing of my inner turmoil.

Although Ben was no candidate for an academic scholarship, I think his action was calculated. He was toying with his fan club, and confirming his top gorilla status among even the eighth grade boys. The fact that he directed his remark to a Catholic kid from the private parish school was another not so subtle reminder of his status. Most of us Jewish guys were fodder for bullying from the tough Irish Catholics in the neighborhood, but they considered Ben tough enough to be a friend. Ben could beat up anyone, or so it was assumed.

I was jealous and desirous all at once. Self-conscious of my voice, and worried that I sounded more like a girl than a jock, I wouldn't dare yell anything out the bus window—even something as innocuous as, "see you later," much less something as ballsy as "suck my cock." I couldn't imagine what the reaction of the kids on the bus would've been to such an audacious move from a middle-ranker like me. The risk of a humiliating response of laughter from the crowd kept me paralyzed, in that and so many other instances.

By this point the rest of us guys were attempting to shake off Ben's testosterone as he ambled to the back of the bus, and sat down next to a very cool eighth grader who, a few weeks earlier, had been the first and only kid to come to school in a pair of elephant bell-bottomed pants. Almost no one else—except Ben—could've pulled off that fashion stunt. But Ben didn't need to.

The bus passed my favorite Tudor style house that now huddled for warmth behind the ice-limbed trees that lined the quiet street. We picked up one last group of kids before turning east towards Hampden. As the bus crossed the bridge over the canal that separated Michigami from the older neighboring town, I watched the steam rise from the contaminated water beneath the ice. Although I knew the steep-banked canal with wide swaths of grass on either side was a sanitation canal, it made for a bucolic winter scene. How peaceful the whole area must have looked 130 years earlier when no one but Native Americans walked among the bears and wolves.

The image soon evanesced into gray reality. I recalled the riots that took place in Chicago's black neighborhoods a few years earlier. I heard more than one person say that if the blacks in Hampden decided to burn things down, as their urban brethren did, we could blow up the canal bridges to keep them from crossing over into Michigami. All had remained quiet in Hampden.

At the far bank, the bus entered the neighborhood of my black classmates whose houses surrounded our school. The homes were mostly older and smaller than those in Michigami, and they were wood framed instead of brick, but as Mom never tired of pointing out, "they are neat, tidy, and well-maintained, showing pride of ownership. The middle class blacks of Hampden are a credit to their race."

I overheard rumors at school, and observed signs of a poorer, "more dangerous" element of blacks moving in from Chicago's South Side to escape the growing black-on-black violence of the city.

CHAPTER FIVE

Same Day.

I looked down from the bus window as we pulled up to the bedlam in front of the still-locked school doors. The colorful, puffy coats, hats, and gloves on all the kids huddling in groups, jockeying for position, or chasing each other looked like an undulating candy display. As the doors to the bus opened, that sweet allusion shattered.

"Get out of the way motherfuckers."

"Cassandra girl, I'll slap you upside your head."

"Honkys get to the back of the line."

I waited my turn to get off the bus, while scanning the crowd for friends. A sixth grade boy who stepped down before I did was knocked aside by a heavyset black kid. The hapless boy's books fell into the slush along the curb. He threw his head back, rolled his eyes, and resolutely knelt down to gather his wet books. Was this a bigot in the making, or had his first four months in junior high already transformed him? Kids behind me who couldn't see what happened were pushing. I jumped down and helped the boy to get his things. Other kids who saw what had happened were laughing and pointing. Welcome to the wacky world of integration in 1970.

Before I joined my friends standing off to the side, a bell sounded and the doors opened. In the rush to escape the cold it was survival of the fittest. Several black kids and a few white bullies pushed and insulted their way to warmth. The rest of us waited for the herd to thin out, so we could walk inside unscathed, and exhale our first invisible breath since stepping off the bus.

My mind drifted above my body, taking note of the chaos, as if I were watching a movie. In fact, seeing a heavy black girl, about six feet tall, yank the collar of an anxious, small, white boy in sixth grade as she shouted, "make room for mama," seemed funny. I often found humor in the insanity around me, unless I was its victim.

Outside the school the ground was shifting, and many were attempting to gain their footing in a world that grew less familiar each day. Inside, we struggled to find where we fit into our much smaller world, and while we felt the spasms taking place outside, our focus was inward, and our concerns parochial.

I made my way to my locker on the second floor relieved to see my best friend Ken's blue parka already hanging on a hook, and his brown paper lunch bag sitting on the shelf of the otherwise empty space. School wasn't as much fun, and felt less safe on days when friends were absent.

Michael Baker was putting things away in his locker adjacent to mine. Tall, thin Michael, who kept his head shaved, accentuating its oblong shape, enjoyed talking about sports and super heroes, and had few close friends. He lived on the Hampden side of the canal in an apartment in the surrounding black neighborhood. His caramel colored skin announced his lineage: black father, a Hampden police officer, and white mother. Michael talked like a white kid, but looked black. You could close your eyes and listen to almost any kid in that school speak, and discern the race of the speaker. There were differences, some subtle and some not, in tone, syntax, grammar, cadence, and vocabulary. Many of our black peers spoke in the manner that would come to be called—at least for a while—Ebonics. To my northern, urban ears their speech held characteristics associated with southern accents, and probably reflected their southern American heritage. Considering the disparate paths our ancestors took to arrive at us, the difference in speech was natural.

Michael's familial circumstances relegated him to the fringes of both the black student body and the white social circle of Michigami. Michael's one friend was Cary Dunst, one of the rare, white Protestants from Michigami. Cary was shorter than average, with a solid build, dirty blonde hair that fell over his eyes, and a broad, turned up nose that gave him a handsome appearance, in a rugged sort of way. Cary and Michael had intense debates about the prowess of various professional athletes and super heroes. During this time of year talk surrounded the Bulls, specifically Bob Weiss and Jerry Sloan, while Superman, Batman, and the other comic book stars had no seasonality. Cary and Michael sat next to each other in class. No one disliked either kid, and yet no one thought to pull the two boys into his or her own clique.

"Hiya, Glen. Damn, it's cold out today. I can't feel my feet," Michael said, stamping his galoshes on the scoffed, and now wet linoleum floor, before beginning the balancing act required to pull the boots off the shoes underneath. I tried not to see the clear snot coming out of his left nostril.

"I know. At least the sun is out. Maybe we'll play softball in gym today." It was a weak joke, but it was all that was needed to show there was no hint of discord between us. Playing his part, Michael laughed with more enthusiasm than my words merited.

We walked into the room together, Michael heading towards his seat next to Cary along one side of the room. With no fear here of verbal arrows striking my balls, i.e. my status, I headed over to the desks in the front where Ken, Gary, and Adam hovered around three girls of our group who were already seated. These were my friends and allies, standing on our part of the hill. Seats weren't assigned, but we kept the same ones we grabbed the first day of class.

I don't know the criteria used to compose the nine, seventh grade classes in my school, but it was clear that my class had a high percentage of good students. The racial and religious make up mirrored the larger student body. Out of the twenty-eight kids, six were black (if you counted Michael Baker), and all of them lived in Hampden. The whites were from Michigami: two Protestants and the rest Jews.

I boldly pulled out the chair next to Barbara Needleman at the narrow table for two. Both Barbara and the girl next to her checked out my appearance starting at about my thighs, and moving their eyes up the nicely coordinated outfit in blue to my neatly combed hair. Some years later, I came to understand that among youth (and gays of all ages) guys were considered much sexier if they didn't look like they gave their clothes and overall appearance too much consideration. A coordinated outfit, outside of the appropriate occasion, was not an effective mating call. It should've been obvious to me. Ben Rubin, for example, always wore blue jeans and cotton shirts that looked a bit wrinkled, and were not completely tucked into his pants. His long sleeves were rolled up part way to reveal his muscular, heavily veined forearms. Guys like Ben who had that rumpled, just-got-out-of-bed appearance, were far more attractive to me than guys who looked like they fussed over themselves. Perhaps it was the difference from myself that attracted me.

My shirts were always pressed (thanks to Grandma's obsession with ironing everything—even my underwear) and color coordinated with my various flared pants. My sleeves remained down and buttoned at the wrist. I rarely wore blue jeans because I found denim from that era stiff and uncomfortable, and it hindered movement. I was unaware that I was subtly giving off signals that would eventually grow to the size of a small billboard advertising "gay."

There was a pre-teen, 1970s' version of sexual tension between Barbara Needleman and me. I thought she was pretty with her long, straight hair, the color I know today to be chestnut brown, and clear blue eyes. Bright and kind, she laughed easily at my jokes. It was normal to think about having a girlfriend to go steady with, and with whom you could make out at parties. Barbara was a good choice. I attracted girls who had a particular combination of looks, intelligence, and a gentle nature that set them above a mall girl. Not surprisingly, their mothers approved of me too.

Barbara was thin, but I wasn't keenly aware of her body or her not having a developed chest—something Ken often pointed out. That didn't matter to me. When I masturbated, there was no room for Barbara, nor any girl, in my fantasies, but when it came to dating it would've been absurd to consider the guys I fantasized about as potential boyfriends. As far as I knew, there was no possibility that two boys, or two men, could date.

I don't know if Barbara talked about me to the girls in our group, but I didn't say too much to my friends about her. The flirting we did in class, the giggles, winks, and notes passed back and forth were obvious, and I was happy to let people think what they wanted. At thirteen, I knew my lack of physical desire for Barbara wouldn't be tested for some time. Kids in my social, racial, religious, economic, and academic demographic—nice Jewish boys—weren't expected to have sex until later. Still, I was beginning to worry. What if I wasn't *normal* by then?

On Saturday nights we often organized class parties. Everyone, including the black kids, was welcome—a nod to a successful result of integration. Contrarily, not many black kids participated nor were the white kids invited to their gatherings. By junior high, I had no idea what my black classmates did on the weekend.

The parties, more ad hoc than planned, were held in someone's finished basement. With Top 40s music as a background, there were lively discussions about the goings on at school the previous week. For most, that's how the evening began and ended. More adventurous members of my class might continue with a silly game such as Goose the Moose, before advancing to the often awkward and rarely fulfilling Spin the Bottle. The fickle, green glass from the 7UP company seldom stopped where the hopeful spinner wished it.

The transition from talk to action started with only hormones as stimuli. Perhaps while James Taylor sang about fire and rain from the record player, a girl would casually lean against the guy she was standing next to in a group conversation. He might receive the advance just as casually, while had it been visible, the frantic activity within his briefs would've betrayed him.

Another couple might pair off, and we'd pretend not to notice them sitting closely together on a single armchair in a corner.

Every minute simmered with the excitement of dancing around our sexuality. You could cut the pheromone-charged air with a knife. The guys and girls tested, manipulated, and teased each other with words, movements, and looks of layered meaning, or outright suggestion.

"I think James Taylor is so sexy. This song should be listened to with the lights down low."

"Maybe someone else will lower them. I don't want to stand up just now."

In spite of the bold words, anything beyond first or second base was not in our playbooks.

Barbara didn't often go to these parties. Her parents tightly controlled how she spent her time, and she never argued with her parents. As a result, she had the reputation of being a bit of a prude. The accepted range of sexual activities that separated prude from a more open-minded girl was whether or not she would kiss a boy on the lips or permit French style. Boys had no limits, but we were supposed to respect girls. A girl risked being labeled a slut if she permitted too much. Oral sex and intercourse were taboo, until at least high school.

No one was complaining. For me, it put off the need to confront my sexuality. The speculation surrounding someone's romantic interest in you—little flirtations, the rare telephone call some evening, the slow dance at a *bar mitzvah*, these were daring, exciting, and fulfilling outlets, and we were allowed to dream about everything that would surely one day follow. I was just happy to be in this group, and to be considered desirable by some of the girls, even if it wouldn't lead to fulfilling my own dreams. Our low threshold for titillation seems quaint now, harkening back to Edith Wharton novels, with men feeling tremors shuddering through their bodies at the sight of a woman's bare wrist. Today's third graders would sneer at our inexperience.

When Tanya Wilkes, a strikingly pretty black girl, with a fashionable wardrobe that accentuated her already developed breasts, entered our classroom, she did so with her head high. The purple sweater that hugged her body that cold day in January featured small animal patches embroidered across her chest. What were those animals? Dogs? Cats? Rabbits? I squinted and followed Tanya with my eyes as she walked towards her desk.

Ken laughed and said under his breath, "Feigman, you dog. You couldn't be more obvious."

How fortuitous! Ken assumed that like he and Gary, and every other boy in the room, I was staring at Tanya's breasts, only not as surreptitiously. I felt like one of the guys. Maybe subconsciously, I *was* staring at her breasts! I smirked at Ken and said nothing. Instead, I turned to Gary.

"Hey Gary, when are we going to see "*On Her Majesty's Secret Service?*"

"I saw it already," Gary said, without looking up at me, without mentioning that he went with his family and my bus mate, David.

"I know. David told me. Real nice. I thought we were supposed to go together. You could've asked me to join you guys."

"Listen to you two," Ken said. "You sound like two girls."

Shit. He was right. I sounded like a mall girl. I needed to cut that off immediately, before Barbara and the others came to the same conclusion. I casually turned to Ken.

"Why don't we go over the weekend, and see who else wants to come with."

"Yeah. Sounds good. Maybe some of you ladies would like to see a movie with us?" Ken was so friggin' smooth, even in seventh grade.

Barbara, Debbie, and Leslie looked at each other, unsure of the right answer.

"I don't know anything about that movie, but I *love* to see movies on weekends." Leslie had an enthusiasm and an oversized personality that was so theatrical; Ken and I speculated that she was making a conscious attempt to imitate Marlo Thomas's character on *That Girl*.

A shriek of laughter from the doorway accompanied by, "she can kiss my black ass," indicated that Pamela Blake had arrived. Bursting with energy one moment, and sullen the next, Pamela had an edge to her. She moved loosely with occasional jolts of energy that could be startling—especially if her fist shot out towards someone. She usually wore a short ponytail, and had bangs cut evenly across her forehead. Her mouth was often wide open in a broad smile, or because she was shouting good-naturedly or antagonistically.

Most of the black kids in class sat together, in the last two rows on the left side of the room. Pamela sat in the first of those two rows, in the aisle seat, and that put her across the aisle and one seat back from me. I overheard many of her discussions with Tanya and another black girl in the class. I think Pamela knew I was listening, and successfully attempted to impress me, with her sexual exploits. She had an older boyfriend whom she referred to as "Bully," and her Monday morning tales to Tanya included descriptions of what he liked to do during sex. This placed one million miles between our two realities. From Pamela I extrapolated that our black peers went much further around the bases than we white kids did. I was grateful to Pamela for giving me the image of a dark muscular body, naked and sweaty under her sheets.

Pamela slid into her seat, and cupped her hands around Tanya's ear as she leaned in and laughed, whispered, and then laughed some more. Tanya's beautiful face showed delight as Pamela revealed her latest secret.

"You are *nasty*, Miss Pamela, you know that?" Tanya said as Pamela sat back smiling. "Mmm, mmm, mmm girl."

As others entered the room, took customary seats, exchanged greetings, sorted through notebooks, and shared conversation, our homeroom teacher Mr. Peterson strolled in wearing his uniform of black slacks that always showed the day's chalk marks, a white dress shirt, with the sleeves rolled up to just below the elbow, and a plain red necktie. He closed the door behind him. Mr. Peterson must've been in his late twenties, although his balding pate and horn-rimmed glasses made me think he was older. He was short, wiry, soft-spoken, and laid-back, the latter a prerequisite for being considered cool. Faculty members had to be cool, if they wanted to be taken seriously. We couldn't learn anything relevant from a teacher who was on the wrong side of the cool vs. queer divide.

Mr. Peterson's wife was pregnant. I'm certain I wasn't the only one attempting to get an image of Mr. Peterson driving into his wife. He was younger than our parents, and smart, often embellishing our textbook material with interesting tidbits about the personal lives of current and historical public figures, making them more like real people. The discussions he led included popular topics, such as the "undeclared" war in Viet Nam, pollution, rock and roll, drugs, music, fashion, race relations, and even sex. On all those topics, Mr. Peterson bore the same attitude as our other role models: rock stars like The Beatles. We excused him for using cool words such as: *hip, groovy,* and *mellow,* because he sounded authentic, unlike our parents or Sammy Davis Jr.

On this morning, after taking attendance, Mr. Peterson reminded us that there would be an assembly at 10:00 in honor of the birthday of the late Reverend Dr. Martin Luther King Jr., which was the next day. Since Dr. King's death less than three years earlier, our school district was among the first to declare his birthday a holiday. Schools were closed. Mr. Peterson explained that we were to go from our first class, math, directly to the auditorium. After the assembly, we were to go to the cafeteria for lunch, and resume our regular schedule.

As he finished his instructions, the door creaked open, and Luella White slowly entered. She was a silent, heavyset black girl who often seemed in a daze. She wouldn't show up at school for days at a time, for reasons unknown to us, and then one day, she would appear and quietly take her seat in a corner. Unlike our black classmates, Luella didn't sport an Afro, or any other African influenced hairdo. Her short hair was pulled back into two pigtails held together with barrettes. She wore old-fashioned jumpers, and moved her large body at a glacial pace. Luella appeared to sleep through the black power and black-is-beautiful movements of the era.

All eyes followed her as she made her way to her seat near the other black students, but slightly apart. After many seconds, Pamela Blake abruptly broke the silence. Quoting a current television commercial about the switch from regular to low calorie syrup, she blurted out, "Aunt Jemima, what *took* you so long?"

Since Pamela was black, the entire class was free to burst into laughter at this clever put down, and so we did. Luella registered the faintest smile as she eased herself down to her seat. Now I wonder if she was mentally challenged, had a difficult situation at home, or if it was something else entirely that created the enigma of Luella. I remember her with sadness instead of mirth.

I watched Mr. Peterson for signs of a laugh, but he did a good job of keeping it in check. I was certain he would tell his wife about it that night.

"Good morning, Luella," Mr. Peterson said evenly, eyes shooting daggers at us jokers. We're talking about the schedule for today—" His voice trailed off as the 8:55 bell sounded. He quickly dismissed us, but we'd already pushed our chairs back, stood up, and headed for the door.

CHAPTER SIX

Same Day

We walked the crowded hallway to math. This was not easy. It wasn't that the hoard of oncoming bodies formed obstacles, although they did, it meant exposing my reputation to threats. In junior high every movement was open to peer review. A walk between classes was no exception.

Manliness meant that a boy conducted every movement and action to a set of unspoken and ultimately ridiculous rules. At our age there was no opportunity to display the nobler characteristics of manhood, such as family responsibility and sacrifice; so to sort he-men from she-men we looked to important signs, such as how a boy held his books as he walked down the hall. Beyond athletic prowess, which was our modern incarnation of the heroic warrior, all that was left to us to prove our manliness was the seemingly simple requirement to not act or react in a girlish manner. The rules could not be found anywhere enshrined on tablets, but we all knew them, and ignored them at our risk.

I was hyper-vigilant, an exhausting state of being as I tried to coax my behavior into the *normal* range for a boy. It was becoming more apparent to me that my normal was not part of the large hump at the center of the bell curve. A masculine boy whose sexual fantasies involved only girls, and who had traditional likes, such as sports, and dislikes, such as dancing, and no serious stigmas, such as a poorly shaped body or a high voice, was the gold standard of male youth. He didn't have to expend energy second-guessing who he was.

The battle inside me was fierce. I wanted desperately to be liked and universally popular. Just a regular guy—but exceptional. Believing I deserved such acclaim, while at the same time fearing I was in reality the universally hated fem, was a paradox.

No matter how comfortable a boy was with himself—and there weren't many in junior high who attained the highest level of self-confidence—he couldn't be completely unaware of the need to monitor his behavior for signs of femininity. The divide between pink and blue was as un-crossable as the Berlin wall.

Boys could not cradle books at chest level, no matter how cumbersome the load; they had to be held alongside the body, with the hand cupped around the book's spine. Perhaps it was a coincidence that this position allowed for quickly shifting the book to the front of the crotch to hide frequent erections.

In the category of movement, sub-category walking the school corridor, the ways not to act like a girl were numerous. Good posture reeked of prissiness. A slight slouch was better, especially when accompanied by the disheveled look. These meant there was no preoccupation with appearance. Slow was better than quick. A tough guy rarely had to concern himself with punctuality—except for an athletic practice.

A boy couldn't walk too closely next to his buddy, heads tilted together in conversation. That was the way girls shared gossip.

The accepted greeting between two boys was the slight head lift while grunting "hey," without opening the mouth too wide. Perhaps opening the mouth would invite the notion of a willingness to suck cock

Perhaps Darwin could explain how these highly charged interpretations of ordinary activities came to be universally employed across America's junior high schools. Could their purpose be to winnow out those who were less likely to propagate the species, thereby reducing the need for suburban homes, which would be detrimental to the world economy?

Boys and girls reached in all directions to form identities as our bodies changed, sometimes kindly, and sometimes cruelly. While our parents' opinions became less charged with relevance, we chased after images and personalities gleaned from thousands of impressions from television, movies, news, older siblings, older students, books, and each other.

With these epic concerns crowding my head, I walked into Mr. Burns's math class. Here was the poster boy of un-cool: middle-aged, with glasses framed in the 1950's; brown, ill-fitting slacks; a rumpled white short sleeve dress shirt, with a solid brown tie; and a square head of gray, greased hair that sat on a neckless, squat body. Mr. Burns was humorless. He either faced the chalkboard or stared into the teacher's manual. He considered our class a unit of uniform intelligence, and made no attempt to apply the information he imparted upon us to the world outside.

I listened for 40 minutes to a morphean talk on sets—no mention of their application to the real world—and then walked with my class to the assembly.

CHAPTER SEVEN

Same Day

The noise in the auditorium ricocheted like the echoes in an animal house at Lincoln Park Zoo. Mr. Burns led us down the aisle, after stopping at the first empty row, he pointed to our chairs. I sat next to Barbara on purpose. Gary was on my other side.

The disheveled teachers looked harried as they half-heartedly attempted to create order. A few made sudden moves here or there to stop or slow the escapades of some of the rowdier kids. The usual suspects among the black kids raced up and down aisles. A black boy called a white boy "football-headed honky" because of his large head. There was a black girl smacking the backs of the heads of each white kid, boy or girl, sitting in a seat along the right side of the aisle as she marched forward. The antics belied the somber nature of the upcoming program. The rest of us sat back, anticipating a good show, not only on stage, but also in the audience. I felt no stake in the day's subject matter, so I enjoyed the chaos the black kids created. I expected the teachers to offer up unintentionally comical behavior, in their vain attempt to maintain a modicum of dignity around the day's event.

The lights were lowered, and the principal, a handsomely dressed black man, attempted a few times to quiet everyone down. When he decided it was as quiet as it was going to get, he introduced the program.

"Today's program honoring the memory of the late Reverend Dr. Martin Luther King, on this anniversary of his birth, is a reminder of the peaceful struggle for equality he bravely led. The fight against bigotry did not end with his assassination. We must all continue the good fight, against all forms of bigotry that would deny a person his or her God-given rights."

I applauded politely along with the other white kids, while the black kids whooped, hollered, and whistled.

The principal exited stage right as three black students from the eighth grade took the stage representing Rosa Parks, Martin Luther King, Jr., and Medgar Evers.

"You go girl."

"You show them."

"Oh, yeah!"

"Uh-huh." Whistles and applause accompanied these shouts of encouragement, while most of us sat silently.

With only wire-rimmed glasses as a prop, and her hair pulled back in a bun to indicate she was Rosa Parks, the speaker looked dignified and solemn—a stark contrast to how she often looked when she pounded on anyone who rubbed her the wrong way.

I leaned over, and whispered to Gary that someone should represent the Jewish freedom riders, some who gave their lives for the cause. Nice guy Gary didn't respond. He never wanted to be on the record for having said anything negative about anyone or any group. His unwillingness to take sides got on my nerves. I believed that best friends should always agree with you in a disagreement with a third party, even if you were wrong. In that respect I thought like a mall girl.

A filmstrip lit up the big screen in the center of the stage, and the three icons of the civil rights movement began their narration. There were disturbing images of "whites only" signs, of black protesters flailing against water cannons, and black and white marchers attempting to fend off attack dogs.

Chaos just short of a riot broke out. The black kids jeered, stood up, and angrily threw wadded up balls of paper at the screen as they cursed at "whitey." I quietly shared their revulsion at the photographs.

I recalled the previous year in Sunday school. I saw for the first time the grainy, black and white documentary films of Nazi atrocities against Europe's Jews, ending in their annihilation—my family among them. I couldn't deny the cruelty of segregation and the immorality of its perpetrators, *but*, I thought, *at least they weren't all denied their lives and the ability to fight another day.* I wanted to tell my black classmates about the Holocaust that transpired only a short time before our births, and of anti-Semitism in America as well. I almost seethed with resentment that there was never any mention that, at the time of the march in Selma, housing covenants restricted Jews, as well as blacks, from many neighborhoods. Hotels freely advertised "no Jews", universities kept quotas limiting the admittance of qualified Jews, and corporate boards of directors resembled Protestant church leaders. If they had been taught these facts, the more hostile blacks who saw each of us as no better than an Alabama sheriff, might've realized we weren't the enemy. We could've been drawn closer together.

On this Martin Luther King Day, there were no Alabama bigots for the black kids to rail against, but there we sat: a soft, fat, easy target of whites, constricted by our sense of guilt at the mistreatment of blacks that we had just witnessed, and by our own lack of physicality. We northern, Jewish, white kids from liberal families made an ironic substitute for Bubba. The black kids had whitey in their sights.

For most of us Jews, our American heritage began after the Civil War, and included our ancestors' struggles for acceptance. I don't know if any of my white classmates had family members who were on the leading edge of the civil rights movement, but none of us had any Klan members in our closets. Social justice was a theme at most of our synagogues and Passover Seders. A history of our parents' voting record would have confirmed a pattern of progressive reform. I never heard any words support-ing racist ideas, but heard plenty on treating everyone with re-spect. The "N" word was unknown at home. Our parents sent us to a school knowing it was integrated.

The commemoration of King wound down, and Mr. Strong, the tall, heavy, black assistant principal of our school, approached the microphone at the podium. "I'd like everyone to rise and join hands as we sing the Black National Anthem." I looked around to see where black hands met white hands. I wanted to see if any black kid rebuffed his white neighbor. My search was brief and turned up empty.

"Lift every voice and sing 'til Earth and heaven ring, ring with the harmonies of liberty..."

I knew this song. We'd learned and practiced it in every music class for the past four weeks. I sang it at home for my parents, who found the lyrics beautiful, speaking a universal message of hope. They likened it to the hope in the Israeli National Anthem, entitled *Hatikvah* (Our Hope).

I didn't like singing it. The song reinforced my growing awareness that much of what we did in school was to make the black kids feel good about being black; and in seventh grade, I couldn't see why it was my responsibility. I wasn't aware that any of my classmates, black or white, had done anything great enough to sing about.

I agreed with black liberation from oppression, but at our school the only oppressors were the black kids: free spirits who misbehaved with impunity. Their speech directed at whites was demeaning. They addressed us as "boy" and "girl," if they addressed us at all. When they weren't segregating themselves, they regularly knocked us around, blocked our paths, and overtly intimidated us, often into surrendering lunches or coins. If any white kid had ever initiated antagonistic behavior towards blacks, I never witnessed it. Were we victims of our own cowardice?

I caught a glimpse of Cleon Jones. We hadn't spoken much since we entered junior high, but there was a bond between us. He caught me looking at him, and we shared a smile. For a moment I felt good about my integrated school.

Looking back on that day's assembly, I suppose the planners hoped to make the white kids more sensitive to our black classmates. What immediately followed did little to help in their objective.

CHAPTER EIGHT

Same Day

The inciting photos of the morning's program energized the black kids. The shoving, tripping and verbal assaults directed at us honkys began immediately as we made our way up the aisle, and out of the auditorium to the cafeteria. Ken, Gary, and I grouped together as we walked to lunch. Barbara and the other girls separated from us. In the cafeteria the girls and the boys chose to sit at separate tables.

Though blacks were a minority of the student body, an indeterminate percentage of them demonstrated consistent hostility to whites, and influenced life at school beyond their numbers. We told ourselves this was a temporary nuisance; someday we would have the ability to separate from them or anyone like them. It wasn't what the proponents of integration had in mind.

Among the black kids was a small, sad group who also received the scorn of their brothers and sisters. Like Michael Baker, they were ostracized for a litany of offenses: befriending whites, excelling scholastically, or being inept at sports. Stigmatized as

'Oreos' or 'Uncle Toms,' like us, they bore these indignities with feigned indifference; but everyone has a breaking point.

I made my daily purchase of a small carton of milk for four cents, and a Fudgecicle for eight cents, exiting the cafeteria line with Ken and Gary. We were secure in the fact that we had a table to call our own, thus avoiding that painful moment of standing alone with a tray searching for a welcoming beacon of light. We walked the long aisle separating rows of Formica and metal picnic bench seating. Midway down the clamorous room we stopped at our customary place on the right where some of the regulars were already eating and engaging in animated conversations. The fare was either the small dried hamburgers on the menu for the day, or the contents of brown bags from home: perhaps bologna sandwiches, Fritos, and some sort of Hostess treat. Hostess advertised their chemical concoctions as "wholesome," whatever that meant. My bag contained a peanut butter and jelly sandwich, Jay's potato chips, and a piece of moist banana cake that Melva had baked.

The room vibrated with adolescent energy let loose from the confines of the classroom. Over it all came the glorious beat of Motown. The black kids claimed the last tables on either side of the aisle. We never attempted to sit there, nor were we invited. Likewise, we never thought to ask any blacks to join us. The minds that pushed integration never noted how we segregated ourselves whenever given the chance. If they did notice, then they missed an opportunity to brainstorm ways to have us mix together at lunch.

At the back of the cafeteria, a daily ritual began. Those fantastic Motown hits came from a small cassette recorder, and black girls began to move rhythmically to the music.

"You go girl."

"Show us what you can do."

"Black is beautiful, baby."

Their shouts of pleasure bounced off the cinderblock walls. The Dr. King assembly seemed to have fed extra adrenaline into the day's dance.

"Hey, how about every time one of them pushes us or gets in our way we say, 'It looks like Martin Luther King died in vain?'" David asked.

"You try it first. You'll probably get pounded a second time." Adam was as short as David was tall. Adam was the organizer of the Stratamatic baseball league, a pre-microchip fantasy baseball game. Stratamatic anything bored me, and my lack of interest only added to the growing feelings of myself as an outlier. While I wondered how those guys absorbed mountains of sports statistics and names of athletes, they couldn't understand how I could name the major winners of Academy Awards since 1928.

The dozen or so guys in my lunch circle would grow up to be good husbands, fathers, and providers. We weren't the jocks, the super-cool dudes, or the geekiest kids. In our quiet way, most of us were the guys who grew into the men who do the right thing by American-Jewish standards for family life. Fortunately for me, the definition of "family" has expanded. Some lost their connection to Judaism, or they never had one, but I contend that for most of us it was Jewish teachings and culture that fueled successful careers and stable home lives. It was presumptuous of me, but at twelve years old I predicted the conventional trajectories my crowd's lives would take. As much as I wanted to fit in, I wanted to someday stand out from these guys, on my own terms.

Derrick Dawson, a heavyset, black eighth grader, ambled over to the table, and came up behind me. I tensed as I quickly tried to guess Derrick's mood. He was one of a handful of black students who roamed the cafeteria at lunch shaking down white students for food or money. The cafeteria monitors, two elderly black men, were either oblivious of this regular conduct, or chose to ignore it. At least Derrick hadn't smacked me on the back of the head—yet.

"Come on *Fag*-man, let me see your Fudgecicle." I hated my last name. It loaned itself to this nasty transformation so easily. Zadie should have bribed someone at Ellis Island to give him a different name. But Zadie didn't speak English upon his arrival, and had no idea how awful Feigman sounds to the Anglo ear. A tough guy, Zadie would've decked anyone who pulled the "fagman" appellation on him. If Dad, a much gentler soul than Zadie, was teased about his name, he never mentioned it.

"You can *see* my Fudgecicle without taking it." I ripped the paper off my dessert, waved it in front of Derrick's eyes for a moment, and then plunged half of it into my mouth.

Derrick smacked the back of my head. "You're an ass, boy. You know that?" He quickly scanned the room, made a quarter turn, and ambled off in search of easier prey at a table of white sixth graders.

My shocked friends laughed wildly at the sight of me jamming the Fudgecicle in my mouth. As soon as Derrick left, the congratulations poured in.

"You sure stoned him."

"That was so cool. I never saw you move so fast as when you shoved that thing in your mouth."

"When you said, 'you can *see* the Fudgecicle without taking it,' I thought I'd piss my pants."

"Hey," Ken added, "you forgot to say, 'it looks like Martin Luther King died in vain.'"

"No way he'd understand what that means. He's too stupid." My feigned confidence belied the knotted feeling in my gut that an encounter with Derrick always evoked.

"Milk bomb!" Another daily ritual.

We all ducked, like we did during our nuclear-war-with-the-Russians drills, as the open milk carton arced from the black to the white tables.

"Awww, yuck!"

The bomb's victim jumped up, swiping frantically at her hair and dress as she bolted towards the girls' bathroom. She fled past the two cafeteria supervisors, their lively conversation uninterrupted. A daily lunch event, milk bombs were an acceptable offense, not serious enough to warrant the supervisors' notice. The chatter that paused for a moment resumed. We were the Elois of H.G. Wells' *The Time Machine*—docile humans farmed as food by the predatory Morlocks—our black classmates.

In one of the few states that funds its schools almost exclusively by local real estate taxes, our parents paid among the highest. I guess the entertainment charge was included. The daily milk bombs, verbal abuse, and a push and shove here and there might not seem like such bad things to someone numbed by today's daily stream of shootings, gang warfare, and the mass killing of kids by other kids with AK47s; but perhaps those heinous activities have their origins in the seemingly more innocent violations of civil conduct that were overlooked in schools like mine.

No kid carried weapons. No one was killed or seriously injured. But the continuous verbal and physical assaults we white kids endured or witnessed came with some costs: the white kids' desire to live in integrated communities vanished along with our certainty that we could ever relate to many of our black classmates. The black kids saw that there was no immediate cost for disrespecting societal norms.

After the sacrifice was made to the god of milk bombs, Ken, Gary and I made our plans for the next day, because school would be closed to observe the King holiday. To my dismay, Ken suggested ice-skating at the university campus in Hampden. Gary agreed that skating would be a really cool way to spend the day, so I reluctantly agreed to go along.

When the bell sounded, signaling the end of our lunch period, we rose as one, and headed for the exit. We passed the tables of black students at the rear of the cafeteria as the omnipresent cassette player blasted out *ABC* by The Jackson Five.

Abruptly, Michael Jackson stopped singing. In his place was the sharp return of plastic and metal smacking against hard linoleum. Everything but two hundred pairs of eyeballs ceased to move. What our eyes settled on were the pieces of the cassette player lying mutely on the floor between the two back tables. From there, all eyes closed in on the now cursed, white, sixth grader who had tripped over the cord, pulling the cassette player to its doom.

Horror replaced oxygen in the atmosphere. It was like watching a car accident in progress. The careless boy, who tripped over the cord, was a hapless Jew facing the injustice of Torquemado. The verdict was a foregone conclusion.

My mind jumped to a class lesson leading up to the King holiday, describing how black men were lynched by mobs in the South simply for bumping into white women on the street. The tales of gross injustice angered me. Today, this unfortunate boy played the part of a poor soul who faced a different sort of lynch mob.

Inexcusably, no Elois stepped in to save him from the Morlocks' dinner table. The cafeteria monitors were actually paying attention to the unfolding drama, but they looked baffled, and stood frozen in place. The frightened boy backed himself up to the exit. With each step, every white kid stepped aside as our black classmates moved in for some kind of attack. Suddenly, the boy bolted. Throwing his books into the crowd, he dashed up the hall to the relative safety of the principal's office as forty black kids took off after him, hurling threats and epithets. Curiosity motivated much of the crowd to follow.

My classmates and I needed to get to biology for a test on the digestive effects of pepsin and other enzymes. We'd hear the outcome of this latest incident later. When the 1:00 p.m. bell sounded in Mrs. Rubens' biology class, we were in our seats, with the exception of some of the black kids. The room buzzed like a small town with a petty scandal on its hands.

"Okay group, I don't know what all the excitement is about, but let's get ready to take our test. Does anyone have any questions before we begin?"

At that moment Pamela Blake came running noisily into the class, very much excited as she relived whatever just happened down at the principal's office.

"Ooooh, Lord. That boy is going to get his ass whupped. Damn. And Mr. Strong? Ha! I have never seen a black man turn that color. Ha! His eyes just about popped out of his head. He didn't know what to do." She laughed robustly.

Mrs. Rubens addressed Pamela who stood several inches taller. As I watched her, noting her relatively large size, I theorized that her ancestors had to be big and strong to survive the miserable trip to America, and a life of slavery. In a leap that would make Darwin proud, I decided that those tragic historical facts contributed to a gene pool that created bodies that were, on average, larger and more mature than those of us descended from Eastern European Jews. My ancestors tried to live their lives unnoticed by the Christian majority that surrounded them. Perhaps only the small survived.

"Ms. Blake, please take your seat now. We're about to take our test on the digestive system." Mrs. Rubens was devoted to biology. She was a fair-minded teacher of about fifty-five who often laughed with abandon. Lovely warmth radiated from her, which kept her off any list of unpopular teachers.

Pam turned around, and started to walk out of the room, announcing that she would return soon.

"Pamela, we are about to take a test, unless you have some kind of emergency, can you please take your seat so we can start?"

"I said I'd be right back. Damn lady." Pam shot back at Mrs. Rubens.

"Pam, come sit down," George called out to her.

This apparently carried some weight with Pam, because she turned around, and sullenly headed towards her seat. As she passed behind Mrs. Rubens, her arm shot out, and her fist landed with a thud on Mrs. Rubens back, causing her to lurch forward. She landed on the desks in the front row, which prevented her from falling to the floor.

"Damn girl. Why'd you do that? Are you crazy?" Charles called out.

"Oh Pam. That was not a smart thing to do," George added in his velvety voice.

I wondered if this incident would end differently from all the others, and this particular story of our race relations would make the 5:00 news. Someone, somewhere would stand up and say, "Enough!" They would bring the cameras, and focus them on the scowling Pamelas, Kevins, Curtises, Serenas, and Juanitas who held sanity hostage, on a daily basis. But alas, there was nothing newsworthy here, because what happened conflicted with the story the media wanted to tell in 1970.

Pam turned, and ran out of the room. Mrs. Rubens, visibly shaken, tried to collect herself as several of the girls in the class, including Tanya Wilkes, ran up, and formed a protective circle around her, and asked if they could do anything. Mrs. Rubens was disoriented and unable to answer. She handed the test papers to a girl in the front row, and asked her to pass them out. She left the room on wobbly legs.

We didn't see Mrs. Rubens or Pamela for the rest of the day. In fact, we didn't see Mrs. Rubens until Monday. In spite of the January temperatures, she showed up to school in a short sleeve blouse, with an uncharacteristically low back, to showcase her large bruise.

After fifteen minutes of speculation, a replacement teacher entered the room to administer our test. When it was finished, without Mrs. Rubens, we were free to flirt and talk about anything. Nothing was said about biology, Pam—who received a suspension—or Mrs. Rubens.

CHAPTER NINE

Same Day

I survived another day of school, and exited the building looking forward to having the next day off. Thank you Martin Luther King. The sunlight and the snow were both faded. I hoped for an uneventful bus ride home as I climbed the two steps to deposit my fare. I sat with the rest of the seventh graders. Something had the mall girls excited. I heard the word "sissy" causing my stomach to form knots. They called out to Bruce when he boarded. Bruce was a fireplug with a handsome face who had the makings of a Jewish hoodlum. I liked him, because even to me, a kid without much life experience, it was clear that Bruce was a good guy who put on a tough front to mask a bunch of insecurities. The rumor was that his father was involved in nefarious activities that when brought to the light of day would make other Jews ashamed.

"Bruce, come here." The mall girls beckoned to him to hurry up.

"We want you to take the sissy test," they said with gleeful anticipation.

I relaxed a bit. They weren't talking about me, but they could draw me into this at any time, so I watched from a safe distance.

The tension that left me jumped to Bruce, and to my well-trained eye, betrayed his bravado. His neck stiffened ever so slightly as he approached, never taking the smile off his face as he asked what they had in store for him.

There were a number of tests going around that had the ability to prove if a boy were a fem or not. One was to catch a boy off guard, and ask him to look at his nails. If he held his hand out, palm down, he was a fem. If he flipped his hand over, palm up, bending his fingers to see the nails, he was "normal." Then he had to demonstrate how he would strike a match. If he drew the match away from his body, he was a fem. Apparently real men have no fear of self-immolation, and draw matches toward their bodies. The last test was to ask the male subject to lift his leg and touch his heel. If he flipped his leg back and reached behind to touch his heel, he was destined to spend life carrying a purse. If he expected to have a house in the suburbs, with a wife and two kids, he needed to lift his leg, turning it in, so he could reach forward to touch his heel.

Bruce's Herculean trial began as he held out his exposed forearm, and one of the girls began to lightly scratch her finger-nails up and down the length of it for a few minutes.

"Remember Bruce, you have to let me do this for at least two minutes. If you take your arm away, you fail the test." The other girls giggled and watched with wide eyes and broad smiles. In spite of everything Bruce had done over the years to be a tough guy, this one test could prove that it was a big lie, and reveal that he was a sissy.

This sounded easy enough, and then blood started to appear along the tracks left by the girl's nails. Bruce continued to smile.

We all looked from his arm to his still smiling face, and back to his arm.

"Times up!" one of the girls shouted. Bruce couldn't completely hide his relief as he put his arm down and carefully unrolled his sleeve to cover his wounds. He was to endure a few days of pain until the raw, bloody skin began to heal under the bandage he wore.

So we had proof, at least for now, that Bruce was not a sissy. It was okay to be ignorant, as long as you weren't a sissy.

Mercifully, the girls canceled plans to test anyone else. Perhaps it was the blood that changed their minds.

I rang the doorbell, and Matzah went into his usual histrionics, barking and jumping at the window. Grandma opened the door with one hand, while holding a rag to her head with the other. "I almost died. You're lucky I'm not dead. She could've killed me. Do you think your Grandpa cares? Abraham Lincoln the second." So far, nothing unusual.

I gave Grandma a kiss on the cheek as I walked past her, and she continued her rant. I patted Matzah's head, and saw Nancy sitting on the living room couch, her eyes red from crying.

"They stole my coat, my new peach-colored coat that Mom and Dad bought me for Chanukah, those bastards." I assume she meant the thieves, and not our parents. "I almost froze to death coming home, even if I did get a ride home. And I get home to find Grandma completely out of control about some attack."

Grandma, rag on head, sunk down on the couch next to Nancy, the plastic slipcover around her seat cushion swelling from her weight. Her dress hiked up to reveal the garters that held her rolled-up stockings. Grandma hated silence, so she filled the vacuum.

"I was in line at the grocery store over by me. Your grandfather thinks they have better fruit than the commissary in the building right next door. Don't ask me. I think they overcharge."

"Grandma, please."

"There are some colored in the neighborhood now, and suddenly we have robberies and hold ups and broken windows, and painted words on everything. It's a wonder people make a fuss when colored move in. You never used to see a scrap of paper in the street. Now there are papers all around the neighborhood. So I was waiting in the line for people with ten items or less. All I had was a few things. Your grandfather and his blue cheese. Who can eat it? Feh!"

She shook her head before continuing. "Well, there's this colored woman in front of me, with a whole cart full of items. She was a young woman with a kid. Your mother and Grandpa always say, 'Talk to anybody like you would talk to anybody else. If you talk differently to somebody because they're colored, then you're being prejudiced.' *Ver Veysach Vos*. They should leave me alone with their nonsense.

"So I lean over, and say to her nice as could be, 'Excuse me Miss, this line is the express line. Next time you should use the regular lane.'

"Well, don't ask, don't ask, don't ask. *Gut in himmel*, what came out of this woman's mouth. I don't know what half of it means. I should live so if I ever heard such a mouth. *Vey iz meer.* She told me to shut up, and mind my own business. She said I was just an old, ugly, honker or something, whatever that is, and she would kick me in the *tuches*, if I said anything else." Grandma thrust her head towards me for emphasis as she said this, her blue eyes unblinking.

"She said *tuches*?"

"No. And she didn't say 'behind' either. You know the other word they use. Well, I got so scared, I dropped the basket I was carrying, and turned to get out of the line. The cashier, I know her. Her name is Maryann. She's a lovely young gentile woman. She just got engaged. *Oy*, the boy she's marrying is no catch, but it isn't my business to say anything, as long as she's happy. Anyhow, she kept her head down, and didn't say anything. She's afraid of them, like the rest of us are. She once told me that they steal, and you dasn't say anything if you see them, because then your life isn't worth a nickel. Then they hold signs up in front of the store telling everyone you're prejudiced."

Grandma continued her story, happy that Nancy and I were now captivated. "So no one says anything except there is another colored woman in the next line, and she says to this woman with the mouth, 'Sister, there's no need to be so foul,' or something. But the woman with the mouth says, 'I'm not talking to you, b-i-t-c-h.' Such language in public! My mother would've washed my mouth out with soap."

It was a bit of a jolt to hear Grandma spell "bitch," even if she did whisper it. She continued.

"Then they started arguing. I tell you, I was so nervous, I ran out of the store, and ran home. I shook the whole way, looking over my shoulder to see if she was coming after me. I had to change my underwear, because I wet myself, I was so scared. I tell you, I was too scared to leave the apartment, but what could I do? You would come home to an empty house after school. God forbid your mother should ever get home a little earlier from school. She's another one. You'd think they paid her overtime."

"Oh Grandma, you're fine. Nobody hurt you. But my coat was stolen, right out of my locker. I am so upset. Glen, I'm telling you, you don't want to go to the high school. It just keeps getting worse there."

"Do you know who stole it, Dolly?" Suddenly Grandma was concerned about Nancy. "Your parents paid good money for that coat, don't I know it. They don't give anything away at Marshall Fields."

"No, but I could guess who it was. No one steals anything at school, except the black kids. I know Grandpa and Mom would get all upset at me for saying out loud what everyone knows, but it's true. I'm sure it was one of maybe three girls who know where my locker is, and who would steal it." Nancy would be proven correct in the future when she saw one of those girls wearing her peach-colored, wool coat, with a broad collar, peach-colored plastic buttons, and a belt to cinch the waist.

"Did they take anything else, Dolly?"

"No. Francine, the girl I share a locker with, her coat was there, but it's an ugly old thing from freshman year." Suddenly Nancy started to chuckle. "Glen, could you picture Grandma running down the street, peeing all the way home?"

I loved when Nancy talked to me like a friend, instead of dismissing me. I laughed and nodded. This aggravated Grandma.

"You think it's funny that some young hoodlum insults and threatens your grandmother? I could be laying dead on the floor in that grocery store, and everyone would be stepping over me rather than confront a colored person." Grandma let out a groan, and shook her head pressing the rag harder against her forehead.

"Grandma, I can't believe you peed in your pants. That is so funny," Nancy laughed and shook her head slowly from side to side, looking at no one in particular. She tossed her long, straight, blond hair back over her left shoulder. Then she tucked it behind her ear. This move, which she repeated too many times to count each day, held her hair in place for about fifteen seconds, before it fell forward again.

Grandma sighed as she leaned on the arm of the couch, and lifted herself up. "My knee hurts me so. I'm sure when I ran, I did something to it."

Matzah barked joyfully in the kitchen as the garage door jumped to life, responding to Mom's electric command.

"Finally," Grandma said as she headed for the kitchen. Nancy and I followed behind her.

We ganged up on Mom, with Matzah leading the charge. He leaped up and down, until she released her purse and book bag, and stroked his head as she made kissing noises.

Grandma knew that Mom would be more concerned about Nancy's stolen coat than her own hostile encounter, so she played an unexpected card, allowing her to deliver the bad news.

"They stole Nancy's coat—the new peach one —right out of her locker."

Mom stopped petting Matzah, and he backed away satisfied, giving the rest of us access to her. "What? Who stole it? You're kidding me. Tell me you're kidding." She looked from Grandma to Nancy, with pleading eyes that betrayed her lack of hope. Nancy's sudden burst of tears confirmed that it was not a joke.

"And this colored woman threatened to kick me in the behind."

Mom was reaching out to hug Nancy, and surprisingly, Nancy let her as she rested her head on Mom's shoulder.

"What? Mother what are you talking about? Who threatened you? Why?"

Nancy lifted her head, and in the midst of her tears she burst out laughing, so I did too.

"What is going on here? What's so funny now? Nancy, why are you laughing?" Mom asked, wriggling out of her brown, leather boots with heels somewhere between sensible and sexy, leaving them on the doormat. She removed her wool hat and matching gold scarf, which Aunt Agnes made for her. Taking off her dark brown wool coat, with black buttons, my mother revealed a plaid skirt that ended above her knee, and a matching brown, pullover sweater with a gold pin, at the base of the turtleneck. Tisk-tisking at the static electricity, she patted the sides of her head, making sure her light-brown hair was mostly in place.

I appreciated the fact that Mom looked good for a mother. It was one less thing to be embarrassed about in front of friends.

Unless someone brought something up about his own parents, the topic of each other's parents wasn't broached—at least not in front of their child, but we all knew we judged parents the same way we judged everything—by how cool they were.

"Grandma told a black woman in the check out line that she had too many items, and she started threatening Grandma, so Grandma ran home and peed in her pants." Nancy grabbed a paper napkin from the holder off the kitchen table, and wiped the snot that came out of her nose from laughing so hard.

"You think that's so funny, Missy? Just wait until you have grandchildren, and see how they talk to you."

"Mother, are you all right? Are you hurt? My goodness, when I left for work this morning everyone was fine. I come home, and hear that my daughter was robbed, and my mother was attacked."

"How should I be? I never heard such language, and in front of everyone she threatened me. I won't sleep for a year. But don't worry about me. Worry about Nancy and her coat. Worry about the whole world because I think it's falling apart."

Maybe Grandma was on to something.

That night, lying face down on the family room couch, with a throw pillow under my chin, I watched *The Ghost and Mrs. Muir* on TV. I liked Hope Lang, but she was no Gene Tierney, and the television show was a sad update on the movie that I loved so much. In the living room, Nancy plodded through *For All We Know* on the piano. Grandma worked the phones from the kitchen, updating her sisters on her near death experience at the grocery store. That left Mom and Dad the dining room to discuss the day's events. I filtered all the noise to hear only them.

"I'm furious about Nancy's coat, Eileen. What the hell is going on in that school, and what kind of kids are going there? We pay the highest school taxes in the area, and for what? We could move two blocks west into Michigami, pay half the taxes, and not have to worry about our kids being crime victims."

I flipped over, so my head was at the end of the couch closer to the door. If I turned off the television they'd know I was eavesdropping.

"Oh come on Jerry, don't be dramatic. We're not sending the kids to new schools. Nancy's a senior for God's sake. And Hampden High still offers a superior education. *The Ladies Home Journal* voted it the best high school in America last year. How bad can it be? Besides, we don't want to give the impression to the kids that the best way to solve anything is to run from it."

"There comes a point when it makes sense. I'm not speaking irrationally. Look at the people we know who tried to stay in their South Side homes as the neighborhood changed. After a few beatings and robberies they figured out the battle was over. They've all left the city. Besides, I don't want to make a point for integration on the backs of our kids."

"A lot of those people moved from the South Side to Hampden because integration seems to be working here. I think you're blowing this up. Nancy hasn't said much else about any goings on in school. I'm not too concerned. And Glen certainly seems happy at the junior high. Could he have better friends? I never hear about any problems, racial or otherwise."

"Well what about that crap we heard about changing the curriculum to be less biased towards whites? What the hell does that mean?"

"I told you, I only heard that from one of the girls in my mahjong group. Remember, we agreed we'd go to the next school board meeting to see what's what."

"Fine. Let's be sure we do. And we should talk to the kids, and specifically ask them if they have any concerns about school."

Oh great. Now I would have to decide how much to tell my parents about the blacks at school. I wondered if I'd be better off saying nothing. I'd heard people say, "You can't shelter kids forever. It's tough in the real world." My cousins in their all-white schools in more posh suburbs than Michigami or Hampden wouldn't last a week at my school. They probably never even saw a black person who wasn't on television or cleaning their house— or cleaning a house on television. I envied my cousins, sometimes. I couldn't imagine what it would be like going to a school without having to worry about getting hit in the head, knocked over, or having my lunch stolen from my locker.

I didn't want my parents getting all up in arms, and humiliating me with a visit to the school, making a scene with the principal. Nancy had a friend in high school who kept getting picked on by a black girl in her class. When Nancy's friend's father noticed a bruise on his daughter, she admitted that this girl had hit her. He showed up at the principal's office the next day, and asked to meet the girl who was beating on his daughter. The principal assumed they would all sit down together for a nice chat, and try to understand the black girl's issue with the white girl. Instead, before the principal could say anything, Nancy's friend's father turned toward the girl, and quietly, but firmly said that if she ever laid a finger on his daughter again, he had friends who would see to it that her head would be found floating in the canal. Amid the principal's protestations, he immediately stood up and left the building. Mission accomplished. The girl never came near his daughter again. But that wasn't Dad's style.

Complicating the issue for me was the fact that I liked some of the black kids at school. The ones I didn't like, often made school entertaining with their antics and their personal vendettas against "whitey." The matter was a true shade of gray. On the rare occasions in gym when I made a good play—like catching a pop-up in softball—they'd offer words of encouragement along the lines of "Way to go, boy," but I knew they meant it as a compliment—mostly.

When a relative would ask me something about school that hinted at problems that they believed inevitably accompanied a black presence, such as crime and violence, I would get defensive and deny it, and claim that everything was great. I believe my answer would have been different, if they had asked me that question at the moment I was confronted by a black kid in the hall who wouldn't let me pass, while calling me "boy."

I could still hear Grandma in the kitchen. "All I did was tell her that she had too many items. What am I, some kind of politician from the South? I never said a prejudiced word in my life. What did we ever know from being prejudiced? I never even heard the word until that King fellow started marching around. I tell you, to them, your life and my life aren't worth a nickel."

CHAPTER TEN

Thursday, January 15, 1970

With the exception of swimming on a hot day, outdoor activities in extreme temperatures tormented me. Before the rise of soccer, the only popular, organized sport outside of school was Little League baseball, and a few of my friends participated. Fortunately, my parents were indifferent to organized sports, and never brought up the subject.

The son of a family friend once chose to have a baseball birthday party in the middle of August. *What a rotten idea*, I thought as I took my position in right field. The temperature hovered around ninety degrees with high humidity as Helios and tears blinded me mercilessly. Bright sunlight, like cold air and wind, caused my eyes to continuously water, rendering me semi-blind out in the field. I failed to see the fun in this exercise. My friend and I didn't go to the same school, so I didn't know any of the other kids, which added to my misery. I kept looking to the mothers in the stands under their umbrellas sipping lemonade searching for a merciful face (Mom?) who might shout out, "it's too hot for those boys to be out there." I wanted to be in the stands with them.

I struck out on my first at bat. After my performance, Mom left to do some errands. My next time up, I hit a home run. Okay. There were four fielding errors, but I was ecstatic as I crossed home plate. It was the closest to a real homerun I would ever get, and Mom didn't see it. By then I had had enough heat, and the sweat was stinging my eyes. I contributed more than my fair share to my team, so I faked a headache. My friend's mother took me into her centrally air-conditioned house, and gave me lemonade. I lay back on her plush, white, velvet sofa that was wrapped in a plastic slip-cover, and I read *Archie* comics and *Mad Magazine* until Mom picked me up.

Now I had another day of outdoor fun ahead of me. Our plan was for Gary's mom to drive us to the stadium at the university in Hampden to ice-skate.

At my request, my parents bought me a pair of hockey skates to replace my old training skates with double blades. I hadn't skated in a long time, but Ken and some of the other guys had taken an interest in playing hockey, and I didn't want to be left out. I liked to say that I owned hockey skates. It sounded cool. They were dark brown and black, and looked tough, but they hurt like hell. This pair of leather torture devises held my shaky ankles in a stiff chokehold, confirming my belief that sports and discomfort are inextricably linked.

I faced a sunny, bitterly cold day as I stood at the opened front door, so I could see Mrs. Kogan's blue Chevy Impala drive up. Matzah and I squinted out the storm door. We each made our own little patch of fog on the glass. Matzah searched in vain for something of interest on the quiet street. Grandma called to me from the kitchen, "It's freezing cold outside. Don't you think you should close that door before we all catch pneumonia? My knee hurts me so today, I can hardly stand."

"Don't worry Grandma. They'll be here any minute."

"Why should I worry? Your father pays the heating bills."

Gary's mom pulled into the driveway, and honked. I shouted "good-bye" to anyone in range, and pulled the front door closed. The sun glinted off the upper part of the blades of my skates that I slung over my shoulder to look as jock-like as possible. I wished we were headed for the comforts of a movie theater, instead of an outdoor ice rink where I'll be struggling along on my ankle-bones, trying to see through teary eyes.

"Hi, Mrs. Kogan," I said, sliding into the back seat with Gary and Ken.

"Hello Glenny," Gary's mom said, slightly turning from her chauffeur's seat in the front. "Hope you're dressed nice and warm today. It's plenty windy. You boys be certain to take breaks, and go inside to warm up, and get some nice, hot chocolate. Okay?"

Gary's mom was a kindergarten teacher, and she talked to us as if we were in her class. I didn't mind, as long as it was Gary's mom and not mine. I could sit back and relax, and let Gary worry, if she said anything queer and embarrassing. A home run was when an argument broke out among a friend's family in your presence, because it was proof that your family wasn't the only abnormal one on the planet.

Mrs. Kogan dropped us off near the stadium, but we still had to cross a large parking lot to get to the skating rink. We walked with our heads down, in deference to the sun. We didn't see the four older boys approach from the opposite direction. I glanced up too late, recognizing four Irish Catholic boys from my neighborhood—members of a group that referred to themselves as the St. John Kike Kickers. I tensed up, but Gary and Ken, still oblivious, continued their conversation about some obscure Chicago Bears statistic.

I cleared my throat, in a vain attempt to get their attention. I nudged Ken who looked up, and nudged Gary. In unison, we changed the angle of our approach to give the bigger guys clearance, but they'd already decided they were going to have some fun with us.

Terry O'Connor stuck out his foot, and tripped Ken, closest in line to the Kike Kickers.

"Sorry girls. You need to watch where you're going." Terry and his three friends, all of whom I recognized from my neighborhood, laughed while epithets of *kikes* and *queers* burned my ears. My abhorrence to any perceived injustice caused adrenaline to surge through my body. I let Gary help Ken to his feet.

I never learned how to defend myself, except for the wrestling holds they taught us in gym, but I had serious doubts that Terry would agree to get into the starting position for beginning a match. Dad never taught me to box. We weren't a physical family; we left that to the Kennedy's and their sort. Dad fought the Germans in WWII, and Grandpa fought them in WWI, but I couldn't imagine either of them in a brawl.

This explosive rage in the face of injustice was dangerous when mixed with my inability to defend myself physically. My friends looked on, mouths wide open in disbelief as I ran up behind the four guys who walked away laughing, with their backs to us.

I zeroed in on Terry's back. Running toward him at full speed, I pushed him forward with enough momentum to force him to his knees. Terry, completely shocked, glared back at me. Uh oh! My anger now released, I had no second act. I suddenly wished I had controlled myself, because all four boys turned to me aching for a fight. As they approached, I started swinging wildly in all directions, like a windmill gone berserk. Ken and Gary started laughing as the four older boys closed ranks around me. One kid held me, while Terry knocked the wind out of me with a single punch to the gut that went through my parka.

That was the end of it. These guys weren't killers. Their parents knew my parents well enough to say "hello" to them in the grocery store. They let me go, and walked away pleased with the outcome of our encounter. I heard almost maniacal laughter as they continued to call out "faggot" and some religious slurs over their shoulders, until they were beyond the range of our ability to hear. Curled on the ground, I tried to catch my breath.

"Nice one, Brains. Are you trying to get yourself killed?" Gary said, hovering over me.

Ken was laughing so hard that he could hardly get the words out. "I wish I had a camera. You should've seen yourself swinging, like some kind of a nut. Great technique. I tell you Feigman, yesterday the Fudgecicle, and today this. You're a wild man."

From my seat on the cold, hard ground, I too started to laugh, and rose to my feet, grabbing Gary's outstretched arm for balance. Convulsed with laughter, Ken closed his eyes, and imitated me with my fists flying in all directions. I pointed to the rip in Ken's pants caused by his fall, and this made Gary and me laugh even harder.

"Hey, thanks for the back up, guys. At least I got back at O'Connor. You could've helped me somehow."

"And miss the show?" Ken said. This sent Gary back into more laughter.

We spent the rest of the afternoon skating without incident. As I had anticipated, I was cold, my ankles ached, and I was half blind from watery eyes. The sky was an intense shade of blue. The weak sunlight offered no respite from the cold. Nothing was melting: not the fat layer of snow on the tree branches, not the icicles hanging from the gutters of the storefronts across the street, and certainly not the hard ice that banged my knees each time I fell. If people were having so much fun, why was there so little laughter? I hated my new skates, and never wore them again.

CHAPTER ELEVEN

Same Day

When I entered the blessed warmth of home, the smell of percolated coffee on the stovetop enveloped me. Scratching under Matzah's chin, I followed voices to the kitchen where Nancy was deep in conversation with Grandma and her sister Gussie in a coffee klatch. Today the smell of coffee is one that evokes a visceral response; I want to hug my beloved grandmother.

"Glen dolly, come sit with us, and I'll make you something to eat. Come on. Sit. Say hello to Aunt Gussie. Go hang your coat up. You must be freezing. Why you have to go out in such a weather." Grandma began pulling things out of the refrigerator.

I walked over to Aunt Gussie, and kissed the soft, saggy cheek she turned up toward me. Nancy and I acknowledged each other with quick glances. I dumped my skates outside the door to the garage, jammed my wool cap and gloves into my pockets, and hung my parka on its designated hook. Matzah, sensing another meal, jumped up, and sat on the remaining empty chair next to me.

Nancy, now a coffee-drinker, continued where she left off, before my entry inadvertently interrupted her.

"Everything about that movie is so cool. The story is really great, and the actors are so neat too. I don't think Clark Gable or Leslie Howard is really that great looking, but still…"

Nancy had just returned from *Gone With The Wind*. The movie was re-released the previous month for its 30th anniversary, and it was held over at Michigami's premier theater.

"I wish I were alive back then, in the Old South, before the Civil War. It would've been so cool to wear those clothes, and live in such a beautiful world."

"Such a beautiful world? The first time you had to *pish* outside in an outhouse, you'd be running back to the future." Grandma was quick to crush Nancy's fantasy, but Aunt Gussie laughed out loud.

"Remember those, Mae? Thank God our Pa had money, and we always had indoor plumbing. But back when we were kids, that was an exception."

"You guys, I'm talking about this beautiful plantation life, chivalry, ladies, and the clash of civilizations, and you're talking about toilets!"

"That's what life is about, Nancela. Everyday things, like toilets, mean more to you on a daily basis than the clash of civilizations," Aunt Gussie said, using her talking-to-students-for-over-forty-years voice. Now retired, Aunt Gussie was respected by her sisters, but not as much for her college education, or the reputation for excellence she earned during her years of teaching. Instead, they were impressed with the amount of her monthly pension that each sister knew to the penny. Aunt Lilly's husband left her more money, but Aunt Gussie earned hers on her own, and she famously held tight to it.

Aunt Gussie and Grandma resembled each other physically, with their stout bodies, ample bosoms, and soft blue eyes, but their minds diverged. Aunt Gussie sought knowledge, while Grandma believed that she was born knowing everything she needed to know—unless it sprang from gossip.

"Your sister just saw *Gone With the Wind*. So you liked the movie, huh Nance?" Aunt Gussie was enjoying having someone so young interested in conversing with her.

"When you were both younger, you wore those long dresses didn't you? And corsets and all that?"

"And how we did. But we didn't have those big hoops. They were long out of fashion, even for our mother. We wore those hobble skirts that made it hard to walk; they were so tight around the bottom. Remember, Gussie, how they used to have to help us get on the street car?" Grandma smiled, and looked at Aunt Gussie for confirmation, but it wasn't forthcoming.

"You were older than me, Mae. By the time I was out of kids' clothes, the dresses weren't so tight." Aunt Gussie's pride in her relative youth was showing, although she was only four years younger than Grandma.

"But Nancy," Aunt Gussie continued, "Do you think life was so good then? Maybe if you were a Gentile who owned a plantation it was lovely, but for Jews like us, things weren't so aye, aye, aye, not to mention if you were colored. Having slaves wasn't right. Remember the Exodus."

"I know that. It just seems that everything was so much simpler then, and so romantic too. I'm not saying the slavery thing was good. But to be honest, the black kids in school are often so mean and wild; I just wish someone had some control over them."

"I don't know what's going to be with these colored today. Look what happened to me at the grocery store." Grandma reminded us of her recent ordeal.

"I'm surprised you have problems in the school here," Gussie said. "I thought they were good colored families living in Hampden. Not like those gangsters in the city. God, they come into the schools, and everything goes downhill. The kids have no respect for teachers—and their parents aren't much better, so from whom will they learn? I blame the parents. They don't seem to give a darn. Teachers take their life in their hands teaching in those schools, and it isn't right. I think I retired just in time."

I devoured the bologna sandwich Grandma made for me, along with the Jay's potato chips and pickles she put on the side as I listened to Aunt Gussie extol the virtues of an earlier era.

"When I started teaching, you respected a teacher. Kids were plenty poor then, but poverty was no excuse for bad manners. The parents backed us up. I don't care if they were poor, right off the boat, and didn't know a lick of English; they still taught their kids to respect teachers. I tell you, I'm glad I'm retired now. I wouldn't want to deal with the garbage thrown at the teachers in the cities nowadays. They can't teach. They're disciplinarians, and the kids behave worse than prison inmates. It's getting to be too dangerous to go into those schools. So much for the future of our country."

"I don't like to talk about it, Aunt Gussie, but I had my coat stolen from my locker this week. When I told cousins Susie and Lisa, they asked me why we don't just move across Lawson Avenue to the Michigami side of town. Sometimes I wish Mom and Dad would sell this house, and move us."

Susie and Lisa were Aunt Gussie's grandchildren who lived in a nearby, all white, suburb.

"Isn't that a shame? When they moved here Hampden was supposed to have the best schools in the country; right at the top," Grandma said, setting a handful of Oreos in front of me. She returned for a glass of milk. It bothered her that Gussie might think her own grandchildren went to better schools.

"That's right, Mae. Somebody must be making some wrong decisions."

"The school is great, Grandma." Outsiders brought out Nancy's loyalty, as well as my own. "I hate for people to criticize Hampden. I think we're much more advanced and worldly than the kids at some of the other schools on the North Shore. Those kids are shallow. All they care about are clothes and shopping. They never get involved in war protests or helping fight pollution and that stuff."

Then my sister went where I rarely did.

"It's just that it could be so much better if we didn't have to deal with crime and insults and assaults and general disruptions caused by so many of the black kids. No wonder all the whites are moving out of the South Side. I honestly can't blame them. All you hear about are the mistreated blacks. People assume the whites are bigots, but do they ask why the whites feel they need to move?"

Aunt Gussie shook her head as if to say, *I have no answers for you.*

"Do you think I'm prejudiced? I know we aren't supposed to be prejudiced, and I really don't think I am. I'm just being honest, which no one else seems to be when the subjects of blacks and integration come up. I could never say what I just said to you in any classroom discussion on race. I'd be lynched," she said with no apparent irony.

Nancy continued expressing the very things my friends and I talked about to each other; and thought about silently around others.

"They're just mean-spirited, loud, rough bullies, and the girls are much worse than the boys are." Nancy was good with words. Mom, Dad, and I had a difficult time winning an argument with her. Mom gave her the most competition. She could always fall back on, "because I'm your mother," as her trump card. Otherwise, Mom just screamed louder than Nancy.

Nancy softened her tone to the *let's not be overheard by Walter Cronkite* voice.

"I feel bad saying it, and I know we support civil rights and everything, and that segregation and racism are wrong, but they make it so hard for my friends and me to want to be integrated with them. After all, they seem to hate us, and would prefer to be by themselves. They act as if we owned those plantations. We've never done anything to them, but they hate us for being white. They don't even get that Jews are the whites on their side. Isn't that true?" Nancy looked to Aunt Gussie for confirmation.

"Ha. Our family was busy getting killed by our fellow Europeans before the Civil War. There wasn't much time for planting cotton in Mississippi." Aunt Gussie leaned back and patted the table as if for emphasis.

"Gussie, remember when Pa bought that poultry farm in Dallas, and we moved from New York City?" Grandma's eyes sparkled when she remembered her childhood.

"Gram, tell me about that again. I love hearing about life in the old days." While it was Nancy who made the request, I shared her enthusiasm. Even if I couldn't wear one of those long dresses and big, feathered hats, it would be cool to live in a time when women wore them regularly.

I loved history. My grandparents were lucky to have lived so far in the past—at least my American born, maternal grandparents. I had the same notions about the early twentieth century, the years of my grandparents' youth that I did about Dickens's London in *Oliver*: it was somehow safer when people's roles were defined.

Silly me. How much better my own childhood would've been, if our roles were even less defined, and everyone was free to be himself, without fear of judgment.

Grandma was glowing at the rare interest Nancy was taking in something she had to say.

"Well, some of our father's real estate deals in New York turned bad in the Panic of aught seven, and he got wind of some opportunities in Dallas from his brother Solomon. Uncle Solly was always up to something, and as smart as Pa was, he let Solly talk him into things. Don't forget, our father came here in 1880 at age thirteen from Vienna, with nothing, and by the time he was twenty, he was worth millions in New York real estate."

"I sure wish we had that money now." That was my first interjection into the conversation. The loss of the Strohman family fortune in the Great Depression was a different story.

"Go on, Mae, tell her about Dallas," Aunt Gussie urged, as excited as Grandma. Her own grandchildren never wanted to hear her talk at all, let alone delve into her childhood.

"I'm telling her. Let me catch my breath. So anyhow, Your great-grandpa bought this poultry farm— by that time they had those refrigerated train cars—and he started sending frozen poultry up to big cities like Chicago and New York, and he made another fortune. Then he sent for Ma and us seven girls to join him in Dallas."

I imagined a uniformed maid opening a heavy wooden front door, fitted with stained glass as she accepted the telegram at the big mansion, in the bucolic Brooklyn of 1909. There was my great-grandmother gathering up her seven daughters for the life-changing move to Texas.

"What did we know from Dallas? In those days, without radio and television, people from New York and people from Dallas were from different planets. And there weren't many Jews there."

"Tell her about the park, Mae, you know, you and Lilly."

"I'm telling her. Give me a minute, will you?" And then Grandma leaned in toward Nancy, and looked from her to me. She and Aunt Gussie reminded me of two conspiratorial children.

"One of the first days in Dallas I went for a walk with Aunt Lilly, and we sat down on a park bench, and all these women would pass us by, and stare at us. We didn't know why they were looking at us. We couldn't imagine. Then one of these nice dressed Gentile women, I'll never forget her, with one of those big hats with fruit and feathers, she comes over and says to us, 'What are y'all sitting there for?'"

"Well, Lilly and I didn't know to whom she was speaking when she said 'y'all.' We never heard that, and we were looking for other people. Who were 'y'all?' Lilly and I were the only two sitting there."

Nancy smiled, and so I did as I swallowed the last bit of Oreo, and picked the crumbs off the plate.

"So then she repeats it, and we guessed she meant us, so I asked, 'What do you mean? We're just sitting looking at the pretty park.' And she says, 'Well, don't y'all know that bench is for colored folk only? White folk should sit over there.' And she pointed to a different bench." Grandma pointed towards the window as if the white people's bench was out on the patio.

"Oh my gosh. That is so bizarre. It's unbelievable." Nancy exclaimed.

"It wasn't so long ago—maybe five or six years—that it was still like that down there," Aunt Gussie said with authority. That startled me. I never thought Jim Crow overlapped my life. Grandma continued.

"Who knew? Lilly and I had hardly ever seen colored people before, and now here she's telling us they have their own benches. I figured colored people must be very important down there to have their own benches. What did we know?" Grandma paused for dramatic effect, and that gave Aunt Gussie a chance to step in again.

"Remember, Mae, how on Emancipation Proclamation Day they'd all come around and entertain, going house to house?"

"I sure do. Such fun. Those were good years in Dallas. Half the time we didn't even wear any shoes. Remember when you were supposed to watch Edna, and you left her in that tree, and she got all bit up with ants?"

Aunt Gussie started to laugh. "Oh, I'd almost forgotten. Oh my, Ma almost killed me when we got home. Poor Edna. To this day I think she holds a grudge, heh-heh. When I think of her covered with all those ants."

Aunt Gussie's laugh was contagious, and Nancy and I joined in, totally enthralled by the two older women's reminiscences.

"See. Wasn't life better then? Grandma, you didn't even have to go to school," Nancy reminded her.

"Sure I did. I graduated public school in New York before we moved. We all did. And the younger girls all went on to high school, and graduated in Chicago, after we moved here."

"Yeah, but eighth grade Grandma. I'd be out of school already. That is so cool."

"What about me?" Aunt Gussie interjected quickly. "Don't forget I went to college. Girls didn't go to college so much in those days. Most girls just got married like your Grandma here. You weren't expected to go to college or work. You didn't work unless you were poor and you had to."

Surprisingly, Grandma gave no indication that she felt slighted by Gussie's implication.

"Pa didn't want you to go to college. Ma told him you were going, and she didn't want an argument." Grandma turned to Nancy. "Our mother let your great-grandpa rule most of the time, but he knew that when she put her foot down he better not argue."

"Wait, Nancy. You were saying life was better back then, but I remember it could be terrible. Whether the past was good or bad depends upon who is doing the remembering." Aunt Gussie's tone turned serious. She folded and unfolded a napkin in front of her when she wasn't speaking, and then suddenly stopped when it was her turn to say something. "One day when I was coming home from school, there was a crowd of people gathered in the park. They had just put up some kind of memorial arch there. Nothing too big, but big enough. Anyhow, I asked a girl I recognized from school what was happening. She said that a colored fellow had raped a white woman, and they were getting ready to hang him from the arch to punish him. The police were there, and they did nothing."

Aunt Gussie paused to allow the shock to register in our faces. Nancy and I didn't disappoint her. She continued, enjoying her role in revealing this horror.

"What they were doing was selling inches of rope for a quarter. They said when they sold enough rope to hang the poor fellow they would do it. Wouldn't you know it that everyone there was giving quarters so fast that soon they hanged him from the arch? I didn't stick around to see it, and when I got home, and told our mother, she wouldn't let any of us out of the house. Believe you me, we were all sick about it. And they left the man's body hanging up there all week to scare the other colored people. Ma kept us home until we heard they cut him down."

Aunt Gussie sat back and became silent, her words lingering over us. I suspect the time and distance from the event kept me from feeling as horrified as I thought I should.

"How awful," Nancy said. "It's sad and it's wrong and awful. But…"

Here came the inevitable "but" that you didn't want repeated on the evening news.

"…I wish somebody could scare the black kids in my school just enough so they'd know that there is some authority to answer to. They don't respect anyone. And it seems that the administration at the school accepts that, as if it's understandable, and the kids have to be forgiven for their behavior, because their ancestors suffered in the way you just described."

Then Nancy became more animated. "Anyhow, getting back to *Gone With The Wind*, I think it would be great if the boys today fought over us girls, and treated us like ladies."

"You girls today don't act like ladies." The immoral behavior of young women was one of Grandma's favorite topics. "The way they dress with their *pipiks* showing. And the way they talk. They don't look like ladies to me. The boys never had it so good. The girls today give the boys everything for nothing. What do they have to fight over?"

"Oh, Grandma." Nancy moaned as she rolled her eyes. But I agreed with Grandma. I liked to see girls in midis and maxis instead of miniskirts. Miniskirts had no elegance. The only things more ugly than bony legs sticking out of mini-skirts were those pathetic granny skirts.

"In my day and age," this was Grandma's favorite way to begin a lecture, "women acted like ladies. Women didn't smoke, and if, heaven forbid, they divorced, you'd cross the street when you saw them coming down the sidewalk. When your grandfather and I dated, he had to have me home by eight o'clock, or my father would've thrown him down the front steps. These women today without brassieres; we never could've left our rooms."

The thought of Grandma's large, ivory-colored, unadorned brassieres that occasionally hung from the shower curtain rod flashed through my mind, but I quickly pushed the thought away. Instead, I sat with my anxiety about living in an era when girls wore miniskirts and no bras, which almost guaranteed that I'd be expected to have sex before marriage. Perversely, I calculated it would've been better to live in a more restrictive time. In 1970, I didn't know that sex with a man would ever be a possibility.

CHAPTER TWELVE

Friday, January 16, 1970

I arrived home from school on Friday, walked through the front door, and Mike Douglas's voice on TV assaulted my ears. I ignored Matzah's insistent jumping, and followed the noise. Grandma was sitting on the couch with her eyes closed, and her head in a position that would cause her to wrap a Ben Gay soaked rag around her neck before bed.

"Grandma, do you mind if I turn this down? It's so loud." I lowered the volume as I asked permission. I startled Grandma, but she quickly got her bearings.

"How was school, Dolly? Are you hungry?"

"School was fine. I'm a little hungry."

"Take a piece of challah."

Grandma lifted herself off the couch with a moan. "I tell you my knee hurts me so. Once I sit down, I can't get up." Grandma walked stiffly, following me to the kitchen.

"So, what's for dinner?"

"What do you think is for dinner?"

"Chicken or brisket."

"You're right. It's chicken or brisket."

It didn't matter. Grandma's dishes all tasted the same. Seasoning meant a teaspoon of salt, a bay leaf or an onion, but I didn't know there was an alternative to bland. The food was hearty, filling, and abundant. Grandma didn't believe chicken or meat was cooked until it was "soft" and fell off the bone. At every meal she asked Grandpa, "How's the meat, Leo? Soft?" For fifty-two years of marriage, Grandpa gave the same robotic response to keep the peace: "The softest yet, Mae."

I opened the refrigerator door to forage, but Grandma wrested her territory away from me.

"Go sit down. I'll bring you some challah and butter. You shouldn't ruin your appetite. I cooked enough for an army, should anyone ask."

Grandma's identity was tied to her housekeeping and cooking, and she hungered for us to recognize her domestic accomplishments. It would've been easy to fill her heart with joy by lavishing praise on her for her brisket or gefilte fish, or her linen closet where each item appeared to be folded with a ruler, but Grandpa was the only one who cooperated. We just didn't think about it. She was forced to fish for compliments, and make bitter remarks.

Matzah knew when it was Friday, and Friday meant additional guests for the Sabbath dinner. He manned his customary station at the living room window, whining with anticipation. Friday also meant Grandma's ritual that we called: *Where the heck is Grandpa?*

Grandpa arrived faithfully for Friday night dinners around 6:00, allowing for the inconsistencies of public transportation. He took the L and a bus from downtown Chicago to within two blocks of the house, and walked the remaining distance. Each week, shortly after 5:00, Grandma would insist that Grandpa was late. According to her puzzling recollection, he always arrived by 5:00. For one hour Grandma shuffled to the window every five minutes, fretting and muttering about Grandpa's tardiness. "Where the heck is Grandpa? What's so darned important at that office that he can't get out on time to get here before the whole meal is ruined?"

"Grandma, no one is even here yet. Dinner isn't for an hour. Just relax."

"What's it to you? Why do I cook all day? I hope he's all right. God forbid he should take a cab from the train. What's he saving his last nickel for. For me? I'll be dead long before he will."

And so it went.

I finished my snack, and went up to my room. It was already dark outside, so I flipped on lights along the way. Whenever I had a moment alone, my thoughts turned to sex and masturbation. Since my masturbatory fantasies were of a homosexual nature, I had tremendous guilt about masturbating. My friends talked openly and jokingly about their obsessive habits, but I kept my mouth shut during those discussions. I feared if I talked about masturbating, I'd reveal the nature of my fantasies. I wondered if I had enough time to beat off before Nancy or Mom got home. Matzah started to bark excitedly downstairs, so I decided to keep my pants on.

Nancy breezed by my open door, on the way to her bedroom. "Hey," she said as she passed. I heard her take the handle of her pink princess phone off its cradle as her door closed.

I thought about calling Ken to talk about the birthday party coming up the next evening. Since it was a birthday party, Barbara Needleman's mother said Barbara could go, so I could look forward to being her boyfriend for a night—even though it was a role that obligated me to make out with her.

I considered giving her my I.D. bracelet. A lot of guys had one. It was masculine to have a gold or silver bracelet with a rectangular plate where your first name was engraved. Giving it to a girl meant you were going steady. When the bracelet was returned at the inevitable break-up, it was accompanied by compulsory tearful drama.

Not counting Pamela Blake's revelations about her sex life, as well as comments made by some of the other black kids, I didn't know of any kids in my grade who "went all the way". There was a rumor that Steve Tompkins, a Protestant guy whose parents were divorced, got a blowjob from a sales girl at a store in Texas when he visited his father last summer, but Steve couldn't be trusted. I never gave him much thought, because I didn't think he was particularly attractive.

I was eleven when I first learned the slang term for fellatio. Nancy's friend, Marla, teased me then about being so queer. She asked if I knew what "blowjob" meant as Nancy giggled and looked at me doubtfully. I tried to put the word into a context, but I could only think of snow blowers, like the one our neighbors owned. Marla was triumphant.

That evening, I was well acquainted with the subject of blowjobs, thanks to Pamela Blake's Monday morning recaps of her weekend activities, and many discussions with my friends. I myself devoted much quiet contemplation time to the subject. Getting one from Barbara was out of the question. The possibility of me giving one to anybody didn't exist.

Mom's brother, Uncle Marty, often gave me signals that I should be thinking about making out with girls. Whenever the subject of my adolescence came up, he'd remind me that I'd soon have the joy of "tuning in the radio." He'd then hold out his hands, as if he were tuning radio knobs—his idea of stand-ins for breasts.

I descended to the kitchen. Mom and Grandma were talking about the plans for the evening.

"Don't forget," Mom said, after I kissed her hello on her powdered cheek, "we have to be out of here no later than 7:30 to get to temple. We have that thing with the black community at services tonight."

"So you'll sit down right away, and I'll give you dinner." Grandma checked pots on the stove, and peered inside the oven door.

"There's still plenty of time if we eat after Dad gets here at 6:00."

"I don't know where your father is already. I told him you wanted to eat early tonight. I hope he's okay."

Mom rolled her eyes, and exhaled deeply. She carefully chose her arguments with Grandma, to spare us endless bickering. She decided to let this last remark go unanswered.

"What thing at the temple? Am I supposed to go? Is this a requirement for my bar mitzvah?" I didn't like going to services. Our rabbi's sermons were unpleasant. He was always railing about the latest anti-Israel or anti-Jewish thing that was happening in the world, and then admonishing all of us to do something about it. There wasn't much that I could do, so I sat there feeling angry at the injustices he described, and helpless to do anything about them.

Friday night services were not well attended by Reform Jews. Who wanted to finish a week of work or school to sit through a two-hour service and a scolding? Years later I attended my first Catholic mass impressed that everyone was in and out within an hour, all obligations met with the efficiency of an assembly line. Unlike the regular reports of Arab attempts to destroy Israel that so concerned us, the Catholics weren't too worried about the future of Vatican City. There was no talk of the persecution of Christians. They left mass smiling, and if they happened to sin again, there was always one hour the next week to clear the books.

"Yes, you and your sister are coming with us. The sisterhood invited members of a South Side church to join us in the service tonight. The point is to bring us together over the things we have in common, such as civil rights and social justice. Obviously, we timed it with King's birthday yesterday."

"Oh man, Ma. That sounds really boring. Does Nancy know about this?" I knew Nancy would hate to give up a Friday night of social activity or hair washing to attend services.

"Yes, she knows, unless she forgot. You mister, should be going to services anyhow. We have your bar mitzvah coming up in a few months. Besides, this is a good example about what it means to be a bar mitzvah. As a *son of the commandment* it will become your obligation to do good deeds, and that includes working for social justice, to help the oppressed, no matter who they are. Is Nancy upstairs?"

"The oppressed? Who's oppressed? I'm oppressed. I'm the one who gets popped on the head, and called 'boy' at school, and the one who has to defend his lunch from being stolen by black kids."

"Don't dramatize, Glen. You go to a good school, and you're learning to get along with everyone. You can see blacks are no different from you."

"Yes they are. They are different. They're violent troublemakers—except for Melva." I adored our housekeeper, and immediately felt guilty having cast aspersions on her race.

"Glen, what's going on? Did something happen in school that I don't know about?"

Where to start? How would I describe the mix of fear and fun the blacks inspired in me, and the chaos that took place in the hallways, lunchroom, classrooms, and assemblies? I learned the three Rs in school, and my courses appeared to be more advanced than my cousins' in their sheltered, homogenous schools, but learning was diluted by the distractions and disturbances. So why didn't I want to tell Mom about those disturbances? Why didn't any of us tell our parents about them? A few kids must've said something, because after sixth grade, the parents of two kids took them out of our school, and sent them to private school. They rejoined the public school system in high school where things were slightly calmer.

For reasons I don't fully understand, we kids kept a pact of silence, leaving our parents to assume our school was peacefully integrated. Standing in the busy kitchen before dinner didn't seem like the time or place to break the silence. I didn't know it, but very soon, the silence would be shattered.

Grandma always said, "There are good and bad in all groups," and my classmates, both black and white, were no exceptions. But that didn't stop my white classmates and me from growing into segregationists based on our daily experiences. Years later, when choosing where to live, it was safer to avoid all blacks for fear the "good" ones would cause the not-so-good to follow.

There was little in my life in 1970, or the years since, to alter these loathsome pronouncements. Moral judgments are easy to cast from a safe distance from the front lines where little or nothing is at risk. But moralists take heart. I doth protest too much; proof that I am wired for either guilt or proper thinking, or both.

Mom tired of waiting for my response to her "what's going on," question, and turned to Grandma, who was peering through steam into a large pot of chicken soup on the stove.

"Ma, are you and Dad joining us tonight?"

"Who is going to wash dishes if I go? I'll have all that food to put away. Besides, I told your in-laws that we'd play *kaluki* with them after dinner."

Grandma had no interest in going to services. She thought they took people out of the house, away from a meal, and out of her control. She taught my mother that it was important to go to services to hear the reading of the Torah, and learn what God had to say, and she sent Mom and Uncle Marty for a religious education. Grandpa's role was to set a good example. Grandma saw her part as the keeper of the stove, so that a meal was ready upon the return from services.

"Is there anything you want me to do Ma?" Grandma loved when Mom posed this question. It put her in charge.

"What's to do? Just sit and eat—if your father would only get here. That man is going to drive me crazy." Mom and I smiled at each other.

Matzah barked as the garage door labored again. Smiling, Dad emerged from the garage, and immediately fussed over Matzah, who idolized him above any of us. Mom, Nancy, and I marveled at how demonstrative Dad was with the dog. I prayed that he never showed this excessive ooh-ing and aah-ing side of himself in front of my friends. Nancy, on the other hand, thought it was cute to see a man being so affectionate. Mom agreed with her.

"Hello, hello, hello." Dad went around the room planting kisses. No one was more receptive than Grandma, although she pretended to be bothered. She loved Dad, and he could do no wrong, even when he teased Grandma in harmless ways. He could charm the support hose right off her.

"I don't need to change for tonight, do I, Dear?" Dad turned to Mom.

"Not at all. You're fine."

"Good. Anyone else coming for dinner besides your dad?"

"Your folks and Aunt Lilly. You forgot?"

"Oh, right. Okay. Dinner at the usual time?"

Dad had directed this question to Mom, but it was an invitation Grandma couldn't ignore.

"Who knows? The food will ruin if we don't eat soon. God knows when Leo will get here, and where are Lilly and your folks? What do any of them have to do all day? Jerry, your father sleeps half a day. I don't know why he and your mother should be late."

"Now, now, Ma," Dad said. Not everyone is as efficient as you are at managing so much. I bet they'll all be here by 6:00, so we can eat at exactly the same time we do every Friday night."

Grandma knew Dad was right, but it was against her nature to agree.

"What do I care? If they're late they're late, and the dinner is ruined."

Dad's parents, Bubbie and Zadie, arrived with Grandma's sister Lilly at 5:45. At 5:55 Matzah excitedly announced that Grandpa had arrived. Out of habit, Grandma fired her usual questions, the light in her eyes belying her apparent annoyance. "Is everything okay? Why couldn't you get away sooner for once? Are you hungry? Are you ready to eat? The meat is so soft it fell off the bone already."

"Everything's fine," Grandpa said, giving Grandma a quick kiss on the cheek she had turned towards him with anticipation. "I'm so hungry I could eat shoe leather, so bring on your wonderful cooking."

CHAPTER THIRTEEN

Moments Later

At exactly 6:00, we stood around the dining room table. Dad put on a yarmulke, and took his place at the head of the table. Nancy and I stood on either side of him. The Friday night regulars had customary seats. Grandma was up more than down during a typical Shabbat dinner as she plodded back and forth to the kitchen.

Grandma's older sister Lilly, a wealthy widow, faced Dad. She was dressed more to preside over a state dinner than a Shabbat table. She often looked regal in expensive suits over her thin frame, and her coiffed hair was dark red.

Grandma hovered by the door from the kitchen, anxiously waiting for the Sabbath blessings to be finished, so she could serve the matzahball soup. Dad placed one hand softly on my head and one on Nancy's. He turned to me and said, "May God make you like Ephraim and Menashe." He then turned to Nancy and said, "May God make you like Sarah, Rebecca, Rachel, and Leah." He then looked back and forth between the two of us and continued, "May God bless you and watch over you. May God make His face to shine down upon you and show you favor. May God grant you peace. Amen."

"Amen," came the echo around the table.

The religious objects on the table—the two brass candlestick holders, the silver wine goblet, the challah cover, and the shawl Mom would use to cover her head for the blessings—were most of what my ancestors could grab as they fled the persecution of Jews in Austria and Russia.

After Mom blessed the Sabbath candles, Zadie raised the *Kiddush* cup, while we sang with gusto the blessing over wine. Zadie's Hebrew was accented with Yiddish, while I voiced the modern Israeli pronunciation that we learned in Hebrew school. If a non-observant Jewish friend joined us on a Friday night, I would hold back my enthusiasm. I was self-conscious and embarrassed by my family's religious observance, because I thought outsiders would judge it to be queer, although Grandpa's disapproving glance would set me right.

Finally, Mom lifted the challah cover from over the two loaves of the Sabbath bread, and we recited the traditional blessing before eating. The bread was passed around the table as each person pulled off a piece.

We didn't eat until the *tzadakah* or charity box went around the table, and each of us put some coins into it. Grandma and Bubbie never had their purses with them at the table, and neither did Aunt Lilly, so as always, Grandpa covered them.

Nancy and I took turns each month picking out a charity to receive the contents of the box. Mom and Dad emphasized the need to give the money to a charity that helped the less fortunate, but Nancy usually selected an animal shelter. I suggested we give the money to Melva, because I knew she was poor, and I loved her deeply. She could've used the money to buy herself tickets to a Cubs game. My parents vetoed my suggestion, but Melva did get a raise out of my intercession.

When the religious rituals ended, Grandma was free to commence hers. She brought in bowls of chicken soup ladled from the big pot. Her face radiated satisfaction for the first time that evening, and it reflected back from the faces around the table. I was old enough to recognize that the grownups were happy to have the family together, safe and healthy.

The table exploded with conversation. Food was the primary topic. Politics and religion were close seconds.

"Mae, how do you get your matzahballs so soft?" Bubbie asked this question every week.

"Delicious, Mae." Aunt Lilly agreed.

"The soup is the best ever, Mae, old girl." Grandpa always added a little something to Grandma's name.

"So how was school, kids?" Dad attempted to involve Nancy and me.

"Fine." We answered in unison.

"That's it? This is an answer? Did you learn anything?" Bubbie asked. She'd never been to school, and saw it as the great privilege of American children.

"Well, you know," Nancy said, picking up the question, "the usual stuff: math, Spanish, English, biology." Nancy pushed her hair behind her ears and leaned over the soup.

"English. Why do American children need to learn English? I should speak such good English as my grandchildren." Zadie's eyes danced with delight at his own remark.

Bubbie jumped back in. "English yes, but Spanish? What can you do with Spanish? Live in Spain?" She looked around the table at the other adults for agreement. Bubbie's black eyeglasses were set with rhinestones in the corners of the frames. The strong magnification gave her blue eyes the appearance of a fish staring through a bowl.

Everyone looked amused except for Nancy. "Bubbie, everyone has to learn a foreign language. We can choose, Spanish,
French, or German. Spanish is the most popular because we live
close to Mexico and Puerto Rico, and everyone takes a vacation
there sooner or later."

"You should know how many Hispanic children we have in
our school now. I'd say a third. Many of them only know a little
English, and most of their parents don't speak any English." From
previous conversations I knew this to be Mom's sore spot. As out-
spoken as Mom was about civil rights, she couldn't accept that a
group that chose to immigrate to America should be considered
a minority entitled to special treatment that no other immigrants
were granted. She would not put them on a par with blacks who
suffered involuntarily through centuries of oppression.

Grandpa added his measure of reason. "It's no different from
the old Jewish neighborhoods at the turn of the century where so
many of the parents spoke Yiddish, and the kids learned English."

"No Dad, it isn't the same. The Hispanics have a different attitude. Jews, Italians, Germans, Slavs, Poles, Scandinavians, you
name it, they all wanted to learn English, and never demanded
that Americans speak their languages. They knew they were lucky
to be here, and that the responsibility was theirs to learn English.
They knew Americans spoke English before they got here.

"But we're getting all kinds of pressure to teach in Spanish as
well as English. They have programs now for teaching English as
a second language. The parents want Spanish translators when
they come to the school for conferences. Signs have to be written
in Spanish and English, as do instructions."

"So what do the others say, the Greeks, the Koreans, etc?"
Bubbie asked.

"That's a good question. What do they say? Nothing. They
learn English, and move on to better schools quickly. And what
truly disturbs me is the Spanish kids say things such as, 'back in

my country.' Can you imagine? They don't think of America as their country. They must be getting this from their parents."

"So why did they come here? When I got off the boat I kissed the ground of this golden land. They should go back to Spain, and speak all the Spanish they want." Bubbie nodded her head once, and patted her hand on the table for emphasis as she voiced her opinion.

Around the table, heads nodded in agreement.

"Do the children do better when they are taught in English *and* Spanish?" Aunt Lilly asked.

"The jury is out, but it doesn't matter. Due to their growing numbers, they have enough clout to have things their way. What I want to know is why the Asians come here in the same situation, make it a point to learn English, and ask for nothing in return? Their kids do the best in the school, and soon move on to a better neighborhood. That's enough evidence for me. The Hispanics should follow their example."

"It sounds to me like an attitude problem." Aunt Lilly had devoted her time and money to helping underprivileged families— mostly blacks—through her synagogue's sisterhood.

She continued. "The blacks went through centuries of discrimination, and I think some special consideration is called for. We have to help them catch up. But what kind of discrimination do Hispanics suffer different from any immigrant? They came here by choice, like everyone else, except the blacks and the Indians."

"Shame on them." Bubbie added.

"They're taking advantage, and their timing is good. Americans have started to feel guilt about the years of mistreatment of blacks, so the Hispanics are riding that wave." Aunt Lilly added.

I glanced at Grandpa for a clue as to what my opinion should be, but I couldn't read his face. He was active in a group of Jewish lawyers who gave free legal help for indigent blacks. Mostly they confronted shady landlords and employers. I loved hearing him talk about the evil white people he helped bring to justice. I rooted for the blacks against the cruel white men, and applauded Grandpa's victories. I took this as evidence that I based my opinions on facts, not races.

"Mae, they did a nice job on your hair today," Bubbie said.

Grandma had just walked back in the dining room, with a tray of brisket. Grandma smiled over the brisket. "They always marvel that my hair never turned gray. They talk about it at the beauty shop. The girl that washes my hair can't get over it."

"It's true, Grandma. How come you never had to dye your hair?" Nancy asked.

"I was always a blonde. They called me towhead in school. With my blue eyes they thought I was Swedish. Can you imagine? Remember Lilly?"

"Who can remember that far back, Mae?" Aunt Lilly smoothed her dyed, red hair back from her temples.

Grandma sniffed at Aunt Lilly. "Anyhow, my hair got a little darker as I got older; it just never seemed to go gray. It just got duller."

Grandma's hair had no color. It was somewhat transparent, like winter straw.

"Now *this* is a good brisket," Zadie weighed in.

"Ma, you outdid yourself." Although he hadn't taken a bite yet, Dad piled on the compliments, and Grandma ate them up.

"Is the meat soft, Leo? It cooked until it fell off the bone."

"The softest ever, Mae, my dear wifey." He completed Grandma's day. "So what's this thing you're all running off to tonight?"

"We invited members of that Jesse Jackson's Operation Breadbasket to speak at services tonight to coincide with Dr. King's birthday," Mom said.

"You know you're all welcome to join us," she added.

"Leo, take more bread." Grandma passed the challah to Grandpa.

"I thought we're having a hot game of *kaluki* tonight," Zadie said. "I brought my pennies from the *pushky*."

"Nancy, *mamela*, why don't you cut your hair? It's always in your face?"

"Nancy, you have such a pretty face. Why hide it with that hair always falling into your soup?" Two grandmas made for an imposing opposition, but Nancy held her ground.

"There's nothing wrong with my hair. It's the style."

"That long hair; she looks like that Cher. What are you going to do with kids? If we want her to cut her hair Mae, we should tell her to grow it long." Bubbie laughed at herself. "Aren't I right Leo? We should tell her the opposite of what we want her to do."

"Sonia, you should have been a diplomat," Grandpa answered her.

Apropos of nothing Aunt Lilly stated, "I've stopped attending religious services." Aunt Lilly dropped this bomb, and then went mute, waiting for the fallout to follow.

"Aunt Lilly, why? I can't believe that!" Mom said. All the adults, except Grandma, grew unusually silent as they looked to Aunt Lilly for enlightenment.

"I'll tell you why. I'm fed up, that's why. As you know, at services we pray for the wellbeing of all humanity regardless of race, creed, or religion. Yet the news comes back to us again and again how Jews are vilified throughout much of the world. It doesn't matter what we do. Who prays for us, and for our peace and wellbeing? Nobody, that's who, so I decided, enough! I'm through being a patsy."

Grandma noticed that Lilly's soliloquy had slowed the pace of food consumption; I sensed her annoyance. Friday night was her show. How long was Aunt Lilly going to carry on? Grandma tried unsuccessfully to force another piece of *kugel* onto Nancy's plate.

"I'm not sure I understand, Aunt Lilly." Mom was nonplussed.

"I just don't think I need to pray to a supreme being for the welfare of those who wish me ill. I'm done with that. We are taught that every life is sacred, and we are our brother's keepers, but no matter what we Jews have contributed to the world, including monotheism, ethics, and the value of life, invariably others see us as somehow standing in the way of their happiness. If they aren't praying for our conversion, they pray for our destruction.

"I can't buy into that, 'light a candle in the dark' malarkey anymore. The Gentiles, the Moslems, whoever it is against us today, they keep spitting out the flame."

Everyone sighed along with Aunt Lilly. Grandma started to speak, but Aunt Lilly cut her off.

"Look at the blacks. For years their cause was our cause, and now they align themselves with Moslems, leaders of the slave trade, and call us the enemy. They don't want our help. Fine. I'm not going to pray for them."

Just as I was getting worked up about the brutalities and injustices Jews continually faced, the mention of blacks conjured up an image of my black classmates seated around their own dinner tables listening to elders, getting themselves worked up over tales of persecution. Our common history of oppression used to bring us together.

Aunt Lilly paused. No one said anything. I wanted to reach for more challah, but felt it would be blasphemous to continue eating during her revelation.

Surely the words were profound—like one of the rabbi's sermons. Somewhere in what she said there was an excuse to get out of services, not that Mom and Dad would buy it.

When no one interrupted her, Aunt Lilly continued. I thought Grandma was going to throw something at her.

"Listen, my decision was a tough one to make. I'm betraying all our ancestors who were cursed to live during the endless centuries of hatred and violence against Jews. I can see irony in my position. No Jews ever had it better than we have in America, and yet I'm the one who gave up. They never gave up. "

"The oppressed usually don't give up," Grandpa interjected. "It's the ones who have it easy, like so many American Jews, who forget their reason for being, and lose site of their original cause."

That also sounded profound. There were hearty nods of agreement around the reference to the good life America provided Jews.

"I hope Uncle Lou isn't turning in his grave. Okay, I'm finished, Mae. You can stop glaring at me."

Aunt Lilly struck her palm down on the table and leaned back, holding her head up defiantly. She sought Grandpa's eyes, and held them. It hit me that maybe she was sweet on him at one time—or even now. They both had the same thoughtful manner of doing things, unlike Grandma's impulsive approach to life.

I tried to relate Aunt Lilly's revelation to my own experience. I didn't think any of the blacks in school were Moslems, although some of them brought up the name Elijah Mohammed from time to time, and he certainly sounded like a Moslem to me. None of them said anything at all about Jews in particular, good or bad. They discriminated indiscriminately. They cursed all whites equally.

"Go on, everyone. Eat!" Grandma said.

"Some Jews are shmucks." This was the first thing Zadie said, since Aunt Lilly opened her heart to us. Compared to her eloquent declaration, it was comical.

"Isaac!" Bubbie sat up, and slapped her hand on the table. "Are you *mishugah?*"

"Go ahead, Pa. Tell us why we're shmucks. I'll tell you if I agree." Dad said this with a slight smile on his face. He wanted to set the record straight for Nancy and me, because Zadie's words were often blunt, unpredictable, and disagreeable to Dad.

Now that Aunt Lilly gave up the conch, I felt it was okay to grab more bread. Grandma appeared less agitated.

"I'll tell you why some Jews are shmucks. The world *pishes* on their backs, and the self-hating Jewish shmucks are willing to believe it's raining."

"Isaac!" Again Bubbie Sonia smacked the table. "The *kinder* are at the table. Watch what you say."

I laughed out loud, and when my parents saw that I found humor in what Zadie said, they joined me in laughing.

Zadie looked surprised that we found his remark funny. He smiled briefly, and the light flickered in his eyes, but only for an instant as his look became steady. This Sabbath eve was filled with lessons, and as we would learn later, danger.

"The world treats us like *drek*, and these Jew-hating Jews find reason to blame themselves. It's easy to blame a victim, because you don't have to fight and defend victims against the bullies. It puts you on the stronger team. To me, that's being a shmuck. Anyone who runs from a fight is a schmuck. Zadie looked around the table now meeting everyone's eyes. The anger in his voice was rising. I sensed Mom's and Dad's growing unease.

"If one Jew finds another Jew he doesn't like, it gives him the excuse he needs to side with the Jew-haters—even to the point of denying us a homeland, which he would fight for and justify for any other people—as long as they weren't Jews. Those Jews are the biggest and most dangerous shmucks of all. If you look at the self-hating Jews, they think they're smarter than the rest of us. Ptooey on all of them."

Zadie turned his head sideways, away from the table and feigned spitting.

"Isaac, please. Don't get so worked up. Mae, I always mean to ask you how much sugar you put in the *kugel*. Yours tastes so much better than mine." Half the things Bubbie said in her lifetime were to distract others from Zadie. It didn't work this time. Grandma hadn't heard the question, and Dad jumped in.

"Pa, I agree with your assessment of Jew-hating Jews, but I don't agree that just because much of the world mistreats us we should stop being who we are—Jews. And to be Jews, we need to continue to do good works as commanded. The Torah that Glen is studying makes this clear. I can get discouraged, but instead I hope that little by little the world will take note. We can't do anything else. If we do, we become like them, and betray our heritage."

Bless Dad. I'm not sure he believed his own words to his core, in the way that Grandpa Leo and Mom did, but I knew he was saying it for the sake of Nancy and me. He didn't want us to take away a lesson of hopelessness or anger from Aunt Lilly's or Zadie's way of thinking.

Mom looked at Dad adoringly.

Aunt Lilly, no slouch, caught on to Dad's motives. "Jerry, you're a good man. Eileen, where did you find this *mensch*?"

Aunt Lilly gave an obligatory smile, and then turned to Dad. "Jerry, you make me feel foolish. What you say is true. To give up, to let them wear me down is to stop being me. In any case, I know one service I wouldn't miss for the world, and that's Glen's bar mitzvah." Dad hadn't changed Aunt Lilly's mind about anything, but I was glad she brought some attention to me.

"Here, here." Grandpa raised his wine glass, and winked at me. He allowed Dad's response to Aunt Lilly and Zadie to stand. He approved.

"And now tell me what's going on at services tonight that we're missing for this hot *kaluki* game where Isaac is going to take my money?"

"It's one of Mom's save-the-world projects. This time it's to make nice to the black community. Big surprise," Nancy answered, brushing her hair aside.

"That sounds like a good project to me, Nancy. Not to you?" Grandpa wasn't going to let Nancy off the hook.

"Maybe if we can get the person who stole my coat to give it back, it'll be worthwhile."

Bubbie and Aunt Lilly looked horrified. "Who stole your coat, *Mamela?*" Bubbie asked as her magnified eyes grew even larger.

"Some black girl at school, I'm sure. She took it out of my locker."

"That pretty peach colored coat you got for Hanukkah? Oy vey."

"Don't forget how that woman attacked me." Grandma had just taken some plates off the table when she turned to get her ordeal recognized. This was too much for both older ladies.

"What? Mae, what happened? I didn't hear anything from anyone." Aunt Lilly was the one sister out of the gossip loop. The younger sisters had the impression that Lilly held herself above trading stories, so they excluded her from their call chain, especially since she couldn't be counted upon to give back anything juicy.

"Hold on, everybody. Settle down. Mother wasn't attacked, at least not physically, and we don't know who stole Nancy's coat, although Nancy seems to think she has an idea about who did."

Mom believed Nancy was right, but she couldn't accept a guilty verdict for a black girl without a fair trial. To her that smelled too much like a lynch mob mentality violating her unshakeable belief in justice for all.

"Don't say I wasn't attacked. That colored woman said terrible things to me, and could've come after me. All I did was tell her she had too many things in the express line at the grocery store. You would've thought I committed a crime. If you'd have been there," Grandma glared at her daughter, "you'd have wet yourself."

"Oy, oy, oy, Mae. I would've died on the spot. She must've been a crazy woman," said Bubbie.

"Mae, you wet yourself?" Aunt Lilly asked like a mischievous child.

"And how! I couldn't run home fast enough. Every minute I expected her to come up behind me."

Nancy and I giggled.

"Do you have insurance for the coat?" Bubbie wanted to know. "Isaac, give her money for a new coat." Zadie suddenly couldn't hear.

"That's okay, Ma. Jerry and I will buy her a new one.

"We can contribute something." Bubbie insisted.

Then Dad said something that shocked me, and earned him daggers from Mom and Grandpa. "You know I was talking to the security guard in our office building in Hampden. He works only part time in our building, but full time on the Hampden police force. He said if it weren't for the blacks in Hampden, they wouldn't need him on the force. In fact, he said they could cut back to one part-time officer, because there's almost no crime that doesn't involve Hampden's black population.

Grandpa was quick to do damage control. "I'm sure he wasn't thinking of the white collar crime that goes on."

"Jerry, how could he say that? And how could you repeat it? You mean there are no white juvenile delinquents or burglars or whatever?" Mom, who moments earlier had looked at Dad with adoration, now looked disappointed. Dad opened the ranks.

"I'm sure he exaggerated somewhat, but he was making a point, and the point should be well taken. Let me ask you something. When you drive through the black section of Hampden, do you make sure your car doors are locked?"

"Oh, Jerry, please." Mom tossed her napkin onto her plate and marched into the kitchen.

"I'll take that as a 'yes,' my dear," he called after her. "And I bet you don't even think about locking your doors as you drive through Michigami. So why do we lock our car doors automatically in the black section of Hampden? We do it because we're all aware that there is a high percentage of crime committed by blacks relative to their population. It's not bad or judgmental to speak the truth. It's when we can't speak the truth that we need to be concerned. We'll never move forward in civil rights, if we can't lay everything out on the table, and speak openly. Just as whites need to own up to our contribution to the mistrust between races, blacks need to do the same."

"I'd give them this, if they tried anything with me." Zadie made a fist of his right hand, and showed it to us all. "Just like we did with those *mumzers* who broke through our picket lines. Brother, it was my fist that helped us get a union, and not some talk."

"Isaac, they don't want you to talk violence in front of the *kinder*." Bubbie said this in Yiddish, but we all understood her.

Zadie answered her in English. "The *kinder* should know what we did. We gave them this." And again he thrust his fist out. "And I did it again when the Polacks crossed Milwaukee Avenue into our neighborhood to pick a fight. This isn't Russia, and we didn't have to take it anymore."

Bubbie shook her head, and looked at Dad as if to say, "I give up. You deal with him."

"Well, I personally don't know anyone who had their car broken into while they were driving through Hampden. Maybe I should re-think my impulse to lock my doors." Mom sat down in her chair, and surveyed the plates on the table to see who needed more of anything.

"So getting back to my initial question, what's going on at services tonight?" Grandpa drew us back into the present.

"Does everyone have enough to eat? I made so much. You're not eating enough." Grandma had lost what little interest she had in the discussion.

"So much food, Mae. I couldn't eat another bite."

"Mae, everything is delicious."

"I never ate such soft brisket, Mae, dearie."

"Ma, you outdid yourself."

"Grandma, can I have more *kugel* please?"

"Oy, my Glen. He knows what's good. Jerry, take more too. Are you on a diet or something?" Grandma asked as she began to place more of everything on Dad's plate, and he gave her a free rein.

"In my day, if we thought someone stole from us, we'd give him this," Zadie said balling up his hand yet again.

"Pa, maybe you and I should go to the school, and give them this," Dad said, imitating Zadie's accent and clenched fist.

"Never mind, funnyman. People like that don't understand anything but a fist. You and Eileen, you're going to talk them into giving back the coat? I'm telling you. We should give Glen boxing lessons."

I shuddered at the notion of putting on those ridiculous gloves, and getting hit by someone.

"Pa, we're supposed to be the People of the Book, not of the fist." Darn, Dad was going back to being the teaching father. I liked it better when he was just funny.

"It's a good thing they don't think like you in Israel, or the Arabs would be dancing on our graves," Zadie shot back, and the topic swerved again. "The Arabs don't know from reason or fair play. Only this." The fist made yet another appearance.

"You know, that reminds me of the man whose wife always told him how she was going to dance on his grave. He got back at her by stating in his will that he was to be buried at sea." Dad sat back smiling as everyone else laughed.

Mom stopped laughing, and turned to Grandpa. "There's not much I can say about our guests. I'll know more when I get there. All I know is they're from Operation Breadbasket."

"That Jesse Jackson is nothing but a crook, according to Melva. She says the women she knows down in her neighborhood say all the money that goes to Operation Breadbasket stays there, and he's just looking to make a name for himself," Grandma said.

"Why don't you kids tell us what happened in school this week—maybe something you learned." Mom played the navigator, steering us away from rocky shoals. She and Dad tried to squeeze in a dollop of parenting on Friday night, in case they were remiss during the previous week.

"Nancy, don't let your hair fall in the plate," Grandma cautioned.

I decided to show how my days in school were relevant to the conversation. "We learned again about how the blacks were oppressed in the South."

"They seem to focus a lot on the blacks. Do they talk about anything else in your school anymore?" Aunt Lilly shook her head. "It's seems a bit obsessive."

Seeing Mom's shock, Aunt Lilly rushed to explain. "I've been hearing we have to give the blacks this and that, because they have it so hard. But you know we used to work with the black community to get them equal opportunity. That's what they wanted and needed. They never asked for handouts, just a fair shake. They were ready to work hard, and go to school. This handout business is un-American. Who was there to give anyone else handouts?"

"Nobody," Grandma Mae responded, followed by "Glenny, *tatala*, eat more *tzimis*. You want to be skinny like your sister?"

"Nobody. Exactly!" Aunt Lilly continued. "If you didn't do for yourself, nobody did for you. A little hard work never hurt anyone. We Jews and the Koreans too, we're a good fit with the Puritan ethic of this country. Isaac, Sonia, you didn't even speak

English when you came here. Somehow you managed. You struggled, and you worked, and look what you have now. What the blacks need is for everyone to get out of their way to let them do their own hard work. Am I right or am I right? Sure I'm right."

"And how, Lilly." Bubbie showed signs of excitement, at recognition from someone as smart as Lilly. "We didn't know to ask for this and that. And if we did, who would've given us anything? We scraped just so we could buy that candy store for extra money to send for my sisters back in Russia. Now everyone feels entitled to money, education, houses, you name it, and they don't want to work for it. Somehow it's my fault that they're poor, so I have to pay for them."

Bubbie managed to focus on two conversations at once as she directed her next comment to Grandma. "I never ate such *tzimis*, Mae. Everything was so good. The Queen of England doesn't eat like this." Bubbie knew how to keep peace with her *machitenista*.

Nancy's face showed disbelief at the comparison between Grandma's cooking and what the Queen ate. Nancy's term for Grandma's dinners was "uninspiring."

Zadie took the baton. "So the *shvartzes* are becoming Moslems? Go figure. From what I know the Arabs still beat on them in Africa. How do they excuse that? But now the colored are Moslems, and they're all best friends. Suddenly all their problems are our fault."

Aunt Lilly grabbed back. "You see children how dangerous ignorance is? You have to go to school to learn the truth, so you can't be mislead like all these people who call their friends their enemies, and think their enemies are friends."

"I don't know Lilly. They may not know their own history but it won't hurt them. Like always, it will come back to hurt us. When the world is ignorant, and people believe lies, we're the ones in danger—not the ignorant ones." Bubbie looked around the table conspiratorially and lowered her voice. "Now the colored will join the rest of the anti-Semites. That's always the way. Weren't all those damned Russian peasants illiterate?" Her voice started to rise. "Their Church wanted them to believe we were devils, we drank their blood, we were taking over the world. Mind you, my parents could barely put food on the table, but somehow we were taking over the world. Such nonsense. What did those *farshtunkinah* Russians want to know from the truth? If the Russian Church told them to beat us, they beat us. Their ignorance was our danger, not theirs. Thank God for America and Israel. Now we can defend ourselves."

As Grandma set the creamer and sugar bowl on the table, she made her usual contribution. "Well, you have to take the good with the bad. That's what I always say. Eileen, can you get a glass of milk for Glenny?"

"Leo, you haven't said much this evening. What do you have to say?"

Aunt Lilly's question reminded me of my new theory that Aunt Lilly might have been secretly in love with Grandpa. Perhaps they were too much alike, so Grandpa was drawn to Grandma instead. Aunt Lilly and Grandpa examined their lives and their place in a larger world, each believing they could somehow contribute in their own small way to the ascent of man. Grandma had no patience for scholarship, and the only things she was interested in changing were linens on washday.

Grandma was born in a sheltered garden, and she thought her job was to till it. Voltaire may have arrived at a similar notion, but Grandma endured no existential crisis to find meaning in life. She took neither the time nor interest in other gardens, nearby or across the globe. Grandma's lack of worldly curiosity served her well, allowing her to focus on her list of chores. Yet she was neither cruel nor uncaring to anyone within her sphere. She just didn't consider what was happening beyond the garden wall.

"Well," Grandpa said, responding to Lilly's question, "I met with a young black man today. His name is Armstrong. I like this young man a lot. He's married and has young kids, younger than our Glen. He works hard, and goes to school at nights. You'd all like him. He's a *mensch*. He's a little behind on his rent right now, but his problems are caused by his unscrupulous white landlord."

Tongues clucked around the table as Grandpa continued. "While we talk about the problems some blacks make for us, and possibly for themselves, Armstrong might be having dinner with his family right now discussing how whites continue to victimize blacks. I couldn't blame him. There are many points of view with subjects as complicated as race relations and culture and religions."

"Ah, go on." Grandma said dismissively. "What's so complicated? Either you're a good person or you're not. I don't care what you are, black or white, Jew or Gentile. There is no excuse not to be a good person."

"Mae, Leo is a good person. Too good a person. He always sees all sides. Leo, you are too good to be true." Was I the only one to think Aunt Lilly still had a serious crush on Grandpa?

"Bah!" Grandma waved Aunt Lilly away as she went to get more coffee cups from the kitchen.

"But Leo, doesn't it bother you," Aunt Lilly asked quietly, "that your wife gets verbally assaulted by a black woman, your granddaughter has her new coat stolen, presumably by a black student, and blacks have found their way to a form of Islam that has a major focus on degrading Jews and Judaism. When do you say 'enough,' and what do you do about it?"

"Sure that bothers me. I'd love to squeeze the whole planet into a classroom, and set them straight about how the world should be according to me. But this won't happen. So I chip away when and where I can, and try not to get discouraged." Grandpa glanced over to see if Nancy and I were listening. Aunt Lilly gazed at Grandpa with admiration. Grandma looked annoyed.

"My son who went to college and dental school will disagree, but any troublemaking *shvartzes* and Arabs and whites and self-hating Jews should get this." For the final time that evening, Zadie's fist made an appearance.

Dad and I laughed, and even Nancy cracked a smile, while Bubbie shook her head as if to say, "I give up."

"Here I'm taking my children to services tonight to hear how much work we still have to do in civil rights, and it sounds like a meeting of the Klan at my house." I don't know if Mom intended that to be funny, but she actually succeeded in making us laugh, except Aunt Lilly who must've felt the comment was directed at her.

"Eileen, dolly, no one is saying the blacks or Negroes or colored, whichever is the respectful term now, are all bad. You know your Uncle Lou, may he rest in peace, and I were anything but narrow-minded. There are plenty of good blacks out there, or at least there were. They were everywhere. Where'd they go? All we see and hear are the black youth that are terrifying teachers and other students. They're burning and looting businesses, defacing property, and killing each other in gangs. They're brutal and respect nothing. They play right into the hands of the real bigots who can say, 'You see? They aren't civilized.'"

I decided that I could shed some light on the topic and gain favor with Grandpa and Mom. "There are some nice black kids at school, Aunt Lilly, but if they're too nice, some of the other black kids call them Oreos, and pick on them, so they don't say much."

Grandma stepped in. "I talked to a woman today at the beauty shop. Jewish woman. Lovely face but very heavy. You'd think she'd be embarrassed, but she carries more candy in her pocketbook than Woolworth's."

"Ma, please get to the point."

"What'd I say? All I was saying is that she said her cleaning girl quit, and she can't find another one. None of the colored women want to clean houses now. What's wrong with being a cleaning woman?"

"There's nothing wrong with hard work, if it's accompanied with opportunity for you, or at least for your children." Aunt Lilly reverted back to type, as the civil rights champion we knew her to be.

Grandma lost interest.

"Well, we're never going to solve the world's problems here. That's what I say. You have to take the good with the bad."

"You just have to be thankful for your health." Bubbie added.

"There's still no country better than this one. You think they can talk this way over in Russia?" said Zadie.

The litany of clichés meant the Shabbat discussion was over. We finished our coffee cake, and headed for either the temple or the card table.

CHAPTER FOURTEEN

Later That Night

The clouds and the snow on the lawns reflected upon each other making for a bright night. For the second time that day I crossed the canal into Hampden, this time in the back seat of Dad's big car. My school hunkered down in the snow at the end of the field along the canal. A brief, gleeful surge coursed through me knowing I could avoid it until Monday. A few blocks later, the twin gothic towers of massive Hampden High appeared against the light gray sky. I squinted on purpose to hinder my ability to see parked cars and streetlights, and I imagined a great castle rising up from an ancient countryside.

The click, click of door locks going down drew my attention as Nancy reached in all directions. We were at a commercial intersection by the school, a popular hang out for blacks in the neighborhood.

"Stop that, Nancy. You're being silly." Mom said, keeping her gaze on the street.

"I'd rather be safe than sorry, Mom. Besides, there's a basketball game tonight. A lot of people will be out on the street."

"You know, I had an interesting experience today at this intersection on my way home from work. Actually, it was something that happens frequently."

I leaned over the back of the front seat to hear my father better. "What happened?" We all turned to Dad as we drove the last half-mile to the temple.

"I was stopped at the light, and a black man stepped off the curb against the light to keep me from going. He knew I had the green light, and he deliberately slowed down to make sure I had to wait for him. I couldn't run him over."

"Yes you can, Dad. You get points for that!" My comment got a chuckle out of Nancy, but a quick reprimand from Mom.

"Then what happened?"

"Nothing. I just asked myself why he did it. I think it's an attempt to claim a little bit of power, in a world where he's mostly powerless."

"That could very well be. I've had that happen to me, too. See if there are any spaces in the parking lot."

Some women expect their husbands to drop them off in front of the entrance of their destination. Not Mom. She enjoyed spending the extra time with Dad, and she always said that Nancy and I should take advantage of any exercise we could get.

Services were supposed to begin at 8:00, but Jews are notorious for not taking starting times seriously, and arriving late—a trait I believe we share with blacks. Maybe it originates in our shared history of being powerless. We entered the noisy, temple lobby with ten minutes to spare. Half as many people were already seated in the sanctuary.

We entered from the left, as we always did, because Dad liked to sit left of center in any auditorium setting, whether a movie, play, lecture, or service. This was a *mishagos* that Mom accepted in all cases except one. She complained that by sleeping on the left side of the bed, Dad put Mom closest to their bedroom door. "A husband should sleep between his wife and the door, in case an intruder enters the room in the middle of the night."

Dad's response was that he had a better plan for the four or five nights each week that Grandma slept over. If the intruder managed to slip by Matzah, the wonder-Schnauzer, then Dad would leap across the bed, and run down the hall to where Grandma slept, to awaken her, whereby she would immediately question the intruder to death, or overpower him with the smell of Ben-Gay cream. Mom couldn't help but laugh whenever Dad mentioned his plan.

I felt like I was walking into a school assembly as Nancy and I followed our parents down the left aisle. I looked in all directions for kids I knew from Hebrew school or Sunday school, but only found a few faces, and they didn't belong to close friends. Two of those kids always went to Friday night services, which made them kind of queer. The Reform movement needed to address this perception.

When my eyes got to the front row, I spotted the ten black guests. Men and women, standing and seated, turned in various directions, and engaged in conversation with congregants who were pleased with themselves for conversing with black people.

The appropriate dress for attending religious services in 1970 was a jacket and tie for men, and dresses or skirts for women. The visiting men wore brightly colored shirts and ties under their suit jackets, and the women who accompanied them sported extravagant hats with all kinds of fruits and feathers. I wished I could try one on.

People were more animated than usual at a Friday night service; they moved around more, and most eyes turned towards our guests, at one time or another. We took our seats when the organist started to play somber music.

I wanted my congregation to make a good impression. I wanted the rabbi to be funny, and the music pretty. It was important to me that the visitors see us as friendly and caring, and that our worship service emphasized the wellbeing of everyone in the world, regardless of race or religion.

During the service, I became obsessed with their perception. Had they ever heard spoken Hebrew or read a book from right to left? What did they think of the Israeli and American flags displayed on either side of the ark? Had they listened to a rabbi or seen a Torah taken from an ark? Did they understand that the ark holding the Torahs mimicked the ark at the Temple in ancient Jerusalem that held the Ten Commandments? Would they report back to the outside world on this experience, and find us wanting? I wasn't as bored as I'd anticipated. To experience services through another's eyes added an unexpectedly exciting dimension.

Rabbi Becker was a tall, fortyish, baritone with dark hair and an imposing chin. When I compared him to rabbis I heard at bar mitzvah services, he was the pulpit master. He began the evening with a harmless joke—a good start. I looked to see if our visitors were laughing, and they were. An auspicious beginning.

The rabbi acknowledged our guests. He said the purpose of their visit was to emphasize how the black community's struggle for justice, felt so keenly on the anniversary of the birth of the Reverend Dr. Martin Luther King Jr., was bound up with the Jewish belief that we are God's partners in perfecting the world.

"It is our sacred obligation to help in the struggle for civil rights, while remembering our own deliverance from the bondage of Egypt, which we relive every Passover at the Seders in our homes. I want to thank the Sisterhood for organizing this lovely event, and you'll be happy to know I will not be giving tonight's sermon. Instead we will hear from one of our guests."

I hoped that whomever spoke from the group of guests would acknowledge the kind of conduct among such a visible portion of the black community that made whites fearful, and flee their neighborhoods. Yet, I knew there would be no talk of vandalism, drugs, litter, graffiti, muggings, shootings, and assaults that frequently occurred wherever black youth congregated or moved. There'd be no mention of teachers, both white and black, who feared for their property and safety in black populated schools; where the students and parents showed little interest in education. The speaker wouldn't recognize that today whites fear for their lives when passing through a black neighborhood. No one will point out the lack of a work ethic, now that blacks were filling the ranks of civil service employees, and that the level of customer service at the post office plummeted to a sad joke.

The congregants would have appreciated if the speaker owned up to any of the aforementioned perceptions and realities. It might've bridged a gap between the two groups, and created a true starting point for honest dialogue. But seeing both sides of the black condition in America was not the reason for the visit. It was to remind us of our share of blame, and our responsibility to correct it. No mention was to be made of any problems in the black community, or the need for blacks to take on a share of the responsibilities for their progress.

Daring to air this laundry in public brought a quick rebuke from blacks and white liberals, yet repeating only one part of the solution thousands of times over the ensuing decades, sabotaged the progress of a generation. If the truth can set you free, then doesn't withholding it keep you in chains?

In spite of my cynicism, I wanted these people to like us, and to be impressed with our beliefs, our rituals, and our hope to bring us all together. I passed judgments as I watched the reactions of the visitors. If their mouths moved with the rest of the congregation when we read responsively, I liked them. Nonparticipation was a sign of arrogance. I took it personally, if anyone looked bored or distracted.

I wasn't the only one whose focus was drawn to the ten black faces in the front row. Whenever I looked around, I spied others stealing glances.

After the Torah reading, Reverend Samuel Tilson, a community leader in Jesse Jackson's Operation Breadbasket, approached the bima. Meticulously attired in a cream colored suit, Reverend Tilson began his sermon, and promptly brought down the temple roof. In contrast to the studied, regal delivery of Rabbi Becker, the words of this practiced Southern Baptist reverend tore through the sanctuary like missiles. He was the most dynamic speaker I'd ever heard.

We were eager to ingratiate ourselves with our guests, and demonstrate through our response that there never existed a bigoted bone in our collective bodies, but we had limited tools at our disposal. A yawn or a glance at our watches was our entire repertoire. When some of the guests in the front row began to supply positive verbal feedback to the reverend, members of the congregation giggled nervously, while others looked on with surprise.

Reverend Tilson spoke of the commonalities between the Jewish and black communities: slavery, repression, and sorrow, "and both held hope in their bosoms for a tomorrow when white Christians would live the words of the Lord Savior Jesus Christ, and love everyone and live by the Golden Rule."

Uh-oh. There it was. The name: Jesus. In one of the great ironies of history, the mention of the name of Christianity's Prince of Peace induces an automatic, visceral fear in many Jews. For two millennia the name was used not to bring peace, but to justify pitiless violence against Jews. Dad told me that it's only in my lifetime that the term "Christ-killer" wasn't acceptable in the public forum of parts of the Western world.

According to the religion that grew from Judaism after the death of Jesus of Nazareth, we killed God's son. When considered within the mysticism of the Holy Trinity, that is the same as killing God. How do you come back from that?

Nothing could throw cold water onto happy Jews with the same effect as a simple reference to Jesus. Separating Jesus from the terror visited on Jews in his name is never easy, but that night our desire for unity was strong, so it only took a few moments to shake off our common gut reaction. We wanted to like the reverend. We had invited him. To show our love, after the collective shiver, everyone pretended not to notice the mention of you-know-who.

When Reverend Tilson finished speaking, Rabbi Becker stood next to him, and the two men placed their arms around each other's shoulders as the rabbi asked us all to join in singing "We Shall Overcome." We had the lyrics on sheets that had been run through a ditto machine before the service. I held the paper up to my nose, inhaling the scent of the purple print, then set it down, having memorized the song in school. Mom looked on proudly.

Earlier that week, we sang the same lyrics amid the hostility heaped on us by the black kids, and the only emotion I felt then was anger. The mood tonight was hopeful, and I wanted to believe the lyrics, even to the point of feeling a shiver down my back when the choir and organist joined in; but as we sang, I shared a glance with one of the kids from my school, and we both rolled our eyes, complicit in our recognition of a farce.

After the service, those who were not programmed to rush out of a gathering to beat an imagined rush to the parking lot, stood around the social hall at the back part of the sanctuary. This part of the room was never used for seating, except on the High

Holidays, when the whole congregation showed up for services—just in case.

Members of the Sisterhood served wine and grape juice, along with the requisite assortment of colorful pastries, which I devoured. Scattered around the room, each of the ten guests was holding court around a small group of congregants.

Mom and Dad gravitated to the circle around Reverend Tilson. Nancy was in the lobby with a girlfriend.

"I'm so pleased that your group could be here tonight. I feel it is so important for our mutual progress," Mom said.

I wanted to let Reverend Tilson know that I supported equal rights, and that I hated mean southern sheriffs, like the one Rod Steiger portrayed in movies about the Deep South, but I also wanted to tell him that many of the black kids in my school were nothing like Sidney Poitier, Diahann Carroll, or the blacks in household products commercials.

The reverend and his friends were disconnected from my experience. I saw no reason to struggle for hateful kids like Kevin McPherson, who constantly prowled for victims of his verbal and physical abuse. He slinked along the corridors, his head scanning like a snake, feeling the air for prey. His agenda each day was to intimidate, steal, and hit as many white kids as he could. Occasionally he would get called on it, but except for the time he was suspended for harassing me in fifth grade, he mostly functioned without interference from authority. He rarely turned in assignments, or participated in class, yet he advanced grades with everyone else.

I wanted to tell Reverend Tilson to stop by my school to speak to the black kids, and tell them that not all honkys are honkys; if they want us to be allies in their struggle, they should treat us like friends, not enemies. I wasn't thinking about all the black kids: not Cleon, Tanya, George, and Michael etc., but Kevin McPherson and all the others who he represented who made life so miserable for almost everyone else, and who hurt our school's reputation. I wanted the reverend to tell the kids to stop the constant hostility. I wanted the reverend to hold them accountable for all the fighting and beating and stealing and disrupting. The threats and name-calling, and the "boy this" and "honky that" had to stop. Instead, I let out an involuntary sigh as the reverend pointed out the difficulties of overcoming white bigotry, because whites had an irrational fear of the black man.

CHAPTER FIFTEEN

Later That Night

Driving home, we lunged into controversial subject matter as Mom went into parental overdrive. We were never far from a controversial topic in 1970: race, war, politics, the generation gap, anti-Semitism, pollution, and more, since everything was up for question.

"What did you kids think of the speaker?"

Nancy jumped in first. "I couldn't believe he was wearing that white suit in the winter, even if it was winter white. Those two-toned shoes were pretty cool though. Dad, why don't we get you a pair of those?"

"That's great Nance, but can we talk about the content of his speech?"

"Mom, you're too uptight about this." Nancy said.

"What is with this word 'uptight'? That's all you hear now are these new words like 'uptight,' 'hassle,' 'groovy,' and God knows what else. On that "Laugh In" show they come up with a new word or expression every week."

"You mean like "sock it to me, baby?"

"Jerry, please! You know I hate that expression. It's vulgar. And in the meantime, Miss, I am not 'uptight.' I'm just curious to see if you got anything out of this. We put a lot of effort into arranging this evening."

I took a turn and decided to be difficult. "I don't know if I got anything out of it. It sounds like the same junk we hear in school all the time. Only there were no black kids in the audience throwing stuff."

"Is that what goes on in school?" Dad sounded concerned. Immediately I regretted opening a potential can of worms.

"You know, yelling things out, throwing things, running around the place, slugging kids. That kind of stuff."

"For crying out loud. Is that what goes on in your school assemblies, or do you mean in class, as well? Where are the teachers? What do they say?"

Rather than calm Dad down, I got him more upset as I continued. "It goes on all the time. Most of us think it's pretty funny. We watch some of the teachers trying to quiet things down, and they get spitballs or worse thrown at them. Other teachers just don't say anything. They kind of look around like they're somewhere else."

"Nancy, are you seeing a lot of that in the high school?"

"To be honest, once I got to high school, and was able to get into mostly honors classes, I don't have to deal with the black kids, except in the halls and at gym and lunch. That's more than enough. I stay out of some of the girls' bathrooms, because they wait there to jump you. We don't have those school-wide assemblies like they do in junior high. Fortunately, there aren't many black kids in honors classes."

That seemed to settle Dad down, but it set Mom off.

"Nancy, you shouldn't say 'fortunately there aren't black kids in honors classes.' That's *un*fortunate. Second, Jerry, you and I should consider bringing up all these shenanigans when we go for the parent conferences."

"Why don't we move across Lawson Avenue, and go to the Michigami schools? They never have to deal with this junk, because there aren't any blacks there. Or we could move up the North Shore. They don't have any racial problems either."

"Glen, don't be ridiculous. The Hampden schools are among the best in the country. That's why we moved here in the first place. They have much better academic programs than the schools in Michigami, and you kids get a much richer cultural education at Hampden as well. You don't need to go to school in Michigami where culture means Little League baseball, and the parents' biggest concern is the latest sale at Marshall Fields. You kids in Hampden are involved in current events. That's important. Besides, you can't run from difficulties and challenges. You stay and try to make things better. Jerry, tell them."

I could swear that Dad hesitated too long to indicate his agreement with Mom, but he backed off and supported her, which is what he did best. "We did move here because of Hampden's reputation for excellence. You're right, Glen, the North Shore has terrific schools, but like your mother said, those kids are rather insulated from the world in the manner of Marie Antoinette. We know what happened to her."

"Yeah Dad, but we're more likely to get our heads chopped off than the kids in other districts. Everyone says Hampden is going downhill because of the blacks. They talk about the crime and the threats from the black kids." Nancy said.

"Why do we have to go to a school with all that stuff? Rob and Amy never have to deal with black kids," I said, referring to my cousins in Sycamore Park. "How come you and Mom are so big on us going to school with black kids? Especially since all they do is pick on us, and steal stuff, and junk like that?"

"Stop the generalizations, Glenny. People use them against us Jews all the time. Let me ask you Mister, why do *you* think your father and I want you to go to school with black children?"

"Because you don't care if we get picked on, and they mess up our classes?"

"I'll get you a job doing comedy at Mendelson's resort next summer. He's another Henny Youngman. In the meantime, be serious for a moment."

"Because you think it's good training for when we grow up. But I don't know why. You don't have to work with anyone you don't want to, or live with anyone you don't want to, so what's the big deal? I bet Uncle Marty never even sees black people. He lives in Sycamore Park, and works in Michigami."

"You never know who you may work with someday. You may actually choose to live in an integrated community, and unless you get to know blacks, and learn that they are no different from anyone else, then you will never make that choice."

Mom was not going to get the answers she wanted from me, because although I understood her way of thinking, my experiences had set me on a different course.

"Now I *do* know blacks, and they *are* different, and I would *never* want to live near them, except Melva and a couple other nice ones in school. So now that I know it, let's move."

Nancy and Dad both chuckled, but Mom wasn't having it.

"Jerry, don't encourage that thinking. The fact that there are a few black kids that you know personally, and that you would like to live near, puts you head and shoulders above other less informed boys your age. But it does bother me." Mom's tone of voice changed, as if she were trying to think something through. "Here your father and I were thinking we were doing a good thing by sending you kids to a school with a history of integration, and you sound as if it's making a George Wallace out of you. I don't know what to make of that. It's a surprise to me."

I started to feel sad that Mom was disappointed, and it was somehow my fault. I regretted not telling her the good things about school.

"Ma, there are some really nice black kids at school too. There is always one or two in any class. Marybeth Mays is a lot of fun. We always joke around. And Cleon is still there."

"How come I never see you kids playing with any black children anymore, like you used to in grade school?"

"I don't know. It just doesn't happen."

"Eileen, you can't control their experience and the thinking that results. We decided where to send them to school. Let's be honest. There were a lot of factors that lead to our living where we do. We weren't exactly looking to put our kids on the front lines of social upheaval. The fact that the schools were integrated was a nice extra, but it wasn't the deciding factor. In fact, hearing that the blacks in Hampden in 1960 were "no trouble," as they said at the time, was more of a positive consideration than the fact that there were blacks there at all. Hampden was ranked one of the top ten high schools in America, and that was good enough for us. We were glad the kids were going to an integrated school, so they could make informed choices as adults. Maybe their choices won't be the ones we expected, but hey, if they choose to segregate themselves it won't be due to ignorance, now will it?" Dad asked.

"Ma, you think every black person is like Diahann Carroll on *Julia* or Leslie Uggams, or that Pearl Bailey who you love to watch on Dean Martin. If Leslie Uggams came to our school she'd probably get her butt kicked, as they like to say, for being 'too white'." Nancy said.

"Yeah, Ma," I added. "I'm not prejudiced. I always side with the blacks in any movies about bigoted whites and segregation and prejudice. Remember how I cried when that old black woman was hurt and sad in that movie *Hurry Sundown*? But they're different from the blacks we go to school with, and we aren't mean southern whites like the guys in those movies. I'm just against the kids that cause all the trouble. It's like everyone's afraid of them. They're mean."

"Yeah, remember how we rooted for Sidney Poitier in *Guess Who's Coming to Dinner*?" Nancy added.

"Yes, I remember. In the meantime, we aren't moving anywhere. Jerry, what's the hold up?"

We'd hit a traffic jam as we pulled up to the block where the high school rose up on our left. Instantly, an explosion of noise assaulted us as a brick smashed through Mom's side window, and thudded onto the seat between her and Dad. Shards of glass flew like shrapnel in all directions, and small fragments seemed to hang suspended in the air, shimmering in the light of the headlamps of cars similarly stalled in the lane of oncoming traffic.

Pieces of glass settled on my exposed skin. Rocks pounded on the roof of the car like hail; some crashed into the windshield, and windows causing small holes with spidery cracks to snake out from their centers. Life shifted to slow motion. Shrieks and indefinable screams of joy and rage flew threw the gaping hole where Mom's window had been. The hail kept coming. Panic welled up among us as we sat trapped in a maelstrom.

Throngs of black kids now ran up and down the street on both sides of the two stalled lines of cars. They were more jubilant then angry. They cheered each other on as they ran to the curb or parkway finding objects to toss at the buses and cars. Where were the police? Where was the law and order we all counted on to keep us safe?

Nancy, my mother, and I emitted girly shrieks with the first concussion. What really unsettled me was the fear in Dad's voice as he yelled out, "What the hell…!"

My ears rang from the incessant banging of rocks on metal. We were trapped by school buses stopped a few cars in front of us. Then the hail of rocks and the accompanying noise abated.

"Dad, get us out of here! Oh my God! What's happening?" Nancy was crying. Mom scanned Nancy and me intensely to assess our condition, while Dad opened his window, which hadn't shattered, to see if he could see beyond the buses.

"Kids, are you okay?" Mom's voice was filled with fear.

Close by, approaching sirens drowned out any remaining noise. The kids who launched the attack were in retreat. I could see them jumping over hedges, and running between houses. The voices now sounded authoritative.

Just as Dad turned toward Nancy and me in back, a black man's face thrust itself through Dad's window. The three of us who saw it screamed with fear.

It was a policeman.

"Everyone okay in here?"

"We aren't sure. What in the heck is going on? A barrage of rocks or bricks hit us. There's glass everywhere in our car." Dad sounded both angry and tense. "Just look at our car, and you can see what happened."

Mom managed to find a bit of her voice. "What's going on? Is it a race riot or something? Can we get out of here?" Her voice rose. "Please help us just get out of here."

"Sorry. We should be able to get you out of here in a jiffy. We're breaking up the crowd. You might want to check in at an emergency room to see if you're cut or anything. We've given them advance notice at Hampden Hospital. You can file a report anytime at a police station. I'm sorry about your car."

"Well, what is it for God's sake? Was someone assassinated? This is nuts." Dad was trying to maintain self-control for our sake, but I could tell he was teetering on the edge.

"It seems that some of the kids didn't like the outcome of to-night's basketball game. They went after the other team's buses as they were leaving."

That was it? Sore losers? How was Mom going to attribute this to white oppression of blacks? The downtrodden were making it hard for Mom to defend them with her claim that they were no different from Nancy or I. Even in the darkened car, set aglow every second with the flashing lights from police cars, I could see the confusion and frustration on her face.

"Looks like you can get moving." The policeman's words washed over us like a welcome breeze. The car lurched forward, and we headed west among a line of cars threading the obstacle course of policemen, squad cars, and broken glass. When we crossed the canal into Michigami, we sighed audibly with relief. Good old Michigami.

Dad tried to bring us back to sanity by focusing on the mun-dane, but his stream of consciousness betrayed him. "I'll have to take the car in, and get an estimate, and then get a loaner while they clean it out, and fix the window, and hammer out the dents. Who knows? Maybe it's totaled? I'll stop at the police station on my way to work on Monday. I can't believe the aggravation this is going to cause. Listen, kids, be sure to be very careful getting out of the car. I don't want anyone getting cut or having glass lodge under your skin. Move slowly. We'll stand in the kitchen and try to remove as much as possible before going further into the house. I hope your grandparents are asleep." He rambled non-stop, until we were in the safety of home. We were too shak-en to stop him.

The house was mostly dark. The card players had left. Grandma and Grandpa were upstairs in the spare bedroom. Behind Matzah's squeals of delight at our return, I heard the familiar sound of the dishwasher nearing the dry cycle. That sound always comforted me. Disorder was washed away, and soon everything would be in its place.

Before we went up to bed, we helped each other remove glass from our clothes and hair, like monkeys picking lice from each other. Just before Mom and Dad's bedroom door closed, Dad said in a voice that betrayed his anger, "Eileen, we have to talk."

The unity service at our temple was obliterated from our minds. We never spoke of it. That night became the night of the basketball riot. Nancy and I told the story often, but Mom selected her audience with care. She never told anyone who had ever expressed a doubt about the benefits of integration, so as not to give credit to their caution.

I've heard that women think, and men act. My guess is that Mom did a lot of thinking about her most basic assumptions about race relations, and Dad came close to deciding to move us out of the Hampden school district. Was it time for them to get our passports in order, and at last concede things could get worse?

For Nancy and me, the night of the basketball riot, remembered in broken glass and the feel of fear for our mortal selves, was just another racial incident—albeit an intense one—along a continuum. For Mom and Dad it must've been transformative, or at least the start of a transformation.

Revolutions in matters of race, sex, age, war, music, and more that we followed on TV over the past six years, birthed wrenching splits to the staid fabric of American society of my earliest childhood. That night, they leapt off the TV screen into our laps. A sense of security Mom and Dad might have held, became collateral damage, no different from Dad's car. We were a part of something big, whether we wanted to be or not, just as we couldn't escape that line of stalled cars as the fury over a basketball game enveloped us.

CHAPTER SIXTEEN

Saturday, January 17, 1970

Mom, Dad, and Nancy were gone, by the time I came downstairs on Saturday morning. Grandpa was reading the newspaper at the kitchen table, and Grandma sat next to him, watching him, calculating her opportunities for getting his attention. I offered her a diversion: I had to be fed.

Ken and Gary arrived together, at about eleven o'clock, and we headed upstairs to my room. I stacked Three Dog Night and Sly and the Family Stone 45s on the record player. The sickening smell of incense wafted from the tiny, brass, pagoda-shaped burner on my desk. I purchased it at the let's-pretend-we're-hippies head shop in Michigami. No actual drug paraphernalia were sold there, but the inventory was suitably mod and psychedelic. A middle-aged Jewish woman ran the shop as a post-divorce attempt at an income. The hipster piled her copper-colored hair on her head in big curls, matched by over-sized, gold-hoop earrings hanging over her flowery, robe-like dresses.

On the wall behind my bed, an unshaven President Nixon looked down from the black light poster of him sitting on the toilet, with a cigarette hanging from his mouth. For lack of anything else to do, we planned to take the bus to PrairieVille Mall and hang out.

I told them about the previous night's basketball riot. They wanted to see Dad's car, but he had already taken it somewhere.

Among the three of us, Ken was the tallest. He had dark brown hair, green eyes, small features and a slight frame. Gary was shorter with broader features and brown eyes to match his hair. I fell in the middle being of average height and weight. I noticed a silver chain around Ken's neck, and pointed to it. "What're you wearing?"

"Isn't this cool? It's a peace medallion my brother sent me from school at Kent State." Ken pulled the chain up from inside his shirt, and it caused something to stir in me, which in turn introduced guilt, my most frequent companion. *Please God, don't let me get any of those kinds of feelings for my best friend.* "Hey, did you notice my choker?" Gary was pointing to an elastic strand of red, white, and blue beads around his neck.

"Yeah. Did you string that? It's pretty cool. I want one." I really did.

"Nah. My sister gave it to me. She and her friends were making chokers and stuff." Gary said.

Ken changed the subject. "Hey did anybody hear what happened to that kid in school yesterday who dropped the cassette?"

Gary started giggling. "Oh yeah. That was something."

"I almost peed in my pants. Did you see his face when he realized what he did?" I asked, chuckling with Gary, and shaking my head. Ken joined in our amusement.

"I saw Kevin McPherson and Curtis May in the back of all the black kids dancing around like this, while clapping going 'Get the honky! Get the honky!'" Ken started dancing around the small room, clapping his hands as he imitated Kevin and Curtis, and our giggles turned into guffaws. "Kevin is a maniac. He's so unpredictable. I'm always nervous walking past him, thinking his arm is going to shoot out, and land a hard punch."

"Hey, hey, listen. It was like that movie "The Naked Prey" they show on TV. Remember this whole African village comes chasing after Cornel Wilde?" Gary added, his face red from laughing.

"So what happened to the kid?"

"Maybe they killed him." Ken said hoping to increase the level of our mirth. "Though we probably would've heard about it."

"I heard his mother had to come and get him, so things could cool down; and Mr. Strong offered to replace the cassette recorder." Gary said as the laughter subsided. "I'd hate to be that kid this weekend thinking about going back to school on Monday."

"Nah. They'll forget over the weekend." Ken said.

"Yeah, right." I scoffed. "I don't think so. Ken, tell Gary what happened in the shop class he missed yesterday morning." I said as I started laughing all over again.

"Oh yeah! It was so funny." Ken fell on my bed clutching his stomach in feigned hysteria. "Oh my God. It was sooo funny. When Larry had his head in the basket. Oh my God. And then...."

"Wait! Wait! Slow down. What happened?" Gary said, wanting to understand, so he could join in the moment that Ken and I were sharing.

"Mr. Spaski was in one of his moods yesterday," Ken said, happy to control the conversation. "He told us he didn't care what we worked on, since we were all useless, and then locked himself in his office. So we were just sitting around. We were supposed to be working on those stupid wooden racecars. Anyhow, you know how queer Larry Kelman is. He and Jeff Fink were reading the stock page in the *Wall Street Journal*, as usual, and Kevin

McPherson came up behind him and said, 'Damn boy! You're real smart, aren't you?' And of course Larry got all nervous and said 'I don't know. Maybe.' But you knew whatever he said would be wrong. Kevin was just looking to pick on a white kid. And the next thing you knew, Kevin had picked up the wastebasket, and dumped it over Larry's head, then left it there. And then he picked up two rulers, and started playing the drums on the wastebasket on Larry's head." Ken could barely get out his last words as he snorted with laughter. Gary and I were right with him.

"But wait." Ken shouted. "That's not all. Spaski comes out of his office, and sees Larry with the garbage can on his head, and starts balling him out. And Larry comes out from the garbage can, and tries to tell Spaski what happened, but he didn't want to hear any of it."

The three of us were now convulsed and feeding off each other.

"Remember the time that Kevin made Fink stick his head in that locker with that bad smell?" Gary contributed. We were on a roll.

"And Fink said, 'wait, can I smell it later, I need to hand in a paper'?" I could barely get the words out.

"And Kevin ran the paper under the faucet?" Ken was nearly choking by this time.

"What about when you stuck your whole Fudgecicle in your mouth when Derrick Dawson wanted to see it?" Gary asked.

"Yeah, and the look on your face the time Evan King said he wanted to see you after school to kick your ass?" Ken reminded me.

"Yeah, Glen. How'd you get out of that one? I don't remember." Gary asked.

We regained some control as I related my story. "Oh. It was so funny. It was like a TV show. I knew I had to get Evan to forget he wanted to kick my butt, so before gym that day I saw Evan in the hall, and I ran up to him like I was all out of breath, and pretended I was looking for him. And I said to him real excitedly, 'Evan, man. I'm glad I found you. Did you hear the news?' I said this like I was so concerned about him. And Evan looked at me like I was crazy, and said, 'What news, boy?' And I said, 'I just saw some eighth grader, another black kid—I don't know his name—and I overheard him say he was looking for you to kick your ass. So I came looking for you right away to tell you,' like we were good friends, and I really cared. And then Evan goes, 'Thanks, man. You sure you don't know who? Well, thanks, man.' Then he took off, and forgot completely about wanting to kick my ass." I finished this story quite pleased with myself.

"Oh my God, Feigman, that is so cool. That's hysterical. It's like on a TV show or something."

"I can't believe you did that," Gary said. "Damn. I have to remember that."

"Damn. What a joke this all is. Can you imagine what school would be like without the black kids? Totally boring." Ken said, grabbing my stack of *Mad Magazines*.

"Gee. Wouldn't that be a shame?" I said melding irony and wistfulness.

"Hey, did anyone see Tanya Wilkes yesterday?" Ken asked. "Oh my God."

"I know what you're talking about. I saw her. You could make out her nipples under that sweater. I saw it. I couldn't believe it. I had to carry my books in front of my crotch for the next ten minutes." I lied.

"You guys got the hots for Tanya?" Gary was intrigued. "I must say, of all the black girls in the school, she is the best. Damn, those tits don't quit. She is sooo sexy. I thought I was the only one."

"You know what they say, right?" Ken said with a smirk. "Once you try black, you never go back."

"Where'd you hear that?" Gary asked. "Is it true?"

"Maybe you'll find out, and tell us." Ken said.

I laughed, but thought silently about George Adams. He was a frequent guest on my late night fantasy list. He was among the most handsome guys in school, with a smooth jazz voice. George wore fashionable clothes, but never blue jeans. His father owned a construction company. He and his three brothers—two were high school basketball stars—were leaders in the black social scene. Those times when George and I conversed one on one, I had a hard time looking him in the eye.

CHAPTER SEVENTEEN

Later That Morning

While we waited for the bus to the mall, Ken wanted us to throw snowballs at passing cars. I thought it was a bad idea, and was surprised when sensible Gary went along. I was born cautious and risk averse. I once joined a friend and his family on their cabin cruiser on Lake Michigan. The big, blue water was calm; we sped along, and everyone smiled from the combination of sunshine, cool spray, and the stunning view of Chicago—except me. I heard somewhere that a submerged log could be drifting along, and if a boat hit it at high speed, it could flip over. My smile appeared when it was time to head back to the harbor.

Not only was I fearful that an angry driver would stop and chase us, but Ken's snowball idea brought back the too fresh memory of rocks pummeling our car, and I wanted no part of it.

I saw the bus approach, and figured time ran out on Ken's plan. At the last minute, he and Gary whipped well-packed snowballs at the next passing car. The impact reported with surprising intensity. The brake lights went on, the car pulled over, and a furious man emerged. Oh, shit!

The bus pulled up, and I jumped on, followed by nervous Gary and laughing Ken. We rushed to the back and sat down. I waited tensely for the bus to start moving, delivering us from danger. Instead, there was a banging on the door, and the driver opened it as a middle-aged man jumped up into the bus. Red-faced with anger, he pointed right at me.

"Do you hoodlums know you can cause an accident that way? Do you think it's funny? Do you want me to have this bus wait, while I find a phone and call the police? You'd better think twice before you pull that again. Do you understand?"

We sat silently with our heads down. "I said DO YOU UNDERSTAND ME?"

"He's talking to you, Feigman," Ken had the audacity to say. I was innocent, but I had no choice, if I wanted this guy to go away.

"Yes, sir." I whispered, mortified as I looked down at my kneecaps. Miraculously the man heard me. He turned, said something to the bus driver, then left.

I was furious at Ken and Gary. Their hormonal surge got me in trouble, and I suffered the embarrassment. They laughed nervously. I was too mad to speak. Thirty pairs of eyes drilled their judgment into me.

We exited the bus in front of Marshall Field's with no particular plan. The holiday decorations were gone, so there was nothing to brighten the day. The plazas between the stores looked uninviting. We headed to the third floor of Montgomery Ward's, drawn, as always, to the IQ quiz game. Across from the receptionist for the personnel department, was a black steel box the size of a refrigerator. For fifty cents, a series of multiple-choice trivia questions appeared on its small screen. We competed against the machine, and each other to see who contributed the most correct answers.

We excelled in different categories. My strengths were in movies, history, and geography. Ken and Gary knew sports and a bit of the other subjects. We competed so intensely against the clock that we wouldn't notice our shrieks of excitement, until a gray-haired personnel clerk would loudly clear her throat, and glare from her typewriter.

We were halfway through our combined five-dollar limit when I noticed a black kid coming up the escalator with his mother. It was unusual to see a black kid at PrairieVille Mall. I quickly recognized Cleon Jones.

"Cleon!" I almost shouted. Gary and Ken looked up as Cleon smiled and waved. His mother revealed her dazzling Marilyn McCoo smile. They walked toward us.

There were greetings, pats on the back, and smiles all around. We invited Cleon to join us while his mother ran errands. She gave us an extra dollar.

I felt good about Cleon playing with us against the machine. Engaging spontaneously with a friend who was black prompted me to note how unusual it was, even for those of us in an integrated school. My cousins in their homogenous schools would never get to know a black kid. The only black kids they would see would be on the news committing crimes. Perhaps they would spy a whole class of black kids on a school field trip to a museum or the zoo.

Mrs. Jones returned to collect Cleon, just as our money ran out. She asked me to give her regards to my mother, which I promised to do. The rest of us ambled over to Marshall Field's where we ran into Steve Tompkins.

The fact that Steve's parents were divorced set him apart. He was the only kid in our grade from a "broken home," and that darkened everyone's view of him. Steve's rebellious affectations didn't help.

"Hey Steve. What're you up to?" I said this casually, trying to sound a bit cooler and more dangerous than I ever could be. It was necessary to sound tough with Steve. He and his sister were rough around the edges. I knew Steve since kindergarten, and he always treated me like a friend, but he got into a lot of trouble at school. In fifth grade he was suspended for three days for taking someone's orange UNICEF box containing $4.00 in change. A suspension was like a prison record.

I was never invited into the Tompkins's large, dark house. I came close when one afternoon Ken, Steve, and I stopped there on our bikes, so he could get his baseball mitt. Steve went in the back door, and stopped us from following him. As the door opened I could see into the shadowy kitchen. Unwashed dishes were stacked everywhere—a foreign scene to me. Grandma washed our dishes before I even finished eating.

"You guys should see what I was doing," Steve said with some pride.

"Yeah? What was that?" Ken asked, successfully invoking the bravado in his voice that I had attempted and failed.

"You know those little square tins of grape jelly in the restaurant? I grabbed a bunch, stood at the top of the escalator, peeled back the tops, and then let them slide down the railing. Anyone walking by the bottom of the escalator would get hit with jelly; get it all over their sleeves. What a joke!"

I couldn't decide if this was clever or the stupidest thing I'd ever heard. Either way, it was typical of Steve. "Did it work?" I asked.

"Well, not yet. But one landed at this lady's feet, and she looked up at me." Sensing we weren't impressed Steve changed the subject.

"Did you guys see the buttons they got in at Ward's? They're these cool, psychedelic stickers and buttons you can put on your jackets with people's names on them. Look here." Steve pulled a packet from his jacket pocket, and showed us the vibrantly colored stickers and buttons that shouted "Steven," "Steven's Room," or "Hands Off! Steven." The colors and patterns were meant to induce the psychedelic images of the Beatles' *Yellow Submarine*. Some looked like the mod flowers on the set of *The Dating Game* or *Laugh-In*. I immediately saw the possibilities for those stickers, and I wanted ones that shouted "Glen."

"Cool." Ken said ogling the packet. "How much were they?"

"Cram that." Steve responded scornfully. "They didn't cost me a cent. Those old ladies there can't see anything."

"Whoa! Really?" Ken asked sounding a bit in awe of Steve's thievery.

"Did you really? Gary asked, shocked.

Steve's revelation made me uncomfortable. Maybe I was more of Aunt Polly than Huck Finn or even Tom Sawyer, but I had a good reason for my visceral aversion to stealing.

When I was ten years old, Ben Rubin came over to the driveway where I was playing HORSE with my neighbors. He showed us some *Archie* comics he had just stolen from Sandberg's drugstore. The other kids seemed impressed. I never thought of stealing anything, but I wanted to impress them too, and show Ben that I was cool. Surprising everyone, including myself, I announced that I was going to steal some comic books. I picked up my bike that was lying on the grass next to the driveway, and pedaled over to the drugstore. The lady behind the counter had known me my whole life. Everyone there knew Grandma, since barely a day went by that she wasn't filling a prescription.

The counter lady was busy, so I walked over to the comic book section as usual; only this time the pressure of fear filled my chest cavity. But no one would suspect Glen Feigman of petty theft. I proved that anyone's faith in my character was misplaced.

I picked up a *Batman* comic, and scurried out like a mouse that scored some cheese. Ironically, I didn't like *Batman* or any superhero comic books. Gary read them, but Ken and I decreed them to be queer, and only *Archie* was cool. What mattered now was that I had stolen something that I could show the others.

Adrenaline pulsed through me as I raced back to the driveway, happy that the gang was still playing HORSE. I jumped off my bike, and let it fall in the grass. With disappointment, I noticed Ben was gone, and unease set in to squelch what should've been a moment of triumph.

"Look what I have," I said, waving *Batman* in the air.

"You really stole that?" My neighbor Mark seemed incredulous, and the other boys standing around didn't know what to make of my stunt. My triumphal moment dissolved into a puddle of shame. I wondered if Ben had really impressed them, or had they been too cowed by his popularity to say anything.

I felt queasy, and my thoughts were starting to swirl. Stealing the comic was easy, no one got hurt, and it was only twelve cents. Now I couldn't imagine why I did it, and wanted to reverse the clock.

Mark's little sister Sandra had been quietly observing the activity. Suddenly she spoke, terrorizing me with her wisdom. "Glenny, you shouldn't have done that, because stealing is wrong, and you'll get in trouble."

My stomach convulsed. *Stealing is wrong. You'll get in trouble.* I made a silent wish for that damn clock to reverse itself.

I was up in my room later that afternoon watching reruns of *The Three Stooges*, trying to ignore what I did a few hours earlier, when Mom called me from downstairs. Grandpa, Grandma, and Nancy were there with Mom. Dad was at his office tightening someone's braces, or he would've been there too.

My stomach— my eternal enemy— knotted and twisted. Lately it seemed to become the nerve center of my body. I stepped cautiously into the family room, as if the floor might open up and swallow me.

Nancy stood in the middle of the room with Mom. Grandpa and Grandma sat in the armchairs on either side of the couch.

It was an out of body experience. It wasn't real. This feeling of alienation from my family was completely new, and I hated it.

"Glen, your sister heard that you stole a comic book from Sandberg's today. Is this true?" Mom's voice was calm, steady, and accusing.

"My Glen wouldn't steal anything. What does that little girl know? I never liked her brother. I bet that boy stole it, and they're blaming my Glen." Grandma would not be a party to the assassination of my character.

"Mother, will you please be quiet, and let me handle this?"

"Mae. Please. Eileen can talk to Glen." Grandpa worked the diplomatic angle.

"What did I say? If I say black, you say white. Better I should cut my tongue out." Grandma answered defensively.

"Mother, please!" Mom pleaded.

"I'm not saying anything." Grandma sniffed.

"Glen, did you steal a comic book, yes or no, and for God's sake, why on Earth would you do something like that?" Mom asked.

I never stopped looking at the floor. I tried to wish myself somewhere else. Samantha could do it on *Bewitched* —lucky witch. I could feel everyone's eyes on me. I pieced together that little Sandra must've seen Nancy on the street, and tattled on me. Goody-two-shoes.

"Glen, I'm asking you a simple question." Mom regained some of the composure that Grandma had taken from her.

"Well, I guess, kind of. I mean Ben Rubin had done it, so I just wanted to see if I could do it, and I forgot to put it back." I sounded pathetic, and it was hopeless. Why did she have to confront me in front of Grandma and Grandpa?

"Glen, you march upstairs, and get that comic book, and you and I are going back to Sandberg's. You're going to give them back the comic book, and apologize. Do you understand me, young man?"

"But Ma..." I started to whine. Couldn't I just leave the twelve cents when no one was looking? Why did I have to draw attention to my sin? I wouldn't do it again—never ever. Lesson learned.

"But nothing, Glen Adam Feigman. I'm ashamed of you."

"He didn't mean it. It was an accident, yeah Glenny?" There was no such thing as incontrovertible evidence to Grandma if it contradicted her convictions. Trying to convince her that I stole would be as fruitless as telling her that the sleeping pills she took were really placebos; being the result of a collusion between Grandpa and the doctor.

Then came the voice that I most dreaded. "Glen." This was a nightmare. "Glen," Grandpa repeated, "the people I admire most are people of good character. They are honest people. They are trustworthy. All we really have is our personal integrity. People with personal integrity are the best people. You were a person of good character, at least until this. Fortunately you're young. You make mistakes. Mistakes aren't so bad if you can take away a lesson, and not repeat them. Glen, go back to being the person of good character that I know you are, and never again give me a reason to think you're not. Agreed?"

I started to cry, but never looked up, and never moved.

Grandpa got up, and put his arms around me as I sobbed on his shoulder. He drove Mom and me to Sandberg's where I began my journey back to personal integrity—a person of good character.

With the lesson of the stolen comic book seared into my brain, the thought of being present for a theft made my stomach cramp.

"Hey, let's head back over to Ward's, and see those stickers." Ken suggested, already moving in that direction.

"Might as well. There's nothing going on here." Gary agreed.

I tried to create a diversion. "We were just there. Let's walk around here and out to the other side of the mall, and see what's going on."

"No. I want to see if they have "Ken" buttons. Maybe I'll *buy* them." Ken sounded like a gangster telling his victim to come for a friendly drive in the country.

We left Steve to whatever mischief he had planned next, and headed back to Montgomery Ward's. We located the display Steve had described, alongside a first floor escalator. The only other person around was one of the rhinestone butterfly employees two aisles over, arranging discounted Christmas cards.

"I can't believe they're out of 'Gary,'" Gary said. "Can you believe they have '*Gerald*' but not Gary? Who names their kid Gerald nowadays?"

"That's why they're still in stock. Nobody wants them. But they have 'Glen' and 'Ken,'" Ken announced. Just my luck.

Ken pulled a set off the hook, and put it in his jacket pocket. It was so easy. No wonder Ward's went out of business. I began to sweat.

"Are you crazy, Ken? You'll get us all arrested. Just like you got me in trouble for the stupid snowballs you threw at the car." This came out as a frantic stage whisper.

"We didn't get arrested. Come on, Glen. Give me a break. They're only ninety-five cents. It isn't going to break Mr. Ward or anything."

"Yeah? Well it isn't going to break you to pay for it, either," I shot back, surprising myself with my quick retort. Maybe I would join the high school debate team.

"Besides, Glen, I see you have yours in your hands already." Ken noted.

"Yeah, but I'm going to pay for it." My hand was visibly trembling. I turned and walked towards the rhinestone, butterfly lady, and with a sudden feeling of superiority, handed her the packet of stickers.

On the way home, Gary sat with Ken, and I took the seat in front of them. I halfway turned back, so I could share in the conversation, but quickly changed my mind. Gary was spouting off some facts about the Bears, and besides, facing backwards on a bus nauseated me.

At home I put "Glen" stickers on my notebooks and on the door to my room. The mod button with the 3D swirly circle now emblazoned the front of my parka. When I received a new bike as a bar mitzvah gift, I slapped a "Property of Glen" sticker on it.

CHAPTER EIGHTEEN

That Night

My budding gay sensitivities raised their little heads, and I labored over what to wear to the birthday party of one of the girls in my class. It was femish to look as if I gave any thought to my appearance, but I couldn't control the urge to coordinate an outfit. My choice for pants was either black stripes, blue stripes, or blue jeans—all with flared bottoms. I settled on the jeans, and then, over my undershirt I put on a gold and blue, horizontal striped, long-sleeved crew neck shirt. I was channeling Billy Bigelow from *Carousel*. I knew all week that I would wear that shirt to the party, so I didn't wear it at school to avoid over exposure. I've since learned that earth tones don't flattery me.

I pulled my desert boots over thick blue socks. White socks with anything but gym shoes were queer. For a finishing touch, I put on the black-beaded choker from the fake head shop. I was glad to live in an era when it was cool for men to adorn themselves with something more than gray flannel and a pocket square.

I brushed my hair, parted neatly on the left side allowing the bangs to swoop across my forehead. In high school, except for some jocks, we would grow our hair, until a teacher or parent said "enough." Barbers had no idea how to style long hair on a boy, so we all looked stupid sporting clumsy wedges and awkward crops. My graduation year of 1975 is certainly the nadir of senior class photos—and that includes black classmates with Afros the size of small planets.

I stopped in my parents' room, and took the bottle of Canoe cologne off Dad's dresser, and splashed it on my face. There was a flash of the early childhood memory of running into Dad's arms as he arrived home from work. That was the smell of safety and certainty.

We assembled at Gary's house. He looked disheveled, and his pants were too short. Ken wore an apache scarf around his neck, folded to two points, like a Boy Scout's scarf, and held together with a silver peace symbol. Very cool.

"Are you wearing cologne, Glen?" Gary asked me accusingly. "You smell like a fem."

My guard bolted up, but I attempted to sound casual. "Shut up, jerk. It's my dad's, and when I get to first base tonight, I wouldn't want Barbara to throw up, like whichever girl smells your b.o."

"Hey, I'm wearing Sweden from my dad's Nine Flags cologne. I love the stuff. I rub it on my dick when I beat off," Ken said. "Want to smell it, Gary?"

Gary's mother demanded reassurance from Gary that he'd be home by 10:30, the community curfew, and she asked for Pam Silverstick's phone number. Finally, we were free.

Pam's mother opened the door, recognized us immediately, and greeted us warmly, but I detected some condescension. *Here are the horny little boys with images of big breasts dancing in their heads.*

"Everyone's downstairs, boys. Take your shoes off, and leave them with the others." We added our footwear to the pile of salt-stained shoes by the door.

Aretha Franklin's voice grew louder as we descended the stairs. The basement was finished with sheet paneling. Two sturdy, large couches, covered in an ancient fabric, sat on the red shag rug in the center of the room. I knew this décor well. It was "furniture from our city apartment, before we could afford a house in the suburbs with everything new." I was certain that upstairs in the living room stood a more petite couch, its cushions protected in plastic.

Michigami's split-level and ranch homes required smaller furniture than the bulky wooden pieces that were left behind in the Chicago apartments. The old pieces looked cramped and uneasy in these newer homes, as if they were afraid they would crash through the floors. The heavy, dark woods that my generation would come to covet were, in 1970, just old furniture. To our parents, they were unwanted reminders of the less prosperous, immigrant past.

Pam's father, an up-and-coming CPA who changed his first name to Michael from Meyer, needed his furniture to reflect his newly acquired status. Like so many of their ilk, Mr. and Mrs. Silverstick imagined themselves in a time when lords and ladies (although, not Jews) ruled over manors. Thus, the Silverstick's had a sort of Rococo thing going on in their living and dining rooms; *Jewish* Rococo was how my college roommate referred to the style.

I tried to focus on the faces. The sexuality of the girls scattered around the basement was on parade. Their sweet scent created a haze in the air that softened the overhead lighting.

The welcome sound of my name eased the tension of making an entrance. Barbara Needleman, in a pink sweater and jean skirt, came right up to me. Her lipstick matched her sweater, as did the little pink earrings in her pierced ears. According to Grandma, at the turn of the century, all girls had their ears pierced, until it became déclassé due to the arrival of so many poor immigrants with pierced ears. Recently, the middle class rediscovered pierced ears, and even Grandma re-opened the tiny holes that had long since closed up.

"Glen, hi. Glad you're here. I just got here too." I was thrilled by Barbara's approach. The grapevine was right; she was interested in something beyond the friendship she showed me in class. I felt no physical attraction to Barbara, but I liked her a lot, and I was thrilled with the idea that she thought of me as boyfriend material; better still, that others might see us as a couple. This was an indication that my adolescence would progress *normally*. I didn't know what to do with my hands, so I awkwardly shoved them into my front pockets.

"Yeah, thanks. You look nice. I'm going to get some food or punch. Do you want any?" Somewhere I learned that a guy was supposed to ask a girl if he could be of assistance.

"Yeah, sure. I'll walk over to the table with you." Before I responded, Barbara stepped in front of me to the metal folding table covered in Happy Birthday paper, and stacked with matching paper plates, cups, and napkins. The design on the paper goods was a mass marketer's idea of a psychedelic, LSD trip interpreted for the middle class. Chocolate chip cookies, pretzels, M&Ms, and a bowl of punch were arrayed along the length of the table.

A scandal erupted at a party a year earlier when we heard the rumor that Steve Tompkins put a single aspirin tablet in the punch bowl. We heard that mixing aspirin in punch could cause psychedelic trips. When I told Nancy about it, she scoffed at my ignorance.

"Sweet Baby James" reached out to caress us from the record player. I looked across the food table into the handsome face of my classmate, George Adams—our black Adonis. He once remarked that his father named him after the English kings. His arrogance added to his magnetism. The cream colored turtle-neck he wore showed off his already well-developed physique. I snapped a mental photo to look at later that night.

In our class everyone was invited to the white kids' parties, but the black kids seldom attended. I guess the black kids had parties too, but none of us were ever invited. George and his girlfriend Carlotta were at the party, because the birthday girl's boyfriend, Louis Gottfried, was on the school basketball team with George, and they were buddies.

The close friendship between Louis and George grew organically from a common interest and mutual respect. Mom would be pleased. They exemplified how integration could spread understanding and racial harmony across America—at least to athletes and demigods.

George and Louis weren't typical kids. Louis had advantages. He was attractive, bright (unlike Ben Rubin), a good athlete, and mellow. He was never in a fight, because everyone assumed he could take on all comers. No blacks insulted or harassed him openly. I snapped another mental photo for later.

The elite black kids at school liked Louis, while the rest of the black kids left him alone. I assumed this gave Louis a different perspective on race relations at our school, yet he raised his own kids in an exclusive, all white suburb.

"Feigman, my man." The friendly greeting from George caught me off guard.

"Your scores are pretty high at those indoor track contests we've been having in gym, and if I remember right, you ran a good 880. Are you going to try out for track this spring? We need some help." George bit into a pretzel stick.

I was stunned. George Adams had just as good as declared me to be Hermes. I had wings on my feet, and at that moment I danced on the clouds. I couldn't have planned this any better. Barbara was standing at my side where she chose to be, and at that very moment, one of the coolest kids in my grade, and a black kid at that, praised *my* athletic ability, and asked me to try out for track. It was true that I was fast and agile, but I had poor hand and eye coordination, so I was mediocre at any sport involving a ball—and that's more of the image that people had of me.

Now I had to give the right response. Panic overtook the glee pumping through my Olympic body. *Don't blow this Glen. Think! Think! What is the right answer?*

"Uh, thanks George. I don't know. Yeah. Maybe. I hadn't thought about it much." *Not bad. Not great, but kind of nonchalant. Not a disaster or anything.*

"Well you should think about it. We need a few more guys on the spring team." George, my new best friend, walked away, leaving me a stranger in paradise. I felt lucky to go to a school where a popular black kid would encourage me to join him on the track team. No white kid ever said anything similar to me. Integration was the answer to all our problems. We could all be friends. Of course, a different reality would set in on Monday morning when I stepped off the school bus.

Barbara and I took seats atop the cushioned lid of a toy bench that ran the length of the room, and we watched our friends maneuver around as Simon and Garfunkel serenaded us. I revisited George's comments. Who was I kidding? I could never understand how kids got themselves out of bed at five a.m. to jump into an ice-cold pool, or chase a ball across a freezing field for the love of their sport. When school let out, the last thing I wanted to do was go back to the gym for some kind of practice. And those awful competitions; how I hated competing. I was and I am a miserable loser. The possibility of losing—and possibly embarrassing myself—terrified me, and kept me from competing many times. As much as I would've loved the recognition and respect that came easily to members of an athletic team, I feared putting myself out there, only to be found wanting.

"What are you thinking about?" Barbara was looking at me with searching eyes. Her hair resembled the Breck girl on the back cover of one of Nancy's magazines.

"I was wondering if I should do the old stretch-and-yawn trick to put my arm around you." I was too cool. George's comments had taken my small talk to mountainous heights.

Barbara blushed and giggled. "That's okay." She lowered her eyes as if she were embarrassed that she revealed herself to me.

In a little while our lips were pressed together. It was unsatisfying to me, but this was what I was supposed to want to do, at any opportunity. Then, at one point, our tongues touched, and it was a whole new experience. We began to explore this way of kissing, and I liked the way it felt—a lot. I liked it so much that I actually looked forward to it the next time, though French kissing Barbara wouldn't find its way into my erotic imaginings that night. George and Louis stood firmly in her way. Pun possibly intended.

CHAPTER NINETEEN

Monday, January 19, 1970

Debbie Spivey and I took our customary seats at the bi-weekly meeting of the ineffective student council. The sponsoring teacher made certain that we followed mysterious parliamentary procedures that she failed to explain, but she let us wander aimlessly through the halls of potential school spirit activities.

Donna Harding, a rep from another class, sat to my right. She was an exceptionally tall, dark-complected black girl, with a large Afro. She was thirteen, but looked at least seventeen. Her silent presence intimidated the toughest bullies. Her voice was deep and strong, which gave her an air of authority on whatever subject she had an opinion.

Through repeated weekly exposure at these meetings, Donna and I got to know each other. She saw me as some harmless little kid, and that's how I felt in her presence. I was surprised and flattered when she began to take me into her confidence, whispering opinions about the proceedings and the people around us. Donna could smell a phony, and with the deadpan humor that many black girls effortlessly mastered, she let the barbs fly. Our council secretary, like all the officers, was elected because she was popular. Donna stated flatly that, "if that dimwit hadn't started stuffing her bra before the election, she wouldn't be secretary."

As council members straggled in, Donna turned towards me, and fixed her eyes on my crotch— more specifically the bulge there.

"What's that?" she pointed between my legs. I looked down quickly, fearing my zipper was open. It wasn't.

"What?" I asked defensively as I automatically raised myself to sit upright.

"What's going on there?" Donna motioned with her head this time as she continued to focus between my legs. Her eyes twinkled mirthfully.

I was wearing brown corduroy pants that were a size too big (*You'll grow into them.* Thank you, Mom), and the extra material tented over my crotch.

"Oh, this is nothing. It's the pants. Everyone has this. It's the material, see?" And with that I pinched the tented material to show there was nothing underneath except more material. Very smooth, Glen. It was too late to retract what I had done, and Donna began to laugh.

"So you don't have anything there, boy? That's okay. You're still young."

Mortification set in. Donna had flustered me, and instead of playing along and acting cool, I reacted like a child trying to clear the record for his mother. Donna's physical maturity and aura of authority emasculated me. My head soon filled with the things I could have said. Additional witty retorts would come to mind that night and over the next few days—Ben Rubin-type replies: *What? This? That's my big cock. My pants can't hold it all. You want to feel it?* Instead, I had just about sworn an oath that my physical attributes had nothing to do with the impressive bulge.

Donna stopped laughing, and smiled at me indicating she played me in fun, and without malice. Eventually, I appreciated the joke, and we laughed together. Our laughter became extreme, and attracted attention. It was cool to be seen as Donna's friend, so I extended my laughter beyond its natural life. We laughed until the president of the student council cleared his throat, and looked at us with annoyance.

My cousins, in their insular schools, would never have the pleasure of sharing a joke with a world-wise, cool, black girl like Donna Harding. Another small triumph for integration.

At 3:15, the inept student council adjourned, as did the rest of the school. Donna and I smiled good-byes to each other as Debbie and I gathered up our books. We let our guard down as we walked the long corridor to our lockers, and we would soon pay for this lapse. I was on gender conformity autopilot; I held my books at my side, and Debbie held her books so the tops rested at the nipple line (Ken's words), her arms crossed around them. I lifted my head only slightly, and grunted "hey," as I passed anyone I knew. Being on gender conformity autopilot allows one to focus on the topic at hand.

Unaware that we were approaching a previously unknown hazard, Debbie and I were watchful for black kids who took particular pleasure in using the crowded hallways as an excuse to shove white kids as they passed. Blacks had different rules from whites. A black person could never give an inch to a white person. Certain blacks went out of their way to block the progress of whites going in either direction around the slower moving black kids. I was aware of the irony that for centuries in the South, blacks had to make way for whites. Times changed, but it seemed we exchanged one idiocy for another. The hall bullies reminded me of the blacks Dad talked about—the ones who slowly crossed in front of his car against the light.

"Glen, do you think I could ride with you to Adam's bar mitzvah next Saturday? I won't need a ride home or anything, but just to the service."

"Gary's mom's driving Ken and me. You could probably come with." "Oh, I wanted to show you this note from Judy. She gave it to me in math. You'll think it's funny."

Debbie opened her notebook, and looked into the side pocket for a piece of paper. I watched her hands as we continued walking. That's when the attack came. A dark-skinned hand and forearm, sticking out of a gold colored sleeve, entered my right peripheral vision. I heard Debbie suck in her breath as she dropped her books. Instantly my eyes exploded with heat, and I was forced to shut them tightly. I dropped my books, and instinctively raised my hands to my eyes. I had a flash of a thought of a movie where a man was blinded by a spitting cobra. I was now acquainted with Mace.

I could hear Debbie crying and bumping against a locker. "Oh my God. I can't believe this. I can't see. What happened? Glen, get me to the nurse." Debbie didn't realize that I was as blind as she.

"I can't see either. We got sprayed with something. Stay against the lockers."

We stood stricken against a wall of lockers, with our books scattered around our feet, and our hands covering our eyes. I wanted to gather up my things from the floor, but I couldn't remove my hands from my melting eyes. Other students soon recognized something was wrong. I picked out Barbara Needleman's voice.

"Glen! Debbie! Oh my God! What happened? What's wrong? Are you okay?" I felt Barbara's hand on my shoulder. Every sense but my useless sight was now on high alert, but overriding everything was the fire devouring my eyes. I noticed the diminution of footsteps as kids stopped around us to find out what happened.

Debbie sobbed heavily, and in spite of everything, I felt comforted by Barbara's touch. She took charge, shouting orders to others to gather our books and papers, telling them to follow her as she guided us to the office. I imagined everyone staring as we weaved our way through the crowd.

CHAPTER TWENTY

One Hour Later

Barbara sat with me in the nurse's office as we waited for Mom. I decided that this experience would bind Barbara and me for life, and we would tell our children about it, and explain that it's one of the reasons we sent them to all white schools.

Debbie and I spent a solid half hour flushing our eyes with cold water. I could hear Debbie's mother and Assistant Principal Strong having a heated exchange from behind the nurse's office door. Debbie and I were able to identity the assailant as a black male, based on the exposed portion of his arm. He disappeared into the hallway crowd, and no witnesses stepped forward.

The nurse caught Mom preparing to leave school for the day. Dad's office was closer, but they always called the mothers.

I tried to predict Mom's response. I knew her first concern would be about my health and safety, but I didn't know how much of a fuss she would make about her son being the victim of a crime at school. She would be perplexed that a black student was the culprit, since it conflicted with her conviction that, if given the opportunity, blacks would rise to be their best selves. Surely, by virtue of attending school in such a renowned district, the black children had the opportunity. On the heels of the basketball riot, my experience that day was not the first, and certainly not the last to shake convictions that she held for decades. By comparison, Nancy's and my experiences at school were relatively recent. We didn't share Mom's firmly rooted convictions

She arrived, and I watched Barbara evaluate her, perhaps as mother-in-law material. I was proud that Mom was one of the better-looking moms. Barbara stood up, but Mom greeted her perfunctorily as she rushed to take my face between her cold hands, and stare intently into my eyes, looking for both injuries and answers. She was satisfied enough to let go of my face, and turn around to engage Mr. Strong who had slunk back to the nurse's office upon learning of "the other mother's" arrival. The scene was ripe for embarrassment.

"What happened to my son? Do I need to take him to a doctor? How is this possible? Who did this?" Thousands of years of honing the maternal instinct to protect a child had taken control. She had one toe left on the ledge of composure.

I held back my knowledge of the race of my assailant, sparing Mr. Strong additional discomfort. Mom would take pains to tell me that the perpetrator's race was immaterial, so I left the revelation up to Mr. Strong, who, as it turned out, said nothing. I would reveal the fact later when I related the story to Dad.

Mr. Strong struggled. He was frustrated to have to meet Mom under these circumstances. If he were to secretly get his hands on the kid who did this, surely Mr. Strong would smack him. He was no fan of the black kids who roamed the school, making his job difficult.

Instead of calming and placating Mom, he came across as patronizing, making everyone uncomfortable. He couldn't get out of his own way.

"Mrs. Feigman, Glen will be fine. It appears he and Miss Spivey were sprayed with Mace or something similar. It was a random act. One of the students must've gotten a hold of the stuff in his home, and brought it to school. It was just a silly prank, as far as I can tell." He read Mom's face, and braced himself.

Mom's usual response to an accomplished black man, such as Mr. Strong, would be one of admiration for succeeding against the obstacles he surely had confronted—that is, if the situation were not challenging her Pollyanna approach to race relations. She tightened the reins against the thought that struggled to break free: that this man might not be up to his job, and that he owed his position to his race and a school board determined to diversify its staff.

Mom's response was muted, and I softly sighed with relief.

"You can imagine how upsetting this is for a parent. I hope you catch whoever did this to make sure that it doesn't happen to anyone else."

Mr. Strong's gratitude for the things Mom left unsaid was obvious as he emoted platitudes. After a few more forced pleasantries, Mom and I drove Barbara home. Barbara's presence in the car was a blessing, since it prevented Mom and me from having to analyze the day's events.

"Thank you so much, Barbara, for helping Glen and Debbie. You're a doll, and your mother should be very proud of you. I'm going to tell her."

"Oh, okay. Thanks." Barbara looked embarrassed. When we turned the car into the driveway of her house, I jumped out, and held her door open. Mom and I walked her to the front door. A little white dog jumped excitedly, and the smell of dinner escaped from the house into the cold air as our mothers conversed in the foyer. The Needleman's house was modest, neat, and comfortable, with some vibrant, and expensive looking oil paintings on the walls, revealing the values of their owners. I spied Barbara's older, sexy brother as he stuck his head out of a room to see who was at the door. Upon seeing me he ducked silently back into the room.

Barbara's mother was thin, with modest make-up and frosted hair. A red paisley apron hung from her chest to her thighs, covering a brown wool dress. A gold chain dropped from her slender neck, and disappeared behind the apron, so I couldn't see the pendant. I knew Barbara's parents from school events. She looked like a feminine version of her father, while her brother was a hot, masculine version of Mrs. Needleman.

Melva waited for us at home. Mom called her, letting her know I would be home later than usual, because I was injured at school, but not to worry. Still, Melva refused to leave, until she saw me with her own eyes. When we entered the kitchen from the garage, I was embraced by the clean smell of Pine Sol that I'll always associate with Melva.

"What happened to you? How's my boy?" Mom told her about the Mace, while I kissed Melva's cheek, and briefly left the world, resting my head on her bosom—the most peaceful place on Earth. I never broke our hugs first.

"Who did this to you? Do you know? I'd like to take a switch to him. It was a colored boy, wasn't it?"

I wasn't sure how to respond. I thought Mom might jump in with a lesson for me about not jumping to conclusions, but she didn't. Melva and I never talked about race, but I occasionally overheard her complaining to Grandma about the black kids in her neighborhood that harassed and even mugged her a few times as she walked home from the L. Before Melva had her beloved German Shepard, Buck, to protect her small apartment, she and her husband were robbed of whatever meager things they had.

"Colored children don't respect anyone anymore. They scare me more than the whites did back South. The whole community is falling apart."

When my friends and I shared jokes at the expense of blacks, we whispered because we knew it was wrong, but it didn't keep us from laughing. Then I would think of Melva, and guilt replaced mirth. It wasn't the family's lessons on the equality of the races that engendered my guilt; it was that I knew Melva, and she was the kindest person I knew. I loved her with my whole heart. Mom and Dad would've found it surprising that it wasn't the day-to-day interaction with my black peers that kept my bigoted laughter in check, but rather my admiration and love for our cleaning woman.

When Melva was convinced that I was fine, and that no one knew who committed the "evil thing," she took her leave until Thursday.

Nancy clucked her tongue, and shook her head to express her disapproval of what happened to me. "What can you expect?" Mom shot her a look of alarm, but before she could say anything, Nancy turned to go upstairs.

Matzah barked in delight as Grandma entered through the front door. Mom prevented the discussion from continuing.

"All right Glen. Let's talk about this later. We don't need to hear about Grandma's experience in line at the grocery store again. I'll talk to Daddy after dinner. Agreed?"

"Yeah, but Nancy might say something over dinner."

"I'm going to talk to her right now; that is, if she hasn't gotten on the phone already."

I missed Hebrew school because of the day's events, and that was fine with me. Monday night was the best night for comedy on television. I was devoted to *Rowan and Martin's Laugh In* at 7:00 and *The Carol Burnett Show* at 9:00. Between shows I could do homework, and take a shower in anticipation of *The Carol Burnett Show.*

We watched *Laugh In* as a family. From time to time, Grandma would comment on the silliness of the program, but Nancy and I thought the show was mod and totally cool, because it was filled with anti-establishment references. They made fun of President Nixon, bigots, and anyone who was against anything progressive in the '60s (or now '70s!). Ken did a great imitation of Henry Gibson, and a girl in my class did a good imitation of Lily Tomlin, as Ernestine the telephone operator. My imitation of Ernestine was better, but I would only do it in front of my family, for fear of being called a fem at school. When the phrase "sock it to me baby" was uttered on *Laugh In*, everyone talked about it the next day at school, because it sounded obscene, and made our parents squirm.

As we watched *Laugh In*, a commercial aired for a cleaning product with three housewives comparing the power of their liquid cleaners. One of the women was black, a relatively new development in television advertising.

The blacks featured in commercials gave me hope, because they were not angry, threatening, or alien in their behavior. Perhaps one day we really would grow to be a colorblind society. I dashed my own hopes when I thought of the blacks swaggering down the corridors in school or the streets of Hampden.

The blacks I saw on commercials behaved no differently from the whites with whom they interacted, but that wasn't my personal experience, and experience trumps commercials every time.

"I see more and more colored on commercials now. Have you noticed?" Grandma asked no one in particular.

After *Laugh In*, I went upstairs. Later, alone in my room, I watched *The Carol Burnett Show*.

I overheard Mom and Dad in their bedroom attempt diplomacy as they discussed whether it was time to consider crossing the great divide of Lawson Avenue to take me out of the integrated school system. Bless them. Mom concluded that she couldn't conceive of taking an action that would be condoned by those angry, anti-busing mobs shown on the news. "If bringing kids together in schools isn't part of the solution, and then what would that leave as an alternative?"

Before Dad let Mom drop the subject, he reminded her of the theft of Nancy's coat, the basketball riot, and some of the recent comments Nancy and I made. His concern was more about the safety of Nancy and me than it was about the larger issue of race.

"We need to monitor what's going on in the schools more closely. You should talk to some of the mothers you know, and see if their kids are saying anything. We definitely need to bring it up at the parent teacher conferences, whenever they are."

"That's a good idea." Then Mom steered the conversation to the subject of the Spanish signs going up all over her school, which continued to drive her crazy.

CHAPTER TWENTY-ONE

That Night

I lay in bed listening to Sly and the Family Stone on my clock radio, reviewing the day's events and the state of race relations at school.

Until I was Maced and missed Hebrew school, the day was like most days. After school, most of the Jewish kids attended Hebrew school or piano lessons, or both. Intramurals, while not high on my list, siphoned off some guys.

Hebrew school conflicted with intramural sports. Some parents pulled their kids out of Hebrew school, in deference to the importance of sports, but in 1970 they were a minority.

Black kids would express frustration that they couldn't get enough guys from their class to form an after school team, because of "that damned Hebrew school." Their frustration wasn't directed at us for being Jewish, but for us having to go to Hebrew school. Some of the black kids weren't aware of a link between being Jewish and attending Hebrew school. All the insults, indignities, and anger that the black students heaped on us were because we were white. Being Jewish had nothing to do with it. I never heard a reference to Jews from my black classmates. I don't know if they or their parents were aware that almost ninety percent of the white kids in the school were Jewish. The black Nation of Islam's demonization of Jews hadn't found fertile ground at our school.

I explored this notion of the unfamiliarity of my black classmates with Judaism, and unwittingly, Jews. Did they know anything about Jewish history, our minority status, and the millennia of oppression? Did they know why the school closed for two days every September or October? Were they aware of the shared struggle between Jews and blacks over the previous decades, or the recent dissolution of that relationship? Even if they knew we weren't Christian, to them we were simply another version of white. Somewhere in this lack of communication and understanding was a lost opportunity to bring us together.

I predicted that the blacks in my school were in for a surprise when they tried to pull their tough act on the Gentile whites in the larger world. That vastly, more numerous variety of white was less easily intimidated, and more accustomed to fighting back. From the exposure I had to Gentile whites through television, movies, and particularly the firsthand encounters with the Irish-Catholic kids in my neighborhood, I was sure that Gentile whites would resist the rise of uncontested black power that flourished in my school. Jews turned the other cheek to our new black oppressors, while the Christians threw the punches back at them.

Nothing in our upbringing had prepared us for the physicality of our black classmates. Corporal punishment rarely existed in our homes. Wrestling matches to resolve disputes were not unknown among my friends, but these were more the exception than the rule. The mall girls resorted to vicious verbal attacks on each other and on some boys, but I never saw them get physical.

Yet there were black girls in my school who slapped and shoved other people with startling frequency.

I fought back to protect my honor the one or two times a white kid physically picked on me. I also had a few physical confrontations when I was an over-zealous patrol boy in fifth grade. My opponents and I were evenly matched, and after a few head-locks and tumbles no harm was done.

Black bullies evoked a different response from my white peers and me. Race must've played a part in this different response. There was a notion floating around in our heads that it was wrong to hit a black person, because of all the unfair beatings they took over the years. Vying for space in our brains was the knowledge that a white kid fighting with a black kid could look racist, and thus was likely to prompt a considerable response from the larger black student body no matter who started the fight.

Consider the source. That hackneyed phrase partly explains my untested theory regarding our lack of physical engagement with our tormentors—along with our fear and inexperience. Guessing that I would be about as popular as a eugenics proponent at Columbia or Berkeley, I theorize that unconsciously we viewed the aggressive black kids as being far enough out of the norm of conduct that there was no dishonor in ignoring, laughing at, or just tolerating the abuse. To be throttled by another white kid was embarrassing. The same throttling from a black kid was somewhat expected and strangely, accepted. I was taught by Grandpa to apply logic and reason to address disagreements, but his advice was useless in the face of an unreasonable opponent.

I wish we had been more physically aggressive in our response. As Zadie would've said with his balled up fist thrust outwardly, "we should've given them this!" While that might've squelched the actions of the more rational provocateurs, it might have provoked any irrational perpetrators still more.

Would the situation have differed if we had been schooled in self-defense, both boys and girls?

I place much of the blame for the growing discord in the race relations at our school on the adults in charge. They hid in corners, or turned their heads. Those that made efforts to intervene couldn't get a grip on the slippery situation due in part to the era. Whites were asked to be tolerant. Blacks were asked what else they would like whites to do for them. Any white in a position of authority had at least one hand tied behind his back, so as not to appear insensitive to the plight of blacks in America. Apparently, to make a demand for the taking of personal responsibility, and to insist on a basic standard of conduct and educational effort was unreasonable and old-fashioned. Any mediator was expected to take into account centuries of black oppression.

No one, near or far, risked the proclamation that lowering standards and expectations would actually slow the progress of blacks in society, and ultimately hurt everyone. Such a decree would be dismissed as insensitive at best and bigoted at worst. The tide of history was pulling with unusual force, and struggling against it was futile, so reason foundered.

CHAPTER TWENTY-TWO

Tuesday, January 20, 1970

The seventh grade annual talent show brought us back to the auditorium, a situation ripe with the possibility for mayhem. As the drama teacher introduced the program, the room was about as quiet as it would get. My gym teacher, Mr. Wendell, got up to introduce the first performer.

Mr. Wendell, a tall, handsome black man who'd played professional football, was one of the first blacks to buy a home on the Michigami side of the canal. There was no resistance in the neighborhood to the Wendell's purchase of the house, and no "white flight." He taught in the district, and his own children went to the schools. It made sense to his neighbors that he chose to live where he did on the "safer" side of the sluggish divide. He didn't appear to be at the forefront of a threatening trend.

The previous year, Mr. Wendell was my homeroom teacher, and a surprising bond formed between us. He found me to be a smart, dependable kid, and I was thrilled that a popular (i.e. young, male, jock, handsome, and hip) teacher saw value in me.

I noted that his neatly pressed Oxford cloth shirts often seemed about to rip open, losing a battle with the muscles underneath.

That year, Mr. Wendell had guided the student council—as ineptly as all the others before and since—and he recommended that I apply to be my homeroom's student council rep. I was elected, and sometimes before meetings Mr. Wendell would ask for my opinion on an upcoming topic.

In gym class he called me *Big Glen*, and while that alone caused my pride to swell, what elevated Mr. Wendell to a pedestal for life, also became the apex of my un-illustrious gym career. During our gymnastics unit, he put us through various exercises on the rings and the parallel bars. To my surprise and joy, I showed promise. Though I was mired in the mid-ranks when it came to team sports, I excelled at the individual skills required for track and gymnastics. As I noted, even George Adams commented on my speed and agility at Pam's party.

On one glorious day in gym class we were seated on risers along the wall. Mr. Wendell set up two horses for the days' gymnastics session. His plan was to have two boys come up and demonstrate various maneuvers on the horse, and then have the rest of us line up and take turns attempting the same moves. That's when he voiced the words that I'll always cherish.

"Let's see. Where are my gymnasts? I need two good gymnasts to come up here, and help me demonstrate what I want you to do. Big Glen, you come up here." I didn't hear who else was called. My heart leaped into my ears. My level of joy left Earth's atmosphere and shot into outer space. Mr. Wendell singled me out as one of his gymnasts, in front of every boy in my class. I bolted off the bench towards the horse. No one snickered! For a moment, I was living Ben Rubin's or Louis Gottfried's life. I desperately wanted to justify Mr. Wendell's confidence in me, and my anxiety must've been apparent, because he looked down at me, and nodded reassuringly, placing a hand on my shoulder.

From then on I felt connected to him. He always acknowledged me in the hallway with a nod and a "How's Big Glen?" Later, after my "incident," I felt I'd betrayed and disappointed him.

Now, at the talent show, Mr. Wendell introduced Ronnie Marks, and the heavy, green velvet curtains parted to reveal a set of parallel bars. Ronnie entered from the left in his gymnastics uniform. Wolf whistles and shouts of "You go, boy!" and "You're okay boy!" shot out from the darkened auditorium. Girls began to whisper to each other, having noticed, as did I, the outline of Ronnie's protective cup through his tight, white uniform. I felt the same combination of jealously and hopeless longing that Ben Rubin evoked in me. Barbara who?

At thirteen, Ronnie's muscular development was apparent and way ahead of most of us. By the time he dismounted, we showed our unabashed enthusiasm for athletic prowess by applauding, whistling, and whooping encouragement. Ronnie's personality paled in comparison to his physique. Having no stage presence, he kept his head lowered, bowed, and walked off. Athletics had given him a solid reputation, and after this display, it was as sure as his grip on the parallel bars. Guys respected him. While girls—and I—fantasized about him. All but some of the angriest black kids gave him a *Get Out Of Harassment Free* card.

Ms. Burnham, the girls' physical education teacher, introduced Audrey Farber who came out in a leotard to do a modern dance routine, another audience favorite. Audrey's red leotard tented the pants of most of the boys in the auditorium. Not one of them watched her feet. It was the girls' turn to experience envy. Ben Rubin and his cocky jock friends stood up in unison to give Audrey a standing ovation. I remained in my seat, unimpressed. Modern dance bored me then and now. If you have something to say, just say it. Don't force me to interpret your movements. I lump modern dancers with pantomime "artists."

These were tough acts to follow, and sadly for Stacey Saylor, she was next. Stacey, a true minority in our school—white Protestant—was a good student, but dull of face and personality. On the flat side of puberty, her habit of wearing frilly dresses and bows, a look disdained by cool girls, didn't help her popularity. Stacey was dressed to fail: frills, bows, ribbons, and black patent leather shoes on parade.

What she lacked mammarily speaking, Stacey made up for in musical talent. A child protégé, she studied piano, and practiced her way to the music solo in the district-wide spring musical and choral concert—an honor usually bestowed on high school students. Unfortunately, there was more appreciation in our school for someone who could flip his eyelids than for Stacey, who could knock out a Mozart piece while sewing another frill onto her dress.

Stacey's biggest fan, Mrs. Everly, the music teacher, did nothing to help Stacey's image. Mrs. Everly was a relic from a past, when children sat quietly at their desks, hands folded. Although probably not more than sixty, her snowy white and tightly coifed hair, powdered white skin, and bright red lipstick gave her the appearance of the little old ladies who lived next door in 1950's sitcoms. Mrs. Everly, in collars and cuffs that resembled doilies, out-frilled Stacey. Then there was that piece of facial tissue sticking out at the wrist. Mrs. Everly had the burden of teaching us the history of music from the time of the Etruscans (and nobody knew who they were) right up through the waltz kings of Vienna. This was subject matter even beyond queer, and she had no idea how to make it relevant.

In her classroom, we welcomed any distraction from her desiccated presentations of slides and filmstrips. There were always black kids, whether in the class or outside, to provide it. Once, while seated at her upright, plunking out the notes to a song more suited to fourth-graders than cool kids like us, Mrs. Everly received shocking notice from outside the high, open windows of the music room when a hail of stones attacked her. One landed on the piano, and the rest landed on the floor around it.

We watched this welcome interruption with delight and amazement as she scrambled across the room, imploring us to remain calm, and run for the door. We moved in the direction of the door, but our laughter got in the way of our ability to walk. The sight of Mrs. Everly waving her arms in terror, combined with the ludicrous, faux hailstorm, delivered one of the year's most memorable days.

We later learned that Kevin McPherson and Curtis May were responsible for the barrage of limestone that rained on Mrs. Everly. We knew what they did was wrong, but we didn't care. No one was hurt, and we escaped from boredom. Those were the small pleasures that I would never have known at an all white school across Lawson Avenue.

In spite of her labors over lesson plans, Mrs. Everly was unable to get an ounce of the respect that we gave freely to her counterpart, Mr. Bowden. To reduce us to putty, the young, shaggy-haired, music teacher only had to lift his guitar, and play a few riffs from a Beatles' melody. He strummed, sang, and found a way to make rock lyrics relevant to the material he was required to teach. He was soft spoken, but we heard every word that emerged from under his bushy mustache. He used the vernacular with ease, and his corduroy bell-bottoms were no different from our own.

Mr. Bowden was brought in half way through the previous year, because another music teacher, Mrs. Peak, "suddenly left." Although we made jokes about her advanced age, which was probably not more than 55, she was well liked, because she had a good sense of humor, and often made fun of herself.

The reason for her abrupt departure was nonsensical and a harbinger of the foolishness to follow over the next decades, and it foreshadowed my own demise at school. Insanity had infiltrated the minds of the administrators and some parents.

What was the sin of Mrs. Peak? In one of her lectures, she properly (but in hindsight, unwisely), used the word *niggardly*. The result was chaos in her class that spilled out into the halls, and it didn't stop until it was brought up for discussion at an emergency school board meeting. There, several vocal, black parents demanded her ouster for her blatant racism.

Mrs. Peak's defense was equally strong. It was repeatedly pointed out that the word was not the horrible "N" word that she was being accused of using, that the word was indeed part of Standard English. Her enemies neither knew nor cared what the word meant, but they did know what it sounded like, and it was therefore unacceptable to use under any circumstance. Certain students, they claimed, would surely suffer a loss of self-esteem. The belief of the mollycoddlers was that self-esteem could be given and taken away, without considering the possibility that someone could earn it.

That meeting was a warning to the parents of some of the students from the Michigami side of the divide. A few "For Sale" signs soon went up on their lawns.

In the end, a compromise was reached—one that satisfied no one. Mrs. Peak could stay on as a district employee, but she would transfer to another school, with a different (i.e. more white) demographic composition. Anonymous threats were then made to Mrs. Peak, and she became afraid to stay in the district. She resigned. The poor, abused children were saved from the 55-year old monster, with the self-deprecating sense of humor. Order was restored at a price that we will never know.

Stacy crossed the stage towards the piano, and most of us politely applauded and offered encouragement. The mall girls were whispering to each other in disdainful tones, unable to ignore the frills and ribbons. Stacy sat at the grand piano, and raised her hands dramatically. Upon their descent to the keys the first spitball bounced off her shoulder. Other paper projectiles soon followed. The missiles were coming from three black boys in the first row, lead by Kevin McPherson. Behavior we knew to be inexcusably rude was also inexplicably funny, and laughter ensued. Teachers and students alike could be heard attempting to shush the crowd, but no single leader took control, and the mayhem escalated.

Booing and hissing, from Steve Tompkins and several groups of black kids accompanied the projectiles that flew from every direction. The din grew louder, until Stacey stopped playing, and wept softly, with her head down over the keyboard. My emotions spun 180 degrees, from amusement to sadness and guilt. Mrs. Everly took center stage, and demanded that we behave and "give this young girl the respect and attention she deserves." She reprimanded us, telling us that we should be proud that Stacey was our classmate, and will represent us in the spring concert.

A handful of paper balls flew at the stage, landing at Mrs. Everly's feet. The audience, including me, erupted in laughter. We knew that as a group there was no penalty to pay for this drastic display of disrespect. I looked around to see who would finally take command of the room as Stacey ran off the stage sobbing. Mr. Strong mounted the steps to the stage. His voice was too tinny for the task at hand, but he puffed himself up, and gave one of his better performances. Looking flustered he shouted out that he was taking down names, and considering a suspension for anyone who didn't conduct himself properly. That quieted all but two or three voices that eventually petered out.

Sadly, Stacey's time had passed, and she did not reappear. Her recognition would come when thousands of parents attending the district's spring concert stood in unison to give her the ovation she earned. Until then, she was just another plain, poorly dressed, unpopular girl at school.

Two small figures rose from seats near the front along the wall—Stacey's mother and an older woman whom I guessed was Stacey's grandmother. They looked sad and bewildered. The two women trudged up the aisle to the exit. I squelched the lump rising in my throat, and wiped tears from the corners of my eyes. I thought of Mom and Grandma enduring a similar humiliation of Nancy or me, and it broke my heart. The dispirited expressions on the faces of those two women devastated me, and lingered in my mind long after we settled down to watch the next group of performers. Three tall, thin, black girls in shiny matching dresses performed a song by Diana Ross and the Supremes. They were a smash.

CHAPTER TWENTY-THREE

Wednesday, January 21, 1970

I hurried to the temple alone down one of Hampden's main streets that cut through the black, residential district. After schools let out, it was common for white kids to walk east through this foreign territory, on the way to downtown Hampden and the white neighborhoods. I kept an eye out for snowballs, and an ear out for threats, but my walk along the concrete sidewalk, framed by a low blanket of white snow, outlined in dirt, was uneventful.

I had a meeting scheduled with Rabbi Becker, before Hebrew school, to review the meaning of the portion of the Torah that I would recite at my bar mitzvah. I would also read a passage from the books of the Prophets, called the Haftorah. The rabbi's job was to make certain I understood what I read, and to make it relevant. I met separately each week with the head of the education department of the temple, to learn how to chant the Haftorah. He sang into a cassette tape that I took home with me to learn by listening and repeating. Sly and the Family Stone, it wasn't.

With the backs of my gloved hands, I wiped my watering eyes as I entered the overheated lobby of the sand colored, brick building. It was cozy, and the big leather chairs outside the door to the Rabbi's study called out, Siren-like. Five minutes early was maybe enough time to rest in one of those chairs—especially if Rabbi Becker were late.

In fifteen minutes the place would be alive with energy from Hebrew school classmates as they arrived from day school. Before I sat down, I put my ear against the heavy wooden door, and heard Rabbi Becker's muffled voice on the other side.

Nancy thought he was sexy, but I didn't see it. His voice was his standout feature. Often gentle—almost seductive —it could swell like the sound of approaching thunder, challenging anyone to ignore his frequent calls to action.

The voice from the other side of the door grew silent. He must've hung up the phone, so I knocked softly. "Come in." Distant thunder, muffled by the heavy, wooden door.

The office was dimly lit, silent. There were no windows, the only light coming from one small brass lamp with a green glass shade that sat at the edge of the rabbi's desk. Three walls were lined from floor to ceiling with books, broken up by a door that opened to the sanctuary. A large, brown, leather sofa backed up to the fourth wall, along with two side chairs of a lighter design. Rabbi Becker's walnut desk, a mover's nightmare, wore what looked like a manila blanket, the result of folders lying end to end across the surface. The total effect was to create an ideal place for a nap or psychoanalysis.

His face lit up with a broad smile as I entered and walked over to one of the chairs in front of his desk.

"Shalom, Gershon, my boy," He stood up and extended a smooth, manicured hand that I shook hard, remembering Dad's instructions to always "shake like a man and not a dead fish." The rabbi's handshake was firm and hearty.

Like most *Ashkenazim* (Jews descended from Central and Eastern European Jews), I was named for a deceased relative. Gershon was Bubbie's father who was killed in the Holocaust. He and my great-grandmother died at the Babi Yar massacre outside of Kiev.

I never felt comfortable saying "shalom," so I just said "hi." Kids who said "shalom" seemed like goody-goodies. Another reason to indict the Reform Jewish educational system of the time.

"You are right on time, my friend, and we have a Torah portion to discuss. First tell me, how are your dear parents and the rest of your family? I didn't see your grandparents here Friday night."

Boy, he didn't miss anything. Was it okay to tell the rabbi that they stayed home to play cards? Saved. He continued before I could respond.

"Your grandfather Leo is a good man. Some of our congregants who are lawyers have helped in his volunteer organization giving legal help to blacks in the inner city. He sets a fine example for you at the time of your bar mitzvah. He is carrying out God's commandments. You should be proud."

I made no comment.

By the way, Gershon, is your family planning a trip to Israel anytime soon? It's the best time in decades to go, you know. Since the Six Day War in '67, we can once again pray at the wall of our holy Temple Mount. Can you believe it, my boy? This is the temple built by King Solomon, son of King David, around one thousand years b.c.e. That's almost three thousand years ago! Well, the Babylonians destroyed the original temple, so this is the remains of the rebuilt temple that the Romans destroyed when they vanquished Israel in 70 c.e. And now that Israel recaptured Jerusalem, we can once again enter our holy city, and visit our holy sites. And not that I'm a pessimist by nature, but who knows if someday they won't take it back. We opened the religious sites to the whole world, but they don't want Jews anywhere near the Old City. Anyhow, I should talk to your parents about our next congregational trip when I see them."

That was a history lesson, right there. Rabbi gave me some historical perspective that I never got in Sunday school.

"Let's see." Rabbi Becker miraculously located a folder from the surfeit of his desk, and leafed through it. His hands were strong, like a ball player's. He used many baseball analogies in his sermons. Was there a link between his athlete's hands and his love of the game?

"Oh yes, our friend Naaman. Yes. Yes. Yes. Naaman. Okay Gershon, did you read the translation of the Haftorah reading that Mr. Kaplan gave you?"

"Uh huh."

"Good boy. Do you have any questions or comments you would like to make?"

"Well, yeah."

"You do?" Rabbi Becker looked up, surprised. Most kids probably sat in that chair, like me, sleepy from the dark silence surrounding them, after a day at school, and uninterested in discussing ancient texts. To make our five-thousand-year heritage interesting and relevant was a daily challenge that most of our parents and educators failed.

My Haftorah portion was from Kings II about Naaman, the captain of the army of Syria who fought against Israel. According to Rabbi Becker, Naaman was a courageous leader who was stricken with leprosy. When his armies invaded Israel, they captured a young girl who became a slave in Naaman's household. She told Naaman, her new master, that Israel's prophet Elisha could cure him if Naaman would seek him out in Israel. Naaman got permission from the King of Syria to go to Israel for a cure. In Israel, Elisha instructed Naaman to bathe seven times in the Jordan River, after which he was cured. Naaman then worshipped

Israel's God, and not the gods of the Syrians. I noted that long before there was an Islam, the Syrians were fighting the Jews of Israel.

"So what is your question, Gershon, my boy?"

"Um, well, I was thinking, um, Naaman wasn't Jewish and didn't worship God, and invaded Israel, and took Israelis to be slaves back in Syria, right? And yet all it took to get him to like us, and to become Jewish was for Elisha to cure his leprosy, right?"

The Rabbi nodded silently.

"So how come with all the people in the world who hate us, why doesn't God just finally show them a couple of things like he did by curing Naaman to show we are right when we say He is God? Then maybe they'll all quit picking on us and Israel, and maybe even become Jews too?"

I thought this a great question, and I wanted an easy answer, but I knew not to expect one, at least not from the rabbi.

"That's a great question, Gershon, a great question." Rabbi Becker sat back and examined me, as if he were seeing me for the first time. "Your question has many dimensions to it, and I cannot give you a single answer, but let's start to analyze it a little piece at a time. You, my young friend, do not ask easy questions, but that's okay. Difficult questions are the best ones. They make us think. They make us use our heads that God gave us. To question is part of our Jewish heritage. First, who are these people who you say hate us."

"Well, Christians, Russians, and Arabs mostly, I guess."

"Okay. Why Christians?"

"Well, even the Catholic kids in my neighborhood call us kikes, and pick on us. They don't really seem to hate us, but it seems to be the thing for them to do. My grandparents tell us how much the Russians and Poles hated them before they moved here, and weren't the Nazis and the people who helped them all Christians too?"

"Well, certainly in name they were Christians, but I wonder if Jesus would have been very proud of what they did. And the Arabs?"

"Well the Arabs hate Israel and Jews, and keep wanting to kill us, and drive us into the sea. I hear it on the news all the time. "

I began to regret my question. It would have been so much easier to say I have no questions, and to go on with the plans for my bar mitzvah speech.

"So *boychikle*, first we have to accept that these groups do indeed hate you and me, because we are Jewish. We know anti-Semitism does exist. It always has, and most likely, always will. So we can ask ourselves is there any way that we can change that, or is it something that would require an act of God, as when Naaman was cured of his leprosy?"

What I was hearing was, "Yes, they hate us and no, we can't do a thing about it."

"Let's look at it this way. When God chose us to receive his laws through Moses on Mt. Sinai, you know Gershon, you saw the Ten Commandments with Charlton Heston, right?"

The rabbi's eyes twinkled. I nodded and smiled.

"Well of course it was a great honor for our people, but it also gave us a tremendous responsibility, some would say a burden, even. That meant that we had to set the example for the rest of the world about the righteousness of God's vision for humanity. In His covenant with us, He bequeathed us this little plot of land—Israel—and He commanded us to be a light to all nations. A light to all nations? It's a heavy burden for a small people, but this is the deal we accepted. To be Jews, we must learn the Torah, try to live by its example, and hope the rest of the world takes notice. Are you with me so far?"

I nodded, sank back in my chair, and attempted to focus on his words. My eyelids were heavy.

"In fact, Israel was admired by other nations during the golden age of King Solomon, but mostly Israel and the Jews have been like the small, studious boy who wants to follow the rules in a school full of bullies. The studious boy can't deny all that he knows just to appease the bullies can he? And you wish that God would do something miraculous in front of the bullies to prove He is who He is? I suppose that would make things easier for this boy and for us."

Damn right.

"Well, we as Jews don't pretend to have all the answers. The Torah has many of them, but they often require digging and studying. One thing it makes clear is how to live a righteous life, one that will help restore the world to a Garden of Eden."

Was he going off track? I forgot my question, but I was curious enough to try and follow him.

"Don't tell my union this, but I don't know if God or Moses or someone else wrote the Torah, but the fact of the matter is, it was a document way ahead of its time, and has not been surpassed. I can say that because there is no one here to argue with me."

He should've been a stand-up comic.

"So let's put this together. Why doesn't God reveal His glory blatantly, instead of mundanely, as in the daily rising of the sun?" I wasn't bright enough to catch the irony.

"The Torah does tell us what role God has assigned to the Jewish people, but it doesn't really tell us how active a role He intends to play in our individual lives. I think He leaves some of that up to us to figure out for ourselves. Maybe He'll play only a cameo as we work to make His vision in the Torah a reality. In that case, we can't wait for God to perform any more showy miracles."

I wondered why God had to make it so hard for us. It reminded me of Glinda in the Wizard of Oz. I didn't buy her line about

Dorothy having to learn the lesson for herself before she could go home. What if she died trying to get the witch's broomstick? What good would the lesson do her then?

"What we do know is that what He's given us is a good thing. Yes, being 'chosen' has been a burden but I might add, we accepted what He offered us. We chose God. It worked both ways. His gift of the Torah is too good to turn away from, no matter what His plan and intentions might be. You and I, as mere mortals, cannot pretend to know what God thinks. If we claimed to know God's mind, and sadly, many of our enemies claim just such a talent, then that would make us gods. It's very dangerous for others when a man thinks he's as smart as God Himself—dangerous and presumptuous.

"So, while it would be truly wonderful if whenever Nazis or Arabs or Russians or whomever attempted to exterminate us, God rode in on a white horse and, to use the biblical term, 'smote' them, or razzle dazzled them. Apparently that is no longer God's way. He did it when we crossed the Red Sea, and we mustn't ever forget that. Our emancipation by God through Moses defines us, and motivates us to this day. You can be proud that our people are the champions of liberty and social justice around the world, even if we aren't always the recipients of it." This comment triggered a memory of Aunt Lilly's recent pronouncements.

"That's a long answer, so here is a shorter one. Because of God's gift of the Torah, we know a righteous way to live, and we can't ignore it. Whether at this point God intervenes on our behalf or not, we know how to conduct ourselves as *mensches*, because that is what makes us who we are. By being true to our Jewish selves, we are being true to God. We can only hope that each of us makes the world a little better by how we live, and there is always the chance that someone else, maybe someone who is not a Jew, learns something from us. At those times we move a bit closer to that Garden of Eden."

"So have I answered your question?" He raised his eyebrows expectantly.

"Well..."

Crestfallen. "Hmmm. I haven't. Tough audience. Tell me. I won't sleep tonight unless you leave here saying, 'Boy! That rabbi is a smart guy.' So ask away boychikle. I do love you, you know that Gershon? You are a good boy, and we're all proud of you."

If he knew the truth about me, he wouldn't be so proud to discover that I thought like a Sodomite about Ben Rubin and other guys. Guilt quickly dug in for a rest somewhere in my digestive tract. To appear to be the kind of kid that adults were proud of came easily to me. I was deceptive, and therefore I was evil.

"But why do they all hate us? The Christians and Arabs?"

"Gershon, I don't think they *all* hate us, but let's look at the historical reasons for the animosity that undeniably exists towards Jews. Ironically, it is mostly in the name of religion that they feel so antagonistic towards Jews. Remember Gershon; the Jews have been around practicing the laws of Moses for a few thousand years. We had our home in Israel with Jerusalem our capital centuries before Christianity evolved from Judaism, and Islam arose centuries after that. They fought their way to become the new kings of the hill, each in its time. To do so they had to dethrone the predecessors. That would be Jews for Christians, and both Jews and Christians for Moslems. Let's just say, they didn't, and still don't, always fight fairly. There is a quote from a Russian by the name of Nikolai Berdyaev that says 'Perhaps the saddest thing to admit is that those who have rejected the Cross have to carry it, while those who welcomed it are as often engaged in crucifying others.' That's a bit complicated, but take a moment to think about it."

I assumed an expression of concentration, looking off to one side, brows knotted, but didn't have time to ponder the rabbi's words, because he kept on rolling.

"Remember too, that in the first centuries after the death of Jesus, the Jews were fighting the Romans, ultimately to the total defeat of Israel in 134. That's when they changed the name to Palestine—to erase us from the map. During this time, the Christians, who had been seen as a sect of Judaism, found it very advantageous to gain favor with the Romans by differentiating themselves from the Jews. They made it clear to the Romans that they were no longer a part of or friends with the people of Israel. They declared many negative things about the Jews during those first centuries, before they took control of Rome; and unfortunately for us, much of it ended up in the texts they ultimately selected for what they call the New Testament. Much of the animosity can be traced back to those texts."

At that moment I wished the kike-kickers in my neighborhood could be there with me, listening to this.

My mind was wandering to the black and white newsreels of mountains of skeletons at Dachau that we watched in Sunday school class. I hated Jewish history courses; they were never pleasant because most of Jewish history since the Roman conquest of Israel is persecution, suffering, and slaughter. There was nothing to feel good about, until George Washington spoke of tolerance towards Jews at Newport, Rhode Island.

"Our Moslem friends are relative latecomers, following Christianity by another five hundred or so years. They believe Mohamed received the last of God's revelations. By the way, don't tell this to the Mormons."

The rabbi's interjections of humor kept me awake and listening.

"Just as the Christians could not tolerate our lack of embrace of their beliefs, the Moslems could not and cannot tolerate anyone who is unwilling to accept the words of Mohamed, their prophet. In the Koran we find a rewriting of much of what had been Jewish and Christian history, and the creation of a new version of the events in the Bible. This time, instead of the Torah seen as the predecessor to Christianity, Moslems see Jews and Christians as part of what to them has always been Islamic history.

"The Koran does not treat 'infidels' kindly. The Moslems of the Mideast aligned themselves with Hitler. They expelled hundreds of thousands of us from our ancestral homes recently in 1948, when the Arabs failed in their attempt to exterminate the Jews of Israel reborn. Jews had been living in those North African and Asian lands for a thousand years before Islam. Of course, Israel took in all the refugees where they now live in relative safety. You don't hear much from the world about *those* refugees.

"The Arabs are one group who haven't disavowed Nazi propaganda about Jews, and the rest of the world seems to be okay with that. Perhaps because Arabs control the flow of oil, they're selling us out for a lot more than 30 pieces of silver."

Rabbi Becker looked beyond me and sighed. After a brief pause he livened up.

"So, *now* are you with me?"

I nodded. His presentation followed a logical path.

"My goodness, I bet we've gone over the time I set aside for you. Miriam is probably waiting outside the door right now.

The rabbi's mood became suddenly dark. The warm room quickly froze. His voice took on the voice of someone speaking under a hypnotic spell, and his eyes glazed over. I stopped breathing, because I was sure my respirations would sound cyclonic in this altered environment.

"If we let go of the land we captured from Jordan in our fight for our very survival, and the Arabs do not agree to accept Israel, by then it may be too late for us. Sadly, the world won't lose any sleep over another slaughter of the Jews. That's why we must never answer to anyone but ourselves ever again." His eyes cleared, a sign he was finished. I resumed breathing.

"I hope you remember your question, because I'm not sure I do. In any case, I hope I answered it. Please say 'yes' so we can finish our discussion." There was that pleasant face again.

"Yeah. I guess so."

I could've stopped there, but decided I liked this one on one with the rabbi.

"Rabbi, couldn't we just tell the whole world that quote by Hillel hanging in the lobby? The one that says (I paraphrased), 'don't do anything to anyone else that you wouldn't want done to you?'"

Rabbi Becker's eyes opened wider than I had ever seen them. I was sure I had said something important. His broad grin confirmed it. He was almost out of his seat.

"Glen! My amazing, beautiful, Glen. You've arrived at the very definition of the Torah. Hillel gave this famous quote when he was challenged to teach the entire Torah standing on one foot. He gave that reply, and added that all the rest was commentary, and that we should go and study it. And to top it off, we have already told the whole world. How many people know of the Ten Commandments? At least half the people on the planet.

"If you understand Hillel's point Glen, and you understand your responsibility is to carry that message throughout your life in every thing you do and say, well then, you have truly become a son of the commandment—a bar mitzvah—even if the calendar says it's some weeks away. I think I'll have you give next Shabbat's sermon. I need a vacation." We smiled at each other.

Guilt was determined to keep me humble. I was unworthy of the rabbi's praise, even if I was suddenly wise beyond my years. I still wanted to lie naked with some of the guys in my school.

Guilt was followed by pity. My life would have been easier if I were born a Christian, or even a Moslem, because I wouldn't have to care about Israel and the Jews. I was part of a fragment of a civilization that was nearly exterminated a mere twenty-five years ago, and as the rabbi said: *Such a burden!* I didn't think the

Christian kids in my neighborhood ever worried about such big, life-threatening matters. If I were one of a billion Moslems, I'd surely feel safe with those odds. Blacks were definitely burdened with American racism, but did they share anything similar to this endless, vicious hatred that Jews had been dealing with for millennia, recently culminating in mass extermination? The blacks in the inner city had more to fear from each other than from any one else.

Why did *I* have to be cursed with the knowledge of the injustice of the world, on such a personal level? Onto the heap of guilt, for good measure I piled anger at my friends who could enjoy their masturbatory fantasies guilt free, because their fantasies were about girls. I was twice cursed because I dreamed about boys. I was on the receiving end of a lot of bum deals.

I had enough. I was exhausted. I wanted to take a nap, or run around the block, or anything to shed the effects of my meeting with the rabbi.

He stood and stretched with an extended "Oyyyyyyyyyyyyyy." I stood up, and offered my hand, but he came around the desk, leaned down, and gave me a strong hug. He smelled clean, like soap. I parted with new knowledge and insight.

My Hebrew class was already in session, and the boredom of the kids was palpable. Bleary eyed, leaning on their hands to keep their heads from dropping, they repeated in Hebrew, "The boy and girl walk to the school." Leaders of Reform Judaism, please take note. This was no way to teach a foreign language.

Our forbearers achieved one of their goals: we were Americanized. Most of the kids in class would rather be playing sports than studying, and after seven years of religious school, I bet not one of them knew the history lesson the rabbi had taught me in only twenty minutes. If they did, they might be more committed to a Jewish future for themselves.

Later that night I thought about what Rabbi Becker told me, and was struck by the fact that in all the centuries of animosity toward Jews and Israel, none emanated from black Africans or black Americans—until only very recently—as blacks began to turn away from Jews, and toward Islam. Mom once commented on how proud she was that Martin Luther King had high praise for Israel.

The antics in school seemed petty when held up to the awful, shared histories of Jews and blacks. Great friendships were built on much less.

CHAPTER TWENTY-FOUR

Sunday, January 25, 1970

Thursday and Friday passed without incident. I faced the daily struggles of adolescence, with neither a gain nor loss of status. I surprised no one with amazing feats of masculinity or destructive feminine behavior. Knowledge of my status on the continuum of coolness accrued slightly, so I continued the Sisyphean task of fine-tuning accordingly.

I heard and interpreted comments from teachers and family about current events, but I'm not certain I learned anything academic.

I spent another Sabbath evening around the table with my family, absorbing the rituals and words, both casual and intentional. I spent the weekend divided between the good (sleep, friends, masturbation) the bad (Sunday school, homework, guilt about masturbation), and the mediocre (everything else).

To hold off the Sunday evening blues, I invited Ken over after dinner. We listened to Nancy's cast album of the Broadway Musical *Hair*. Over the past couple of months, I'd listened to it so often that I memorized most of the lyrics, including new words such as sodomy, fellatio, cunnilingus, and pederasty—which were contained in one song. Ken, Gary, Adam, and I worked out the definitions once we could decipher the lyrics.

My parents surprised some of their friends by taking Nancy and me to see *Hair* when it was staged at one of the big theaters in downtown Chicago. I hesitated because I thought it might be queer to see a Broadway musical, but my friends told me that to see *Hair* was cool, because it was a cool show with a nude scene. Other kids' parents wouldn't take their children to the play, because the material was "too adult" for twelve year olds, and this convinced me to go and boost my level of cool.

Standard attire for men and boys when downtown, no matter the reason, was a jacket and tie, so I wore my Sunday school clothes, since the temple and downtown shared the same dress code.

A sense of excitement accompanied any trip to downtown Chicago. Riding in Dad's 1969 Buick Electra 225 past the big houses in Hampden that commanded the lakeshore, we approached the amassing glow that was Chicago. Apartment buildings of varying heights walled us in, until that magical moment when they stood back in deference to the entrance to Lake Shore Drive.

On our left was the wide-open expanse of the parks, beaches, and choppy waters of Lake Michigan. At night the lake could appear a black void, but on this night the moon rose over the water, and laid out a shimmering path from land's end to the horizon.

During the day, the various moods of the lake, its harbors, beaches, and paths were a warren of activity, and dared you to look away, but at night the action was landside. Tall apartment buildings sparkled on the right side of the road as it wended its way downtown where the buildings piled up like the Emerald City, punctuated by the new, hundred-story John Hancock

Center. Standard Oil and Sears were planning even taller towers, including the world's tallest.

Mom made the same comment every time we drove down Lake Shore Drive. "I don't think any big city on Earth has a prettier shoreline." None of us had traveled much, except Dad during the War, but no one disagreed.

From behind their desks, uniformed doormen managed the coming and going of residents, while taxis and buses crossed paths on the Inner Drive. Grandpa and Grandma and a few of my great-aunts lived along Lake Shore Drive.

"I recently heard that there are 30,000 Jews on LSD," Dad announced, seemingly apropos of nothing.

"Are you serious Jerry? That's terrible? Where did you hear that?"

Dad laughed. "Not drugs, honey, Lake Shore Drive!"

We groaned. "That's pretty good, Dad." I knew I'd repeat the joke in school on Monday.

Nancy must've been watching the passing buildings. "I'd like to raise my kids in one of those apartment buildings, with a butler, like the kids on *Family Affair.*"

"A butler? You'll have to marry rich to have a butler and private school tuition." Dad said.

"Jerry, you can't generalize like that. Why private schools? Remember, I teach in the Chicago Public Schools," Mom said, turning her attention from the passing scenery to Dad.

"I believe the reason that we moved to Michigami, along with just about everyone else we know with school-age kids, was not only for the chance to buy a nice home, but also because we weren't happy with what was happening in the city's schools." Whenever Dad corrected or contradicted Mom, there was a hesitation in his normally relaxed speech as he calculated the best route around a confrontation. Mom gave criticism a chilly reception, but appreciated his efforts, and stifled her reflexive resentment.

"Still, it's sad what's happening in the city, and not just here but all around America," Dad continued. "All the old neighborhoods we knew as kids are changing. It seems like one after another they're going from white to black overnight on the South and West sides. And the immigrant element on the North side isn't so aye aye aye. They have those poor whites from Appalachia moving into Uptown. They're taking those great old homes, and breaking them up into little apartments."

"Well, I can't say I have any answers." Mom confessed. Nancy and I looked at each other, silently acknowledging this rare response. "But I don't want to generalize. Just because neighborhoods change from white to black, isn't necessarily bad for a neighborhood." Mom looked over her shoulder at Nancy and me, as if we needed reminding that her comment was for our benefit.

Dad must've been feeling brave, or else he was just careless. "Based on the evidence, Honey, I don't see how you can say that. Name one neighborhood that improved by any measurement that went from white to black. Can you blame it all on economics, or is there a cultural aspect that needs to be addressed as well?" He kept his eyes on the road, afraid to face Mom, even for a moment.

"It's a complicated situation, I know." Mom was uncharacteristically thoughtful. "I understand whites are afraid to loose the money invested in their houses, and they're afraid of the crime that seems to follow blacks. They aren't all out-and-out bigots. But I'm sure most blacks just want to make better lives for themselves like anyone else. Like all of us, there are good and bad black people. Pardon the pun, but it isn't a clear-cut, black and white situation."

"It's sad," Nancy said staring out the window at yet another tall apartment building slipping past. "There's no more romance in the world. All grown-ups talk about today is how everything is falling apart and getting worse. You guys get me depressed. I feel like I was born too late."

"What do you mean, Nance?" Dad asked.

"Well, you guys always talk about how nicely you used to dress for school and for dates, but now everyone wants to look like a bum in blue jeans. You talk about how boys and girls used to dance together romantically to beautiful music, but now we don't even touch each other when we dance, and nobody's even quite sure how to dance anymore—especially guys."

The folks were clearly intrigued and amused by Nancy's rant, because they listened without interruption. "You talk about how great your neighborhoods were in the city, and how much fun you had going places like Riverview Park, and too bad it's closed down now because the neighborhood got bad, and no one felt safe, just like all the other neighborhoods. You talk about ballrooms that nobody goes to anymore. There is no ballroom in the suburbs, that's for sure. All I hear about is how no one had to lock their doors, and you could leave your keys in your cars without worrying."

Nancy was on a roll. I think she impressed herself in that she was pulling together the threads of dozens of conversations into one coherent thought. Maybe this was evidence of our Hampden education.

"Whenever we pass new apartment buildings in the city, someone always says how cheap the construction is, because no one cares about doing good work anymore. 'There is no craftsmanship,' they say and, 'the buildings won't stand for long,' and 'isn't it a shame they tear down those old beautiful homes to put up that junk?'

"I keep hearing how fashion used to be elegant, and everyone wore pretty dresses instead of granny skirts or pants. It makes me feel like the present is ugly. I'd rather live in the cities you see in the old Fred Astaire and Ginger Rogers movies, when they were glamorous, and everyone flocked to them from small towns."

"I thought you said you wanted to live on a plantation in the Old South," I said, recalling her comments after viewing *Gone*

With The Wind, and trying to show my parents that I was as sharp as Nancy.

"That too," Nancy said. "I'd live any place in the past with romance and beauty and drama. There's nothing romantic about modern suburban life. It isn't like the small town in *Our Town,* or like the plantations Tara and Twelve Oaks, or like the prairie of *My Antonia,* or any other place worthy of writing about. In the future, I can't imagine people will look back, and write romantically about the suburbs. Who would feel nostalgia for them?"

"You might be surprised Nancy. The past can look deceptively better once we've moved away from it. You might also be grateful that the suburbs aren't like the other side of things in the past. Remember the book *The Jungle,* by Upton Sinclair? The city didn't sound so great in there, did it? We can romanticize the past, but it is hard to do with the present. Still, I'm thrilled to know you ponder these things, and that you're enjoying the books you read in school." I foresaw Mom proudly relating Nancy's comments to her teacher friends in school on Monday.

As we pulled up to the uniformed valet at the restaurant, all conversation ceased. The specialty of the house was prime rib, and by the age of twelve, I knew it to be a rare treat. I looked around the dining room filled with complacent, middle-aged men in ties, accompanied by women in shiny dresses and lots of jewelry. There were a few kids besides Nancy and me. Among the staff and patrons I didn't see a single black face, giving weight to the claims of the media that we lived in a segregated city. Based on my experience at school, I wasn't convinced that this was a bad thing. I smiled thinking about the black kids in school tossing one of their milk bombs in this fine room. I bet they'd get arrested.

The restaurant was housed in a seventy-year-old building that was built as a private home. "Nowadays, no one can afford to live in houses like this, and keep them heated, and pay enough servants to run them. The dollar isn't what it was in 1900." Mom didn't foresee the new Gilded Age that awaited us at the end of the twentieth century, when every old mansion in Chicago was snapped up, restored, and staffed with servants.

"There you go again, Mother. That's the point I was making," Nancy said. "No mansions and servants, because of practical things like bills and taxes. It's just like in *Dr. Zhivago*, when everything became bureaucratic and gray after the Bolshevik Revolution. All the romance of life under the tsars was dead. Everyone dressed in plain dreary clothes. All the balls and parties in St. Petersburg ended. They even renamed St. Petersburg into something boring like Leningrad."

Mom scoffed. "Just remember, your father's parents lived in Russia under the tsars, and their lives were hell, no matter how charming it appeared in *Fiddler on the Roof*. They didn't know from any parties and balls. They were lucky they had food on the table. Remember what I said about romanticizing the past."

Still, I wondered if Nancy was on to something. I remembered *Oliver* from New Years Eve. In Dickens's world there was the safety of enforced behaviors and rules. We were living in a world without order. Like Nancy, I too heard all the tales of how better things used to be, especially from my grandparents and great-aunts. Even in the Great Depression, my parents would say, they didn't know how poor they were, because they had such happy childhoods. Could it be that an elegant night like this one was among the last remnants of this dying, wondrous past, and we were witnessing the end of the world of fancy restaurants, downtown theatre outings, and grand old buildings? In its stead was rising a world of riots, revolutions, crime, and mediocrity—not to mention hideous fashion?

Surely there were some good things in the new world, such as television and plays that featured naked people. How *did* my folks survive without television? I imagined that some day I might bore my kids with tales of wonderful nights in Old Chicago, in the last of the good old days. I considered the impressive building we were entering compared to the split-level houses or apartment buildings that looked like Soviet housing blocks.

After dinner we walked past the ornate movie palaces in the Loop that were showing black exploitation films, and Mom clucked her tongue as she related how movies used to open in downtown movie houses, only to arrive weeks later in the sub-urbs. Even I remembered the last vestiges of that era; we went to see *Mary Poppins* and *My Fair Lady* at their Loop premieres, I wore a tie and jacket, while uniformed ushers wore white gloves. Nobody dared to talk during a movie. I suppose if texting were available back then, anyone attempting it would've been expelled from the theater.

We walked into the lobby of the palatial theatre where the excitement was transmitted in hushed voices, in apparent rever-ence for the surroundings.

"They don't build them like this anymore Glen," Dad said leaning toward my ear as we walked down the aisle to our seats. "They can't afford to put up this kind of theatre anymore."

"I heard that, Dad." Nancy said. "Cut it out already, will you please?"

I felt cheated. I appeared to be living in a time of falling stan-dards and lowered expectations.

With each row we passed as we walked down the aisle, I felt superior to everyone seated behind us. I didn't know these peo-ple. I never saw them before, and never would again, but I felt su-perior based on the seats that Uncle Marty was able to get for us.

I forgot about the terrible times I lived in when I made out the naked men on the darkened stage towards the end of the first act. The nude scene was too brief and a let down. None of the guys in the cast were fantasy material. Still, I was glad to be living in a time when a play with a nude scene was acceptable fare for kids—at least in my family.

The rest of the play held my attention, although the messages were dated. I already knew that Viet Nam and bigotry were bad; rock and roll and marijuana were hip; and sex before marriage was commonplace, although I hoped I could somehow avoid it, and still be cool. Who didn't know that long hair on guys was in, and that crew cuts and the military represented the old establishment? But I loved the songs. Nancy did too, and on the way out of the theatre she insisted that Dad buy the cast album.

From that night until this Sunday night with Ken, I'd often go downstairs to Nancy's and my old playroom, in our finished basement, and listen to the album. With incense burning in the small brass incense burner from Michigami's faux head shop, I'd turn on the black light above our Rolling Stones poster, lie on the couch, and feel like part of the "in" crowd.

Back at school I became a semi-celebrity when people found out I'd seen *Hair*. No one else around our lunchroom table, except maybe Ken, had any chance of seeing the musical, and Ken was only going if his grandmother decided not to use her ticket. The questions came at me fast. *How much could you see? Did you really see tits and some bush? Could you make out the nipples? How long was the scene? How many girls were in it? Were any really cool?*

No one asked about the cocks, but I conjured them up frequently, including that night in the basement as I relaxed in an old chair, hanging a leg over one of the arms. Ken sprawled out on the couch, with his feet off to the side resting on a white vinyl hassock—the furniture from my parents' apartment before they moved to Michigami. The oppressive smell of incense wafted from the small brass burner. An old torchiere, set on the lowest wattage, glowed soft yellow. Mick Jagger glared down at us from his poster. Over the music, fire engines wailed in the distance.

"I hate Sunday nights," Ken mused, starring up at the ceiling. "There's nothing to look forward to, but a whole week of school."

"I hate it too." Like Ken, I spoke without moving, as if in a drug-induced stupor. "Friday nights are my favorite, because you have the whole weekend ahead. Saturday nights are fun too, except I have to get up for stupid Sunday school on Sunday mornings. So Friday nights are better. And then comes Sunday, and you know the whole day that the next day is Monday. Blah."

"Lately, though, I've kind of been looking forward to school, because it's fun goofing around with the girls in the class all day. You know what I mean?"

"Oh Ken, come on and say it. You mean you like goofing around with Sandy Marsten. Come on Kennyboy. You've got a real crush on her. Everyone knows it. You guys keep making eyes at each other. She's really pretty, you know?" I was trying out this use of "Kennyboy," as well as the overall tone I was taking to see if it came across as cool, believable, and most importantly, masculine. No on all counts.

"You think so? She's got tits like torpedoes. I love them. I want to marry her tits. I want to take them home with me."

I laughed. Lately, Ken was one-dimensional, focusing only on tits, and I found it funny, despite my own indifference to the subject. I tried to compare it to my almost constant thoughts about guys' bodies. I envied his ability to voice his fantasies with total comfort, knowing they were perfectly *normal*. Ken and I had been friends since kindergarten, and we used to share all of our thoughts openly. Since entering puberty, I had to learn to release my thoughts through a hastily constructed filter.

I changed the gender in the question I next posed to my best friend. "Have you ever fantasized that you could be like a bar of soap in a girl's house or something? And you know, she would use you? You know?"

Ken sat up a bit. "Feigman, you sex fiend. Hell yes. I can't believe you said that. I think about that every night, like maybe the first time I beat off. By the second time, I'm an insect that can follow her around, and watch everything without her knowing it. Or maybe I'm her bra, and I get to hold her tits all day."

"Ha! I know exactly what you're saying," I said enthusiastically substituting jock strap for bra in my mind, and bouncing my leg that was resting on the arm of the chair.

"Did I tell you what happened the first time I beat off?" Ken asked.

"Uh, uh. But if you tell me, I'll tell you," I said, deciding I was no longer going to sit out the frequent discussions and jokes about masturbation.

"I had started locking myself in the bathroom after school thinking about all the girls I saw in school that day, and laying on the floor of the bathroom on my back with my dick in my hands."

"Oh my God, Ken. I swear. I started the same way," I said excitedly since this was a sort of confirmation that I was normal— except of course for that damnable content of my accompanying fantasies.

"Cool. So listen. I wasn't sure what I was doing, but I knew it felt good touching my dick, and laying there with my eyes closed, thinking about the girls, and doing things to them, or them doing things to me..."

"Like blowing you," I interrupted, confident that this would be one of Ken's fantasies.

"Oh yeah. You bet. And one of those times I started moving my hand up and down. No one told me to do it. I never read it or anything. They never told us how to masturbate in sex-ed class in fifth grade. I just started doing it, and all of a sudden I started jerking around uncontrollably on the floor, and a little drop of liquid came out of my dick. Like I mean a drop. I thought I was having a heart attack or something. Or maybe God was punishing me. Then I remembered about sperm, and I put it all together from class, and I said 'whoa man. I know what this is. Damn. This is crazy.'"

Ken's vocabulary was cooler than mine. He used swear words with ease, which I attributed to time spent with his older brother. We idolized guys in college, unless they were in ROTC.

"Wait, wait, you have to hear what happened to me. I was on the bathroom floor too. I swear to God. I did the same thing." I skipped the fact that I was looking at a photo in *Life Magazine* of some guy from an Italian movie in tight jeans, with his shirt undone to reveal olive-colored, rippled abs, and a dark treasure trail descending from his navel.

"It was early last year. When I had my first orgasm, nothing came out of my dick yet! Can you believe it? I was too early, and I didn't know what was happening either. I was shaking like crazy. I swear, I thought I was giving myself a heart attack too. And I swore I would never touch myself like that again."

"Yeah, right. How long did that last, pervert?" Ken laughed.

"About two days I think. But I didn't go far enough to have an orgasm for a few months. And then one time, I reached the point of no return, and there it was. One drop, and then, like you, I put it all together. Man, was I excited. I wasn't going to die from this."

"The sad part is we probably won't use our dicks for a couple of years. Can you imagine any of the girls we know even giving you a hand job?" Ken asked.

"Yeah. Maybe. I don't know. Sure. Who knows? Maybe Sandy will be the one. Damn. Can you imagine a girl actually touching your dick?"

Oh, how I wished it were in my future to touch a dick other than my own.

"Well yeah, I can imagine it. I imagine it about every minute of the day, and I guess I imagine it when I sleep too. You know, wet dreams and all. Are you having any of those?"

"Yeah, I think so," I remembered the first time I woke up in the middle of the night, and felt something wet on my stomach. If I hadn't remembered the dream I was having as I woke up, I would've thought I peed in bed. I fell back to sleep hoping semen didn't stain the sheets for Melva to see.

"It's like we're sperm factories working in overdrive," Ken said, his pride showing. "If we don't keep up with production, the goods get shoved out the door anyway." We chuckled.

"Hey, speaking of dicks," I said, "how about Tom? He used to be so unpopular, and now it seems all the girls are interested in him. I can't figure it out. It drives me crazy. Maybe he's getting better looking or something to them, but did you see at Pam's party how Debbie Spivey was leaning on him all the time? He still wears those dumb looking Hush Puppies, or whatever they are."

"I know. It's like since going to junior high, different people are turning cool, and some cool people are going backwards."

That remark made me think about myself.

"Hey," he continued, "we used to be good friends with Ben Rubin back in third and fourth grade, remember? We were always doing stuff with him. That's when we were really cool too. Damn, he's the most popular kid in the whole school. I never talk to him anymore. Do you?"

"Nope. He's too cool to pay attention to us now. He's got Darlene Fine now. He gave her his I.D. bracelet. At least, that's what Gary told me. His sister told him. She's friends with Darlene's sister. Even they think Ben is cute. Every girl talks about him. I don't know why they think he's so great (*big lie*). But I wish I were as good as him in sports.

"He's a dick. He'll get pimples like his older brother. Did you see him lately? Then the girls will forget about him. But that Darlene Fine sure is fiiiiiiiiiiiiiiiiiine. She can blow me any day of the week. Her tits don't quit."

We were back to tits, and I laughed. In spite of my secret, I felt this was one more conversation that helped to bond Ken and me. Having him as my friend made me feel less weird, as if the fact that I didn't share his interest in girls didn't really matter. Ironically, in spite of my lack of interest in girls as sexual beings, I still wanted them to want me, and I was troubled that recently Ken was starting to get a lot more attention from girls than I was. I was smarter than Ken, but he had a natural coolness, and that was more important than being smart. I was going to have to monitor the situation; maybe be less obviously smart in class, and try to imitate some of the things Ken did that girls found attractive. I had started to un-tuck my shirts like Ken. Of course, I had to wait until I left the house to do it, because Grandma put up a fuss the first time she saw me about to leave the house that way. Then she put up another fuss when I forgot to tuck my shirt in before I arrived home.

I didn't want to think about it, but maybe I was becoming more feminine as I got older instead of masculine. Since Ken's fantasies were normal, he was naturally becoming a man. My stomach contracted.

"And speaking of dicks again," Ken looked over at me more seriously now, "have you noticed how small Archie's dick is?"

"Yeah," I said excitedly, "oh my God, I noticed in the locker room the other day when we were going to the showers. And he has no hair there."

"It's weird. I guess he's just slow growing up."

By seventh grade, most of us had reached puberty, so the endowment differences were less striking than they were in sixth grade. Still, hiding our parts behind towels as much as possible was our preferred method of walking to and from the showers. I had seen enough to know that I had nothing to hide, but I couldn't bring myself to act like Norman Garfinkel who not only loved flaunting his nakedness, and making jokes about dicks, but occasionally tucked his dick backwards between his legs, so it looked like he had a vagina. Then he'd walk up and down the locker room asking everyone if they could help him find his dick.

"Then of course there's our black brothers," Ken continued to ponder the sights of the locker room. "I still think they look weird, you know—the uncircumcised ones. Don't you?"

"Oh yeah. It looks really weird. But you have to give some of them credit. Damn. It's like a kosher salami or something."

"You mean un-kosher," Ken threw back.

"Yeah, definitely un-kosher."

From the stereo came the lyrics from *Hair*: *I'm a colored spade, a n----r, a black n----r, a jungle bunny, jigaboo, coon, pickaninny, mau mau, Uncle Tom, Aunt Jemima, Little Black Sambo...* and Ken and I sang along.

Ken beat out the rhythm on his stomach, while I patted out the same rhythm on one arm of my chair. The song was an indictment of racism, and the use of all the slanderous terminology employed by bigots against blacks, so it was okay to sing out with impunity. These taboo words were often on the tips of our tongues at school after any number of outrages, but we never gave them voice so as not to disappoint our parents or teachers, or to risk getting our heads pounded.

Nancy shouted from the top of the basement stairs. "He guys, come up here. There's something on television."

"What?" I whined. "Tell us what it is." But Nancy was already gone, and since it was rare that Nancy wanted to share with me, it had to be something worthwhile.

"C'mon," I said as I rose from my chair, tugging my Hanes white briefs under my blue jeans from up where they had crept.

Dad, Mom, and Nancy were seated on the couch. A special local news report had interrupted *The Flip Wilson Show*. I watched as flames ate away at a large building, and black smoke billowed upwards.

"Cool. Where is that?" I asked no one in particular, and without looking away from the screen.

"It's right in Hampden. That's the lumber company where you and I went to buy that screen door a few years ago," Dad said, with his hand in a bowl of popcorn, and his eyes also on the screen.

As we've been reporting, firemen were hampered in their first attempts to stop this fire before it got out of control, as they were attacked by rock throwing youths from the surrounding neighborhood.

"You hear that?" Nancy asked. "The lumber company is right in the black part of Hampden, and the kids want the place to burn. Figures."

"Yeah. Figures," Ken and I said almost simultaneously.

"Can you believe it?" Nancy said. "Can you imagine the kids in Michigami throwing rocks at firemen? It would never happen. This is terrible publicity for Hampden," she added. "Now I'll hear more from everyone I know at Sycamore Park how Hampden is slowly becoming like the South Side ghetto."

"Oh, take it easy, Nance," Mom said reaching into the popcorn bowl on Dad's lap. "Don't get carried away. I agree that I hate for Hampden to get that kind of publicity, but I hope people realize it's probably just a few troublemakers. They should've said how many kids were involved. I bet it's only a few."

Then Mom thought it out further. "Still, where the heck are the parents of those kids?" The troubled look on her face stayed there until *The Flip Wilson Show* returned, and she directed her gaze at Ken and me.

"So what are you to up to down there in your clubhouse? I can smell that incense all the way up here. Feh! Doesn't it give you boys headaches?"

"No, Ma," I said, afraid that if this conversation continued, one of my parents would say something really un-cool, and embarrass me.

"Do you boys want me to make you some Jiffy Pop? I can deliver it to you down in the inner sanctum within twenty minutes."

I looked at Ken who was looking back at me nodding his head. "Yeah, alright. Thanks. C'mon Ken. Let's go back down."

"See ya," Ken said over his shoulder. We slipped away on our stocking feet.

CHAPTER TWENTY-FIVE

Friday, January 30, 1970

Shabbat dinner arrived with its attendant revelations and lessons, intended or otherwise.

The blessings completed, Grandma and Mom carried in the soup. Mom's younger brother Marty and his wife Marion were at the table with their children Rob, who was Nancy's age, and Amy, a year younger than me. Grandma and Grandpa were pleased to have all of their grandchildren present. Uncle Marty's family only observed Shabbat when they joined us.

Although Grandma carried on her usual parallel conversation about the food, Shabbat dinner was more about moral lessons for the kids; one was implied by simply joining together each Friday evening for something spiritual, and the other was explicit, given my elders' blatant attempts to use the occasion to enforce proper ethics, and root out potential moral pitfalls.

"How about each of you kids tells us something he or she learned in school this week?" Dad asked, looking with hope at our young, vacant faces, while he balanced half a matzahball onto his spoon.

"That is so queer," I said looking at the other kids to support my bold statement.

"I think it's a nice idea," Aunt Marion added, before blowing on her soup. "Rob, you start."

Rob rolled his green eyes. "All right. Fine. I learned what a 'doobie' is."

"A *what?*" The adults asked simultaneously. Only Grandma said nothing from the kitchen.

Nancy and Rob laughed. Amy and I were bewildered, but we didn't want to let on, lest we appeared un-cool.

"A doobie," Rob repeated. "You know. A joint. Marijuana."

"Marijuana?" Aunt Marion asked with a raised eyebrow. "Is that what they taught you in school this week? Is that what Frank Sinatra was really singing about when he sang, 'doobie doobie doo'?"

Bubbie looked stunned, but Zadie remained focused on eating.

"Don't be such a smart Alec, Mister," Uncle Marty frowned at his suddenly troublesome son.

"I'm not being smart. You asked what I learned in school this week. That's the easiest thing I remember."

"Well I never heard that term. And I can't imagine why it should come up at school." Aunt Marion offered.

"Aunt Marion, I know of kids who get high at school." Nancy interjected. "I hear more about it all the time. Ma, remember Debbie Zippstein? We used to be kind of friendly."

"Sure I do, she was a nice girl. She looked a little like Haley Mills," Mom answered, clearly curious now as she handed Grandma two soup bowls that were already empty.

"Well, she was at Woodstock last summer with some other kids. They hitchhiked there, and ever since she's become a real hippie. She talks like a hippie, and she dresses like one, and I think she and her friends are high a lot. Maybe they do LSD."

"She hitchhiked? Oh my God! Is she crazy? Doesn't she know girls get killed doing that? Mamela, I hope you never ever do such a thing," Grandma stopped shuffling plates long enough to stare at Nancy.

"Don't worry, Grandma. I don't hitch anywhere."

I couldn't tell if she was lying.

"Be sure you never ever do," Dad said looking directly at Nancy, and waiting for her eyes to meet his.

"So, Nancy, you mean this nice Zippstein girl smokes dope, and used LSD too? My God, such a tragedy for her family. LSD? Ach. It breaks your heart to hear about these kids," Mom said, glancing at me after she finished.

"It's that Timothy O'Leary causing that LSD trouble." Aunt Marion added, blotting her lips with her napkin.

"That's Leary, Marion, not O'Leary," said Uncle Marty. "He's not the husband of Mrs. O'Leary of Chicago fire fame."

"Where would a girl like that get LSD? That's so sad. Does her family know? What about the teachers?" asked Mom, frowning.

"The kids take dope in school today? *Oy vey iz meer.* Now I've heard everything," Bubbie chimed in, with her hand on her heart for emphasis.

"Well, you kids better keep your distance. It's illegal, and you can get arrested, and ruin your life for something stupid. It could be harmful. No one knows enough about it. Just stay away from it." Mom was emphatic.

"Ma, can I have some salt, please?" Uncle Marty foolishly asked Grandma.

"I remember this Debbie when she was a little girl playing dolls here with Nancy. Oh my. Such a shame. What gets into these kids?" Mom again.

"It's all of those rock and roll singers and hippies. They think if they get high, and talk about love, it will solve all the world's problems," Aunt Marion said. "Look at those hippies on trial here in Chicago. To some people they're heroes. I'm embarrassed that some of them are Jewish."

"Salt? Since when do you eat salt? I didn't put any salt on the table. I didn't think anyone would need it. You don't need salt. All of a sudden I don't know how to flavor a brisket?" Grandma asked, insulted.

"Imagine. When we were kids, it was a big deal to chew gum at school. Huh!" Uncle Marty laughed. "Now they're using drugs. And yes, Ma, you know how to flavor a brisket, for people who don't like to taste their food. Now can I please have the salt?"

"Marty, don't joke about it. I'd die if I heard the kids were using drugs. Are any of your friends? Where in Sycamore Park do they buy it?" Aunt Marion asked Rob.

"Don't worry. I don't know anyone using it; at least I don't think so, at least not yet. And I wouldn't know where to get it. But it's definitely out there, even in Sycamore Park," Rob said. He brushed his fingers back through his curls.

"Rob, don't touch your hair at the table."

Rob scowled at his mother.

"Mae, if he wants salt, give him the salt," Grandpa said, and then added, "It will be interesting to see how this trial ends. It should end soon. That Judge Hoffman is a character. I've met him. But it's good to see young people concerned and active, trying to make things better. Don't we all agree there is merit in that? Their tactics might be naïve, but they sure have everyone's attention." No one followed Grandpa's lead to discuss the Chicago Seven trial.

"Glen and Amy, are you kids told about the dangers of drugs in your junior high schools?" Dad asked.

"Fine. I won't cook any more. After fifty years I can't cook a brisket?" Grandma said leaving the room to get the salt.

Not surprisingly Amy said "no," since the administrators and parents of Sycamore Park assumed drugs were an urban problem. Amy ran her fingers through her long, blond bangs and batted her blue eyes.

"Kids, I said don't touch your hair at the table!"

"Yeah. We have this police officer come to our class," I added. "He's this big, tall black guy called Officer Flynn. He comes to our health class, and he brings this big suitcase full of different kinds of pills. He tells us what they are, and what they do, and not to take them. There are a million different colors and shapes of pills." I was pleased to note everyone was listening to me.

"Marty, why do you have to start with your mother? Would it kill you to eat it without salt?" Aunt Marion chided.

"Has anyone offered you pills at your school, Glen?" Grandpa asked.

"Uh-uh. I never saw any pills other than the stuff Officer Flynn has. I don't know anybody who takes any drugs. I don't know why they waste time showing us all that stuff. It's really boring when he talks. Nobody pays attention for long." I thought of Officer Flynn; his monotone voice droning on about the different names for each pill he held up.

"Why would they teach all of that to junior high students, unless they have some reason to fear someone is pushing drugs on the kids?" Aunt Marion asked.

Grandma handed Uncle Marty the salt. "You'll be up all night drinking water now. You'll see. I should have named you Morton instead of Martin."

I laughed, surprised at Grandma's clever comment.

"Well, I hope they're over reacting to something. Certainly it's better to be pro-active, but why create a problem where there isn't one?" Mom asked the assembly.

"Thanks, Ma. You're a real peach," Uncle Marty said, laughing and liberally sprinkling salt on his plate. Grandma shook her head with disgust as she moaned and walked back to the kitchen.

"They should break the heads open of anyone pushing drugs on children." Zadie finally ventured into the discussion.

"Pa, for once I agree with you about knocking some heads." Dad said to his father. He continued, "Now, before we leave this wonderful subject, can we all agree that none of you kids do or will take drugs, and you will always come to one of us if you have any questions, even if we don't know what a doobie is? And let's not forget, Zadie here," Dad pointed to his father. "He's our enforcer. So you better heed my words. Now who else learned something in school?" Dad was relentless.

"Uncle Marty, can I have some salt?" I asked mischievously, glancing at Grandma for her response as she returned from the kitchen.

"Glen, I'll box your ears if you start that now," Dad said, laughing. I was filled with pride that Dad and Uncle Marty appreciated my joke.

"I learned that Marcy Feldman from down the street, the one who is a senior this year, is dating a black guy at school." Nancy said delighted that once again she would plunge us into a controversial discussion, unlike anything Dad had in mind.

Grandma was all ears. "That nice lady, Mrs. Feldman, I see at the beauty shop, her daughter?" She asked.

"Yeah. That's the one." Grandma shook her head.

"Now, how would you handle that one?" Uncle Marty asked no one in particular.

"Oh my. I can't even imagine." Aunt Marion almost shuddered as she looked at Amy.

"Nancy, are they seriously dating, or are they simply friends?"

"They're serious Ma. All lovey dovey in school. Together all the time."

"Well, is he a nice boy? Are his parents nice? Is he a good student?" Mom asked trying to demonstrate a thoughtful approach to what was an uncomfortable subject.

"Does it matter, Eileen? He's black. How would you feel if Nancy were dating a nice black boy?" Uncle Marty asked. "Wait. Don't tell me. I know. As long as he were Jewish, you wouldn't care. Am I right?"

"Marty, what are you starting with your sister for?" Grandma asked, irritated.

"That's exactly right, Marty. We teach the kids to judge on the inside. Not on the outside. Good character has no color. If he were Jewish and a good boy, I could have nothing to complain about." I was sure Mom was playing to Nancy and me, while praying she would never have her magnanimity tested.

"Do you agree with my sister, Jerry?" Uncle Marty asked Dad.

"I always agree with your sister," Dad said laughing. "After almost twenty-six years of marriage it's served me well. And if you were smart, you'd agree with her too."

"You guys, I can't believe you're talking about me like this, anyhow," Nancy admonished everyone. "I think I might have something to say about this. I'm not interested in black guys, so I don't think you need to argue about it."

I detected sighs of relief from around the table in addition to Bubbie's, "*A Gut a danke.*"

"How many for coffee?" Grandma asked as hands went up around the table.

"Ma, please let everyone eat their dinner before you start clearing the plates for coffee. And Nancy, I just want you to know that your father and I are consistent in what we teach you. Like Spencer Tracy said in *Guess Who's Coming To Dinner*, I'd worry if you chose to marry a black man, because you would have a lot of difficulties in life. I don't think most of the world is ready for it. But our major concern is you marry a Jewish *mensch*."

"Eileen, you never change," Uncle Marty said shaking his head and smiling.

"Eileen, you're a saint." Aunt Marion added.

"Our Eileen is a *guta nashuma*—a good soul," Bubbie added. I knew it from the day my Jerry brought her home to meet us."

"So what does that make me?" Uncle Marty asked, with mischief in his voice?

"You're a *putz*." Aunt Marion said laughing to her husband. The four of us kids found Aunt Marion's quip hysterical.

"My Marty is a good boy." Although she practically lived with her daughter, and despite his use of salt, Grandma's preference for Uncle Marty over Mom was as clear as her preference for me over her other grandchildren.

"Speaking of dating blacks, how are things at old Hampden, anyhow? Still having troubles keeping order there?" Uncle Marty asked, deciding to keep the discussion heated.

"When are you going to sell this place, and move up to Sycamore Park? Then you won't have to deal with all that commotion over at Hampden," Aunt Marion asked, not realizing she was brushing up against a beehive.

"We are not moving to Sycamore Park, thank you very much. We love our house and our neighborhood. Our kids have great friends, and they're happy in school. They're getting a great education. Marion, I don't think it's a nice thing to say, to be honest."

I didn't want to be disloyal to my parents, but I was glad Aunt Marion brought up the subject of moving. I knew there was little chance of Mom and Dad entertaining a move from our house, and I wasn't sure I wanted to leave my friends, but every time someone mentioned it, it chipped away at the wall.

Uncle Marty stepped in to defend his wife. "All Marion means is that while we know how strongly you feel about the struggle for civil rights and all—and we agree—you don't have to put your kids on the front lines. You think the blacks are going to thank you some day?"

"What front lines? Are you crazy, Marty? What do you think is going on in Hampden?" Mom was starting to lose her temper, and some of us were getting uncomfortable.

Uncle Marty wasn't one to avoid an argument. "We hear about the growing crime. Is it the white kids that are committing it? I don't think so. Every time our kids' school plays Hampden in some sporting event at Hampden, there's some incident of theft or violence in the parking lot, or things get thrown at our kids' buses. Or parents' cars get broken into. We have to provide extra security for when we play Hampden. Why is it only at Hampden? It doesn't happen at the other North Shore schools. Who do you think is throwing stones at the buses? You can see who it is. I'm sorry if it sounds bad, but it's the truth. I know by speaking the truth I'd be called a bigot, but why? Anyhow, there's nothing wrong with wanting to keep your kids away from that element, black or white. A parent instinctively wants his kids to be safe. It's the honest, bold-faced truth that the trouble at Hampden, as well as the rest of the city, is caused by blacks."

Surprisingly, no one said anything. Emboldened by the lack of a counteroffensive, Uncle Marty continued. "If I get hit over the head by a black man, and I call him on it, I'm damn sick of being called a racist for it. And another thing that bothers me..."

"I didn't know so much was bothering you, Marty," Aunt Marion interjected.

"Let me finish Marion. I grew up in the same house as you Eileen, and I listened well to what Dad said, but whenever he talked about helping blacks gain equality, we had this belief that they were just like us, with the same values, and they just wanted to work hard, and get a good education, and raise good children. How could someone stand in the way of that?"

"Well that's right." Mom said hoping she and Uncle Marty were going to agree. Then came an addendum. "But it seems a large number of them aren't so interested in working hard or studying in school. I don't know what they're teaching their children at home, but from what I hear they're disrespectful and disruptive.

"It's a poverty issue, Marty." Mom fought back.

"Aw, don't blame poverty. Plenty of immigrants were poor here, but they taught their children to respect authority, and value education. The blacks in Hampden aren't poor, anyhow. How goes it at school Glen and Nancy?"

"That's right. Anyone hits you on the head you give him this," Zadie said as he balled his hand into a fist, and hit it into his other hand."

"*Shah*, Isaac. It's not our business," Bubbie put her hand over Zadie's fist.

Before Nancy or I could answer, Uncle Marty continued. "The blacks have some problems in their community that have nothing to do with white oppression, and its time they own up to it. I'll be damned if I'll accept that all their problems are someone else's fault. Eventually, you have to take responsibility for yourself."

"Are you saying that they haven't suffered unfairly?" Mom asked.

"Of course not. You know I don't think that. I'm well aware of the cruelties they endured. I can't even imagine the pain of living in a segregated South."

"I can't even imagine," Aunt Marion echoed, shaking her head.

"That's right, I remember in boot camp in Georgia going to a local home for Thanksgiving, and the father was saying "N" this and "N" that, and the maid was right there serving the dinner. I was horrified. I couldn't get out of there fast enough."

Uncle Marty's example shocked me. I thought of Melva. It would've broken my heart if she were subjected to that. Uncle Marty continued.

"But now isn't the time for blacks to look for excuses when finally, they're being given all kinds of opportunities. Now is the time to take action. And I don't mean join gangs and take drugs. I mean they should go to school, go to work, get involved in the political process, and make something of themselves. No one can do it for them, but we can stay the hell out of their way. And that's what I'm advocating. Staying out of their way."

"Eileen, Marty and I donate to the NAACP. We do. But we don't know that there is much else we can do. We vote for politicians who support civil rights. In the meantime, if some nice black people moved into our neighborhood, I'd be delighted. But I wouldn't want to live in the middle of a black neighborhood where your life isn't worth a nickel. I don't think that's prejudice. That's just being sensible. Isn't it?" Aunt Marion looked to her sister-in-law.

Mom withdrew, and just looked at Aunt Marion. "And this busing business is crazy. How would you like it if they took your kids out of your neighborhood that you and Jerry worked your whole lives to move into, and bused them into some high crime area, with miserable students just to achieve integration? And they make the parents who protest this out to be bigots. There's so much more than race involved in that," Aunt Marion said shaking her head as she buttered a piece of challah. Grandma took note.

"Anyhow, I don't know if it's racist or not to compliment a whole race, but I must say, I love watching those black church choirs on Sunday mornings. They move so effortlessly with the music. They really have a rhythm that I just don't see in whites. Is that a bad thing to say?"

"Aunt Marion, I know what you mean, but what I want to say is that they want to integrate the schools so the blacks will get the same educational benefits as the whites. They don't get enough money at their own schools," Nancy said. I was surprised that she came in on Mom's side of the discussion.

Uncle Marty's tone became gentle. "You know Nancy, you can throw money at schools, but in the end, if the kids aren't there to learn, and their parents aren't supporting the notion of education when the kids get home from school, you might as well throw the money out the window. Look at Hampden. No one pays higher school taxes than your parents for Hampden's schools. Your schools are loaded with everything you can dream of, yet it doesn't make a damn bit of difference for any kids that aren't there to learn."

"Look at your father, Nancela," Bubbie pointed out. "When he was a boy, we had nothing. The whole neighborhood had nothing. But your father and his friends knew they had to learn. If they didn't bring home good grades, they'd be afraid to come home. That's what makes the difference. The schools can't do everything. It's the parents."

Mom came back to the discussion, but she sounded more uncertain than determined.

"These are crazy times. Sometimes I feel the whole world is turning upside down. As parents we want to do the right things by our kids; as Americans, for our country; and as Jews, we want to do what's right, period. Don't forget our Glen will be a bar mitzvah soon. I don't want to be a hypocrite telling him to be responsible for his fellow man, only to act irresponsibly myself."

I saw Grandpa looking at Mom with pride, but Uncle Marty looked dismayed. Here was a possible reason that he chose to be a White Sox fan, while Grandpa and everyone else in our North Side family rooted for the Cubs.

"Are we the only family tying ourselves up in knots lately, struggling with all the changes going on around us, or is everyone else going crazy too?" Dad asked.

Uncle Marty took up Dad's question. "I'm sure we're not alone. Look how much has changed in the last ten years. Can you imagine that Eisenhower was still president ten years ago? At least we had Kennedy to look forward to. Now all we have is two more years of Nixon."

There was a collective groan from around the table.

"The truth of this whole race issue is that it's not black and white. It's not pure good vs. pure evil. Yeah, there are things that are clearly good or bad, but there is also a lot that's in shades of gray. Everyone has to do their share to make things better."

Grandpa saw his chance to teach a lesson to the grandchildren. "I'll say one thing for us Jews; I'm proud that we vote our social conscience, and not our wallets. Every other group in America reaches a certain economic level, and suddenly they turn Republican, but we Jews don't switch. We hold onto our ideals.

"Good point, Dad." Mom said.

Grandpa didn't need encouragement. "They don't give a hoot for the welfare of their fellow Americans. All they care about is that they think Republicans will cut their taxes—and at the expense of somebody else, of course. Per my Republican associates, government is there to help business, and business will take care of America. End of story. That's their answer to everything. But we Jews stick to our principles. We vote for the well being of our neighbors. I confess to be a bit baffled that people who call themselves good Jews or good Christians can vote for the party that puts business ahead of people and the environment. Where in the Bible does it say we should sacrifice our humanity for the good of the corporation?"

"You're right, Dad. You kids should listen to your grandfather." Mom looked briefly at each of us around the table.

Then Uncle Marty made a point that was hard to reconcile with what Grandpa said. "You know, Dad, those Dixiecrats are hardly the ones you want to affiliate with."

"Good point, Son. But you know which aspect of the Democratic Party I'm referring to. Besides, I believe Mr. Nixon is figuring out how to rally those southern whites to the Republican Party, with some winks and nods at their issue.

"I have to say though, Dad, I hear Nixon might sign some environmental legislation involving clean air and water this year. I have to give him credit, if he does the right thing, even if he loses the support of some of his business friends who generate the pollution. That takes leadership—real leadership. Now Viet Nam, that's another story."

"Please, Jerry. Let's not talk about that now. Let's talk about something pleasant." Mom looked at Dad as she stood to help Grandma in the kitchen.

"Marla said her parents are thinking of becoming Republican because they don't agree with the idea of quotas or something like that," This was Nancy refusing to accommodate Mom's request, so Mom followed up.

"Really, Nance? I'm sorry to hear that. That's a tough stand to take."

"It isn't so tough. How can a Jew support quotas?" Zadie asked setting both fists on the table on either side of his plate.

"What do you mean, Pa?"

"You know what I'm talking." Zadie lifted his fork, and pointed it at Dad. "Quotas were used for years to keep us Jews out. They kept us out of schools and jobs and whatever else worthwhile, with quotas on Jews. It was like back in Russia. Here in America we worked hard, and earned the right to get in, so now they're going to tell us to step aside to make room for people who are less qualified, and don't work as hard? Well I say, *no way buddy*. Let them earn their place with hard work. You want a colorblind society? That's a colorblind society."

"Don't get yourself worked up," Bubbie said, pulling Zadie's raised hand back down to the table.

"He's right, Sonia," Grandpa said thoughtfully. "You know, I came up against quotas getting into both college and law school. The admissions director at Northwestern came right out, and told me they had enough Jews already, and turned me down without batting an eye. Let's hope that our black friends don't let this point come between years of friendship and working together towards the larger goal of justice for all."

"Grandpa, I didn't know you were rejected because you were Jewish. That is so kooky," Nancy said. "Did you fight them?"

"There was no one to complain to. It was accepted practice, and pretty much the same everywhere: housing, schools, businesses, and hotels. That's why we of all people are sensitive to the indignities experienced by blacks."

I always suspected that whatever Grandpa and Mom said was calculated to benefit Nancy and me, but I wondered if they were struggling in the face of disturbing signs in the black community; particularly the black leadership's recent rejection of Jews as partners in the civil rights struggle, to which Aunt Lilly and Grandpa recently referred.

"As bad as it may have been here, it was still better than anywhere else in the world." Bubbie never missed an opportunity to praise America. "At least in this country they didn't kill us, and burn our synagogues and homes and businesses. Back in Russia and Poland they didn't just keep you out of hotels and schools. They ran you out of your own homes, and killed you when they felt like it."

"I thought we were going to talk about something nice, like Glen's bar mitzvah. What is it now, about six weeks off, and I'm going crazy with the planning." Mom put her hands on either side of her head, and shook it back and forth for a comic effect. She decided that Nancy and I had enough of an education for one night.

Everyone's eyes lit up at the mention of my bar mitzvah, but it could have been a coincidence, since Grandma entered from the kitchen with a tray of coffee cakes at just that moment.

CHAPTER TWENTY-SIX

Friday, April 10, 1970. Bar Mitzvah Weekend.

I view the bar (or bat) mitzvah as an inflection point. The child's link is officially attached to the chain of millennia. Until that day, parents are to have worked diligently at the forge, firmly but lovingly hammering in morals and values, while teaching respect for and the knowledge of how they came to be handed down. Finally, the child must understand the obligations that accompany such a heritage. If done right, when the link is forged, the child should have a solid base on which to build a life, and to make the better of the myriad choices that he or she will face through the years.

The reasons that chains lay broken, and some Jewish children follow questionable paths, would lead one to look at the parents and their time, or lack thereof, back at the forge. Either they failed to do their part, or knowingly or not, emphasized the wrong elements.

For parents or parental figures to give children the support and tools needed to lead moral, productive lives is not unique to Judaism; but In Judaism, the parental responsibility and the rite of passage is so important, that it's formally enshrined by the bar mitzvah service. The jump from child to adult is symbolized simply enough by having the child read for the first time in front of the community, directly from the Torah, the original source of moral laws for Jews. The party extravaganzas that now follow the bar mitzvah service are a questionable manifestation of the prosperity of post World War II American Jewry.

Governments, societies, and even teachers have their own responsibilities and agendas, and cannot replace nor make up for parents who abandon their work, or who haven't the knowledge of how to raise the next generation.

The activities surrounding my bar mitzvah were typical of the era. Our Friday night Shabbat dinner was moved to the family room to accommodate an extra table. Grandma's sisters and out of town relatives from both sides of my family were well represented. Their animated interaction provided entertainment for us grandchildren.

Melva arrived on Thursday, as usual, but stayed the weekend to help Mom and Grandma in the kitchen and elsewhere. She took pleasure in receiving as many compliments as Mom on my behalf.

The gossipy ladies of River City, Iowa lived on through Grandma and her sisters. All that they lacked were the big, feathery hats. They talked over each other, complained, reminisced, and laughed themselves to tears. I had never experienced a major loss in life—except the occasional goldfish or turtle—so I was oblivious to the ephemeral nature of the gathering. One by one they would pass from the scene, but here they were in all their glory.

Grandma couldn't hide her pleasure in running the show for her extended family. When Grandma was a little happy, Grandpa delighted in it, and the rest of us savored the peace. Grandma's voluminous display of cooked dishes gave her the gift of knowing that later she would have a legitimate reason to complain about her aches and pains.

With disappointment, I had to break away from the fun, and join my immediate family to attend Shabbat services. Rabbi Becker brought my parents up for the honor of opening the ark when it was time to retrieve a Torah during the service. As the weekend progressed, I was told repeatedly how wonderful my achievement was, and how hard I must've worked to reach this day. I didn't do anything different from my friends, and as far as I knew, I never had the choice to do otherwise. I went to Hebrew School, but so did everyone else. The classes sometimes got in the way of fun, but they were never a big deal. Learning and memorizing whatever I needed to for the bar mitzvah ceremony came easily to me. I listened as people told me what a remarkable young man I had become, and I wished them to be right. Their praise and high hopes were not enough to overcome the nagging feeling that eventually I would be revealed to be a fraud and a pervert, and it ate away at the edges of my feeling of accomplishment. Occasionally the tangible love of my family, and the presence of so many people peppering me with affection and praise, broke through the veil of guilt.

That night I went downstairs to the basement where Melva would sleep, and we played dominos. She asked if I were nervous about tomorrow. I said I wasn't, and that I was more excited about the fact that everyone I knew would be there, and that the luncheon afterward would be a lot of fun. "I'll be sorry when it's all over, and everything goes back to normal."

On Saturday, Grandma woke me earlier than I planned, but I was eager to start my bar mitzvah day, so I didn't argue. I anticipated a day of special treatment, deserved or not. Mom greeted me with a kiss on the forehead as she reminded me that this day was indeed special. Dad was still in bed taking advantage of one of the few Saturdays when he didn't have to have his hands in some kid's mouth.

We arrived at the temple a half hour before the service to meet with Rabbi Becker. The air crackled with surreal and positive forces. Perhaps the feeling was akin to a bride's on her wedding day. It's all about me. I pleaded for each second to last two seconds, but still time raced. Nature, always indifferent, kept me humble.

Grandma, Grandpa, Bubbie, and Zadie were in the front row with Nancy and Melva. I stretched my neck to look around the doorway that lead from the office to the sanctuary, and saw family and friends trickling in. It was exciting to see all those people dressed up and present on a Saturday morning just for me. I noted the juxtaposition of my family with my friends, and decided I liked it.

The service was unremarkable, except to those who loved me. Bar mitzvah boys were supposed to be nervous, but I was happy—almost cocky—feeling certain I had mastered my part.

We had a tradition at our temple that made it clear that what was happening was the continuation of an unbroken chain of thousands of years. The Torah was handed to Zadie, who handed it to Dad, who then placed it in my arms. My link was now soldered to the chain. Every bar or bat mitzvah should ask himself or herself if he is going to be the one to break the chain, or see that it continues on. In becoming a bar mitzvah, the wisdom of almost two hundred generations of our mothers and fathers was to live on in me. I carried in my arms all the laws and ethics that sustained the Jewish people for millennia, but I didn't dwell on whether or not I was up to it, nor did I think about how I would keep the chain going if I weren't to have children. Instead, I worried about dropping the Torah.

When I gave the speech that interpreted my Haftorah portion—the one I discussed with Rabbi Becker—it was obvious that I had an editor in him. Rabbi made my point much better than I had in my draft: *If people can put aside their differences, they can help each other, learn from each other, and make those differences seem less important. We never know how big an effect any small, but righteous action can have on the world.*

At 11:55 a.m., after years of anticipating this day, the serious part was over, and what was left was a celebration. I smiled and waved at the audience like a politician.

My parents planned a boilerplate luncheon, at a hotel that hosted the most bar mitzvah parties that year. From the table cards, centerpieces, and food, to the band, dance contests, and snowball dances, my bar mitzvah party was quintessential 1970.

Zadie said the blessings before the meal, and Grandpa Leo made a toast. I remember he paraphrased Einstein, and said, "The pursuit of knowledge for its own sake, an almost fanatical love of justice, ...these are the features of the Jewish tradition that make me thank my stars I belong to it." He never left the forge.

One thing unique about my bar mitzvah celebration was the presence of Melva at the head table. Most of my friends had black housekeepers, but none had a relationship to match the one I had with Melva.

She was given the honor to light one of the thirteen candles, in a ceremony common to bar mitzvah parties. When Melva's name was called, everyone in the room simultaneously stood, and gave her an ovation. No one else received such adulation. Joyful tears streamed down her face as she made her way to where I stood next to the special candelabra on the center of the dance floor. After she lit the candle, she leaned down, and set her cheek against mine for a photograph. A framed enlargement of that moment hung in her living room, until the day she died.

That night, all was quiet except for the sound of water pulsing through the dishwasher. A faint smell of coffee mixed with an amalgam of perfumes and cigarette smoke lingered. The celebratory sounds of family and friends were gone, and contentment blanketed the house. I walked barefooted and in pajamas through the darkened kitchen, and descended to the basement where a light and the sound of a talk radio program indicated that Melva had not yet gone to sleep.

So as not to surprise her, I called out her name before I reached the bottom step.

"Come on, Baby," Melva's voice of honey and smoke called back. She began to cough, and I knew she had a cigarette hanging from her mouth. She was in a blue nylon dressing gown and pink house slippers as she sat at the card table reading a copy of *Ebony*. The big sofa was made up into a comfortable bed.

"What are we playing, Baby, cards or dominos?"

"Let's play dominos. Okay?"

"Sounds good to me."

I loved this time with Melva. During the *Big Snow* of January 26, 1967, Melva was stranded at our house for several days. We spent some of the time playing card games that she taught me, as well as dominos, and we listened to WGN talk radio programs. She baked and cooked, and I was in heaven. Buried in snowdrifts, the house was warmed by the smells of corn and banana breads, and fried chicken. Grandma and Mom took note that the only time I would eat meatloaf was when Melva made it from her own recipe.

I brought the domino set to the card table, and we began our first game. We didn't talk much about the bar mitzvah. I confessed to Melva that my friends and I were thinking we were old enough to skip school, and take the L by ourselves to a Cubs game.

"You kids need to be careful. There are crazy people out there. Better you go with your Grandpa, like you always do."

"You could take me, couldn't you?" I asked innocently.

"Baby, I've never been to a Cubs game," Melva shocked me.

"Melva, you've never been to a Cubs game? You, their biggest fan? How come?"

Melva laughed, coughed, and took the cigarette out of her mouth. "Let's just say it isn't easy for an old colored woman like me to sit herself down on the North Side at a ballgame in the middle of the day."

"You should go. I'm going to ask Dad and Grandpa. You have to go. I want to go with you. We'll have a blast. You'll love it."

Melva said nothing, but I saw the ends of her mouth turn slightly upward.

"Mel, when you retire will you move in with us, I mean, you will won't you?"

Melva laughed again. "Glen, how could I move in with you? What am I going to do about my husband? Besides, I can't even afford to think about retiring. I think I'll just fall over the vacuum some day, and that'll be the end."

We laughed together. "No, seriously. Listen, Melva, I've been thinking. I'm going to be rich some day. I'll be a doctor, and have a lot of money, and I'll buy one of those big houses, with the white pillars in front, like the White House, with a big front porch. You and your husband can come and live there. We'll get you a big rocking chair, and all you'll have to do is sit and rock all day, and we can listen to the Cubs games together. Maybe I'll be rich enough, and we can have Ernie Banks and Billy Williams over for dinner and stuff. They'll be retired then, and have plenty of time. Wouldn't that be cool?"

Melva was quiet for a moment, and I wondered if I had somehow insulted her. She appeared to be studying the dominos in front of her, but then she looked up with a big smile, and I could see that her eyes were moist. "Glen, that would be real nice. I'm going to look forward to that."

I sat back contented, because I made Melva happy. I never forgot my promise to Melva, but I passed into adulthood unable to fulfill it. Now, regret envelops the memory.

We played several rounds of dominos and one hand of gin rummy before Melva said it was her bedtime. I moaned, but didn't argue. I put away the cards and dominos, and gave Melva a kiss on the cheek. "Pleasant dreams, Mel." She wished me the same.

CHAPTER TWENTY-SEVEN

Monday, April 13, 1970

My bar mitzvah didn't break new ground, so the feedback was sparse, causing me to fish for the compliments that Barbara, Debbie, and Leslie graciously offered. Soon everyone moved on to the topics of weekend sports highlights and other activities. Although I never dwelled on anyone else's bar mitzvah weekend, I was hurt that a day that was elevated far above the ordinary days of my life meant little to my closest friends. As part of a recurring pattern, I took insult that anything special to me wasn't of interest to the rest of the world—especially to my friends. The self-absorption of the insecure.

To further darken the day, Mr. Wendell announced we would play dodge ball in gym class. Figuring out how to get my hand, arm, and body in a position to launch the ball like an accurate missile was my Manhattan Project, only there was no Oppenheimer to lead me. I failed. Others made it look so easy. The ball was a natural extension of their arm. On me it was like a mutated cyst. Why didn't gym teachers take us limp-wristed boys aside, and actually work with us on our throwing technique?

The first time I held a ball that day, I threw it weakly, yet it hit not one, but two guys, because the ball ricocheted off the first one. "Attaboy, pussy!" came the welcome cry of praise from my black teammate, Charles Dawson. The *attaboy* not only cancelled out the negativity of the *pussy*, but it rocketed me to the stratosphere. That was the first *attaboy* I'd ever gotten in dodge ball, and it came from a black kid, with great athletic ability. The *pussy* addendum was a given. I felt an instantaneous bond with Charles Dawson, and if anyone were to interview me at that moment, I would confidently crow that I would never trade my integrated school for any mambi pambi, lily-white school.

In social studies that afternoon, Pamela Blake insisted that there were more blacks than whites in America, therefore, blacks would eventually dominate the country. When Mr. Peterson pointed out the demographic facts—that blacks were a minority in the U.S.—she was skeptical. He told her that once you left Hampden, there were cities and states with hardly any blacks. Pamela picked up the gavel that Mr. Peterson kept on his desk, as a means to get the class's attention, and announced she would use it to pound the head of any kid who annoyed her that afternoon. Other than a few of us who chuckled, no one paid much attention.

CHAPTER TWENTY-EIGHT

Thursday, April 16, 1970

I was lying on the couch in the family room, watching an episode of *The Ghost and Mrs. Muir*, while mulling over sexy George Adams and the upcoming track season.

Becoming a jock, the highest level of anything attainable among American youth, was perhaps in my grasp, thanks to my speed and agility, but I lacked the necessary passion. In spite of the perquisites that accompanied jock status, including rarely being called a fem, I didn't want to put out the necessary effort. Without a passion for, or even a simple enjoyment of the game, motivation was allusive, and jockhood a labor without the love. I hadn't forgotten that George Adams himself, one of the recognized leaders of both black and white kids, had suggested I try out. Demonstrating to friends that I had the ability to excel at something non-cerebral would be cool, yet…there was another barrier that kept me on the couch, and out of the jock section of the locker room: the possibility of losing a race. I was a sore loser.

If I couldn't win, I didn't want to play. If I put myself out there for the world to see, I wanted a guarantee that I wouldn't fail.

Stretched out, and leaning on my hand facing the TV, I didn't immediately answer the question Nancy posed from where she was seated all evening, at the card table across the room as she took notes from a textbook.

"Glen! Answer me, you queer. Is *That Girl* on next?"

"No, stupid. *Bewitched* is on next, and thennnn *That Girl.* Don't you know anything?"

"You are so queer sometimes. Just for that, I won't tell you what Joel Needleman told me about Barbara."

Instantly I was up. I jumped off the couch towards the table where Nancy sat looking smug.

"Tell me! What did he say? Something about me? What did he say? Does he even know me? Did Barbara say anything about me? Since when are you friends with Joel? Tell me what he said," I demanded.

Nancy laughed. "Look at you. You're all ears now. Suddenly you want to talk. Sorry, I need to do my homework. Quit annoying me."

There was too much at stake here. My reputation, my cool factor, my entire future could hinge on what Joel Needleman told Nancy regarding Barbara. The knot in my gut told me I was desperate.

"Nancy, you better tell me, or I'm telling Mom and Dad that I know for a fact that you and Marla smoked pot." I took a chance on this. I had no idea whether or not Nancy and Marla got high, but I had my suspicions, and needed a wedge to get to her.

Nancy stopped smiling. "You lie like a rug. You don't know any such thing."

I had hit on something. "Oh, now look who's excited? I won't tell them if you tell me." My ploy was working, but I had to keep it going, and get the information from Nancy, before she discovered I was bluffing.

"You jerk. You better tell me now who told you that I smoked pot. I want to know, or I'll tell Barbara Needleman that you wet your bed, or something like that."

My eyes widened explosively, and I shrieked like a parakeet, my voice soaring to its highest pre-pubescent tones. "What! Are you crazy? Wet the bed? That's a lie, and you know it. You are so mean I can't believe it! I'll tell your friends that you still stuff your bra." This was spiraling out of control, and I was no closer to knowing what Joel Needleman said. I decided to throw myself on Nancy's mercy. Typically, she won every argument with me, because I became flustered, and she used her superior verbal acumen to trounce me.

"Okay, forget it. I don't know about you and Marla smoking pot. But why won't you tell me about Joel Needleman? Just *tell* me."

"Joel didn't say anything about you. He doesn't even know you. I just said that because you wouldn't answer me. I know you like Barbara. It was obvious at your bar mitzvah. You chose her to represent your girl friends, and you picked her to lead the snowball with you. Why would someone as cool as Joel Needleman even care what you do?"

From a conversation I overheard between Nancy and Marla, I knew she had a crush on Joel for a long time. I read the columns he wrote in the Hampden school newspaper about how important it was to protest against the war in Viet Nam, pollution, and the older generation in general. Barbara told me he was accepted at Harvard.

Joel was hot. When I spied him outside Barbara's house playing basketball, it made me uncomfortable because I recognized my attraction to him was far greater than anything I felt for Barbara. His curly dark brown hair, his smoky green eyes, and the way his butt filled out his torn jeans filled me with anxiety. I couldn't look at him directly. It was like staring at the sun during an eclipse. Forbidden.

The sudden ring of the phone grounded me. Nancy jumped up to get it.

I could hear Grandma's agitated voice coming through the receiver. Though I couldn't make out what she was saying, she was clearly upset, and Nancy was only able to offer an occasional "uh huh."

"Grandma, I think it's great that Grandpa wants to ride a bicycle," Nancy squeezed in quickly. "That's so cool that he *can* ride a bicycle, and that he wants to stay healthy." Grandma interrupted, clearly unhappy with Nancy's response, and sounding more agitated. Then came the words that I dreaded.

"Gram, Glen wants to talk to you. Talk to him. He's right here." Nancy smiled as she held out the phone to me. I must've looked horrified, because she laughed. "It's for you Glenny, Grandma's little boy."

I lifted myself off the couch with a groan, made my way to the phone table, and slumped into the adjoining armchair. "Hi, Grandma." That was the last thing I said for the next five minutes.

"After fifty years of marriage I'm now certain that Grandpa has lost his mind. I'm going to have a nervous breakdown, so help me. The doctor told me this aggravation will kill me. Grandpa came home with a bicycle. Did you ever? *Hernoch*, he plans on riding it around Lincoln Park when the weather gets warmer—for exercise. Exercise? Is he joining the Olympics all of a sudden? I'm sure he'll fall and kill himself, if a car doesn't hit him first. I should be the one to identify his body? Is that what I have to look forward to? If he wants to kill himself he should buy a gun, and I'll hit him over the head with it. I always knew he was crazy, even when I married him. I should've known that his family was crazy, and run in the other direction. Imagine his father quit a banking job at $40 a week to take a job at a Jewish school. No wonder he has no sense."

I thought about Nancy's frequent observation that we lived in an unromantic time and place. Yet, on this night, over our new touch-tone telephone, in a suburban family room, over the din of the Thursday night line-up on ABC, Grandma revealed her fifty-year love for Grandpa, albeit without poetry. Here was an aging woman, terrified of losing the man who meant security to her, and in whom she somehow found a purposeful existence. No one would call their marriage great, but it survived half a tumultuous century. In my eyes, by virtue of its longevity and the era in which it unfolded, their relationship achieved a modicum of romance. Born into the vestiges of Victorian morality, they were briefly separated by the First World War, and then lived through the ages of cars and planes, jazz, the Great Depression, World War II, nuclear weapons, and even a moon landing. From a distance of time, it's the kind of romantic backdrop Nancy mourned.

Relief for me came in the form of Matzah barking and whining, announcing Mom and Dad's return from a high school board meeting. I recognized the scent of Mom's perfume before she entered the family room. Matzah leaped from Mom to Dad and back again as they scanned the room to get their bearings.

"Grandma, Mom and Dad just got home. Do you want to talk to Mom? Okay, Grandma. Thanks. I love you too. I'll tell Dad you want to talk to him." I saw my mother shake her head and shrug as if to say, "So what else could I expect?" Dad laughed and took the phone from me to talk to his mother-in-law. I relaxed knowing Dad would know what to say to her.

"Hello Ma. How are you, Gorgeous?"

Mom laid her coat over the arm of the couch, and sat down with a sigh. Matzah jumped into her lap, and tried to lick her face. Mom lifted her head so Matzah licked under her chin as she scratched behind his ears.

"Hello, Mommy's baby boy. How's my *sheyna punim?*"

"How was the meeting? Anything we should know?" Nancy asked setting her homework aside, while on TV, Endora placed a spell on Darrin.

"Your father and I are very disturbed about the meeting, and we aren't sure about what to do." Mom shook her head.

"What are the choices?" Mom was pleased that Nancy showed an interest in conversing with her. She probably noticed that I was listening as much to Samantha Stephens as I was to her.

"There's this group of parents from the black community that believes the reason the percentage of black students in honor classes is so low is that the courses are written for white sensibilities, and that blacks can't relate to them." Mom stopped here to see how Nancy would react. It didn't take long for a response.

"That's ridiculous. I can't believe that." Nancy said matching her words with a look of disbelief.

"Why do you say that, Honey?"

"Because it doesn't make sense. They aren't in honors classes because they aren't interested in school. They're all too busy complaining about white oppressors, and boasting about black power, and black pride—that is when they aren't ditching classes or busting heads in the girl's bathroom, or breaking into lockers. They shun the few black kids who *do* make it into the honors classes for being 'too white,' for being 'traitors to the black power movement.' I don't suppose anyone at the meeting mentioned any of this." Nancy sounded exasperated as she tugged on strands of her hair.

"No one said exactly that. But your father actually questioned how courses in math and science could be taught to either white or black sensibilities. He said physics, chemistry, and algebra are color-blind. That earned him evil stares from some of the black parents.

"It's true. Look at Anna Ling. She's a straight-A student, and she's Chinese. It has nothing to do with her sensibilities, and everything to do with her attitude and her parents' expectations of her."

"It's funny. I agreed with your father, but I felt we were somehow on the wrong side of the argument. It's one of those situations where you wish to address previous wrongs, but in this instance, perhaps—just perhaps—the black parents have it wrong. They make no mention of individual responsibility, hard work, and the importance of applying oneself in school."

"What else?" Nancy asked, her voice laced with skepticism.

"Well, Ralph Peterson—isn't that Kathy's father?"

"Tall bald guy? Yeah. What'd he say?"

My mother's hands were at her sides, and Matzah pawed her arm to encourage more head scratches.

"Well, he said what your father has often said, and now you just confirmed. He wanted to know that if the courses were taught with white sensibilities, then why did the Orientals, like your friend Anna, I guess, have such a high percentage of their children in honors classes, especially since some of them come from homes where English isn't the first language. And that's the same thing I've been saying about the Hispanic kids whose parents insist they be taught in Spanish. Other immigrants don't get that consideration, and they do better than the Spanish children. It's so obvious, but either they don't see it, or no one wants to admit it.

"You know it might be a cultural thing and not a race thing at all. The Orientals and some of the other groups moving to America are determined to do well in school, and they're encouraged at home. They're like Jews. Education comes first, or it used to, before Jews found the religion of after-school sports."

"Why is everyone afraid to say the truth?" Nancy said, sort of looking at Mom and sort of past her. "I thought that there was nothing better than the truth?"

"That's a good question, Nance."

"What's the question, Sweetie?" Dad asked. His conversation with Grandma ended, he walked over to the couch where I sprawled, my head on a throw pillow, Mom sitting at the end of the couch, at my feet. Lifting my legs, so he could sit next to Mom, Dad plopped down, and then arranged my legs on his lap.

"We were just talking about the meeting, Jer."

"Oh, that. Don't get me started again." Dad rolled his eyes, and patted my calves.

"Nancy wants to know why no one will say what she thinks needs to be said, about why the black children in school aren't doing as well as the white or Oriental children." Through her tone she was indicating to Dad that Nancy's question should add to his pride in his daughter.

"There's so much guilt out there. Anger too. It's all mixed up with history and politics, and some garbage. It'll be a long, long time before good people can sit down, and talk honestly and sensibly, without worrying about igniting some kind of powder keg. I hope they don't do more harm than good for those black kids, until that day arrives."

"Hey, Dad, try wiggling your nose and make it all better." That was my brilliant contribution using *Bewitched* as my source.

"Yeah, wouldn't that be nice? Anyhow here we are, the lucky generation, doing what all people do who live in interesting times. We try to adapt as things change around us. We try to hold onto the familiar and the things we cherish, and we fight in varying degrees against what we see as wrong."

"You sound like the rabbi, Dad."

"Why thank you Nancy, I think. Too bad I don't get paid for pontificating. Anyhow, being in a school like yours, at this particular time in history, is like living on the front line of some kind of war or revolution. It's messy and difficult and things aren't so clear cut, are they?"

"Well, I think the right thing for everyone to do is pretty clear cut. What isn't clear is who are the bad guys, and who are the good guys, or is everyone a little of both?"

"Eileen, I think we are raising the first female Secretary of State."

Nancy beamed. Mom smiled proudly. It was my turn to groan.

"I'll tell you though, I'm thinking of what Marty said, and asking myself if I really want my children on the front line of a revolution." Dad said directly to Mom.

"Are you saying you don't want the kids in Hampden now?"

"I'm not saying anything with certainty, but after hearing some of those parents tonight, not to mention recent activities, I got the feeling that reason isn't going to prevail in those schools. Is it fair to ask our kids to deal with the fallout? Let's see, there was the riot after the basketball game, Glen's eye incident, and Nancy's stolen coat. I'm not so sure education can thrive in this environment, at least not textbook education.

"I see the national trend of catering to the lowest common denominator coming to roost here in Hampden, and that's a recipe for failure. Do you think in ten or twenty years Hampden will still be ranked among the ten best high schools in the country? My guess is that we're at the start of a decline."

"What's so bad, Jer? The kids are getting a *good* education, they have great friends, and I love this house. Let's not get carried away. Nancy's close to graduation, and Glen loves school, don't you Glen?"

Oh boy. I didn't want to be placed between my parents, a smart position only when I needed to play one against the other. In this instance I didn't know what I wanted. The waters swirling around school were murky. I wasn't among the most popular kids in school, but I wasn't close to pariah status. I was part of a comfortable clique of kids that included attractive girls, average athletes, and brainpower. Who knew where I would stand at a new school?

I felt loyal to my school simply because it was my school. I knew it, understood it, and saw the good as well as the ridiculous. My friends and I often spoke about how much we hated the trouble the black kids caused us, but we were always quick to defend our school against any well-intentioned relative who might cast aspersions.

"You really mean we might move?" I was buying time.

Mom jumped in. "No Glen. We aren't moving so fast. I just want to make sure you're happy at school. It's important that you can learn, so you can get into a good college."

"Would we get a bigger house, with a swimming pool? Would it still be in Michigami, only just on the other side of Lawson Avenue?"

Dad laughed at the notion of a bigger house with a pool, while Mom fielded the question. "No one is getting a pool. That's all I need. Your grandmother would never sleep. She'd be out there all night making sure no one drowned. And you're changing the subject. Do you like your school, Glen?"

I looked at Nancy. No help there. "Yeah. It's okay, I guess. I like a lot of things about it, but some of the black kids really get on my nerves sometimes. They think they're so much better than anybody, and they're constantly trying to hit someone or steal something or interrupt class. I wish I could stay at my school, but without so many black kids there."

My parents traded glances. Mom was crestfallen, and my feelings of guilt rose as quickly as her spirits fell. She hadn't expected me to direct my anger so explicitly at my black classmates. How could a child of hers, the daughter of Leo Epstein, harbor antipathy to blacks? If her words and Leo's example had not repelled bigotry from taking root in her children, then surely by sending them to school with nice black children would save them from its malevolent growth.

The guilt quickly settled around my digestive system. I caused Mom disappointment, and I would suffer for it.

"Mom, don't get the wrong idea. I like the school. We have a good time there, and I think I'm learning more than our cousins at their schools. I can tell when I talk to them." I might've been killing my chances to free myself from black oppression, but I couldn't bear to be the cause of Mom's disappointment. I knew my parents thought they were doing a good thing by sending me to school in Hampden, even if they found themselves defending their choice with increasing frequency among friends or family.

"Listen Son, your mother and I always want you to be honest. What you said was honest, and it doesn't matter if it was what we did or didn't want to hear. Never worry about that. Your mother and I aren't going to make any quick decisions about moving based on this discussion, but we want to make sure that you're safe and happy in school each day. Do you feel safe at school, or are you ever concerned for your safety? Be honest."

I thought of the times I'd been shoved against a locker, had the back of my head smacked, my lunch money taken, been tripped, or had books knocked out of my hands, and then answered. "Yeah. I feel safe at school, I guess. I mean no one has ever gone to the hospital hurt or anything like that. It's just a lot of stupid stuff."

That was true. I didn't anticipate sustaining life-threatening injuries at my junior high school. The serious violence, including beatings, knifings, and even gunshots lay in Hampden's future. The ripples of physical and verbal assaults that most of us experienced on a regular basis were the leading edge of the waves of violence to follow. Their course was prepared daily by the good intentions of those who indulged the perpetrators: the enablers of what I see as a historic decline. These were the adults in our school who avoided confronting the growing mindset of placing blame on others; the decline of taking responsibility for one's self; and the near collapse of standards of what we used to call good conduct. They bought into, or feared opposing the trending idea that the traditional methods of teaching and controlling behavior carried with it a serious risk of damaging the fragile self-esteem of budding hooligans. The time was not right for questioning the theory: if black is beautiful, then whatever black does is beautiful—or at least acceptable.

"Glen, that really isn't a good enough answer. What do you mean? Are you ever physically or mentally threatened or harmed in school, beside the time you were Maced, which is more than troublesome in itself?"

I didn't want to sound like a sissy. I also didn't want my parents to know how frustrating every day could be, and cause them to get upset and overreact, possibly setting off an unstoppable chain of events that might include scenes at school.

At least the black kids gave us things to laugh at, and provided welcome distractions from schoolwork. My friends and I enjoyed observing the antics of the black kids as they flustered our teachers, and tormented the really queer kids. The classroom and auditorium became carnivals when the black kids would shout whatever was on their mind, and run up and down the aisles looking for trouble.

That and the occasional "Attaboy, pussy!" made me forget my anger, albeit briefly.

To further convince myself that all was well at school, I made a mental line-up of all the black kids with whom I had some kind of positive relationship, and would be sorry not to see again.

I was ready to answer Dad. Having decided that the status quo was safer than unknown territory, I directed my gaze back to the TV, and told my parents, "I'm okay with school. There's no danger or anything."

"By the way Jerry, what did my mother want?"

"She's all upset because your father bought a bicycle, and he's determined to ride it for his health."

"Well, it'll get him out of the house, so that'll help him right there." We all snorted a sort of laugh.

CHAPTER TWENTY-NINE

Saturday, April 18, 1970

I sped through my morning routine, bounded down the stairs, and rounded the corner into the kitchen. Mom, Grandma, and Melva sat around the table, coffee mugs in hand. Matzah filled out the foursome; the morning paper sat opened in front of him.

Melva smiled at me. Grandma jumped up and said, "Sit down, *Tatala* and I'll give you something to eat."

"Good morning, my sweet boy. This should be a good day, huh?" Although I agreed with Mom, all I could muster as I took the seat next to Matzah, was "uh huh." I wasn't one of those TV kids who sounded orgasmic over a snack cake or a Tonka trunk. Matzah pawed at my arm with desperation.

"Later, Matz. I don't have anything yet." In an act of futility, I pushed Matzah's paw aside.

"Looks like you have a beautiful day today. Lots of sunshine," Mom kept up the cheerful patter, between sips of coffee.

Grandma set a bowl of oatmeal, covered with brown sugar and raisins, in front of me. "I made the oatmeal with milk. You better dress warm today. It's going to be cold there by the lake. I hope Grandpa wears a warm coat. I don't know why they play baseball in April. The weather's so unpredictable."

Melva and I traded smiles. It could've been twenty degrees outside; it wouldn't have kept me from going with Melva to her first Cubs game.

"I'm packing you plenty of food, so Grandpa doesn't have to pay those prices for hot dogs. You all have bologna sandwiches, Fritos, and apples. And I put some pop in there, too," Grandma said with authority, as if she anticipated resistance. "Oh, and there's a special bag with cherries in it. Don't ask what I had to pay for that."

I loved cherries, but I knew I wouldn't eat them at the game, because of the pit problem. I didn't want to be caught spitting a pit out of my mouth, at the exact moment when a television camera had me framed. Spitting out pits was fine for most, but I couldn't accept the vulgarity in myself.

"Thank you, Mrs. Epstein," Melva said over her shoulder to Grandma who was back in the kitchen, pouring a glass of orange juice for me.

Dried leaves that remained from autumn swirled suddenly in a corner of the patio. "I hope the wind is going out of the park today. Then you'll get to see lots of homers, Mel."

"As long as they're not for Montreal. I still can't believe I'm going to the game. I bet I'm more excited than you, Glen."

"You've never been before?" Grandma asked Melva as she placed two pieces of buttered rye toast in front of me.

"No, I haven't." Melva offered no further explanation.

"Well, I'm glad my dad was able to get these four tickets from his client," said Mom. She pushed back from the table and stood up. "I'd better throw on some clothes, so I can drive you to the L."

Matzah watched Mom leave the room, and then turned back to me, scratching at my arm again. I tore off a small piece of toast for him. Within seconds his paw was back on my arm. The doorbell rang; he jumped off the chair, and tried to get traction on the kitchen tile, barking all the way to the door.

"Who is it?" Grandma yelled to the front door.

"It's Ken, Grandma. Open the door, please." I shouted.

"I'm in here, Ken." I wanted to get Ken away from Grandma as quickly as possible.

Ken marched into the kitchen, Matzah excitedly trotting behind him.

"Hi, Melva." Ken turned to me. "Hey." He gave me the ever-safe, heads up nod.

Ken was dressed in Cubs gear, and carrying a mitt. He sat down on my right as Matzah returned to his chair on my left.

"Sit down Kenny. I'll give you something to eat. You want a piece of toast or some oatmeal, Dolly?"

"No thank you. I already ate." Ken said to Grandma.

"Don't be shy Kenny. We'll tell everyone you ate anyway. How about a little sweet roll?" Grandma persisted.

"Um, okay. What kind do you have?"

"Oy, another Mr. Particular. We have all kinds, so long as you like apple. That's all that's left. You'll eat and you'll enjoy."

In spite of the optimistic predictions, the Cubs did not do great in '68, and they ended up far from fine in '69, giving baseball one of the greatest team collapses in history. It was just as well that we had no rhyme for 1970.

Melva, Ken, and I discussed Leo Durocher's management style (I mostly listened), Kenny Holtzman's pitching, and Ernie Banks's team spirit. Grandma quickly lost interest, and picked up the newspaper as the doorbell rang, and Matzah leaped off his chair. He squealed with excitement he reserved for his favorites. Grandma and Melva raced for the door.

"Get out of the way, Matzah. It's Grandpa. Let him in. Melva, don't fall over the dog." There was a short pause as the door opened, and I could hear mumbled greetings. "Glen, Grandpa's here."

Ken and I joined the group in the entry, just as Mom came downstairs wearing a pair of black bell-bottom slacks, and a white and red paisley blouse. She had put on lipstick, and combed her hair. I silently approved.

"Hi, Dad. What do you have there?" Mom zeroed in on a big box wrapped in a blue bow, tucked under Grandpa's arm.

Without saying anything, Grandpa made his way into the living room, and we followed him the way Matzah followed anyone with food.

"By the way, Melva, I don't think you'll need your coat today."

"I won't?"

"No you won't because you'll have this." Grandpa handed Melva the box.

"Mr. Epstein, this is for me? Are you kidding?" Melva was both giddy and embarrassed.

"In honor of your first Cubs game Melva, we can't have anyone questioning your team loyalty.

"Open it, Melva!" I was as excited as she was.

Melva sat down in an armchair, held the box on her lap, and carefully untied the blue bow. She lifted the lid, and pulled aside the neatly folded white tissue paper to reveal a shiny blue jacket, with the Cubs insignia sewn on the left breast.

"Cool, Melva! You have a jacket like mine!" I told her. "We match!"

"Cool," Ken added.

"What's that? A jacket? Oh isn't that nice," Grandma said in a way that made me guess she was trying to remember the last time Grandpa brought her a box with a bow.

Melva hadn't said anything. She sat smiling broadly, and shaking her head. She held up the jacket, and then stood up.

"Mr. Epstein. Oh, Mr. Epstein. This is beautiful. Are you sure it's for me? She laughed."

"Yep, I'm sure. In case Ernie Banks looks your way today, you should be wearing a Cubs jacket."

I had the feeling that Grandpa meant this to be another lesson for me. He wasn't going to let my bar mitzvah pass, and take its significance along with it. By doing good deeds—*mitzvahs* — Grandpa lived a rich life, and he wanted the same for me.

"I hope this is a big size to get around all of me." Melva said, still smiling as she tried on the jacket, and preened in the hall mirror.

"It fits like a mitt. Wear it in good health." Grandpa said.

"Yes, Melva. Wear it in good health." Mom added, looking to see my reaction to the scene Grandpa had orchestrated; another clue that this was for my benefit.

"More important," Grandpa added, "you should wear it to a World Series!"

"Amen," Mom affirmed.

"Amen," Ken and I echoed.

Grandma swung into action to get us out the door in time, making sure we each had a lunch bag, and reminding us to zip up our jackets. Finally, she warned Grandpa not to let "the boys" out of his sight with all the *mishuganahs* running around loose in the city.

We threw out appeasing "yeses" and "don't worries," as we made our exit. Melva left her old coat in Grandma's hands.

Grandpa rode shotgun, and Melva, Ken, and I sat in back as Mom backed out of the driveway. We headed east into Hampden. While Ken and Melva discussed the possibilities of the Cubs taking the pennant, my mind wandered.

I had no passion for baseball, though there was something about the Cubs and baseball that kept me mildly interested. Basketball was tedious, but I didn't mind playing a game of

HORSE. Football meant attempting to throw or catch a ball that wasn't even round. There was no pleasure in spending hours in freezing temperatures, with watery eyes that blurred my vision, listening to odd words or phrases, such as "line of scrimmage," and "kick or make?"

Baseball was an early sort of beard for me, my female date to a business affair. It helped me *pass* among my friends. My feigned enthusiasm typically would dissipate when we took our seats in the ballpark. The only honest link I had to baseball was Melva. I knew she was near whenever I heard a Cubs game on a radio. I wanted to share the Cubs with Melva, because they were important to her. I don't know how the daughter of a poor Arkansas sharecropper, with little formal education, latched on to baseball and the Cubs.

The basic rules of baseball were familiar enough, but then there were details, exceptions, and statistics that annoyed and confounded me whenever my friends delved into them. They must have been studying the endless lists of statistics and players for every college and professional sport played by humankind, at the same time that I was reading about historical disasters, and the history of the hoop skirt.

On this particular game day, my excitement was inextricably linked to Melva's presence.

As the car crossed the canal into Hampden, I instinctively looked to see if our door locks were down. Both back buttons were up, but out of deference to Melva, I resisted reaching over to lock them. We proceeded without incident to the Hampden L station where Mom said her good-byes.

"Remember Dad, when you come home, call from the Evans Avenue station, before you get on the Hampden line, and I'll come right away to meet you right here. We should get here about the same time."

CHAPTER THIRTY

A Few Minutes Later

Grandpa paid our fare, and we climbed the stairs to the L platform. My blood began pumping faster in anticipation of the coming journey. The ride on the L into the city always felt like an adventure, and then after the game maybe Ken would stay for dinner, and we could get together with Gary and some other friends, and go to a movie. I shivered involuntarily with anticipation.

As we waited for the train, I looked around to see who else was on the platform. There was a white, teenage couple holding hands and giggling under their Cubs' hats. Beyond them, leaning on a steel column, was an older black man. Judging by his clothes he was a housepainter. Next to him was an attractive black woman wearing a business suit under her unbuttoned cashmere coat, and clasping the hand of a very small child, in a red bow tie, and a dark blue suit. Two teenage girls sat sullenly on the bench behind them, next to a woman in mod pink pants who was thumbing through a magazine.

The voices that ascended the stairs to the platform caused my spine to stiffen. Three black male teens emerged from the stairwell at the far right end of the platform. One of the boys picked at his large Afro as the boys pushed and shoved each other, laughing loudly and shouting obscenities that made me uncomfortable in the presence of Grandpa and Melva. They wore brightly colored bell-bottom trousers and high platform shoes. Their parkas, all unzipped and slightly off their shoulders, were too warm for that day's temperatures.

One emptied the remains of a bag of Cheetos over his upturned face. After eating the last few orange curly puffs from the bag, he let it drop onto the platform. My blood began to boil.

Another threw an empty pop bottle on the tracks where it shattered. He and his friends sauntered along the platform toward us. My jaw clenched. Their presence had the same effect on me as a downed power line, jolting back and forth on the platform. What would happen next? How to avoid it?

Grandpa instinctively moved to the front of our group, placing himself between the approaching boys and the rest of us. The platform was wide, and we stood several feet from the edge, leaving plenty of room for anyone to walk either in front of or behind us. The three boys were determined to walk right through us, just like so many of the black kids in the school hallways. Moving around us would've been an unthinkable act of submission.

They were headed for a collision course with Grandpa, who by this time had dropped any pretense of being unaware of their menacing approach. They continued roughhousing with each other as they approached, but all three sets of eyes were on Grandpa daring him to stay put. Melva grabbed my hand and Ken's shoulder, and pulled us back with no subtlety, leaving another few feet in front of us. Grandpa was not fast enough. With two of the boys on his left, and one on his right, they knocked Grandpa's shoulders from both sides.

"Out of the way, boy," one snarled. Having made their point, they continued to the far end of the platform.

Grandpa was shaken. "Hey, young men. What is the point of that?" They let this go, although I could make out the words "old honky" in their laughter.

"Are you all right, Mr. Epstein? Colored boys are crazy nowadays. They could've just walked passed us with no bother. That happens to me on the South Side every day."

Melva was squeezing my hand so tightly it began to hurt. I think she was trying to keep herself from shaking.

"I'm fine, Melva. Boys will be boys, I guess."

No one else on the platform said anything.

I knew the encounter disturbed Grandpa terribly, and he rubbed one of his shoulders. He was angry with the kids for the harm that belligerent behavior like theirs did to the cause of racial harmony. Grandpa once told me that as a result of history, blacks, and particularly, black youth, would have to realize that for better or worse, they were ambassadors for their race. He said it was related to the way Jews everywhere cringed whenever a single Jew committed a crime.

"It's a *shanda fer de shlaynim*," Grandma would say upon reading any Jewish name associated with wrongdoing. Her Yiddish words meant, *it is an embarrassment for the neighbors*, and every Jew understood the implication that the misdeeds of one Jew would reflect poorly on every Jew, in the eyes of any Gentile looking to justify anti-Semitism.

Grandpa was probably most angry about the effect our encounter might have on me. He paid attention to my comments about school at Shabbat dinners, so he was aware that I felt a growing hostility toward blacks. I wouldn't tell him, but I hated those three guys, and I wouldn't care if the L rode over them.

Grandpa sighed as the train pulled in, and we boarded. The three boys chose a car at the other end of the station giving me some relief, but I was still on guard.

The train wasn't crowded yet, and we took seats next to the doors that faced each other across the aisles. Grandpa sat with Melva, while Ken and I shared the other seat.

We rode silently through Hampden, stopping along the way as the cars filled up. The end of the line was Evans Avenue, a Chicago terminus for the CTA. We changed to an Evans Line B train to the Addison stop near Wrigley Field.

The sun forced me to squint as we pulled into the station. My eyes began to water, but I could see the B train waiting across the wooden platform. Like us, people streamed out of the L cars, and crossed the platform to the other train. I scanned the crowd, but I didn't see the three black guys. The prevailing color of the crowd was Cubs blue. Melva grabbed my hand again, and Grandpa had his arm around Ken as he shepherded him onto the train.

The pretty black woman with the little boy entered our car, relieving my anxiety somewhat. A number of people, all white, were already seated on the train. Grandpa gestured to an empty seat for Melva to take, and then pointed to the one behind it, for Ken and me. After we were situated, he sat down next to Melva. The two bench seats met back to back, and when the train lurched forward, Ken and I were riding backwards, which made me a little dizzy.

The conductor's voice came over the loudspeaker, in the usual nearly unintelligible manner of a CTA conductor.

"Blah blah is next. Next stop is blah blah Avenue. No smoking, spitting, or radio playing on this train."

This was typically an exciting moment for me, but instead I felt uneasy, so I looked around for signs of reassurance. The crowd of jovial Cubs fans calmed me. Several groups of young teens throughout the car laughed, teased, and occasionally switched seats as the L train clattered south into the city. A rowdy white crowd rarely caused me anxiety—unless they were the Kike-Kickers from my neighborhood.

Riding backwards, Ken and I watched as the back porches of Rogers Park apartment buildings glided past. At times the train passed so close to the buildings, I could've reached out and touched the dark bricks through an open window. These were the neighborhoods that I heard about; the ones families like Ken's and mine had departed some years earlier. They had seen better days. Their re-discovery and renaissance by the gentry lay in the future. On that day, even in the sunshine, they looked tired and used up.

An elderly man in the seat in front of us had fallen asleep, and the side of his face pressed against the window. Before we pulled out of the next station, two black boys walked past the window, and smacked it hard enough to make a loud cracking noise. The old man jolted upright. The two boys laughed, and one of them spit a huge gob on the window, before walking away. His sputum stayed on the glass next to the old man for the rest of the trip. I added them to the three guys who bumped Grandpa to my hate list. The specter of a southern lynch mob would make them think twice, I thought, and then felt a pang of guilt, at the thought of Melva and Grandpa seated behind me.

The train made stops at major east-west arteries whose names I vaguely recognized from earlier trips downtown, or from family conversations. They were long commercial streets lined with stores that no longer could compete with the lure of suburban shopping malls. Here were doctors in their last years of practice; diners, with elderly patrons on fixed incomes; and other businesses that might succeed, if only they could provide more parking. A few blocks to the east were the backs of the tall apartment buildings that lined the lakefront.

At one stop, the doors flung open, and people piled on. One young black woman had a small pre school-age girl and an even smaller boy in tow. They each held a large, colorful sucker. I smiled warmly and hypocritically at the children. I wouldn't have bothered if they were white. They looked back at me with vacant eyes.

"Come on, and just sit down and shut up. And keep that thing away from your sister's jacket. If you get that on her jacket, I'll knock your head. Just sit there, and don't move." She pointed to a newly vacated seat that was in front of Ken and me, while she stood in the aisle hovering over them. Her butt faced the black lady and child who had boarded with us in Hampden.

Grandpa had his back to this group; otherwise, I'm pretty sure he would've gotten up to offer the lady his seat. I mulled it over, and decided I could hide behind being a kid, and remained seated.

The two children were barely tall enough to climb on the seat, and they said nothing to their mother who was now rummaging through a large handbag. She pulled out a bag of corn chips, opened it, and handed it to her little boy. "Give me that sucker, and take this. You can't eat that sucker without getting sticky everywhere." She took the sucker from the little boy who looked deflated. He held out his hand for it, and his mother pushed it away.

"No. Maybe later. Eat those chips, and turn around and be quiet."

I glanced across the aisle at the other black woman, with the neatly dressed little boy. She was turned sideways, staring out her window, using her back to deflect from her son and herself what transpired in the aisle. She kept one arm wrapped tightly around her bow-tied son as he silently took in the small drama.

I turned my gaze back to my window. A loud noise startled me as the doors behind us that separated our car from the next, burst open. The loud trio from the platform in Hampden pushed into our car, apparently on an illegal march through the L train.

"I'm right behind you fucker. Keep on moving."

"Hey ya'll, no one is here neither."

"Like I said, boy, keep moving."

Ken and I looked over our shoulders to watch the three make their way up the aisle, forcing standing passengers to press against seats. When they arrived at the far end of the car, at the sign that said, "No Passing Between Cars," they opened the door to the next car letting in more noise as the train rattled along. The door slammed shut behind them, and a group sigh of relief followed. If the three young men's mission that day was to reinforce a negative stereotype, they succeeded.

"Addison. Addison is next. Wrigley Field."

Ken and I looked at each other, smiled and stood up. Grandpa craned his neck to look over the back of his seat. "Let's go boys."

We exited the crowded train, along with hundreds of others, and fell into a line for the stairway that emerged at Addison Street. The crowd herded west to Sheffield Avenue. Shielding my eyes from the unconfident early April sunlight, now directly overhead, I found myself looking at the high walls of Wrigley Field. In the midst of small apartment buildings, it appeared to rise organically right out of the sidewalks.

The noise of street vendors and traffic police whistles streaked through the thin spring air. Upon approaching the ballpark, the bulging throng narrowed at the turnstiles.

I adjusted my eyes to the shadows as we entered the concourse around the stadium. Grandpa bought three program books. I was looking forward to showing Melva how to fill in the information for today's game. It was my usual habit to update the scorecard, until about the fourth inning when I inevitably would lose interest.

We emerged into daylight, and approached the boxes that weren't far above the first base line and the opponent's dugout. My senses gorged on the sights and sounds of Wrigley Field coming to life, for the game that was still an hour away. Unlike the tiny front lawns outside the park, the April grass was emerald green, although the legendary vines that climbed the red bricks were still bare. Scattered players from both teams casually tossed balls, while the familiar voice of the announcer and the booming chords from the organ welcomed us.

The half empty seats would be filled by game time. We continued to walk down the aisle, and I understood why Grandpa had kept the location of our seats a secret.

"Grandpa, did we really get such good seats? This is so cool. Can you believe this?" I looked back at Ken who was smiling broadly.

I felt like royalty as the Andy Frain usher stood aside, and we took our seats just three rows up from the field. I sat between Melva and Ken. We set our lunches at our feet, and I immediately opened my program book to show Melva how to use hers. But when I looked up at Melva, she was looking elsewhere. In fact, she was looking everywhere. Her eyes moved up and down as they took in the entire scene at the ballpark. From the flags fluttering high above Waveland and Sheffield Avenues to the white numbers painted on the red bricks across the field, Melva scooped it up in her arms, and splashed it over herself with relish. Her head shook slowly back and forth, and she seemed to be humming softly. I decided to leave her alone for a few minutes. The announcer encouraged us to welcome our home team, and the Cubs made their official entrance onto the field. We stood up cheering, and I pointed out the players to Melva.

"There's Billy Williams, and that's Santo and Beckert, and that's Kenny Holtzman who's pitching today, and look Melva, number 14! Ernie Banks!" I had never been as excited at a ballgame. Through Melva's eyes, I was seeing the Cubs for the first time.

Melva had a hand over her heart as she followed her hero's steps across the field.

"Come on, Glen, let's get his autograph!" Ken shouted as he took off down the aisle towards the wall along the field. I grabbed Melva's program book and my mitt, and followed Ken.

Other boys waving mitts, programs, and baseballs toward the first baseman joined us. Ernie Banks smiled and waved as we pleaded with him to come over to the wall. We cheered spontaneously as he trotted over to us.

I made futile attempts to cajole autographs from players before, but this time I had a head start from our VIP seats. I was stunned as Ernie Banks took the program out of my extended hand, signed it, and handed it back to me. He continued granting autographs for a few more minutes, and the crowd grew. I panicked. The program book was for Melva, but he hadn't signed my mitt. I encouraged him to look at me again, but I couldn't recapture his attention.

"Okay kids, that's all for today. Thanks for coming out. Let's play ball," said our idol as he headed back to his pedestal at first base. There were groans of disappointment, but not from Ken, who had a signed mitt.

We proudly marched up the aisle with our booty, and returned to our seats. Inner conflict dimmed my enthusiasm. "Look, Grandpa. Melva, look. He signed the program book, Ernie Banks. Right here. See? Ernie Banks. He looked right at me. I touched his hand when he handed the program back to me. He's a really nice guy."

"Yeah and look, he signed my mitt right here," Ken proudly displayed the signature.

"Wonderful, boys. Now what are you going to do with that program book, Glen? It's a very important souvenir, isn't it?"

Grandpa was up to something, and I wasn't happy about it. I assessed my position. My plan was to have Ernie sign the program book for Melva, and the mitt for me. I wanted that signature. It held a status. I glanced at Grandpa who was looking at me expectantly. I knew what he wanted me to do, and for an instant I was angry with him, but I turned to Melva.

"Here Melv, this is your book. Ernie Banks signed it for you."

Melva's joy permeated my skin, and filled every cell in my body, leaving no perch for regret. She gently rubbed one hand over the signature as she held the book. She slipped it under her jacket, and told me she didn't want to write in it, but she would watch me fill out my program book.

Kenny Holtzman pitched a great game. The man who sat in the centerfield scoreboard came out several times to add runs for the Cubs as the innings progressed. By the top of the eighth inning, when Montreal was down six to one, shadows had completely overtaken the fragile sunlight. With cold indifference to the date, the air at Wrigley Field turned wintry.

Seasoned Cubs fans held their breath until the last out, but Melva's first game was a Cubs victory. We stayed for the last out. Grandpa said that when the Cubs were ahead, even by seven runs, you had to stay until the end, or you might be sadly surprised when you got home.

The crowd around us was animated by the win. Before leaving the stands for the gloominess of the concourse, Melva stopped and looked back at the field once more, as if trying to memorize it.

We moved in unison with the crowds east on Addison to the L station, and climbed the stairs. Melva, a cigarette dangling from her lips, held the railing as she huffed her way up the steps. Her program book was safely tucked under the top of her dress next to her bosom. She thanked Grandpa again, gave Ken a hug, and then she and I embraced as I kissed her on her cheek.

"I'll see you on Monday, Baby," she said as she entered the waiting southbound train. Grandpa, Ken, and I entered the northbound train on the other side of the platform.

There were random sounds of laughter at times from various quarters on the L car, but in spite of the victory, the atmosphere was more subdued than the ride to Wrigley Field. Somewhere between Addison Street and Evans Avenue, evening had arrived. We stood the entire way to Evans Avenue where we changed trains for the Hampden L. Before we boarded, Grandpa used a pay phone to alert Mom of our pending arrival.

The cream colored Buick Skylark pulled up, just as we stepped onto the sidewalk.

"Perfect timing. Did you have a good time, boys? Your dad told me they won easily," Mom said over her shoulder, while Ken and I slid into the back seat.

"Yep. Great game. They really looked good." I tried to sound like more of a fan than I was.

"Yeah, really good," Ken echoed.

"The boys got autographs from Ernie Banks," Grandpa added.

"You did? That's wonderful." Mom drove the car west towards Michigami.

"Yeah. He signed my mitt," Ken offered.

"Wonderful! Did you get your mitt signed, Glen?"

"He signed my program, and I gave it to Melva," I said seeking approval for my *mitzvah*.

"Oh, she must have been thrilled to get that. That's wonderful. Did she enjoy herself?" Clearly Mom didn't recognize the extent of my sacrifice.

"I think she really did," Grandpa responded.

"Well that's good. You did a *mitzvah* taking Melva to that game," Mom said to all three of us.

"What are we doing tonight?" I asked.

"I thought we'd have dinner at Max and Moe's instead of eating last night's leftovers, and then we'd go to see that Doris Day movie at The Hampden. It's called *With Six You Get Eggroll.*

"Are Mother and I included in these plans?" Grandpa asked.

"Yeah, Dad. Ma wants to go, so you're going. Kenny, would you like to join us? We can ask your mother when we stop at your house. Instead of dropping you off, you can come with us."

I looked at Ken, hopefully.

"Oh thanks, but I'm supposed to go with my parents to some relatives' house tonight."

"Where are you going?" I asked Ken, almost insulted.

"To my stupid cousin's house in Morton Grove. You know my dumb cousin Mark who wears white socks with his regular shoes?"

We pulled into the driveway of Ken's house, which I thought was prettier than our house, at least until I grew older, and developed a sophisticated palate. Ken's house was gaudy. The typical suburban tri-level home, with the neatly manicured lawn. The facade glowed brightly from the colored floodlights hidden behind the bushes in front of the house. Draperies, with thick gold ropes holding them back, framed the large, picture window. The address over the garage was written out in an elegant script. Inside, thick, powder blue, shag carpeting covered the floors of the living room and dining room. The furnishings were white with gilding, and covered in powder blue velvet fabrics in imitation Louis XIV. A chandelier, heavy with fake crystal prisms hung over the dining room table.

Ken's mother opened the front door as we pulled up, and she stepped outside to wave at us. She was attractive and slender, mid-forties, and appeared to be dressed and made up to go out for the evening. She wore a dark blue pants suit, with flared pants and black patent leather shoes, and adorned herself with southwest style turquoise jewelry. She waved, smiled, and mouthed a "thank you" toward Mom.

"You're welcome," Mom said through her open window. "He was a perfect angel, as always." I wondered how Mom knew, since she hadn't been with us all day.

"I hope it didn't cost too much to feed him," Ken's mother shouted back.

"Don't be silly. It's our pleasure. Anytime."

Ken slipped into his house behind his mother.

CHAPTER THIRTY-ONE

The Same Evening

We piled into the Buick, and headed to Max and Moe's Delicatessen on Lester Street in Michigami; an unplanned hodgepodge of strip centers and stand-alone fast food restaurants. Narrow parking lots squeezed between the sidewalks and the buildings screamed, "no one gave a damn about aesthetics."

In the western sky, a dawdling pale orange that the night had not yet swallowed, served as a backdrop to deep purple clouds and a knot of electrical cables, telephone wires, and TV antennas. Nancy's romantic sensibilities were offended, and she bemoaned the contrast of the sunset, which might have been beautiful, before our hometown was developed, with its fluorescent street lights, tangled cords, isolated trees, and low rooftops.

"It's all hideously unromantic."

Dad attempted to maneuver the car into the small lot alongside the restaurant.

"Look at that Cadillac pulling in right in front of us. You can barely see the backs of their heads over the seats," Dad said to no one and everyone.

"You can see her big red hair sticking up," Nancy said.

"Yes, and he's wearing a hat, which means he's a terrible driver," Mom added.

"What do you mean?" Grandma asked.

"It's my observation that men who wear hats when they drive are terrible, slow, oblivious drivers. All my lady friends agree with me," Ma said matter-of-factly.

"I think that's because the only men who wear hats nowadays are old in years or in spirit, and their driving skills aren't what they used to be," Grandpa contributed.

"They're mostly old Jews around here," Nancy said. "If you see a Cadillac driven by a man in a hat, that's double trouble."

Grandma laughed. "I never heard of such a thing. Did you Leo?"

Grandpa chuckled. "I'm not surprised. It makes me think of my brother Irv."

"Perfect example, Grandpa," Nancy said.

There were two angled spaces next to each other, and the Cadillac in front of us made two painfully slow, unsuccessful attempts to maneuver into one of them. With the behemoth straddling two spaces, the little captain was satisfied. The engine stopped, and the driver's door opened.

"Is he crazy? He's got both spaces? Where are we supposed to park?" Dad was incredulous.

A small foot in shiny, oxblood loafers led the emergence of a short, blue and red checkered pant leg out of the open door. Then the open-collared, white shirt under a dark blue sport coat followed. A similar revelation came out of the passenger side where there emerged a leaning tower of dyed red hair overlooking large, rhinestone choked glasses that rested on a powdered nose. A bright green dress peaked out from beyond the hemline of a belted car coat, stopping short enough to reveal a short but surprisingly shapely leg that came to an abrupt halt upon disappearing into sensible, rubber-soled shoes. The two delicatessen-bound seniors were oblivious to our car that sat askew in the parking lot, its entry into the now blocked second space aborted.

"Now don't make a scene, Jerry. We probably know half the people here," Mom cautioned.

"I'm not going to make any scene."

"Run them over, Dad. You only get ten points because they're old, but it's still points," I urged.

"Glen, *Tatala*, what kind of talk is that? Grandpa and I are probably older than they are. Would you want someone to say that about us?"

"It's only a joke, Grandma. My friends and I give points for pretending to hit people who get in front of your car."

"In my day, that wouldn't be considered so funny." She shook her head.

I looked at Nancy and rolled my eyes.

Dad opened his window and leaned out. "Excuse me. Excuse me." There was no response from the plodding couple that had locked arms as they met up behind their Cadillac. "*Excuuuuuuse me, Sir.*" Dad said loudly. This got a response as the two looked up to see where the voice was coming from. When they saw Dad was indeed trying to get their attention, they smiled broadly, and the woman waved at us. Although they couldn't really see into the dark interior of the car, they assumed they knew us. After all, this was Max and Moe's Delicatessen, the Jewish watering hole of our Serengeti Plain. Nancy and I burst out laughing.

"To whom is she waving?" Grandma wanted to know.

Dad opened his door, got out, and walked over to the little couple who greeted him warmly. Dad gestured towards the lines of the parking space, and the couple turned around to look where he pointed. They shrugged. The next thing we saw was the elderly man hand Dad his keys, and step aside. Dad parked their car squarely within the yellow lines, and handed the keys back to the man who smiled as he shook Dad's hand. The happy couple turned once again toward our car, waved, and slowly spun around, and plodded arm in arm to the restaurant. "Those people are why other people don't like Jews," Nancy said suddenly.

"Why is that, Nancy? They're harmless and they were actually quite charming," Mom responded with amazement.

"Don't you see how they look to non-Jews? They drive a big Cadillac, dress to excess, and then park their car oblivious to everyone else. That seemed totally rude. It says, 'as long as *we're* comfortable, to heck with anyone else.'"

"So, are those such crimes? This is a reason to hate people? Have they hurt anybody?" Grandma asked.

"No, but if someone already doesn't like Jews, this would give them more reasons to dislike us." Nancy answered her critics. "You don't see older gentiles in Hampden dressed like that, driving big Cadillacs, and not caring how they park."

"What do you see?" Grandpa asked quietly.

"I don't know. They just look more tasteful, and act more modest."

"Nancy, you sound like a snob," Mom said.

"She sounds anti-Semitic to me." Grandma added.

"Well, why do they all have to drive those big Cadillacs?" Nancy persisted. Older Gentiles seem to drive Fords."

"Fords? Do you know why Jews don't drive Fords?" Mom asked, sounding almost angry. "Because when I was a girl, Henry Ford would accuse the Jews of causing all of America's problems. He sponsored Father Coughlin's radio program, which was a platform for spewing Hitler's anti-Jewish ideas. He funded the printing of those books, "The Protocols of The Elders of Zion," all over the world spreading lies about Jews drinking the blood of Christian children to make Passover matzah, and that Jews conspired to take over the world. You want to buy a Ford from that family? No thank you. No decent person, Jew or Gentile should buy a car from a man like that."

This was new information for me. I thought of all of our Catholic neighbors and their Fords from the McNamara dealership in Michigami. Grandpa watched for Nancy's response that was not forthcoming. Dad opened the door to get in, and the cool evening air that entered with him made me realize the air in the car had grown stale.

"Are they something? Characters." He shook his head. Dad effortlessly pulled into the parking space, and we entered Max and Moe's where Uncle Marty always noted in those pre-credit card days, "It's an all cash business. They make money hand over fist here." With the exception of Grandma and Grandpa, who were unlikely to recognize anyone there, we looked in all directions to scan the faces hunched over mountainous corned beef sandwiches. Standing between us and a booth or table was the hostess's stand and cash register manned by Moe's wife Evelyn. She always wore a black dress and open-toed, pink house slippers that clicked as they flapped with her every step. Mom knew Evelyn through a mahjong club. Next to the cash register, gum and mints were displayed, along with charity collection cans that promoted research to cure various diseases.

To the left was a separate room with the delicatessen counter. People were lined up, looking resentfully at anyone holding a lower number as they waited to buy lox, bagels, cream cheese, smoked fish, onions, and the other staples for a Sunday morning brunch.

Dark, veneered walls enclosed the restaurant. Gold vinyl booths with wood veneer frames lined the perimeter of the room, and dark brown Formica topped tables and chairs cushioned with gold vinyl pads filled the open space. Amber colored glass sconces lined the walls, while matching lanterns hung from the ceiling. The room was alive with animated conversation, punctuated with cackling laughter. Over it all hung a thin cloud of cigarette smoke.

Evelyn smiled at Mom. "I see you've got your whole *mispacha* with you tonight. That's nice. Six of you, Dolly?"

Mom gave a closed mouth smile back to Evelyn. "That's right. How are you?"

"I could use a seat right about now, but otherwise, I'm not complaining. Who would listen anyhow?"

Mom laughed weakly, and Grandma, who never missed out on a conversation, nodded in agreement.

Evelyn gathered six plastic, slightly sticky menus, and handed them to Helen, indicating the round table as ours. Helen, like our waitress at The Gold Coin on New Years Eve, was from central casting for diner waitresses.

I could see my mother deciding if we could accept this first offer of a table, but knowing their clientele, Max and Moe had prepared for protesters, and it seemed no table was near a door, a draft, a bathroom, the kitchen, or the stand for dirty dishes. The lighting over the tables was uniform. The only choice was booth or table, and for our party of six, the table was the right choice. Seeing that the table had no visible dirt, and the chairs appeared to be dry, Mom silently accepted our assignment.

"Someone could wipe the *schmootz* off of these menus once in a while. It isn't as if they're giving away the food here." Grandma clucked, helping to make Mom feel better about having accepted the first table offered to us.

Mom's eyes roamed the room. "There's a draft here, isn't there? Is it from the door or is there a vent here?"

I overestimated Max and Moe's attempt at preemptive thinking.

"Should we move, Honey?" Dad asked attentively.

"Ma, that is so typical," Nancy said sounding more annoyed than Mom.

"What's typical? Be quiet, will you already, Nancy? Aren't you cold Mother?" Mom looked to Grandma for a rare moment of commiseration between the two.

"What did I do?" Grandma asked, having heard her name but nothing else.

"Aren't you cold, Mother? Isn't there a draft?" Mom asked again.

Grandma shrugged. Apparently she didn't feel it, missing the chance to agree with Mom about something. "As long as I don't feel it on my neck. I would hate to wind up with a stiff neck."

"You guys, please. You sound so typically Jewish again." Nancy persisted.

"We are Jewish, in case you didn't notice." Mom snapped. "And you are too, Miss. And what? We aren't allowed to comment on a draft?"

"Why is it we can never just sit down and eat without complaining about something? There is always something wrong with the table we get, anywhere we go." Nancy looked down into her menu, avoiding the confrontation her words were likely to provoke.

"That's not true, is it, Jerry?" Mom suddenly seemed unsure and unhappy about the stereotype.

"Is what, Dear?" Now Dad's face was buried in his menu. "What are you getting, son?"

"Corned beef on rye and a chocolate phosphate," I said quickly.

"Sounds good to me," Dad said, putting his arm around my shoulders, and pulling me in closer for a brief hug.

"Daaaaaaad, cut it out," I whined, though I secretly loved when Dad displayed affection.

"Daaaaaaad, cut it out," he mimicked me as he gently rubbed my head with his knuckles, and grimaced, pretending to make it hurt.

If Dad's plan was to distract Mom and Nancy from their tiff, it worked. We ate our meal in relative peace.

After dinner, I enjoyed the movie, which starred Doris Day. I was unaware that I identified with her, and not the male lead.

CHAPTER THIRTY-TWO

Monday, April 20, 1970

My bar mitzvah present from Uncle Marty and Aunt Marion was a Schwinn, three-speed, twenty-six inch bicycle. It was a bit tall for me, and much faster than the neon blue Stingray it replaced. My neighbor David said I should've asked for a ten-speed, but I found a choice of ten speeds intimidating, and I didn't understand their purpose. I lived in the Prairie State, and even our sledding hills were man-made.

We were well into April, and spring was no longer a meaning-less date on the calendar. The mild weather meant I could ride my bike to school where I kept it locked to the bike rack.

After school I rode my bike to Sandberg's drugstore. Sandberg's was like Max and Moe's without the food. All the Jews from the surrounding area had their prescriptions filled by Bill Sandberg, a frustrated Borscht Belt comedian. Bill's sister-in-law, Bess, sold perfumes and cosmetics, while working the cash register, and there was never more than two degrees of separation between patrons. Bess was the woman I'd shamefully faced back when I returned the stolen comic book.

At the little shopping strip near our house, people rushed in and out of Sandberg's, Grandma's beauty shop, Solly's Cleaners and Tailoring, and the grocery store, in anticipation of sundown and the beginning of Passover. We were a later day version of the Jews of Anatevkah preparing for the Sabbath.

I jumped off my bike, and left it unlocked (this was Michigami, and not Hampden) against the side of the building. As I approached the glass door to Sandberg's, the reflected sunlight prevented me from seeing the man on the other side as he prepared to exit. I pulled, he pushed, and we bumped into each other.

I'd seen this man at Sandberg's many times; usually he bought a Yiddish newspaper. During short-sleeve weather, the numbers tattooed on his arm identified him as a Holocaust survivor. There were many in Michigami.

"Sorry," I mumbled as I pulled back. I didn't look directly at him, because his damaged face made me uncomfortable. An ugly scar on his left cheek descended from the patched socket that once held his eyeball. I rushed passed him to the magazine racks and the familiar face of Alfred E. Neuman.

Looking over the latest *Mad Magazine,* I quickly forgot about the man with the soft white hair that peeked out from under his ever-present blue cap, and the light blue eye that seemed to search in all directions for its lost partner. When I did remember him, I knew enough to be thankful for where and when I was born.

Back home, Grandma, Mom, Melva, and Matzah were tripping over each other in the kitchen. Passover, with its special recipes and food restrictions meant stress for Grandma, and everyone in her orbit. She dictated assignments to her two sous-chefs as she examined the contents of the various cast iron pots on the stove and the pans in the oven.

The dining room table was set with our finest dishware, along with the *Seder* plate and other items that were brought out for only this holiday. On each chair lay a *Haggadah* that we would recite from as we retold the story of the Exodus. For my family Judaism was focused on social justice and the dignity of every human being, so Passover was a goldmine of material for teaching Jewish values. Mom, Dad, and Grandpa mined it thoroughly.

The usual cast of characters sat around the table: both sets of grandparents; Uncle Marty, Aunt Marion and their kids; and Aunt Lilly.

Grandpa Leo was the undisputed leader of our *Seder*, but he let Zadie handle the traditional Hebrew blessings. We took turns reading. Mom and Grandpa emphasized how our struggle for freedom from bondage represented every person's struggle for his own freedom, with a particular emphasis on the civil rights movement in America, and the plight of Jews in the Soviet Union.

When we got to the ten plagues, Nancy and Rob smirked the first couple of times the reader said, "and Moses stretched out his *rod...*" I finally understood what they were smirking about.

As Grandpa had reminded me on New Year's Eve, during the recitation of the ten plagues, per tradition, we removed ten drops of wine from our cups to symbolize a reduction in our joy. This was to acknowledge the suffering of the Egyptians who drowned in the Red Sea.

Aunt Lilly said this was just one more thing that aggravated her. Here we are in the midst of celebrating delivery from 400 years of slavery, and we pause to think of the suffering of our captors. "Who else but us Jews would do such a thing? Would our enemies give us a second thought?"

We didn't know that in three years, on Yom Kippur, our holiest day, Egypt would once again attack Israel.

She humphed with indignation and we continued.

CHAPTER THIRTY-THREE

Friday, April 24, 1970

A warm April day in Chicago has a balmy feel to it. The warmth cooked our pubescent hormones, and at lunch a group of us went out to the field, and played Red Rover. George, Carlotta, Tanya, and Charles—four of the black kids in my class—were among our group, and I noticed with approval this display of successful integration.

The call went out: *Red Rover, Red Rover, let Glen come over.* I called on my considerable speed to build momentum. My neurotransmitters interpreted any physical or mental challenge, as a life or death situation. To live with a public display of defeat would mean years of agonizing rumination and replays of, "if only." I could've played it safe, and targeted the grip between two girls, but that'd be a pathetic choice. Attempting to breaking the link between two boys came with uncertainty; I could never cope with uncertainty, so I settled for the middle path and easily broke a boy-girl bond. Good cheer wafted on the wind that day, and calls of encouragement arose from both sides of the field.

To my joy, George Adams said something about how, "that boy should've joined track."

Those first warm days allowed us to explore the relationships that had been developing under the fluorescent lights of winter. The sun foretold of good things to come. My friendship with Barbara would surely grow in the warm light of spring. I exuberantly circled back in my shirtsleeves, and took Barbara Needleman's hand. My trophy willingly followed me back to my team's side of the field.

At the end of the day, the windbreaker Grandma insisted I wear that morning was a burden, so I tied it around my waist. I strode over to the bike rack filled with Friday afternoon anticipation. Ken and I had plans to go to a movie on Saturday with Barbara and Sandy. My good cheer even shielded me from the irritation of two large black girls from the eighth grade who stared me down angrily in the hallway on my way to my locker, refusing me berth. Without word or expression, I let them pass.

I felt suddenly sick to my stomach as I neared the bike rack, and saw the empty space where my bike should've been. I knew immediately what happened, because the broken combination lock and chain were on the ground next to the bike rack. My good mood and positive energy were extinguished, replaced by outrage, exacerbated by impotence. "Damn them!"

A few kids mounting their bikes nearby stopped and looked at me. The faces I knew, the names I didn't.

"Someone stole my bike," I said angrily, to no one in particular. I didn't get a response beyond a few blank stares, some tongue clucking, and shakes of the head as they all continued on their way. I was today's sacrifice.

"You definitely need a good lock around here, advised one before he pedaled away. "You should report this."

I picked up the defeated chain and lock, and ran back in the building on a mission.

"Here, fill out this form. Do you need me to call someone to give you a ride home?" The indifference of the black lady behind the desk couldn't have been more evident. I wanted someone to hug me, and share in my indignation. Instead I received a bureaucratic response. I imagined she was protecting the thief, possibly her relative.

My friends were long gone leaving me to walk home alone. I wasn't looking forward to telling Mom and Dad about the theft. A little pity would've been nice, but I didn't want them getting worked up, and igniting another heated discussion on race and crime at my school. Was I growing up? Here I was, willing to give up sympathy and consolation from the grown ups who loved me, in order to avoid upsetting them, and causing a heated family discussion.

As I approached the canal bridge out of Hampden, my thoughts were interrupted when something sailed past the left side of my head. It was immediately followed by something similar that just missed my right ear as it flew by. I felt a sting at the base of my neck just at the line of my collar. I whipped around to see three black kids, maybe a year younger than I was, on the other side of the street. They were throwing 45-rpm records like Frisbees, trying to slice cuts in the necks of passersby. Their poor aim and my shirt collar saved me, but not a white kid from high school sailing his bike west out of Hampden toward the bridge to Michigami. A disk flew into the spokes, and he went flying over the handlebars, falling on the pavement. His bike lay in the street. I ran over to him as cars stopped, and people jumped out. The three assailants disappeared at the sight of angry, white adults.

The boy was dazed, and there was blood on his hands. A man threw the bike in his car, and took the boy somewhere, presumably home or to a hospital. I hurried home.

I arrived home bike-less, and at our Shabbat dinner, the theft of the bike caused the stir that I hoped to avoid. I didn't even mention the whirling records.

"We didn't buy that bike for Glen so that some damned hooligan could ride it around. This makes me really angry." Uncle Marty's brows gathered tensely above his nose. He glanced in the kitchen presumably to make sure Melva wasn't there. "Let me guess who stole it. Some black kid no doubt. You're never disappointed when you expect nothing but the worst of them. Assholes."

Eyebrows were raised. Grandpa reacted quickly. "Marty, please edit your comments. What you said is unnecessary, false, and it won't help Glen get his bike back." Everyone played his usual part in these discussions. Mom and Grandpa bent over backwards to rationalize. Uncle Marty represented something closer to my own feelings, and I felt guilty for siding with him against Mom and Grandpa. Dad looked uncomfortable trying to walk a line between the two groups. Zadie's balled up fist made an appearance. Grandma and Bubbie talked about the end of civil society, and the cost of food.

Uncle Marty didn't back down. "Dad, when will you admit it? Blacks have a problem with criminal behavior way beyond their numbers. I'm sick of the censorship. Until we can lay everything on the table, and whites can talk honestly about their feelings, without fear of stepping on oversensitive toes, the race dialogue will get nowhere in this country. In the meantime, Glen's bike was stolen, and the solution is for Eileen and Jerry to admit their cause is lost, take the kids, and get the hell out of this neighborhood once and for all. Everyone blames white flight on the whites, when the truth isn't all about hatred of blacks. It's fear based on experience, whether firsthand or observed. It is *not* irrational. I repeat: it is *not* irrational behavior to want to shield your loved ones, and protect your assets.

"My kids have never had a damn thing stolen at school or on the way to school or coming home from school. They've never been threatened. Yes, there're plenty of spoiled brats who could use a swift kick in the ass, but no budding gangsters. Who needs that nonsense? Why even *try* to play nice with them?"

Uncle Marty looked from Grandpa to Mom, who said nothing, so he continued. "You think that your noble talk is ever going to change them? They don't understand your high-falootin talk. They have their own agenda, and it's going to make all of you bleeding hearts look like fools when they don't live up to your expectations, and they kick you in the ass, and take your lunch money, so to speak. I say don't play with them at all, until they grow up, and act responsibly. I'm not talking about their kids. I'm not saying oppress them or stand in their way, either. I'm saying get out of their way, and you'll see, they'll languish and kill each other, and continue to blame you. And like self-hating fools you'll agree with them! I say divorce yourselves from them completely. You remind me of the Jews who find every reason they can to blame themselves for millennia of atrocities."

Rather than address Uncle Marty's words, which in another place and time might have provoked an intense response, Dad moved quickly to pragmatism.

"Marty, don't worry. Our homeowner's policy will cover the bike. We never did claim Nancy's coat. Maybe we could claim them both now, and that will be enough to make it worthwhile to pay the deductible."

"Never you mind, Jerry. Marty and I will buy a new bike, right Marty?" Aunt Marion looked with hope at Uncle Marty.

"Yeah, yeah. Don't worry, Glen, we'll get you the same bike. And this time we'll get you a black-proof lock too." Uncle Marty snorted, and I smiled at him. Mom was horrified and momentarily stunned into silence—but only momentarily.

"Marty, enough already. Let's not make matters worse by impugning a whole race, because some kid stole Glen's bike. I'm unhappy about it too, believe me. But these incidents don't have to be blown up into bigger issues. And stop with the talk of the neighborhood already. Nobody is moving anywhere." Mom looked at Dad for confirmation that didn't come, so she looked to Grandpa who still looked disheartened by Uncle Marty's tirade.

"Marty, you can't run from the world and hide from its problems," Grandpa said. If you aren't part of the solution, you're part of the problem. We *are* our brother's keepers. We Jews should know that better than anyone."

"Aw, Dad, please. Those things sound nice, until you get mugged or beaten. Whether it's from centuries of slavery or segregation I don't know, but the truth of the matter is, a lot of our black brothers don't seem ready to take their place among us as law-abiding, hard-working, responsible Americans, and if you look at what's happening to our great cities, it seems to be getting worse, not better. Can you imagine here in the United States of America, in the middle of the twentieth century there are whole parts of our major cities that none of us could walk into, without facing the high risk of being beaten or murdered simply because we're white? And yet, they're still beefing about the old laws that kept them out of white neighborhoods, and we're still apologizing. Isn't it horribly ironic?"

Again, Uncle Marty took the silence as a signal to continue. "Of course I'm not talking about a whole race, but enough of them to make one want to give up trying to help. God helps those who help themselves. I say let's give it a shot."

"Hey, do we always have to talk about these things? Can't we talk about something fun for a change? These dinners are depressing." Nancy looked around the table.

"Leave it to my Nancela to make sense," Bubbie offered.

And with that the state of race relations in America was completely swept aside for a discussion on fashion. Like any heated argument in the family, it came to an abrupt halt, and in seconds not a trace of it hung in the air. I wondered to where all of those thoughts and questions evaporated. Did they drift in the ether somewhere, until someone snatched them back?

Aunt Marion was wearing a pants suit, and Amy was wearing a midi-skirt. As with the subject of race in America, everyone had an opinion about fashion.

Bubbie sounded flustered. "First, mini, then maxi, and now midi. *Vey iz meer.* Who can keep up?

"Not me. I gave up a long time ago. My stockings still have seams." Aunt Lilly looked around with a smile to indicate she was making a joke. I smiled obligingly.

Bubbie continued. "Things change so fast now. It seems everyday somewhere someone is trying to change something else in the world. Things that we thought would be the same forever now last two weeks. In the past I didn't change a hemline for fifteen years. I wish the world would slow down."

I agreed with Bubbie. What was cool today wouldn't be cool tomorrow. Falling behind wasn't an option—unless a kid wanted to risk the scorn of his peers. Unseen and unknown forces worked to change every aspect of life, and make it modern (i.e. cool) or just different from how it was yesterday or years ago.

I associated the rise of these forces to the historically linked assassination of President Kennedy and the appearance of The Beatles on *The Ed Sullivan Show*. These transforming events took place less than three months apart, and as if floodgates opened, the old rules began to fall almost daily, and the rate of change picked up velocity.

The junior high cafeteria walls were lined with enlarged black and white photographs of dances held only eight years earlier. The kids looked hopelessly out of date. Girls had roughed hair, and dresses that ballooned over petticoats. The guys wore horn-rimmed glasses, crew cuts, sport coats, and neckties!

Change for the sake of change was viewed as positive, and the rate of change brought unease to many, and widened what the media called "the generation gap," as well as the distance between hippies and rednecks.

Feeling unsettled about my identity, and not knowing where all the rapid change was leading made me anxious and fearful. An increasing openness about sex would surely cause the discovery of my secret sexual desires, and leave me shunned. I couldn't conceive of the idea that the easing of sexual mores would eventually lead to my liberation. In 1970 there was no deliverance from my torment on the horizon. Listening to my elders talking about the calm certainty of their "day and age" left me wistful and nostalgic for a time I never knew.

The next month, I saw an older black kid in downtown Hampden on my bike. On the handlebar bell was a "Property of Glen" sticker that I had placed there with pride. I didn't chase him. Nothing positive could have come from the encounter if I caught up with him. The confirmation that the thief was black fed my growing animosity.

CHAPTER THIRTY-FOUR

Saturday, April 25, 1970

The girls wanted to see *Airport*. Ken and I didn't care what we saw. We were too caught up in the excitement of having a sort of date.

Sandy's mother didn't think Sandy was old enough to date, even if it was a matinee, so Sandy didn't mention to her mother that Ken and I would be there. Barbara's mother must've had a soft spot for me, because she told Barbara, "If by chance Glen is there, it's okay to sit together, as long as you behave like ladies and gentlemen." She planned to pick up Barbara and Sandy as soon as the movie ended.

"Can you believe about my bike?" I asked Ken on the way to our rendezvous. The bus rolled past the small Michigami ranch houses.

"What'd your parents say? Are you getting a new one?"

"I can tell they were mad, but they acted like it was no big deal. You know my parents. I think they're afraid to show anger about the black kids at school, because it might make me prejudiced."

"Oh, then I suppose you didn't tell them the joke about the black physicist. Ha!"

"Yeah, right. I don't think that would've gone over too well. My Uncle Marty would've liked it. He was really mad about my bike. He and my aunt were the ones who bought it for me. They said they'd get me another one."

"School would be really boring without the black kids. You know what I mean? They're always making something happen to keep things funny in class, like the other day when Derrick Dawson squeezed that orange on Jeff Fink's head."

"Ha. Poor Jeff. Yeah, he was really cased."

Ken changed the subject. "You think they'll be there? I mean you think Sandy and Barbara are going to show up at noon?"

"Yeah. Why not? Barbara and Sandy told their mothers they wanted to shop around PrairieVille before the movie, so that they could get dropped off there, at around eleven o'clock, then we can head over to the movie together. We just have to remember to split up after the movie, before Barbara's mother sees us."

"Sandy's mother's so damned old-fashioned. It makes Sandy seem like a prude, but it's all her mother. She treats Sandy like a fifth grader. Ha! Her tits aren't like any fifth grader. That's probably what her mother's worried about. Or maybe it's her father. I never thought of that."

"Hey, I was wondering how long it would take before you brought up Sandy's breasts." I never felt comfortable using the word "tits." I still don't.

"Well, I was wondering how long before they were felt up. Get it?"

We laughed, and I nervously looked around to make sure no one was looking at us disapprovingly. Any number of older women on this bus would be shocked by our conversation.

"So, are you going to do that stretch thing, and put your arm around her?" I asked Ken.

The night before, my stomach felt like it did at the starting line for a race in gym class. I went over the different ways I could act around Barbara at the movie, and tried to anticipate the various outcomes. Most of my friends and their families believed that going to a movie with a girl was a date, and that thirteen was too young, so I wasn't sure how to act. Even if it were a date, I didn't know if it was all right to put my arm around Barbara at the mall where there were likely to be people we knew.

Barbara remained a riddle to me. Although we never officially talked about going steady, she treated me like a steady boyfriend in the few ways available to us. She sat next to me at school when it was practical. She mostly chose me to dance with during "snowballs," at bar mitzvah parties. She stayed with me at school after I'd been Maced. Most importantly, she made out with me at Pam's and subsequent parties; Barbara was not a girl who took making out lightly. Yet I doubted Barbara's commitment to being my girlfriend. Her schoolwork took precedence over exchanging notes with me, or talking with me in class, whereas I always put the opportunity to interact with Barbara ahead of anything else. Finally, there was the fact that Barbara never wanted to partake in any plan that meant lying to her parents about her whereabouts.

In any movies I'd seen about young lovers, the girls did anything to see their boyfriends. When my grandparents took me to see *Romeo and Juliet* two years earlier, Juliet lied to almost everyone. Of course Romeo and Juliet were a few years older than Barbara and I were, and they even slept together. I would've slept with the actor who played Romeo, in a second. I envied Juliet when I thought of the scene where they woke up together, clearly naked.

It was normal to want a girlfriend, and to fret over the relationship, and I wanted to be normal. Barbara needed to play her part to demonstrate that I was her man. If I lived in a world where her brother and I could be lovers, I'd send Barbara packing pretty quickly.

"I was thinking more like resting my arm on the armrest next to Sandy, and bending my elbows sort of like this," Ken demonstrated this technique in answer to my question, "so that my elbow might bump up against her tit. Or maybe I'll just put my hand on her leg."

I nodded, noting how every part of a girl's body was sexy to Ken, and then imagining how excited I would be if I were going out with Ben Rubin, and had the chance to touch his leg.

I thought of something Nancy and Marla talked about as they whispered and giggled. "Hey Ken, do you know the popcorn trick?"

"Nope. What is it?"

I felt very cool. "All right, you cut a hole in the bottom of a popcorn box, and hold the box in your lap. Then you shove your dick up into it, and offer your girlfriend some popcorn. Eventually she grabs you instead of the popcorn."

Ken exploded with a loud "Ha!" and added, "I love that idea." I loved his reaction. An elderly lady in the seat across the aisle turned to look at us. She shook her head back and forth, and then returned her gaze to the window, in time to see the community hospital glide by.

When I spotted Barbara and Sandy they were engrossed in conversation, sitting on a bench at the bus stop by Marshall Field's. A few butterflies launched themselves in my stomach. It wasn't Barbara specifically who had me excited, but the thought of being anyone's boyfriend, and in a position to build my popularity.

A breeze caused Barbara's silky hair to fly around her face, instead of resting calmly on her shoulders as it usually did. She tucked it behind her ears as she continued speaking. Sandy, who was known to be obsessed with her long, straight, brown tresses, took a hairbrush out of her purse, and began a futile attempt to defeat a spring wind in Chicagoland.

Ken and I stepped off the bus. Barbara and Sandy frantically whispered to each other, and stood up giggling. I instinctively put my hand over my pant's zipper to check if it was pulled up. It was.

"Hi."

"Hi."

"Hi."

"Hi."

From that inauspicious beginning, the conversation proceeded even more awkwardly. The girls related how they had been hungry, and decided to eat at Walgreen's lunch counter, instead of shopping.

I thought that Barbara's naturally pink lips were more attractive than Sandy's, which were covered in white lipstick.

"Well, we should head over to the theater." There I was, the ever-practical one trying to keep the world under control.

We made our way through the outdoor mall amid a myriad of colorful spring flowers. Barbara occasionally attempted to keep her hair tucked behind her ears, while Sandy continued to clutch her hairbrush. At one point I noticed Ken place his hand on Sandy's back guiding her across a little bridge that arced over a small, decorative pond.

The movie theater stood like a painted, white brick island rising out from a dark asphalt sea. As we approached the box office, I realized that Ken and I never discussed whether or not we were going to treat the girls to the movie.

I knew boys were supposed to treat their dates, but this wasn't really a date. We made our plans as part of a discussion in class among the four of us. I didn't call Barbara to ask her to go out on a date. We were just four friends going to a movie. I never paid for Gary or Ken. But Barbara wasn't just a friend. She was kind of my girlfriend, wasn't she?

I tried to get Ken's attention, but he was busy entertaining Sandy with a story about his brother's protest activities at Kent State. The box office loomed.

"Ken, can I talk to you?" Ken and Sandy stopped and turned to look at me.

"Huh?"

"I need to ask you something."

"What is it?"

"Um, could you come over here for a second?" I jerked my head to direct Ken to move in toward me. "Can you guys give us a second?"

Barbara and Sandy looked at each other, and shrugged.

"Okay. Sure." They stepped to the side putting distance between us, and whispered to each other, which made me queasy. Mine was not a cool move, but I didn't know what else to do. I wished I were home listening to Grandma and Aunt Gussie reminisce.

We were Ricky and Fred trying to hold a conference behind Lucy and Ethel's backs. I leaned in to Ken, and asked frantically about who was supposed to pay for the movie.

"Hmmm. Didn't think about that, and didn't bring that much money. Figured I'd buy the popcorn for Sandy and me, but didn't plan on paying for her ticket. You paying for Barbara?"

"I don't know. Never thought about it."

"I mean it isn't a date or anything, is it?"

"Don't know. Is it?"

"Forget it. I'm not paying for Sandy. She can pay, and I'll buy the popcorn or candy or whatever, like I planned."

"Okay. I guess that's not a bad idea. So who goes up to the window first?"

"Aw, shit. I don't know. You know they're going to be wondering if we're paying for them."

"I'll feel funny going up to the window and getting one ticket and leaving her standing there."

"You got the money?"

"I think so. I don't suppose it would be cool to say "two children" would it?"

"Yeah, right. That'd be real cool. Darn. Hmm."

"I'm going to pay. I just hope she doesn't want any candy or anything, or I won't have enough."

"Well if you pay, I'm going to have to pay, too. Shit."

We glanced at Lucy and Ethel. They looked uncomfortable pretending not to notice this desperate huddle. Ken and I broke apart, and walked back over to them.

"Okay. Sorry." I offered meekly as I came up alongside Barbara.

"Is everything okay?" she asked without sounding very concerned.

"Yeah. Let's go."

I took the lead as we approached the box office, and asked for two tickets. I turned to Barbara, and extended a ticket toward her.

"Here."

"Glen, oh my God. Thank you. That's so nice. You didn't have to do that." Barbara smiled broadly as she took the ticket. She looked radiant. I wanted to tell her that it was nothing, and that it was only the beginning. I wanted to tell her that when we got older, and I was a successful doctor, and married to her, that I would buy her a mink coat or something, and lots of diamond jewelry, but all that came out was sort of a grunted acknowledgement of her gratitude.

When we passed the concession counter, Barbara said, "I always used to eat Jujubes at the movies, but that's a no-no with braces."

"Yeah, I'll find out next year. You know my dad's an ortho-dontist, so there's no way I'm not going to have braces."

Barbara laughed.

"Do you want any popcorn or anything?" I prayed for the right answer, since I didn't have enough money.

"No, but thanks. You're so nice."

I hoped she didn't notice my relief. I came off looking good without spending an extra cent.

We walked down the aisle until we agreed on a row about halfway to the screen. Barbara entered the row first, followed by me, then Ken and Sandy. Barbara stopped at the fourth seat in, and we all sat, giving Sandy the aisle.

More people meandered up and down the aisles selecting seats. An elderly couple stopped right next to Sandy, and began to scour the entire theater for just the right seats. They selected the two directly in front of Ken and Sandy.

Ken rolled his eyes and clicked his tongue.

"It figures. The place is half empty and they have to sit right in front of us."

"You want us to move down?" Barbara asked looking down the row towards Ken.

"Can you see?" Ken asked Sandy.

"Yeah, I'm fine as long as she takes her hat off."

"We're okay. They're short."

The lights faded, the curtains parted, and the screen lit up with previews. *Mash* looked like it would be funny, although war movies usually bored me.

Sandy and Ken were whispering and laughing, so Barbara and I looked at them, and I asked what they were laughing about. Before either of them could respond, the old man in the aisle seat in front of them turned around.

"Listen, you don't seem like bad kids, but do me a favor and keep quiet. I know you want to have fun, but we didn't pay to listen to you."

"Okay. Sorry." I said.

"Yeah, sorry." Barbara and Sandy said in unison.

We all exchanged wide-eyed glances. Ken leaned back in his seat, and opened his mouth making a face, as if he had just seen something shocking. Barbara put her finger to her lips to indicate we should be quiet. I started to say something to her, but she shook her head, and pressed her finger over my lips. At the touch of her finger and the scent of *Wind Song* coming from her wrist, I felt an odd sensation. It wasn't pleasurable, just odd.

The preview at that moment was for a Disney animated film called *The Aristocats,* which wouldn't be released for months. Both girls made the kinds of noises that adults make when spying a cute baby. I liked nothing better than an animated Disney movie, but I hesitated to show any enthusiasm for something that might appeal to children and girls.

The doors at the back of the theater were still open, allowing the sunlight from the lobby to stream in, along with late arrivals.

"Come on. Get your ass in here boy."

I tensed up. I recognized Kevin McPherson's voice, and met Ken's eyes briefly as we both turned to see Kevin McPherson and Curtis May coming down the aisle.

"Boy, I don't want to sit back here. Let's go up front."

"Hell. You can sit up front. I'm not sitting up front. I want the middle."

All eyes in the theater turned toward the two boys making the noise. I could feel the entire audience tense up, as if it were a single organism. I prayed silently, *Please God, let them sit as far away from us as possible.*

The commotion approached. I kept my back to Kevin and Curtis, and tried to make myself as small as possible, hoping my companions were doing likewise. It was no good. The noise stopped abruptly at our row.

"Hey, it's cool Ken. How're you doing, boy? And my man, Feigman. All right." Curtis held up his hand to "high five" Ken, and then reached over to slap hands with me as well. He then nodded "heys" to Sandy and Barbara, and they smiled "heys" back at him.

Kevin stuck his head over Curtis's shoulder. "Ooh, you boys are on dates. I see that. Uh hmm. You boys are going to try and get you some, aren't you? I know that. These boys are slick, heh-heh." Kevin and Curtis laughed.

With Curtis and Kevin hovering over us, I felt like a neutered puppy. Wherever this meeting was going was in their hands. I tried not to notice that Kevin's words were insulting to the girls. I decided not to get offended, or I'd have to defend their honor. Instead, I chose to feel relief that Kevin seemed to be in a good mood. Curtis's friendly greeting was not only surprising, but flattering.

I was sensitive to the elderly couple in front of us, and recognized their discomfort at the commotion directly behind their heads. Yet the old man, while quick to shush my group a few moments earlier, now said nothing to the much noisier Curtis and Kevin. Kevin lost interest, and took a seat two rows in front of the elderly couple.

"Shhhhhhhhhhhhh." The shushing sound came from somewhere across the theater.

"Fuck you," Kevin shouted back to no one in particular.

Meanwhile, Curtis held his palm up to Ken who returned the gesture.

"You all enjoy the show. My man, give me five again. All right. That's cool. Peace brother." Curtis walked off.

"Peace," Ken called after him.

I couldn't get myself to say "peace." Ken believed himself to be authentic in his use of hip words, but at that moment I thought Ken sounded like someone *trying* to be cool. Curtis or almost any black kid who wasn't considered an Oreo was naturally cool. I sounded like a complete queer when I tried to use hip words.

I was grateful that Curtis, whose behavior in school was unpredictable, demonstrated such camaraderie. Perhaps Curtis and I would become friends in school having shared a moment together. I was almost gleeful that the encounter with Kevin and Curtis didn't involve getting smacked on the head.

Kevin and Curtis spread themselves out three rows ahead of us causing the elderly couple in front of us to confer with each other numerous times. When the movie began the two boys reacted noisily to the events on the screen. They called out advice, and commented on the actors, the dialogue, and the scenery.

"Hey, will you boys please be still." The old man in front of us hissed.

"Who you calling "boy," honky?" Kevin stood up and glared at the old man.

"Hey, shut up!" a masculine voice called out from across the dark theater.

"You shut the hell up." Kevin shouted.

"Sit down, Kevin. Watch the movie, man." Curtis said in a loud whisper.

"Fuck you, Curtis."

The old man huffed, and stood up along with his wife, and they headed up the aisle.

We looked at each other, unable to follow the movie. The atmosphere was unsuitable for brushing against Barbara's arm, or placing mine around her shoulders. Ken must've been thinking the same thing, because his elbow was nowhere near Sandy's breast.

The elderly couple returned followed by a teenage boy in a sport coat and tie carrying a long, silver flashlight. The old man pointed to Kevin and Curtis as his wife and he sat down saying, "they're the ones."

The teenager nervously cleared his throat. "I'm going to have to ask you to please be quiet."

"We aren't saying anything, faggot." Kevin responded angrily.

"Okay, then. We've had a complaint that you're making noise, so please keep quiet."

"That old man's making all the noise with his "shhh" and "shut up," and clearing his throat like he sounds like he's dying."

"Will you shut up over there?" The masculine voice from before shot out from the dark.

Kevin stood up, and turned towards the voice. "You come over here, and make me, pussy, or I'll come there, and kick your white ass."

I couldn't imagine a white kid shouting the reverse in a theater full of blacks, and coming out alive.

Trying not to panic, the teenage manager intervened. "Sir, if you'd like I can give you your money back, and you can leave. That is, if you'd like." He cleared his throat again.

"Sit down, and watch the movie." Curtis commanded Kevin.

"I want my money back," Kevin demanded of the manager. "I don't want to see this honky-ass movie." He shoved the manager aside as he stormed up the aisle.

"All right," the anonymous voice cheered from across the room.

"And I'm kicking your ass," Kevin shouted back in the darkness.

The manager hurriedly followed Kevin up the aisle. A few moments later, Curtis mumbled something, stood up, and left the theater.

The relief in the theater was palpable.

"Are those delinquents your friends?" The old man turned around to ask us.

"We know them from school," Barbara said.

"You must live in Hampden," the old man said as he turned back around.

The remark stung—not the reference to delinquents—but the one about Hampden. I thought of things to say in response, but in the end I said nothing. We processed the old man's remark individually in silence.

It was twenty minutes into the movie; an hour later we were caught up in the hijacking of the jet. I placed my arm alongside Barbara's on our common armrest. I made certain that our hands touched. She didn't move. A good sign. During a particularly tense moment on the screen, I raised my hand slightly, and let it rest on top of Barbara's hand. In the world of Edith Wharton and me, Glen Feigman, this was a bold move. There was still no movement from Barbara. Another good sign. It was time to put my arm around her, but the mental strain of planning and executing the hand move had exhausted me, so I made no more advances.

The movie ended, and the lights went on.

"Cool movie." Ken said.

"I loved it," Sandy added. "That old lady, Helen Hayes, is so cute. She reminds me of my grandmother."

"I know. She's adorable," Barbara added.

The old man and woman were putting on their coats. They smiled at each other, upon hearing our verdict on their contemporary.

"So you guys need to leave first, right?" I asked responsibly.

"Yeah. My mother should be out there waiting for us," Barbara said sounding disappointed.

"Okay. We'll watch from the lobby, and we won't leave, until you get in the car," I reassured her.

"Thank you guys. That'll be great," Sandy said. "And thanks for the movie," she turned to Ken.

"Yes, thank you Glen," Barbara said looking at me. "We'll see you guys in school on Monday."

"Okay. Maybe we can do this again soon," Ken dared.

"That'd be great," Barbara replied.

I beamed. For once I wished it were Monday morning, so we could be together in school, and continue what I decided was indeed a date.

CHAPTER THIRTY-FIVE

Friday, May 1, 1970

In Social Studies class we discussed the US invasion of Cambodia. I'm not sure what any of us could contribute to the discussion, other than to repeat what we might've heard from our parents or older siblings. My parents and grandparents had mixed feelings about Vietnam. Grandpa and Dad, veterans of two world wars, were at first appalled by the young people protesting the undeclared war and the draft. The burning of the American flag made them dyspeptic.

"They are ungrateful, unpatriotic, and naïve. The sacrifice for liberty is constant." That could've been either Grandpa or Dad speaking. Then, as the fighting dragged on, and the end-game muddled, they grew frustrated and indecisive, until finally calling for an end to the combat.

I agreed with Mom's friend who said at a dinner party, "I don't understand why we can bomb them up to here," she indicated her knees, "but not up to here," she added pointing to her hips. "Either you bomb them or you don't, but don't do it half way. What they're doing accomplishes nothing." The women nodded agreement.

Their husbands were frustrated that America was afraid to do anything to upset the Russians or the Chinese. "If it's in our interest to keep the Commies out of Vietnam, and I'm not sure it is, then damn what the Russians or Chinese say. What are they going to do, bomb us?"

Grandma, who anguished over the departures of Grandpa for France in 1917, Dad for the European theater in 1942, and Uncle Marty for Korea in 1951, wanted the soldiers home. "Let them send Nixon to fight. When I was a girl in school, you never even heard of these crazy countries. Who ever heard of Vietnam or Cambucktu or whatever they're calling these places today? Who cares what happens to them? Our boys don't need to die for some cockamamie place that no one can find on a map. There's plenty of places right here where we can spend our money. Let them start with the potholes on Evans Avenue. I get such a head-ache by the time I get off that bus."

Nancy and her friends modeled the opinions of their rock star and college idols, and were therefore, uniformly and vehemently anti-war.

From pop culture media, I learned that any young person in favor of the war sported a crew cut or spoke like Jethro on *The Beverly Hillbillies*. His parents were called "rednecks," and likely to be bigoted, pollution-loving Republicans.

Back in class, Joel Tresly, a future Jewish Republican, insisted, "We have to keep the Communists out of Vietnam." Joel was not popular. "Otherwise, every other country over there will eventually become communist. You know, like the domino theory says, and they'll eventually come over here to attack us."

Ken, whose opinions were shaped by the older brother he idolized at Kent State, immediately attacked. "Oh sure, Joel. The Vietnamese are going to cross the Pacific in their rowboats, and invade America. Ha!" He sat back satisfied as the class erupted in laughter. Some of the boys rowed furiously in their seats, adding emphasis to Ken's point.

Joel's vision seemed plausible to me. Since the time that I was old enough to understand, I heard that Communists were intent on taking over the world, country by country. Right now they were after Vietnam. If it were to become Communist, surely the Communist leaders would then set their sights on the next country, and so on. I wondered why so many cool people felt that this scenario didn't hold up, and thought it best to leave the country to the Communists. Could so many cool people be wrong? I just didn't know everything John Lennon knew, so I laughed—but only half-heartedly—at Joel's expense.

Our teacher enjoyed seeing us in a lively discussion. He told us to write a prediction of what the newspapers might say about the subject over the weekend, and then to bring in a newspaper clipping on Monday that substantiated our prediction.

That evening, we did not know that my family faced an abrupt end of an era. Whether in a state of constant anxiety or reverie, no one can predict when his or her world will be jolted by an unseen, outside force.

We sat around the Shabbat dinner table discussing the expanding war in Southeast Asia. With support from Bubbie, Aunt Lilly, and Aunt Marion, Grandma restated her belief that countries that no one every heard of could be worth "our boys" dying over them.

Grandpa, Zadie, Uncle Marty, and Dad were torn as to whether the US could really just "give up," or finally declare a real war, and mobilize the country to "get the job done like we did in 1941." There was agreement all around when Grandpa said that in hindsight we should never have gotten involved in Vietnam.

Having reached no solution to our international dilemma, we turned our attention to local news—specifically Zadie's recent spate of fender benders that he blamed on the epidemic of drug use among hippies. That segued to today's youth not knowing the joy of dancing with a partner, since "all they do is jump around separately as if their feet are on fire."

Aunt Lilly, bringing herself and everyone else to tears of laughter, retold the story of her trip to the mineral baths at Hot Springs, Arkansas with Aunt Gussie. In spite of Gussie's frequent complaints of stiff joints, she found the energy to climb a fence at the Hot Springs racetrack, in order to claim the cheapest seats.

Punctuating the conversations: the topic of Grandma's meal, with repeated emphasis on the brisket.

After dinner, Uncle Marty, Aunt Marion, and their kids headed back to Sycamore Park. Nancy excused herself, and went upstairs to gab on the phone.

I played a card game of *Kaluki* with Bubbie, Zadie, and Grandpa. I chose this over going to Ken's house, even though his parents were out for the evening. We would've made phony phone calls or real calls to Barbara and Sandy, but I enjoyed the gentle banter of my grandparents' as they mostly reminisced.

Mom, Grandma, and Aunt Lilly comfortably chatted in the kitchen while they washed the dishes. Dad reclined in a chair near the card table, reading the newspaper. This Rockwellian moment had me swaddled in a warm, protective blanket. But danger never sleeps, and I was soon caught with my guard down.

At evening's end, the elders prepared to return to the city, and the good-bye ritual commenced with embraces and kisses, followed by vows to be together the following Shabbat, if God were willing. Admonitions to be careful followed, as did promises to be certain to call to say, "We got home safely."

I changed into pajamas, and stretched out on the couch in the family room to watch an old Rosalind Russell movie on TV. Ensconced in a wool afghan that Bubbie crocheted, I fell asleep.

CHAPTER THIRTY-SIX

Sunday, May 3, 1970

M r. Kaplan gave me a sad smile as he placed his arm around my shoulders and walked me silently to the temple's lobby. I was confused when I saw Dad waiting for me. Today was the Berlesman's car pool day, and Dad never missed those opportunities to sleep late on Sunday.

"Dr. Feigman, here's our little man."

I tried to read Dad's face for a clue to what I had done to bring about this unplanned meeting. Dad smiled weakly, leaned down, and drew me close for a gentle hug.

So I wasn't in trouble. Something else was wrong.

"Come on Glen. Let's go home. I'll explain on the way. Goodbye, Mr. Kaplan. Please thank Rabbi Becker, and tell him we'll see him later or tomorrow at our house."

This caught my attention. Rabbi Becker was coming to our house?

We headed west through Hampden, past the high school and the black section of town that was now quiet and sleepy on this sunny, Sunday morning. Something was terribly wrong, and I thought if I kept silent, it might right itself.

Once Dad began to speak there was no going back—not to yesterday, not to last year, not even to earlier that morning. Only minutes ago I sat in Bible class with my friends, trying to stay awake, and unable to find any relevance in whatever Mrs. Heferman attempted to explain to us. That was my former life.

What Dad revealed to me thrust me across a line, into a new reality. Instead of my bar mitzvah, was this the real end of childhood?

"Glen, you can guess that something is wrong. I wish I could tell you differently, but…listen, Glen. Something happened to Grandpa Leo, and it isn't good. Grandpa died this morning."

Maybe it was my fault. Could my unholy desires have brought on whatever happened to Grandpa? I would give up masturbating to make this go away.

Dad waited. I was supposed to say something, but it took a moment to find my voice.

"What happened?"

Dad sighed deeply, keeping his eyes straight ahead.

"Grandpa was out riding his new bicycle." Dad's eyes started to tear up, and he held back a sob. "Remember how excited he was to buy that bike, and ride in the park for exercise?"

"Uh-huh. Yeah." I was looking ahead too. It was painful to look at Dad's anguish. "Did he fall off? Was there an accident?" I couldn't say the words, "hit by a car." They were too awful.

"Well, two kids ran up to him, and stopped him, and tried to rob him, I guess. They hit him on the head with something, and he fell over. The doctors aren't sure yet if he died from the hit or the fall or both."

Of course he died from the hit, I thought. He wouldn't have fallen if they didn't hit him.

Grandpa, the man whose eyes lit up whenever I presented good grades or demonstrated I was on my way to becoming a *mensch,* was dead. He never raised his voice, and yet his praise or reproof could elevate or collapse my spirits more dramatically than anything Dad or Mom could say.

Surely, he'll be waiting at home in his light blue cardigan to tell me this is a mistake. When I kissed him good-bye on Friday night, it wasn't meant to be forever.

"Did anyone see it happen?" Now I was holding back a sob.

Dad regained some control. "There was a witness who saw it happen from her apartment window. She's the one who called the police."

Powerful forces roiled inside me. Sorrow, disbelief, anger all banged against each other, the walls of my stomach, the lining of my throat. Their effect was to render me paralyzed. Dad drove, his arm stretched to reach around my shoulders, his eyes darting from the road to my face. I don't know what he saw, but focusing on me may have been a distraction from his own thoughts.

As the car neared our street, I struggled to find my voice. "Were they black?"

Dad stared straight ahead. "Yes."

I learned later that he'd asked the same question when he heard about Grandpa. As details of the crime got out to family and friends, the unfortunate truth was that no one was surprised to learn that the two boys were black.

CHAPTER THIRTY-SEVEN

Monday May 4, 1970

The rabbi customarily spent an hour or two with a grieving family before a funeral to gather information on the deceased for the eulogy, and to answer questions about death and Jewish custom. Grandpa's sudden and tragic death required Rabbi Becker to devote more time to us. In addition to the grief that accompanies death, we were attempting to manage other conflicting emotions.

Uncle Marty's response to Grandpa's violent end was pure anger, which left no room for grief. In talking about the eulogy, he wanted the rabbi to talk about the irony of Grandpa's death at the hands of two blacks in search of money, since helping the disadvantaged was a significant motivator for Grandpa, and played an important part in his life. Uncle Marty wanted to point out a double standard.

"If two whites killed an elderly black man, the city would erupt in a riot." I agreed with him.

I witnessed physical confrontation every day in school when black kids thrust themselves in the path of their white school-mates. There were frequent demands by blacks to turn over our money. It made my stomach hurt to imagine gentle Grandpa coming face-to-face with it as his life came to an abrupt end.

Mom wanted no reference to how Grandpa died spoken at the funeral, other than to acknowledge that it was unexpected. She said Grandpa's good deeds would stand without setting them off against the cause of his death. "Everyone knows how Dad died. It's in the newspapers and on the TV. I don't want his funeral to be a referendum on race relations."

My family declined to give interviews to the media. The news-papers gave Grandpa almost a full-page obituary due to his ac-complishments in life, and the circumstances of his death. The irony was there for whomever wanted to see it.

Uncle Marty finished venting at Rabbi Becker, and acknowl-edged that Mom was "probably right." I detected a tiny sign of relief from the rabbi.

From the couch in our family room, Rabbi Becker turned his attention to Grandma, seated quietly in an armchair. He reached for her small hand, with its surprisingly smooth skin, and held it in his as she related her story. Subdued at first, she gained mo-mentum, almost resembling her feisty self, but it was a temporary resurgence.

"Leo insisted on riding that *mishuganeh* bicycle yesterday morning. I warned him not to, but when does he ever listen to me? 'Leo', I said, 'you're too old, and it's too cold. You'll catch pneumonia,' I said. He doesn't listen to reason."

I noted Grandma's use of the present tense as she continued. "I said the bike was dangerous and the machines...you know... the cars, wouldn't see him when he crossed to the park. I told him he'd break every bone in his body if he fell. He could've ended up in the lake. I told him not to come to me, if he fell and drowned.

Rabbi Becker's look was tender.

"I was a nervous wreck. I couldn't wash the dishes from breakfast. I tried, but got my robe all wet from the sink." Grandma turned to Aunt Marion. "Marion, you know the pink housecoat you bought me from Marshall Field's about ten years ago? I kept it in a drawer until last year. I should've left it in the drawer."

"Ma, please focus on telling Rabbi your story, and forget about the robe."

Within the first few years of a purchase of clothes or linens, Grandma and her sisters kept them unused, in preparation for the next Great Depression.

"Never wear new clothes," Grandma told me, "until you have them for some time, because only poor people have to wear new clothes right away."

Grandma turned back to Rabbi Becker. "I sat looking out the window at the park trying to see Leo, but who could see through the trees and down twenty floors. That's when the doorman called to tell me two policemen were coming up to talk to me. I tell you, I never felt so sick in my life. I went to unlock the door right away, but I couldn't stand there, and wait for them. My legs were giving out, so I almost crawled to the couch waiting for them.

"Leo hadn't been gone an hour when the police came in. I must've looked like the wreck of the Hesperus sitting there. I couldn't even talk. One of the policemen, a nice fella, young, Irish, I think, reached down to help me up to go with him. He must've thought I was crazy, because I didn't want to get up, and I called for Leo. I didn't want to hear anything they had to say. I told them to tell Leo whatever it was they were telling me when he got back. I told them my husband takes care of everything.

"They starting talking about Leo being taken to the hospital, and I should go with them. That's when I told them to call Eileen. I don't know how I remembered the number."

Mom stepped in. "When I picked up the phone, first I heard Mother screaming for Dad in the background, and then the policeman introduced himself, and said Dad was assaulted and taken to the hospital. I had them put Mother on the phone, and told her to go with the policemen to see Dad in the hospital. Then, my legs gave out. Thank God Jerry was here to take charge."

"Tell me more about Leo, Mrs. Epstein. I've heard from almost everyone else. Now you tell me something."

For a moment, Grandma seemed less frightened and tentative. She had everyone's attention, and her eyes came alive, but in another era.

"Leo and his family lived in an apartment building near our house. My father had a big house in Wicker Park, and Leo's poor family lived on another block, in an apartment. I knew his sister, and she introduced us. He was so handsome. I never dated anyone before Leo."

Mom's, Aunt Marion's, Nancy's—oh hell—everyone's eyes overflowed with tears as we listened to Grandma's story.

"My father was very strict. One time Leo rang for me at eight o'clock in the evening, and my father told him not to come back. He said nice young ladies are home where they belong, at such a late hour.

"My sister Lilly said I should marry Leo. I think she liked him too, but she was already engaged."

So there was truth to my theory about chemistry between Aunt Lilly and Grandpa.

"Anyhow, President Wilson declared war, and Grandpa enlisted and was off to France. He was so handsome in that uniform with those leggings they wore. I thought his legs looked skinny, but then I felt ashamed for noticing. Nice girls weren't supposed to notice a man in that way."

For an instant, Grandma smiled almost coyly.

"I worried about him so much when he went across. It took months for letters to go back and forth. So many died of flu, even before they got there. Anyhow, we got married when he came home after the Armistice. We all had celebrated downtown at State and Madison. There must've been two million people there. Such fun, and I finally relaxed, knowing Leo would come home."

Rabbi Becker interrupted. "Mrs. Epstein, family here all spoke of how important everyone was to your husband, and how charitable he was with his time and wisdom. They said his goal was to leave the world better than he found it. Do you have anything you want to say about that?"

Grandma's light dimmed. She withdrew. "Leo was always helping somebody. He did a lot for the colored. I was busy running the house, and taking care of my parents when they got older. I suppose he talked to me about his work, but I don't remember too much. They can tell you everything, I'm sure." She gestured slightly towards the rest of us.

"He's a good man. I worry about him, though. He's stubborn, but he takes care of things. I don't even know how much money we have. He gives me the little I ask for, for the groceries and the kids, or whatever. What do I need? I don't spend much of anything. I don't know what I'll do. I never even went to the bank. What am I going to do?"

Grandma started to show signs of panic, but we all quickly comforted her. When Rabbi Becker left, she was sitting quietly, looking quite small in the armchair. We remained nearby, so she could feel us around her, but her gaze was inward, perhaps to Grandpa and things that only she knew.

CHAPTER THIRTY-EIGHT

Tuesday, May 5, 1970

The funeral home was as quiet as a... funeral home. The furniture, dark, heavy, and comfortable. The air, cool. Dim lamps gave off a healthy, pinkish glow to the living—and the dead. Caskets at Jewish funerals are typically closed, but the family gets to peek at the deceased privately before the funeral. Earlier, when the lid was raised for us to cast our eyes on Grandpa for the last time, his gray skin looked soft and warm under the pink lights. He was dressed in his uniform from the First World War. Mom said Grandpa took tremendous pride in serving the "US of A," as he called it, and he would like the idea of resting eternally in his soldier's garb.

In the private family lounge, Nancy, my first cousins, and I sat in a semi-circle around Grandma. Her grief rendered her smaller than usual, like a Victorian doll, blue eyes vacant under her little black hat and simple black dress.

At once, all eyes were drawn to Aunt Marion entering the room like a movie star, in a wide-brimmed black hat, with a veil over her eyes. Looking more subdued, Mom followed, and the rest of us made room for the two ladies to sit on either side of Grandma.

I never saw Grandma so passive, showing no sign of impatience or nervous energy. On her left hand, Grandma wore her silver wedding band, the one with the tiny hearts carved around it. Silently, in a rare display of affection towards Mom, Grandma took hold of her hand.

Dad and Uncle Marty entered the room with Rabbi Becker—all wearing yarmulkes and dressed in black. Rabbi Becker asked Mom and Grandma to stand and join him and Uncle Marty. Mom helped Grandma to stand. For the only time I could remember, Grandma made no complaint about her arthritic knee as she slowly rose. The three mourners came close to the rabbi, and he pinned a small black ribbon near each of their collars. He made a small tear in the ribbons as he recited a Hebrew prayer. He explained that for the next thirty days, they were to wear these bits of rent, black cloth symbolizing the rent garments worn by Jews in mourning since the time of Moses.

The closed casket, draped in an American flag, stood alone in the front of the large chapel under the "eternal" light. Thirty minutes before the funeral was to start, an attendant led us from the private room to the front row of seats in the chapel where we were to receive personal expressions of condolence before the start of the funeral. Grandma sat, semi-dazed, in the center of the row. Uncle Marty's group sat to her right and Mom's group sat to her left. I sat between Mom and Dad. Grandpa's brother Irv, his wife, and Grandma's sisters sat in the second row.

Uncle Irv's usually mischievous eyes were now still, and he looked his seventy-eight years. The night before, he confessed to us that oddly he felt guilty that he wasn't there to protect his younger brother. When they were boys, he defended Grandpa whenever Polish kids, looking for a fight, crossed the street that divided the Polish from the Jewish neighborhood.

For two days I cried on Melva's shoulder, but now she was back at our house helping to prepare for the *shivah* that followed the burial. So I sat stiffly in my bar mitzvah cum funeral suit, missing her.

The funeral director prepared for a large group, yet there weren't enough chairs. The assembly reflected Grandpa's busy life. Among relatives from both sides of my family were Grandpa's associates, representatives from the various charity organizations and community groups that Grandpa supported, and generations of friends.

I looked over my shoulder. Many seats were filled, while others had purses or jackets on them, like placeholders at an entertainment venue. The receiving line of mostly familiar faces snaked out the door.

As the slow, somber line passed before us, my emotions mimicked those of my elders. If Mom wept in the arms of Grandpa's childhood friend, my throat closed up. When Grandpa's law school buddy reminded Grandma of better times, the faint smile that broke through her inscrutable expression caused the corners of my mouth to lift.

Barbara Needleman and a few of the girls from class were suddenly in front of me, giving me a jolt. Like me, they wore the clothes they wore to bar mitzvahs. I hugged each of them, feeling gratitude, but nothing more stimulating.

The grim, downward faces, familiar and unfamiliar, continued to pass. I awkwardly shook hands with Gary and Ken who were there with their families. Ken's parents were shaken from the previous days' news from Kent State in Ohio. Although he wasn't hurt, Ken's brother was at the protest when the National Guardsman started firing at the students. My family was too focused on our personal loss to pay attention to a national calamity.

Recognizing the parents of some of the Catholic kids on my block coming through the line gave me a moment of comfort. They said such kind things to Mom, Dad, and to Grandma that I hoped it would lead to a turning point in my tense relationship with their "kike-kicking" kids.

I shivered suddenly. When I looked up, I was face to face with a handsome black man in an ill-fitting suit. He offered his hand to Dad.

"I'm Armstrong Bryant, and I admired Mr. Epstein very much. I feel like I know your family. This must be Glen," he said, gazing down at me. "Your grandfather told me all about you. You had a bar mitzvah recently. He was so proud."

I nodded, and mumbled something affirmative.

He shook my hand. "I'm sorry for you and your family. Your granddad was a great man. He helped me out when no one else would or could, and I'll miss him."

My hand looked tiny and white, enveloped by Armstrong Bryant's hand. I couldn't look him in the face. "Thank you," I said softly. Guilt, along with grief, consumed me—guilt over my hateful thoughts over the past two days.

Mom stepped in to greet Mr. Bryant, and took his hand in both of hers. Grandma's stiff response to Mr. Bryant relaxed a bit when Mom explained his connection to Grandpa. He was the first of several blacks who came to pay respects that morning—each with fond memories of Grandpa.

Among the many other voices, there was an occasional undertone of anger, accompanied by pronouncements about the collapse of morality and decency in America. Mom gave a cool response to match Uncle Marty's encouragement.

I jumped at the next voice. To my left stood Mr. Wendell, my gym teacher and ego booster, chatting with Nancy. Dad, who was almost six feet tall, looked short and narrow next to the broad, tall frame of Mr. Wendell moving down the line from

Nancy. Offering Dad condolences, Mr. Wendell fixed his eyes on me.

"You have a fine young man here, Dr. Feigman. Glen is one of our better young men in school, and he's a good athlete."

I was overcome. I stared at my feet. I loved Mr. Wendell for saying that. No one had ever used my name with the word athlete in the same sentence.

Mr. Wendell shook my hand and added, "Glen, if you feel the need to talk in school, you come see me, you hear? I mean it."

I nodded. I would soon come to regret that I didn't take him up on his offer. "I will. Thank you." I gave Mr. Wendell a closed mouth smile as he moved down the line to Mom and Grandma.

More than thirty minutes had passed, and the line still stretched out of the room. Rabbi Becker stepped to the podium near the casket to encourage everyone to take a seat, so the service could begin. There were a few moans from the people near the front of the line. Others persisted in attempting to speak to Mom, Uncle Marty, or Grandma. Eventually everyone found a seat in the great room or in chairs set up in the lobby just outside.

When the rabbi invoked Grandpa's name, a lump settled in my throat. Each reference to the end of life or eternal peace caused tears to stream down my face. Rabbi Becker summarized Grandpa's life, recounting his early years of poverty as the son of immigrants who fled the dangerous pogroms of the Russian *shtetls* to the streets of the immigrant ghettos of Chicago. He spoke of the loves of Grandpa's life that guided his every step: learning, the *Torah* with its emphasis on doing *mitzvahs*, and his family, particularly Grandma and their children and grandchildren.

My pride grew with every sentence, knowing my friends and neighbors were witness to the eulogy. I was especially pleased that Armstrong Bryant, Mr. Wendell, and Grandpa's other black friends were present. I saw them as a potential conduit to carry Grandpa's example to the entire black community. They must relay that my family is a kind family, and that we shouldn't have been brought to grief at the hands of blacks perpetrating cruelty, and criminality.

Shadowing me as it often did, a state of conflict persisted. I didn't want the rabbi to say anything that might be construed as a negative reflection on the black community, which would likely cause Mr. Wendell and the other blacks in attendance, to feel uncomfortable. Mr. Wendell was a mentor, and the thought of anyone saying anything negative about blacks around him made my hackles rise, in the same way as when my friends berated the blacks at school, and I would think about Melva.

When the rabbi asked everyone to rise for the final prayers, I felt relief that soon this part of the ordeal would be over. Yet with each step of the grieving process, the permanence of Grandpa's death would reveal itself. Each passing moment carried him deeper into the past, and increased my sense of loss.

CHAPTER THIRTY-NINE

Wednesday, May 6, 1970

*S*hivah—Hebrew for seven—is observed for the seven days following a funeral, except for the Sabbath, when mourning is
eclipsed by gratitude for the gift of the day of rest. There was little
opportunity to feel bereft—perhaps that was the wisdom behind
the custom—as a continuous flow of familiar and strange faces
quietly entered our house, bearing food and offering words of
condolence. The bountiful trays and baskets of fruit, decorated
the house like colorful art. People gathered in every room of the
first floor, and noisy kids were relegated to the basement. Melva
presided over the kitchen where Mom's friends organized a daily
schedule of tasks and meals.

On the afternoon of the day of the funeral I sprawled out on
my bed; face down, my nose running onto my pillow. I'd closed
the door to escape the din and the smell of cigarettes mixed with
perfume, the sounds and scents that normally meant a celebration. Melva knocked gently, and opened the door.

She moved in on Sunday night, and stayed through the week, taking pride in the number of women who stopped by the kitchen to pay homage to an icon of our family.

The previous night, with the dishwasher humming over its last load, she slowly descended the steps exhausted, ready to sleep, only to find me waiting with dominos in hand. Her eyes rolled as she exhaled deeply, and then laughed, asking if I were serious. My silence transformed her weariness to sympathy, which was good for a few games.

That afternoon when she peeked in my room, and made her way to my desk chair, she wore the white dress she wore for holidays.

"Glen, I want to talk to you, just for a minute. Okay?"

I wasn't the brooding type, and not one to close myself in my room to be left alone, so I'm not sure why I decided to do just that. Perhaps I was subconsciously playing the role of some actress in an old movie. It didn't suite me, until that moment when I had an audience.

Melva pulled the desk chair over to the bed, and sat down with a groan. I sat up, and leaned against the wall behind my bed. She patted my knee.

"I only have a minute, but I've been thinking, and I don't want to forget what I want to tell you. You know me, I don't talk too much, so who knows if I'll remember what I wanted to say?"

I took a tissue from my nightstand, and wiped my eyes and nose as I had seen countless grieving women do. I was in the habit of keeping a box of tissue next to my bed, but not for tears.

"Glen, I'm worried about you. I know your heart is hurting right now, and I know you're sad. I just don't want you to be filled up with hate. Don't give it any place."

I was surprised and uncomfortable with the direction this conversation was taking, so I didn't say anything. I studied the tissue in my hand, on my lap.

"I know you're thinking if it weren't for those two colored boys, your grandpa would be here right now. It's true and I know it. They took him from you. No one in this house is going to let you say it. Your folks are too good about that."

I felt that now familiar lump in my throat as Melva invoked Grandpa. There he was, quietly explaining the world to me as we crossed a street hand-in-hand, on one of our educational excursions around Chicago.

"Oh, now don't make me feel like I'm making you cry. I don't want you to cry, but it's okay to feel sad. It *is* sad. We're all sad. But don't feel hate too."

"I don't feel any hate, Melva." I lied.

"You know this here is Melva, and you can maybe read books better than me, but I can read you better than anything. I know you must be hating those boys. They did a terrible thing, and I am not excusing them, no way. Uh-uh. But how do you think I know how you feel? Hate is a bad thing to feel. It knots you up, and ruins your life.

"How *do* you know, Melva? You never hated anyone, and who could ever be mean to you?" I gathered Melva was attempting to cheer me up in some peculiar way, with this talk of hate. Melva was incapable of ill will; she was pure goodness.

"Hate will eat you up, and make you mean. Look at how your ma's friend Rina, with that red hair, is so angry all the time. I know she hates her husband. I see it. Every time I see them together here, I just shake my head. Listen to me now: hate makes you mean.

"Really?" This discussion kept me off balance, and I wasn't prepared to say anything; I didn't know where it would go next. "Who became mean Melva?"

"Me." She let this sink in, before she continued. "I know we don't ever talk about the fact that I'm a different color from you, because that doesn't usually matter here. But my color gives me experience that you don't have. I don't want you to end up like some Arkansas mayor because of these two boys. Hate can grow and spread, if you don't watch out for it. So I'm telling you to watch out for it."

Melva was right about the fact that we never talked about race. I heard her conversations with Grandma, about how dangerous the black kids in her neighborhood had become, and how it scared her, but this was the first time she brought race into a discussion with me, other than when she asked who squirted Mace in my eyes.

"You know, Glen, I don't go to church often as I should, but I think the good Lord made sure I'd be here today, so I can teach you something to keep hate out of your heart."

"Who did you hate Melva? I can't picture you hating anyone. You were never mean or anything. You're just saying this."

"Listen to me, Glen. I don't need to say everything, but you know I come from Arkansas, and life there wasn't easy for people like me. I was born back around 1915, at least that's what my ma told me, and the hate there grew right alongside the cotton. People who didn't know me hated me, because I was colored. That's just how they were. I was a good girl, and my folks were kind, decent people, but sometimes the white people did terrible things to folks I knew, even to my daddy. So I hated them back— all of them; I mean, all the white people I saw, whether I knew them or not. One of them had hurt my daddy, so I hated all of them.

"What'd they do to him?" I remembered seeing a photograph of a lynching.

"That doesn't matter. I don't talk about it much. I just want you to know I felt the way you do now, but it didn't do me any good. It just made me mean and miserable.

"So what happened, Melva? You aren't like that now."

Melva smiled and sat back in her chair. "You know what happened, Glen? I'll tell you what happened. When my husband got out of the service after the War, we had enough of Arkansas, and like a lot of colored folk, we rode the train north. He got a job working in a West Side hardware store, for a nice Jewish man. I tell you, Glen, we didn't know what that was. We never heard of Jews in Arkansas, but this man, Mr. Mandell, he was a nice man, and he treated my husband real nice, like he respected him."

I smiled as I imagined Melva and her husband trying to figure out what a Jew was. Maybe she thought we came from a country called Jewishia.

"Anyhow, my Dion was in school already, and we needed money, so my husband asked Mr. Mandell if he knew any families looking for a cleaning lady. That's the only work a colored woman could get. By then I heard that Jewish families gave colored folk work, and sure enough, Mr. Mandell talked to some woman up in Rogers Park, and she hired me."

"Really Melva? Who was that? My mom?"

"No. I don't know if you remember the Farbers. They lived in the building next to where your folks lived. Anyhow, after a while Mrs. Farber connected me with your family, and I started working for them too. Nancy was still a few years away. And you were a few years after that."

"Melva, was it Mr. Mandell that made you stop hating?"

"Mmm, no, but maybe it started with him. He was a good man, but I just minded my business. I still didn't trust white people, because of the things I'd seen growing up. I thought they were all the same. Can you believe that? As far as I was concerned, Mr. Mandell might turn out to be no different from the whites back south. Was that fair? Not when no one was ever more nice or respectful to me than Mr. and Mrs. Mandell."

"So, what changed you?"

"Glen, you're sounding like your grandma now. Hold on. I'm going to tell you right now. I worked for your family and a few other families by then, and we got along okay. Nancy came along, and she was a cute baby, but she was someone else's baby, and not too special to me. And then you were born." She paused and sat back a little, her eyes twinkling. "And I was there when they brought you home from the hospital, and you know what Glen? I swear you were only a few days old, but you looked at me, and first thing you did was smile and grab hold of my little finger."

Melva stopped again, and smiled broadly. She kept her eyes on me as she held up her little finger and laughed.

"Your little bitty hand couldn't even go around my little finger, but you sure tried to grab on."

I loved this story. I tried to imagine what had gone through my mind at the moment when I reached out for Melva.

"And you know what, Glen? After that, it didn't matter who was holding you. When you saw me, you reached for me. And you always were smiling for me. You could be crying like a cat, but if I came into the room you stopped crying, and smiled at me, and reached out your little arms. My own boy didn't pay me mind the way you did." She lowered her gaze a little.

"Really, Melva? I did?"

She looked back at me. "You sure did. Everyone noticed. They joked that maybe there was a mix up at the hospital, and you were my baby." Melva chuckled.

"Anyhow, I didn't think about it at first, because these things happen, before you take mind of them. Just like I didn't pay attention when hate came into my heart, I didn't notice when it went away neither. I guess there was no more place for it. How could I hate all those white people I didn't even know, when that little baby boy loved me like he did? He loved me, and he was born blind to my color. You just loved Melva natural, right from the start.

"I told you before, I should be in church more, but I knew that the Lord brought me to your house to wash the hate from my heart. Our old preacher used to say something about how a child will lead us, so I figure in my case it was you. You know animals and children give honest love, and you can't turn away a gift like that."

I was overwhelmed and embarrassed that I had unwittingly played such an important part in Melva's life. Guilt, by now my constant companion, saw an opportunity here, and gripped my soul, reminding me that I hadn't done enough for Melva—other than to cleanse her heart inadvertently.

"Like I said, I didn't notice it at first, but I was happy. I couldn't wait to come to your house every few days, and see you. I don't think I cleaned so good then, because I spent too much time with you. You never wanted me to put you down."

We laughed together.

"I was still poor, and my arthritis was starting to bother me; my husband wasn't doing so good then, but my life seemed better than I could remember. I never to this day can forgive or forget some of those folks back south, but I don't blame the world anymore. You know why I'm telling you this?"

"I think so," I said meekly.

"Tell me what I'm saying, Glen. I've got to be sure you know what I'm saying, so I can go on doing what I need to do here."

I looked around the room as I thought. "Um, you're telling me not to let those guys that...hurt Grandpa...ruin my life by making me hate so much, because of what they did 'cause that will do me more harm."

She sat back, satisfied. "You got a lot to bear right now, and a lot to think about, but I want you to remember my story, and in a little while, when you aren't feeling so weighed down, you go on being a happy boy in school. Okay, Baby?"

I drew into myself a bit at Melva's last remark. Her image of me as a happy boy suddenly put some distance between us. I didn't see myself as a happy boy. I was fearful and guilty of awful thoughts, and I anticipated more unhappiness to come.

She raised herself from the chair with a groan, and held out her arms. I stood and rested my head against her shoulder.

"Why don't you come downstairs, and I'll fix you something to eat?"

I nodded as she left the room, and I sat back down on my bed.

Something important had just happened, but my encounter with Melva left me uneasy. Her lesson seemed like a step toward adulthood, towards rationality, and away from the familiar emotional thinking of childhood. Regardless, I was not prepared to grant Melva's wish to give hate no quarter. Grandpa's murder was certainly the worst, but not the only incident of black aggression that was personal. My horizon encompassed three years of mayhem and insults on a daily basis, and I was not charitably inclined.

In spite of all the nice black kids I knew at school, thoughts of them were crowded out by an image of violent, mean, and rude people.

Those pejorative images were based on my experiences, my exposure to the news media, and what I'd heard from family and friends who lived through changes in their safe, clean neighborhoods when blacks moved in

If I chose to avoid blacks, it was because I was applying Dr. King's standard of judging by character—as reflected in behavior—instead of color. I don't think I was using his words perversely to excuse my learned response.

I was so conditioned to blame whites for any racial discord that to my own ears I sounded like an unapologetic racist. In reality, I was an apologetic racist.

It didn't matter that my black classmates singled me and other whites out to receive their anti-social behavior every day, based on the color of our skin. It didn't make sense that their behavior wasn't considered racially motivated.

There were plenty of white groups to avoid, and it had nothing to do with race. It had to do with their behavior and values. They weren't black, so it was easy to call them out without fearing the bigot appellation.

I learned later in an advertising class that, like it or not, what one perceives is one's reality. At age thirteen I was certain that very few people, white or black, would choose to share a school, home, office, store, movie theater, street, or bus, especially at night, with a person or group with a reputation for violence and a lack of common courtesy. I wanted someone to explain to me why it was anything more than plain old common sense to want to avoid such people.

I swung my legs over the side of my bed and stood up. Emotions ruled our national dialogue. It didn't matter how much I might be growing into a rational adult.

CHAPTER FORTY

Thursday, May 7, 1970

Mom said my life had to go on, and she wanted Nancy and me back at school before the end of *shivah*. I didn't think I was ready. I felt like my planet jumped its orbit, and Grandpa's death created a barrier separating me from the life I had known. Even the newspapers described what happened to my family as tragic. How do you reset after a tragedy?

I wanted the world to know that I was from the tragic family written up in the paper; that it was my grandfather who was murdered, and I needed the world to adjust accordingly.

Through Mom's simple act of waking me up at the usual time on Thursday morning, it struck me yet again that life was forever changed. Before Grandpa died, Grandma would've been the one to wake me. But Grandma was sleeping a lot, and uninterested in her usual obsessions.

Melva prepared my breakfast, and packed my lunch. She and Mom kissed me good-bye. Grandma was conspicuously absent.

This was the first time I stepped outside since the funeral. I felt vulnerable and uncertain of the kind of attention I would get as a result of Grandpa's highly publicized death.

At the bus stop, I squinted in the early morning sunlight and said "hey" to Mark and David. In unison they gave me the heads up nod, grunted, and quickly looked away.

On the bus, all chatter stopped, and I detected a number of eyes on me. I took an empty seat. David and Mark sat behind me.

"I'm sorry about your grandfather, Glen. It's really sad." I was shocked to see Nancy Lefko, the mall girl so desperately in love with Ben Rubin, leaning towards me from across the aisle. I stammered to answer, but could only muster, "Oh, thanks. That's okay." Guilt again. I sensed I was enjoying her unusual attention as a result of losing Grandpa. During all those years of mall girl snubs, I didn't know I could've had their attention by having a simple family catastrophe.

Unexpectedly the image of Grandpa's coffin being lowered into the ground on its slow, final descent caused tears to leak from the corners of my eyes. One actually escaped before I could wipe it away. I decided to be strong like Scarlett O'Hara, and not let anyone see me cry.

Spring jackets undulated in front of the school's entrance, coming together and breaking apart like an amoeba. The edges of the mass occasionally came apart as someone pushed his or her way through the mass.

As I waited my turn to step off the bus, the boy in front of me was immediately knocked aside by two large black girls. His books scattered under the bus. "Out of the way, motherfucker," one of the girls growled as the two continued walking. This was a familiar scene.

This sudden violence rattled me with a surprising intensity. My nerves were coiled on top of my skin, and I kneeled down to help the boy retrieve his muddy materials. He muttered a soft, "damn them," and thanked me quietly without looking up. Another American bigot born.

I located my friends before exiting the bus, and once I finished my good deed, I headed in their direction. I received a warm welcome from Ken, Gary, Barbara, and others in our group. For the first time that morning, I was glad to be out of the house. The school doors opened, and the crowd funneled through the gap.

Ken and Gary stopped to talk sports with someone, so I continued upstairs to my locker where Kevin McPherson and Curtis May were carrying on boisterously.

"Hi, guys. I just need to get to my locker." I said.

They ignored me, their goal now to inconvenience me as much as possible. So much for the bond we formed at the movies.

"Come on, guys. If I can just..." I stopped as Kevin moved his head in my direction.

"Can't you see, boy, that we're having ourselves a little conversation here? Now if you'll just wait, we'll be moving soon." He turned back to Curtis who was smiling broadly.

One locker over, Michael Baker heard the commotion.

"Come on, Kevin. Can't you just let Glen in there? What's the big deal?"

A switch flipped in Kevin, and he slammed his fist into my locker, and directed his angry glare at Michael.

"You shut the hell up, boy. You're really a white boy, you know that? You're always working hard, reading your books, playing your stupid games, with that faggot white boy Cary, your only pussy friend. Boy, you are an Oreo. You act like these two white boys. Always so smart in class." He was gesturing towards Ken, who now stood at my side, and me.

"Oh, that makes a lot of sense." There was fear, but also indignation in Michael's voice. "So if I did poorly in school, and caused trouble, and didn't have a white friend, I wouldn't be an Oreo? That's got nothing to do with black power and black pride. That's just stupid."

Michael was playing with fire, and others felt the air charging up around us.

Pamela Blake must've sensed trouble, and came out of our classroom to join the *fun.*

Now the harassment focused on Michael. A four-hundred-year perspective might've explained the roots of this scene, but I had neither the time nor the patience to follow that path. I was frustrated at the silly, antagonistic behavior, and felt pressured to act as Kevin stepped up his insults at Michael.

"You better shut up, Oreo. Watch who you're calling stupid or I'll kick your booty, boy. Come on, Oreo boy, you're so smart. Let's see you fight." He shoved Michael against the lockers.

Hippies, flower children, and rock bands sang about peace and love in this Age of Aquarius at Woodstock, but it was only wishful thinking. We were at Altamont. I flashed back over the violence of my childhood: John and Robert Kennedy, Martin Luther King and the ensuing riots, Charles Manson, Richard Speck, and now Grandpa.

Michael took the heat off me, but I couldn't leave him with my mess. There was no adult presence to cool the situation down; more kids gathered making a semi-circle around us. Some of the black kids shouted encouragement to kick the Oreo's butt. Most of the white kids, recognizing that this was a fight between two blacks, appeared only curious.

A barely audible voice of reason came from the crowd. "Come on guys, leave him alone. He hasn't done anything." It was Cleon. He was well liked among his black peers, and perhaps they'd heed his request.

"Hey Cleon, we're just having fun with Oreo here. Don't worry about a thing. Be good, and be quiet."

"I just don't..." Cleon started, but was quickly shut down.

"Don't make me come after you next, Cleon." Kevin said through clenched teeth, without taking his eyes off of Michael.

"Yeah, Cleon, don't be an Oreo too," someone added.

Cleon backed off.

"Why don't your honky friends help you, Oreo boy? You're all just faggots. You know that? A fucking Oreo, honky faggot," Kevin said leaning in close to Michael's face, and laughing.

Marybeth Mays broke through to Michael, and took his arm to guide him to the classroom, but Curtis knocked her arm down.

"What are you doing, girl? Get out of here."

"You boys are crazy." Marybeth said, but she backed off, too. Everyone knew about Curtis' temper.

With tears streaming down his face, Michael shoved against Kevin's chest, causing Kevin to step back a few paces. The black kids called out "Oooooooooh boy," and someone added, "Michael's going to get it now." Kevin had the excuse he needed to land a punch. He pushed Michael hard against a locker, and his head caused the metal to reverberate.

"Leave him alone!" I shouted as my genetic loathing of injustice released the hormones required to set me in motion.

"Look at that white boy," Pamela said. You better be careful Kevin. Glen looks dangerous." She turned towards me. "Boy, you know I know you, and you're a nice boy, but you need to stay out of this."

"What'd you say, boy?" Kevin strode towards me, his chest puffed out. With the exception of Ken, the others moved away from me. Rather than regretting my action, my blood boiled, and Kevin was the source of heat. There was too much emotion coursing through my body, and I was sure my voice would crack, and I would cry in front of everyone. Instead it came out strong, angry, and determined.

"I said leave him alone, Kevin. Why do you have to be so violent? Why do you always have to pick on someone? Michael didn't do anything to you."

"Boy, I'm going to kick your ass." Kevin put a painful headlock on me and flipped me onto my back. "You're just a fag, boy. You know that? A white-ass faggot." I was lying on the floor when Kevin kicked me in the side causing more pain.

Ken broke out of the group, and tried to knock Kevin down when Derrick Dawson shoved Ken so hard he fell on *his* back.

"Stop it!" Barbara Needleman and Tanya Wilkes shouted simultaneously. They both arrived on the scene to find Ken and me on the floor. Barbara rushed over to me, and tried to help me to my feet, while Tanya attended to Ken. In the midst of the chaos I made a mental note that there were positive examples of integration at work, demonstrated by Cleon, Marybeth, and now Tanya.

"Hey Kevin. Be cool. Leave them alone. They're good guys," Tanya offered on our behalf.

And then came the toughest voice of all. "Kevin! Leave him alone if you know what's good for you." It was my friend from student council, Donna Harding. No one could safely ignore her command.

"No white boy tells me what to do." In spite of his combative response, Donna gave Kevin pause.

"I'm telling you what to do, and I'm no white boy." Donna's authoritative voice thundered through the corridor.

"I'll see your sorry white ass after school, faggot. Honky ass motherfucker," Kevin said pointing at me.

Donna took aggressive steps toward Kevin as if she were about to strike, and Kevin quickly backed off. God bless Donna. I loved her at that moment.

Mr. Peterson finally came running out into the hall. He saw Barbara attempting to help me to my feet, and Ken brushing off his clothes as he stood up. Mr. Peterson assessed the scene and sent a student to get Mr. Strong.

"Okay, everyone go to class right now. Kevin, you stay here."

"Fuck that," Kevin said and started to walk away.

"Mr. McPherson, I said stay here." Mr. Peterson put his hand over Kevin's shoulder to stop him, and Kevin knocked Mr. Peterson's arm aside.

There was fire in his eyes. "Don't you touch me, honky. Nobody touches me. That honky started it, so I finished it." He pointed to me.

I stood with Ken, Michael, Barbara, Tanya, Donna, and now George Adams, who arrived to join our clutch. Most of the other students from my class were out in the hall. Others, sensing the worst—or best—was over, drifted to their classrooms. Kevin turned his wrath on Mr. Peterson.

I can't believe that this is happening on my first day back at school, after two kids killed my grandfather. Why is Kevin doing this? Why is he and so many like him, this hostile? Why can't they just stop all this violence and race stuff?

Out of nowhere, Barbara Needleman gave voice to everything I had been thinking and more.

"Stop it. Just stop it. No more 'honky' this and 'boy' that, Kevin. None of us ever did anything to you. No one here ever owned a plantation, or had slaves. No one here owes you anything. We go to the same school. We root for the same team. We aren't your enemy."

"Shut up girl." Mean Serena showed up.

"Yeah, nobody asked your opinion. I never liked your goody-two-shoes ass," Pamela added.

"Honky faggot needs his girlfriend to defend him." Kevin spouted.

"Maybe you should listen to her, you jerk," I said.

Kevin ran passed Mr. Peterson, grabbed me, and wrestled me to the ground which caused my head to make contact with the hard floor. The pain was instantaneous, and I actually saw those proverbial sparks. Tears finally came, along with the pain at the back of my head.

Donna, Tanya, Barbara, Ken, Michael, George, and Mr. Peterson all lunged towards Kevin.

Pamela Blake smacked Barbara on the back, and Curtis grabbed Ken's arms holding them behind his back, until Donna broke them up, while George and Mr. Peterson tried to pull Kevin off me. I watched it all through a haze.

In rapid succession I saw Grandma looking lost, and Melva sharing her history with me as she attempted to teach me not to hate. Michael Baker's tear-stained face was in my line of sight, as was Barbara trying to fend off Pamela's heavy hands.

Kevin wouldn't get off me, and I stared up with glazed eyes at his angry countenance. Anger, pain from my injuries, and despair worked together on the prehistoric part of my brain. It automatically set my lungs, vocal cords, and finally my mouth on a suicidal mission. I produced a soft sound that my lips, tongue, and teeth grabbed unto and shaped as it entered the world as, "N----r." I won't even put it in print.

Everyone was busy, and no one seemed to hear me, including Kevin. Still under the prehistoric part of my brain, I said it louder. "N----r." Just a single word.

The universe stopped: breathing, movement, time. Life as I knew it was over for the second time in less than a week.

There it was. I said it, and I couldn't take it back. The word I had formed metastasized, and nothing could control what I unleashed. I knew my life was changed. I simply closed my eyes, lying and waiting for whatever came next.

CHAPTER FORTY-ONE

Moments Later

Mr. Strong came running around the corner bringing motion back to the scene, and unaware of what he was facing. He soon learned he had little power over the unfolding drama. Initially my use of the forbidden word had stunned everyone into frozen silence, but now as the news spread like fire up and down the hall, the scent of blood tainted the air, and a mob quickly formed around me. I struggled to my feet while Mr. Strong and Mr. Peterson tried to salvage some order.

I crossed a line to a forbidden and dangerous place. "Boy," "honky," "whitey," "pussy," and "faggot" were called out incessantly by my black peers, but the unwritten rules forbade the use of any derogative term to describe blacks—unless used by another black. The "N" word stood at the top of the pile of forbidden epithets. I had cast myself hurtling towards a terrible reckoning.

As the calls for beating and even lynching me arose from the black students now emptying into the hallways, I was suddenly yanked away and lifted above the crowd by a pair of strong black hands. I found myself riding on broad shoulders, carried at full speed along the hallway and downstairs to the gym. Mr. Wendell did not stop until he had me in the relative safety of his office with the door locked. He lowered me to the floor, and motioned for me to sit in the chair opposite the desk. Mr. Wendell looked at me, shaking his head as he let out a sigh.

"I told you to talk to me if you needed to."

My mind spun like a blender on high speed: whirling around with fear, regret, and a paralyzing anxiety.

Mr. Wendell's face was an unreadable mask. I wished this were all part of the nightmare that began last Sunday at the temple. If only I could awaken to last week when my greatest concern was whether or not Barbara and I would make out at the next party.

If Mr. Wendell would just go out there, and tell everyone that I was upset because of Grandpa, they'd all understand, feel sorry for me, and just forget all this. I felt ashamed in front of Mr. Wendell. My use of the angry epithet seemed a grievous mistake—perhaps an unforgivable act. He must understand that I was driven to it. I only meant to refer to Kevin, who'd acted so brutishly. Mr. Wendell knew my family. He knew we weren't the kind of people who hurled poisoned darts freely.

Would my parents be ashamed of me, or would they understand my state of mind? I couldn't imagine either of them ever using the "N" word. Then again, my parents never went to my school. I recalled Mom's telling me about her experience with integration in the 1940s. She attended Chicago Teacher's College with a group of elegant, light-skinned black women whose only social sin was that they were a bit snobbish.

Nancy and our friends wouldn't be shocked to hear about my outburst. What I said was nothing that they didn't think about at least once each day at school.

I actually felt a flash of relief knowing that Grandpa wouldn't hear about my scandal. He would've been the hardest person to face other than... Oh, God! Melva! What if this got back to her?

While Mr. Wendell and I sat silently and uncomfortably across from each other, outside the locked door, a chain of events was set in motion, and my hope of a pardon died a stillborn.

Using the threat of multiple detentions and even suspensions, Dr. Lincoln and Mr. Strong coaxed students back to their classrooms. Some black kids couldn't resist using the disruption as a reason to loiter in a stairwell or side corridor, but eventually order was restored. The air was electrified with the potential for unrest.

Black students conferred in their section of seats within each class as they considered what to do with the racist white boy. Later, I learned they and their parents wanted to know what was to be done to address the injustice and blatant bigotry of not only this one boy (me), but also the entire white student body and the school district. I was the embodiment of the bigotry endemic to the system. I was the proof that roadblocks to the academic progress of black students were intentionally erected. I was a reflection of the recently elected school board that was too cautious about integration.

Although Dr. Lincoln and Mr. Strong were both black, to doubtful black students, their blackness was compromised by their position of power in an organization that was so clearly a product of white values. To these doubters, the two men held their positions to falsely demonstrate the district's commitment to equality. They were puppets hired to reassure the white parents that they weren't too black. They even spoke like honkys. Black men, such as our two school leaders, could only have come so far in life by betraying their black brethren.

By lunchtime a handful of black parents arrived at school demanding both an explanation from Dr. Lincoln, and action to be taken against the bigoted child. They wanted the boy identified, and they demanded assurances that he would be expelled; their children could not be expected to attend school with an evil bigot. Until the expulsion took place, they would keep their children home from school. These knee-jerk reactions snuffed out any opportunity to gain mutual understanding.

Earlier, Mom was called to the school, and reassured that I was unharmed, but not given any details. As she later explained, she couldn't understand why Dr. Lincoln told her to go to the side door leading from the gymnasium. Adding to the mystery, he told her that if she got there soon, the students would be out on the field, and she could enter the gym unnoticed.

Dr. Lincoln met Mom at the gym door. He wore a strained smile as he silently ushered her into Mr. Wendell's office where I still sat frozen. I noticed how tired she looked.

Mr. Wendell stood up, and extended his hand to Mom. She noted that nothing seemed physically wrong with me except that I had been crying, and after briefly shaking Mr. Wendell's hand, she looked him in the eye and asked what was wrong.

Dr. Lincoln stepped in. It was getting crowded in the office with the two big men and my mother standing around me.

"Mrs. Feigman, first let me offer you my sympathies. We were all very sorry to read about the tragedy in your family."

I looked at Mom for signs of a breakdown at the mention of Grandpa. She simply nodded her acknowledgement. "Is that what's bothering Glen?" Then turning to me, "Glen, are you not ready to be back at school? Do you want to come home?"

"Mrs. Feigman, Glen got involved in an incident with some other students today, and in the heat of their battle he used a racial epithet that I'm afraid is going to give us all a problem here."

"What? What happened exactly? I don't understand." She turned to me confused, but concerned, and softly asked me to explain what happened.

When I opened my mouth to speak, the sobbing started. Mom immediately bent down, and put an arm around me, and reassured me that everything would be okay.

"Take your time, and tell me what happened."

Once again that morning, I was overwhelmed by emotion. My head ached from the beating, while shrieking questions and the voices of my assailants and friends bombarded it. Was I a victim or a villain? Was I entitled to any pity or even understanding from Mr. Wendell and Dr. Lincoln? Would Mom be compassionate or disappointed in me? Could these three representatives of the safe and orderly world I had known, until last Sunday, make everyone else understand that I was not an evil person, or was the damage irreversible?

"I didn't do anything bad," I sobbed. "Michael Baker defended me, and so I defended him against Kevin, Curtis, and Pamela, and some other kids that were picking on us." Then I looked over at Dr. Lincoln, "They said Michael wasn't black enough. Then they picked on me too for sticking up for him." Mr. Wendell looked over at Dr. Lincoln who was looking more uncomfortable. I thought I detected the light of reason in Mr. Wendell's eyes.

"They punched me, and kicked me. Mr. Peterson tried to stop them. I was just trying to reason with them, but you can't. They don't listen. They're just mean."

I sidestepped the matter of my use of the forbidden word that swamped everything else combined. Mom didn't push me to say more. Instead she turned toward Dr. Lincoln.

"This is the second time I've been called to this school in a matter of months, because my son was the victim of violence. I know my child, and he's neither violent nor a mean boy. So what gives, gentlemen? What's going on in this school under your oversight, and where are the parents of the children who struck Glen? Why was I called and they weren't?" She glared at Dr. Lincoln. "How is it that you allow this violent behavior? My son doesn't live in a home where intolerance is accepted. His grandfather, who we are currently mourning, was a champion for the dignity of all of us. My son is no bigot." This last declaration gave me yet another stab of guilt. "I can imagine what he said here, but my goodness, is he now going to become some sort of pariah? Is anyone looking into what could drive a quiet, gentle kid to shout obscenities?"

Despite the knot in my stomach, and the guilt that was now wailing away at me like never before, Mom's description touched me.

"The fact is, Mrs. Feigman, Glen used a word that many find offensive to say the least. Now we have a situation. I think that for now it's best to cool things down, so you should take Glen home quickly and quietly, while I work with the parents and students who need some calming down. Then we can all decide how to proceed."

I detected a slight trembling in Mom's voice. "Must I argue the obvious here? My son tried to stop a fight, and he was beaten for it, so he has to leave school? Are the parents who might be so upset aware of anything but the use of a word? Do they know about sticks and stones breaking bones?"

"Mrs. Feigman, surely this is not a good time for you. I can only imagine how difficult things must be right now at home. Maybe Glen could use a little more time there."

Mom pounced. "Don't patronize me, Sir. I don't believe you can imagine how things are with me right now, and I don't care to go into it. And do not presume to tell me what is best for my son. What's going to happen if my son stays in school?"

"Mrs. Feigman, I don't think you realize the hornet's nest Glen, innocently or not, stirred up. He could be very uncomfortable here, and perhaps not completely safe. I'm suggesting you voluntarily keep him home, until we sort things out here, and cooler heads prevail."

"This is absolutely absurd. You people have lost control of your school. Maybe I'm crazy, but you know what Dr. Lincoln? I *am* going to take my son home, but not because he doesn't belong in school, getting an education. I'm beginning to wonder if he *can* get a good education at this school where standards and education come second to his having to worry about who is going to attack him next, while you lower all accepted standards for good behavior and education, so as not to offend anyone. If you set low expectations, you'll get substandard results."

Dr. Lincoln was clearly relieved to hear that I would be going home; in fact, I doubt if he heard anything else Mom said.

I had an out of body experience as I watched Mom and me slip out a side entrance. My school had become an enemy camp from which I had to escape. As we pulled out of the parking lot, I reentered my body in time to feel the nausea that wouldn't leave me for the next several days.

CHAPTER FORTY-TWO

That Evening

"That's enough of this nonsense, Eileen. We're pulling Glen out of that school." From my bedroom, I could hear the anger in Dad's voice. He and Mom were in their room to prevent any *shivah* attendees from overhearing them.

"Don't worry, Eileen, we won't have to move. Nancy can finish up at the high school, but we'll have to find out what it costs, and we'll pay to send Glen to the Michigami schools on the other side of Lawson Avenue. I didn't want to bring it up during all of this, but I understand other families are getting out of the district for similar reasons."

Silence from Mom. At some point I would ask Dad who those families were. They were probably the parents of sixth graders who quickly deduced that the toxic atmosphere at school was incompatible with learning.

"Eileen, I don't want our boy having to put up with bullying and wild behavior in the false name of combating bigotry. I've been thinking a lot about this, and I'm not comfortable with the quality of education that he can receive; not when so much energy has to be spent trying to keep order, and placating a group demanding special treatment."

"Jerry, haven't you felt the same way as I have all these years? Didn't you believe in the vision my father and I shared, and believed in all these years? Were you just going along?"

"Honey, I believe in you, and I always have. From the start I loved your passion for justice for all. I love your belief in our better angels. I admire the rose colored glasses you often wear. I've always supported you, and I want to continue to support you, but the direction in the civil rights movement away from Dr. King, and the change in tone of the discussion, cause me to step back and rethink what our role should be. I'm beginning to see that we might be sacrificing what's best for our own children in terms of not only their education, but also their physical safety. The school board's approach really does a disservice to the cause of social justice and civil rights. It's not going to help the blacks in our community attain better lives for themselves. In fact, I think this approach of placating and walking on eggs to avoid speaking hard truths is going to set them back."

"You really are a good man. My father always said you were. You know he loved you.

"Damn them," Mom muttered. "Damn them all for doing this to us, for putting us in this position. And my God, Jerry, look at my poor father. Have I ever once said anything about the fact that his murderers were black? Have I? I don't even know what to think about that. Should I even consider that?"

"It won't do you or anyone else any good. Your brother does enough thinking about that for everyone anyhow."

"No matter what those outraged parents are saying, we're not bad people. They think *we* are the problem. Has the whole world gone crazy? I'm sorry, Jerry, but it seems to me that taking Glen out of school is an admission of some kind of guilt, and it will send the wrong message to the children. What would my father advise us to do?"

Now Dad was silent. Mom continued.

"I'm done in. I'm confused. I'm worn out. My brain is tired of trying to find reason in a world that's going crazy. I'm as upset as you are, but I have to believe that if we talk to the parents who are upset because of Glen's use of that word, and explain the whole situation, surely they'd understand. I think my father would suggest that, don't you?"

"I think you're being naïve, Eileen. At this point in history we're fighting a relentless tide. They don't need to understand anything. The onus is on us. Glen is just a means to extract more concessions, or find more ways to excuse themselves from taking personal responsibility for their behavior."

"That sounds hateful, although I know you don't mean it that way. How did we come to this, Jer? This doesn't sound like us or what we want or how we want things to be for our kids."

"Honey, I think our children are just fine, and they already have a good sense of right and wrong. There's a limit to how much you can cry victim. Some of these parents and their kids have crossed the line. I'm not having my son become a sacrifice at the altar of *let's-make-eternal-amends-for-American-history*. Let's face it Eileen, when kids want to learn, they learn. We were packed forty in a classroom. Remember? It didn't keep us from applying ourselves, and learning our lessons."

"Jerry, I just can't help thinking of my father. It's as if his efforts for social justice were in vain, and we're part of the reason. I just know he wouldn't want us to walk away from this. He would want us to make things right at Glen's school."

"Your father would be as proud of you as he always was. You haven't betrayed anything he stood for, and neither has Glen. He was standing up against bullies. We need to make sure he understands he was wrong to stoop to name calling, but Glen is an ethical boy."

An ethical boy who hates half the blacks in his school, and beats off thinking of naked guys.

"As Glen's father, I'm making a decision here that I think is for his own good. I really believe there's nothing we can do by ourselves to make things right at his school. It's like fighting a lynch mob. Talk about irony!"

Good one, Dad. He was right. It was ironic that whenever the black kids smelled blood, they were off and running, and well beyond the reach of reason.

"They think pandering is the right way to handle educating the black student body."

Dad sounded like the smartest guy in the world to me. Too bad his opinions were so out of favor.

"If only blacks didn't see education and every other issue through the filter of race. Maybe it's too soon into this civil rights movement we're in."

"But Jerry, I want our kids to be able to get along with everyone, and to have all kinds of friends".

I imagined Dad pacing back and forth, his eyes on his feet.

"I've been giving this a lot of thought. First of all, no one gets along with everyone. There are plenty of white kids whom I'm sure Glen wouldn't choose for friends, just as I'm sure there are black kids with whom he's friendly. It comes down to what Dr. King said about character versus color. I don't want him to think that having to protect your lunch money each day has to be a normal part of an education, if you want to co-exist with blacks. Maybe some folks think it will make him streetwise. I don't see any benefit going down that street."

Now Dad had probably stopped pacing to look directly at Mom.

"Let me ask you something, Eileen. We like to think of ourselves as good people. We try not to judge others unfairly, we firmly believe in social justice, and we like to think we're open-minded, right? Well, where are our black friends? When did we ever have a social circle that included blacks beyond when our paths might have crossed through the school or through some of your dad's efforts?"

It was true. My parents didn't have any close black friends that I knew about.

The silence told me that Mom didn't know what to say.

I was trying to grasp the fact that I might never go back to my school, and that I would face the scrutiny of a whole new group of judgmental, junior high school peers.

"Hon, does the fact that we don't really have any black friends mean that we wouldn't support civil rights, or that we would stand in the way of its progress?"

Silence.

"Like everyone else on the planet, we're most comfortable around the people who are the most like us."

Silence.

"We live our lives, and try not to hurt or interfere in anyone else's life. We don't lead any parades, but we do march in some."

Still there was no reply from Mom, so Dad continued, apparently tapping into a reservoir of old, and unspoken thoughts.

"Let's not beat ourselves up."

Dad must've sat on the bed next to Mom. His voice was less agitated, more tender.

"How would you feel if a black family moved in on the block? I think I know the answer to that. You'd be the first one at their doorstep with a pie—albeit store bought."

Maybe she smiled. He continued.

"But how about two or three or ten black families? I confess I'd be worried that crime and vandalism and gangs and drugs would follow, just like in so many other places. The money we invested in this house might disappear. But you know what I hope would happen?"

No response.

"I hope we would stay, and my fears proved unfounded. I hope that the black families would show all of us that they want the same things for their kids that we do, and that we share the same values. And their kids would show up at school ready and willing to learn."

"My gosh, Jer. Such questions you ask me, and so much to think about. What happens to my responsibility to protect my children when doing so conflicts with my belief in digging in, and fighting for integration? Or what if we've been wrong all these years? What if my father was wrong? What if integration will never unite blacks and whites? What if both groups are happier apart? That's an awful thought."

"Well, just think about all of our friends who finally had to give up, and leave their South Side neighborhoods. They tried hanging on to make a point that integration could work. So what happened? Their kids and their property were attacked. So they left. Does that make them bigots? Are they bad people? Most of them are still fighting the good fight, although they had to retreat some to do it. Wouldn't it be nice if we could have an honest dialogue about this? But no one is listening. Everyone is too busy shouting."

"I feel sick to my stomach. The year is almost up. What are we going to do, pull him out of school with a few weeks to go?"

"All right, Dear. Let me change direction for a minute. While things don't look good right now for racial harmony in our case, that doesn't mean that integration won't work in other circumstances at other times. Let's at least acknowledge that our kids had some good experiences, and made some black friends. They'll never be able to accept a blanket statement of bigotry when they remember those faces. That's some sort of victory isn't it?"

"I suppose."

"It's too bad those parents think they're helping their situation by removing a boy like Glen from school. They ought to sit down with Glen, and learn who he really is."

"Wouldn't that be something wonderful?"

Yikes. If they found out who I really was, they'd like me even less.

"I don't see it happening. For the situation to get better at that school—and I am not just talking about Glen's incident or the Mace or the thieving or even the basketball riot at the high school, but the whole damned question of race and education—it would require two sides coming together with an open mind, and no scores to settle. We just aren't there."

Another silence. They were each in their own thoughts.

"I'll talk to the principal to see if we can arrange for Glen to do whatever work is left for the year from home. Then we can register him in Michigami, and pay whatever tuition we need to. It's going to be expensive."

Now I'm costing my parents extra money.

"I'm really sick about this, Jer. It's part of this whole nightmare that started last Sunday. Damn it all. Damn, damn, damn."

What a horrible child I must be to bring this added stress to my parents, at such a difficult time.

"When Glen leaves they'll be convinced that we're the enemy. *We*, Jerry! How can that be? How have we become the enemy? Between this and my father, it's too much, and I don't have the energy. We'll do what you say. I don't know what's right anymore."

CHAPTER FORTY-THREE

Immediate Aftermath

I never again entered my school. I never rode the bus or had the privilege of sitting in the back seats as an eighth grader. Through high school graduation there wasn't a black in any class. No one shoved me into a locker, blocked my passage down a hallway, tripped me, hit me, or stole from me. I was no longer "boy." But I also never shared a funny moment with a Marybeth, Donna, or a Cleon.

School assemblies at PrairieVille Junior High School in Michigami were quiet, orderly, and dull. At eighth grade commencement, just as the principal requested, families held their applause until the last name was called.

The socio-economics of the white (and mostly Jewish kids) of the two school districts were similar, but my new classmates were provincial and naïve about the world outside Michigami. Humor in my Hampden class was juvenile, but at PrairieVille it was infantile. I felt superior to my new classmates.

PrairieVille's bullies and troublemakers were minor leaguers who would've crumbled when faced with a Kevin McPherson, Curtis May, or Serena Gibson.

All the usual characters walked the halls at PriairieVille. Jocks sat at the top of the hierarchy. Queers (in the old sense of the word), nerds, clowns, bullies, and fems filled out the ranks. Since everyone was white, if you were picked on, it was because of your character, not your color. Obeying the universal rule, effeminate boys were tormented by bullies, jocks, and PrairieVille's version of the mall girls. As I progressed through high school, the snickers of "faggot" fell on my ears with greater frequency, and they hurt no less than the physical pain that Kevin inflicted on the back of my head. I felt nostalgic for the appellate of "boy" or "honky" whenever I heard "faggot" from some white kid.

When asked about the dangers at Hampden, I defended my old school. But Hampden continued to let me down. When PrairieVille's basketball team played at Hampden, our team bus was almost flipped over by a mob, even though we were trounced.

I recalled the black kids whom I genuinely liked, and I missed the interaction with kids from a different demographic. If anyone spoke disparagingly about blacks, it was Donna and company, and Melva who came to mind, and I defended their honor. Dad was right. I couldn't accept a blanket statement of bigotry thanks to my time at Hampden. That was a victory for Grandpa and Mom.

After "the incident," for the three weeks of class that remained of the school year, and with the blessings of the administration, my teachers worked out a plan for me to work from home. Everyone at the Board of Education and in the administration breathed a sigh of relief when my parents notified them that I would not return to school. Concerned black parents had their pound of flesh, and could safely allow their innocents to return to school without the threat to their well being that I presented.

Among my friends, feelings were confused. To a few—particularly Ken, Gary, and our friends around the lunch table—I was a hero for giving back some of the verbal abuse we endured for two years. To others, even though they knew me well, I was tainted. Mouthing the "N" word indicated that I possessed a degree of carelessness, bigotry, or evil. Others were simply jealous that I left Hampden.

That first summer progressed like any previous summer. Michigami friendships lay in the future, so I hung around Ken, Gary, and the rest of our group. Once school started, I made new friends. Although I was invited to some of the bar mitzvahs of my Hampden friends, we had less to talk about since we no longer shared daily experiences.

I took Barbara Needleman to my first Michigami party. My new friends were impressed with her. Barbara never asked me back to her house, because her parents were uncomfortable with the reasons for my departure from Hampden, but that didn't stop me from making my relationship with Barbara out to be more than it was, so I wouldn't have to make out with other girls.

People had the need to classify me in familiar categories so they looked for clues. The "f" word reared up when it became clear I couldn't field a well-hit ball, and lacked interest in joining intramurals. Like in Hampden, I fell in with the bright, not totally uncoordinated, middling set. Without black kids opening doors to mischief at PrairieVille—sort of the way older siblings beget parental leniency for their younger brothers and sisters—the kids at PrairieVille were better behaved than the white kids in Hampden. Lower standards for what was considered proper conduct hadn't crossed Lawson Avenue.

CHAPTER FORTY-FOUR

I n the years since "the incident," the U.S. has become more diversified, and the pendulum remains stuck on the side of accommodation. The widely understood code of proper behavior during my early childhood and of earlier generations, particularly towards elders and educators, has all but disintegrated. Crossing Lawson Avenue is no longer a guarantee that you'll be met with civility.

No one in the Hampden school administration asked me to explain the events of that day in May of 1970, or to voice my criticism of their approach to integration.

I wore the "N" word like a self-judged Hester Pryne, and I was genuinely sorry for using it. My regret deepened rather than dissipated with time. I wanted a do-over. I wanted to personally apologize to all the black people I had known who never wished me any ill will, and often proffered their hands in friendship.

I didn't dislike all blacks, just a group of kids in my school, and others I now see on the street, in move theaters, on public transportation, or in the news; like the kids who killed Grandpa, who refuse to conform to anything close to the norms of civilized behavior. I feel no differently about whites who fit the same description—it's just that I rarely encounter them where I live or travel, or where local crime is covered.

My family's equilibrium was permanently reset by the events of that May. For a woman who saw the world in black and white, Grandma now found it hard to make simple decisions. Chicken or brisket? She talked less but didn't listen more. She looked smaller, more fragile.

By year's end, Grandma moved in with us. At 5:00 on Friday evenings, acting out an old ritual, she peered out the front window towards the bus stop. After a moment she would mutter as she walked back to the kitchen.

The legal wrangling surrounding Grandpa's youthful killers was a continuous assault on our family, and Mom in particular. The defense attorneys assigned to the case claimed the boys had no personal responsibility for their actions on that Sunday morning, because society was at fault. The two had been condemned to being raised by absent fathers and indifferent mothers. We were all to blame if they didn't know right from wrong. They lived in a violent environment of our making, one that had its own code of conduct.

Mom was as confused as she was outraged. She railed against the "creeping sickness" in our country that granted blanket exemptions from personal responsibility for entire groups of people, and she didn't care if Nancy or I heard her. Yet, she asked to meet with each boy, with or without his family. Dad was against it, but Mom said it was something she had to do. She wanted the boys to know something about the man they killed. She also hoped to somehow bring something good out of the horrific event. She wasn't sure what that would be, or how she would do it, but she felt the answer might lie with the two boys.

Dad insisted on going with Mom to the juvenile detention home. Although it was an unusual request, especially since the trial was not over, the two counselors, each representing one of the boys, allowed it.

Darius was the name of one of the boys, and his mother was in attendance. Mom said the mother couldn't have been more than twenty-five years old. Darius's mother said her son was sorry for what he did, and that he didn't mean to hurt anyone. When she asked Darius to confirm this, without looking up, he mumbled, "yeah." When Mom attempted to tell Darius something about Grandpa, and how he wanted to help children like Darius to achieve good things for themselves in life, neither Darius's mother, nor Darius seemed to understand why Mom was telling them this. Darius's mother asked Mom why she wanted to put her baby through this legal stuff.

"He said he was sorry. He should be going to school, and not in this place. If that old man wanted to help boys like Darius, you should let him go."

Mom was stunned. She wanted to forgive Darius, and she did, but she never thought she would be asked to let him go free from facing the consequences of his actions. She looked at Dad with desperation in her eyes. She needed someone, someone like Grandpa to tell her the right thing to do.

"We should go, Eileen," Dad said. Mom didn't say anything. Later, Dad told me that Darius's mother called after them to let Darius go home.

The counselor for Antoine, the other boy, accompanied him to meet with Mom and Dad. Mom started to ask him why he set out to rob and hurt someone, and Antoine became immediately defiant, so his counselor abruptly ended the visit. As he led Antoine away, Mom apparently called out, "I forgive you, Antoine," but only Dad heard her.

The boys were tried as juveniles, found guilty of manslaughter, and sentenced to a juvenile home. There they would be exposed to more violence, and an ineffective system of education and remediation. About the time I would graduate from high school, they would be of legal age, and set free, with permanently sealed records of their crime. The likely outcome of this "justice" would be two lives of perpetual criminality.

The judge decided that the boys had set out to create mischief, and did not mean to kill Grandpa, but only scare him, and take anything of value. He believed, as the defense attorneys claimed, that Grandpa's death from the beating on his head was unintentional, although the beating itself was not. The boys themselves seemed unimpressed that their actions had mortal consequences.

Uncle Marty was horrified that any excuse could be made. He said once gain that if his son and his son's friend had attacked a black man who accidentally died from the attack, the city would go up in flames. He compared it to when Arabs kill a Jew, the world calls for restraint. But if an Arab accidentally dies when the Jews of Israel defend themselves from attacks on Israeli civilians, in an astonishingly cruel perversion of history, the Moslem world, with tacit approval from others, accuses the Israelis of attempted genocide.

The combination of Grandpa's death, the aftermath of my incident at school, and finally, the court proceedings, shook Mom like a violent seizure. No one was more rooted in Grandpa's ideologies than she. In the past, Grandpa could help her process cognitive dissonance. Now she turned to Dad whose influence over her increased. Rather than one of Grandpa's thought-provoking questions to her questions, Dad gave her practical advice and opinions that sounded more like Uncle Marty than Grandpa.

Mom became more energized in her opposition to the elevation of Spanish speaking immigrants over other groups, proclaiming it "un-American." She tried to convince any Hispanic school leader who might listen that granting special treatment while lowering expectations was no formula for success. She had seen that it did not appear to be working for the blacks of Hampden, so she had little hope it would elevate the Hispanics of Chicago. This put her in direct conflict with the emerging, clout-heavy Hispanic community, and she was eventually transferred to an all black school on the South Side where Spanish wasn't spoken.

When Dad and her friends told her that teaching on the South Side was too dangerous, she refused to pay attention. Perhaps she felt nostalgic to take a bullet for the old team—even at the risk of real bullets. Grandpa and Mom once said that to assume the South Side is dangerous is synonymous with believing all black people are dangerous, and so she found the warnings an unacceptable generalization. She would carry Grandpa's legacy forward. "You'll see. I'll meet wonderful people, and implant the love of learning that is innate to the human soul. These people are hungry for knowledge, and their just waiting for the right teacher."

Within a few weeks at her new school, she was threatened at knifepoint, her purse was stolen, her windshield was smashed, and someone tried to break into the car while she stopped at a light near the school. She found no way to break through the violence and the anti-education attitude of the students and families. If she got through taking attendance, her day was a success. Mom debated about transferring to a suburban school, but instead she chose to retire. Moving to an all white school, she reasoned, would be an admission of the defeat of Grandpa's belief that if given the chance, blacks would seize any opportunity at education, and work to advance themselves.

Mom's was not so much a complete makeover, as it was a blurring of her neatly outlined views about race. Stereotyping or making derogatory remarks, serious or in jest, remained punishable offenses in her company. She remained outraged at what she perceived to be a social injustice—only now she recognized that victims of injustice come in all creeds and colors.

Uncle Marty felt vindicated for having said that Mom's and Grandpa's lopsided view of race relations would bite them in their butts, and he took pleasure in giving back what he had gotten from them at so many family dinners.

But at Shabbat dinners, the topic of school and race were mostly avoided after Aunt Marion commented that she was happy I was "out of that school system," and Mom reflexively snapped at her that there was nothing wrong with the Hampden school system. Uncle Marty asked her with glee if she could then explain why she moved me to Michigami schools. She seemed stunned for a moment, and then answered weakly that there were some unreasonable parents who'd made my move necessary. Uncle Marty viewed this as a defeat for "the bleeding hearts club of guilt-ridden whites," but he chose to keep quiet.

I figured out a way to blame myself. Surely it was I who handed Uncle Marty this victory over Mom and Grandpa, even if I agreed with him.

Among Mom and Dad and their many close friends, communication was circumspect if any party was uneasy discussing either Grandpa's death or my abrupt exit from Hampden's school system. One exception was Phyllis Reznick, one of Mom's friends who had moved to Hampden a few years earlier, after her newly integrated South Side neighborhood became inhospitable to whites. She remained an unapologetic liberal who took issue with Mom's decision to send me to PrairieVille Junior High, "a segregated island of middle class mediocrity."

She sat with Mom over coffee at our breakfast room table one Saturday afternoon, and I overheard Mrs. Reznick say, "Being tormented a bit by black classmates is a necessary burden if we're to bring blacks fully along the path of equality. You can be proud that your kid was smacked a little once or twice. He wasn't killed, for crying out loud.

"And being called "boy" and "honky" are steps towards true empathy with the oppressed."

She wanted me to return to Hampden, and issue a formal apology to my black classmates and their families. "What Glen said is inexcusable under any circumstances. There's nothing equally foul that a black could say or do to a white." She didn't feel I was owed an apology for my beating, which had come first.

Her oldest son later attended Hampden High School, and was beaten up in school and on the street. This didn't seem to bother Mrs. Reznick, although as soon as he was old enough, her son moved to Montana.

"Jerry, how was I ever friends with that nut case? I must've been as crazy as she is. Was I just blind?" Mom never spoke to her again.

CHAPTER FORTY-FIVE

Autumn 1980

My first gay sex experience was approximately one year before AIDS began to attract minor notice. In October of 1980, I was twenty-three, and working on a master's degree.

When I was an undergraduate, if anyone wanted hetero sex, it wasn't difficult to find a willing partner; the guys were always willing, and no girl wanted to be the last virgin on campus.

Anxiety, self-loathing, isolation, and a whole laundry list of misery occupied my college years as I strived unsuccessfully to be attracted to the sweet, pretty girls I dated. The news from Ken, Gary, and my other "normal" friends was always upbeat, with updates about the girls they dated, craved, or "nailed" (that would be Ken), and the plans they made to travel with women post graduation. There was no doubt in my mind that Gary, an icon of stability, would marry his college sweetheart, and he did.

There was one, openly gay student on my entire campus, an exchange student from Denmark. He appeared happy and self-assured in his flamboyance. Even this gay Dane, who every guy I knew called "faggot" under his breath, was better than me.

I decided to see a college counselor, something none of my friends felt the need to do, thus reinforcing my identity as sub-normal. The counselor, instead of being a bearded, avuncular academic, with patches on his corduroy jacket elbows, was a thirty-something, over-achieving, psychiatrist Adonis who drove to campus in a late model Mercedes convertible. There was a photograph of a beautiful woman with a pretty little girl on his bookcase, which I assumed to be of his wife and child. *Now I know the reason so many of the girls on campus made counseling appointments,* I said to myself.

Here I was, face-to-face with this dazzling man, trying to admit that I *might* have some gay thoughts from time to time (like at that very moment). I was too ashamed to speak the truth, so he became aggressive in his questioning.

"What are you trying to say? Do you think about sucking cock?"

I almost had a spontaneous orgasm as his words invaded my inner ears, directly from that sexy mouth; his dark eyes held me with some sort of glue-like testosterone. We were seated in facing armchairs; his beefy thighs spread apart. I had nowhere else to look.

My reflexive response was nothing less than the lie of the year. "No!"

"Well then, just what do you think about?"

"I don't know."

He surely knew, but he couldn't bring me where I wasn't ready to go. He prescribed Valium for the anxiety, and told me things would get better. They didn't, but I did have someone new to add to my fantasies. When I remember him, I wonder what would've happened if I'd answered his question about cock-sucking with a resounding, "Oh, yes! And I want to suck yours more than anyone's." I heard some years later that he was arrested for having sex with female clients. Perhaps he was kinky enough to have considered me.

I carried my misery to graduate school. That's when I met Andrew.

Before Andrew, I found the courage to make regular visits to a large, all-night newspaper and magazine store in the city. Along with *The Financial Times of London, The Wall Street Journal,* and *The Economist,* they sold gay pornography in the form of cheap novels, and magazines with alluring covers of half naked men who were fully naked within the covers. When driving there, my pulse would quicken, and guilt would launch butterflies throughout my abdominal cavity. The first few times I dared to enter, I grabbed some magazines, went to the counter, having also picked up the obligatory copy of *Sports Illustrated,* and paid the clerk without ever making eye contact. After some weeks, I was a bit less frantic.

The effect of devouring the porn novels was to believe that the only way to have sex with a man was to be abducted by a motorcycle gang, and become an unwilling sex slave. All the men in the stories and photographs were exceptional physical specimens, skewing my notion of the kinds of guys with whom I could be having motorcycle gang sex.

On a sunny, but cold October Saturday at the university library, I sat in a cushy armchair in the reading lounge, highlighting passages in my marketing textbook, and occasionally glancing at a cute guy seated in the chair next to me. I had already fantasized about being abducted and taken on his motorcycle to a remote cabin for sex slaves, when he leaned over and asked if he could talk to me. He was close enough for me to smell his minty-fresh breath. I looked into his watery brown eyes, and I liked what I saw—and felt.

"Sure," I said. He asked me to follow him to an area where talking wasn't discouraged, causing a small rush of endorphins to flood my brain. *So this is how the kidnapping begins.* As I walked behind him, I noticed he was slightly taller and broader than I, and his butt filled out his khakis.

We walked into an empty room that was enclosed by glass walls and windows that looked over a small courtyard. There were inviting groupings of chairs and couches from which my mystery man picked out an isolated area, and motioned for me to sit. Our chairs formed a right angle, and when he sat down, he let our knees touch. After more than a decade of despairing that this could ever happen, a grade school fantasy about Ben Rubin had finally been fulfilled, with this stranger a worthy substitute for Ben.

"I'm Andrew," he declared, waiting for my response.

"Hi. Glen here. Nice to meet you." We didn't shake hands. I looked at him expectantly. His aura of calm, self-confidence complemented my neurotic nature.

"Listen, I've seen you in the gay section of the newsstand…"

My ears started to ring, and my vision blurred. I fell backward into an alternate universe. For the first time in my life, someone had hard (no pun intended) proof that I was gay—or of the unlikely possibility that I was doing extensive research into gay pornography. The implications overwhelmed me.

"I don't know what you're talking about," I started to get up, but Andrew put a strong hand on my arm, pulling me back down.

"Glen, please. I'm sorry. I didn't mean to confront you. I should've realized you might not be out to yourself at this point."

If he hadn't been so attractive, I might've pulled away, but in an instant I decided to let this play out. My brain was processing furiously, the only outward sign were the tears pooling in the corners of my eyes. Soon the floodgates opened and I began a stream of consciousness confessional to Andrew. With every word that left me, an element of euphoria filled the void, until I was lifted, along with the weight of my entire life until that moment, into a parallel world filled with hope and a glorious light.

It was more than Andrew had bargained for, but he was a perfect gentleman. After many minutes he held up his hand to quiet me, and told me to come with him to an off-campus diner to continue our talk. I would've followed him anywhere—even if there were a motorcycle gang waiting for us at the diner.

We talked for hours over coffee and pancakes. I finally let him tell me about himself. He was two years older than I, and one semester away from a law degree. He grew up in a conservative Christian home in Indianapolis, and for the first time in my life, I found myself falling in love with someone who could possibly love me back.

Without knowing what would happen, we went back to his apartment, a typical student's this-is-only-temporary-until-my-real-life-begins apartment. I looked in the bedroom, and noticed the unmade bed and some clothes on the floor. It struck me as sexy as I thought about my own bed, made up with hospital corners.

I stood in the middle of the entry hall, frozen in place, expecting Grandma to awaken me for school at any moment. Instead, Andrew turned towards me, and brought me to him in a hug. I would've wept with joy, but I didn't want to dampen his soft, fisherman's knit sweater. We stood like that for many minutes. I feared that if I broke the hug, he would say, "Good-bye." When he did pull apart from me, he told me that he was interested in me, but clearly I wasn't ready for "anything." I wasn't as sure, but didn't want to argue with him—yet. We sat on his couch, and talked as our reflections began to take shape in the windows against the growing darkness outside. We had much to tell each other, and the words came without effort. When he noticed I couldn't keep my eyes open, he covered me with an afghan, and I fell asleep on his couch.

Some hours later he awakened me with a kiss. What a kiss! A guy, a cute guy, kissed me on the lips. So this is the thrill that all my friends felt and talked about since we were adolescents at make-out parties.

I left Andrew's in the middle of the night, determined to tell my family that I *might* be gay, that I was through making myself miserable, and that I needed to explore to be sure. That meant having sex with Andrew, but I would leave that part out.

Between times spent with Andrew, I could think of no one else. We talked on the phone at least once a day, and met for lunch in the cafeteria whenever possible. Suddenly, I was impatient to be done with school. Isolation was lifting, and the world was decidedly changed. A spirit of adventure had overtaken me with surprising alacrity. On Friday, Andrew asked me to join him and some friends for lunch on Saturday.

We walked into a restaurant together, and self-consciousness overcame me. Surely everyone was looking at us disdainfully, and declaring us to be fags. The feeling increased as we sat at a table where four other guys—all gay—waited our arrival. They scrutinized me as closely as anyone since my last physical. I was thrilled by the idea that Andrew might be presenting me to his gang as his new boyfriend. I wanted their approval, and for the first time in my life, I could get it by being the real me. No need to mute my emotions or worry about the angle of my wrists. Ecstasy. The beauty of the dream that began with Andrew only one week earlier continued to wax.

I experienced some disappointment, that I never knew their world existed, and that there was no Peter Fonda of *Hell's Angels* look alike in the group. But they were all educated, outwardly well-adjusted, everyday guys. When we left en masse, I sensed judgmental looks from every direction.

We hadn't made post-lunch plans, but Andrew and I ended up at his apartment. We decided to order-in pizza for dinner, open a bottle of wine, and watch TV. I felt unworthy of the joy that filled every cell of my body.

After pizza and two glasses of wine, Andrew dimmed the lights, lit some vanilla scented candles (to this day, they remain my favorite), and instead of TV, he put Art Garfunkel's *Breakaway* on the stereo. By the third track I had my first view of Andrew's naked body, bathed in candlelight stretched out before me, a Greek god. Before the track ended, I had my first orgasm with another human being. Andrew understood my lack of control. My first experience would never make it past the editors of those trashy novels. It took until the middle of the flip side for my second release.

All things gay consumed me. Time spent with anyone who wasn't gay, was time lost. The construction of my new life began, and I was determined to quickly build it with new friends with whom I could experience everything in life all over again, only this time, as the real Glen.

The Wednesday after that first love-making session, my parents, Nancy, her fiancé Ron, and I sat at the kitchen table over a dinner of lamb chops when apropos of nothing, I said, "I think I'm bi-sexual, or something."

"I knew it," Nancy said without missing a beat, earning an odd look from Mom. Ron refused to look up from his plate.

"What makes you say that?" Mom asked.

"I've wondered for a long time. You know I've been unhappy and making myself crazy. I can't do it anymore. Since I've decided this, I've never felt better."

"Well, okay. It might be just a phase. I mean it might take a few years to get out of your system, but it's probably something temporary."

Dad, who hadn't shown any outward reaction said, "Just be sure you always seek out people with good values, just as you've always done. You can't go wrong if you do."

"Of course, I will. Don't worry."

I consider that my official coming out, made easy by incredibly loving and wise parents. Thus began my parents' gradual understanding of me as a gay man, and the subculture I was to inhabit, until being gay became almost mainstream—at least in our circle.

After several weeks, Andrew's perfection started to show flaws, or I began to look for them. *Why couldn't he make his bed?* It wasn't long before I decided there had to be someone better for me. His graduation plan was to move back to Indianapolis, which gave me a reason to distance myself from him. Ironically, it was I who felt abandoned and insulted when he easily acquiesced to my suggestion that we see less of each other.

There must be a kernel of truth to the twin beliefs that you never forget your first love, and you never completely stop loving them. Andrew was the best thing that could've happened to me in the autumn of 1980.

CHAPTER FORTY-SIX

Friday, April 10, 1987

The morning of my thirtieth birthday, six and one half years after my coming out over a lamb chops dinner, I woke up to a phone call from Mom.

"Your father and I wanted to catch you before you went to work. We won't sing now. We'll save it for tonight at Shabbat dinner. What time will you be here?"

"What time am I always there on Friday?"

"I just thought maybe for your big birthday you'd want to come earlier."

"I can't get out of work early. I'll be there by six as usual."

"Wait, Dad wants to say something. I love you. Happy thirtieth birthday, Glenny."

I heard what sounded like protests from Dad as she handed him the phone.

"All I wanted to say was 'happy birthday,' old man. When I was your age I had already fought in a world war, was married, and had a child."

"We're all grateful to you for your service to our country. Sorry I couldn't arrange another war for me. And about that wife and child..."

"Just giving you a hard time. You know that. We want you to be happy and healthy. And we don't want you to end up alone."

"Don't forget rich." I interjected, hoping to add humor, and veer away from the topic of a permanent relationship.

"The older you get, the less that matters."

"Yeah, but you know what Grandma always says, "Rich or poor, it's good to have money.""

"Well, you know it does no good to argue with your grandmother. She'll be waiting at the window at 5:00, wondering why you're late."

Mom said something in the background.

"Your mother says to get off the phone or you'll be late for work."

"I'm going running now."

"Be careful. Be sure you're wearing good shoes. You know you can damage your knees and shins otherwise."

"I'll be fine. Thanks for the birthday call."

"We'll see you later. Your mother says to be careful running by the lake. Don't trip. You can fall in the water, and no one would know. People drown in Lake Michigan every day."

"Good-bye. I'm hanging up now."

Why did I immediately feel free-floating guilt after talking to Mom and Dad?

I ran down the 15 flights of stairs, wished the doorman a good morning, walked the short distance to Lincoln Park, and began my daily run along the lakefront. The sun had emerged from its night's liquid slumber under Lake Michigan, and now sat above the watery horizon. I listened to my regular cassette, and by the third disco song the runner's high set in, and I reflected upon my life.

I worked on the creative side of an advertising agency in downtown Chicago. To be out at work was the exception, and I was no trendsetter, although the savvier of my co-workers figured it out. I declined to play for the firm's softball team, having served my time in high school.

When Carlos, the first black to be hired in our division, came on board, although it was unspoken, the belief among the staff was that he was an affirmative action employee. No one but me recognized that he was gay, yet we didn't come out to each other. He was extremely closeted, because ironically, the black community was deeply intolerant.

When introduced to him, I said I grew up in Hampden, which was code for: *I grew up with blacks*, thinking this might ingratiate me to him. To silence the silent doubters, I hoped he'd turn out to be a creative superstar. Fairly or not, when he barely broke average, I joined the others in assuming he was an affirmative action hire.

Our receptionist, Cassandra, was black. We laughed together frequently, because she had that same sense of humor that drew me to so many of the black girls in Hampden classes.

From the time I crossed Lawson Avenue to finish my education, until I met Cassandra and Carlos, I had little day-to-day contact with persons of color, with the exception of Melva, the doormen in my building, and a few neighbors.

During my freshman year of college, the resident advisor was a genial black sophomore named Devin—one of the few blacks in the dormitory. The rest of us quickly sized him up, determining him to be an affirmative action student. We were polite, respectful, and friendly, but no one took what Devin said seriously. He was usually holed up in his room beating off to *Love to Love You Baby*.

After graduate school, I bought a condominium in a high rise in a section of Chicago that was gaining a reputation as

Boystown. Like much of Chicago, it was gentrifying rapidly. Just to the north was Uptown, an island of low-income housing and a black population encouraged by an alderman with dreams of a communist Utopia. Uptown nights brought bullets, vandals, and muggers to the streets.

My new, non-Jewish friends and white neighbors openly acknowledged to each other that Uptown's problem was its low-income, black population. No one analyzed it. Little effort was made to conceal a fear and dislike of blacks based on their limited exposure, unless a black person was present.

In spite of Grandpa and Mom's best efforts years earlier, I found no reason to defend the criminal class. When a group of young black men headed my way from Uptown, the smart thing to do was to cross the street. It was sensible to avoid the L stop in the middle of their neighborhood. Both steps reduced the chances of a mugging or beating. Urban whites morphed into the persecuted blacks of the Old South. When in Uptown, we didn't let the sun set on our backs.

I loved my apartment, my neighborhood, and my social life. I remained friends with Ken, Gary, and some of the guys I had met at Michigami. There was a period of adjustment when I came out to them, but as we got older, their comfort level with me, and mine with them, found our equipoise.

I was happiest with my gay friends, who were mostly Christian, and white. Gay life reflected all life in Chicago, and that meant racial segregation.

A black woman named Lorrina lived with her young son, Alden, on my floor. He was a sweet child. I almost said "boy," but I can't comfortably use this word for a black, even when he's only five years old.

Sports products that clients gave me made nice gifts for Alden. He let me pick him up and hug him whenever he thanked me. It was impossible to ignore the mixed race element of our friendship; there was a feeling of satisfaction that wouldn't be there if he and Lorrina were white.

A stud-like, arrogant snob of a Jewish guy named Stuart lived down the hall. I imagined anti-Semites who met him found justification for their hatred of the rest of us. Is there a critical mass of Stuarts required to bring disdain to a whole race, religion, or other differentiator? Did it only take one? I thought for a moment that I might have missed my calling in anthropology.

CHAPTER FORTY-SEVEN

That Evening

I took the L and a bus from downtown to what I still called "our" house. I discerned Grandma's tiny, 91 year-old frame in the dining room window as she maintained her weekly vigil. I walked up the driveway, and she left her post to open the front door.

Latke, the miniature schnauzer Mom and Dad brought home after Matzah died, was a geezer himself. Still, he jumped and squealed upon my arrival as best he could.

"You're late. I was worried. There are so many crazy people out there nowadays."

I kissed Grandma on the cheek, set down my briefcase, and picked up squirming Latke. "Grandma, I get here at this time every week. I'm not late." There was something poetic about Grandma's opacity. The tradition of Grandma's Friday night window vigil didn't die with Grandpa; she reset her focus on Dad. When I finished college and began attending Shabbat dinners, she watched for me. "Happy birthday, *Tatela*. Did your friends at work do anything nice for you?"

"Yeah. They brought in a cake, and decorated my office."

"Oh, that's nice. Your mother is in the kitchen. I hope we eat soon. I don't know how long she can cook a chicken without it falling apart."

Since Grandma's abdication, Mom cooked Shabbat dinners. Grandma looked frail, but her doctor said she was healthy "for her age." She took weekly walks to the beauty shop where those who knew her for decades continued to marvel that her hair hadn't turned white; to me it was still colorless. Other than that, her life consisted of visits to the doctor, and accompanying Mom and Dad to wherever they took her. The rest of the time she talked on the phone with Agnes and Gussie—her surviving sisters—skimmed the daily paper, kept the television on, and talked incessantly to unsuspecting visitors.

As Mom lit the Shabbat candles, I looked around the dining room table, and wondered if I should feel nostalgic on this milestone birthday. Nothing differed from the week before, or even the year before, so I reached back to a time when other faces looked back at me. I paused at the last time all of my grandparents sat around the Shabbat table together; it was the year of my bar mitzvah, Grandpa's death, and the "incident." *I'm getting old,* I thought. More years had passed since my Bar mitzvah than the thirteen years that preceded it. Who will be around the table in another thirteen years, or twenty, or more?

Dad said the *Kiddush* and the traditional blessings for children over my two-year-old niece, Leda. Nancy encouraged her daughter, named for Grandpa Leo, to lead us in the Hebrew blessing over the *challah*. She could barely construct a sentence in English, but we were anticipating big things for Mom's and Dad's first grandchild.

Nancy's life was a cliché. She studied elementary education in college where she met Ron, a graduate student in law school. Nancy was pretty. She still wore her honey-colored hair long and straight. At 5'6" she was taller and leaner than Mom had been at Nancy's age, and she towered over Grandma who seemed to get shorter before our eyes.

Ron was considered a good catch. There was nothing controversial about his thoughts or actions; he planned and followed a straight path, laughed easily, had average athletic ability, and that straight guy knack for knowing the current statistics of every professional and college sports team. He was as handsome as a straight guy needed to be to interest a girl of Nancy's status. The result was a man who fit comfortably in any social or professional situation that he was likely to find himself.

Nancy graduated college the same year Ron graduated law school. He took a position at a law firm downtown, while she gave up any thought of a career. They lived in the city. Ron laughed at my jokes, which granted him my approval. He took an interest in my work and, not surprisingly, avoided asking about my personal life. He had more in common with Uncle Marty than with Dad, because they could talk endlessly about sports. Dad was more interested in discussing Ron's legal work. After a hint from Mom, Ron began to volunteer his legal services at least once a month.

Before Leda begins kindergarten, Nancy and Ron will pack up their city condo, and move to Sycamore Park or somewhere close to it. Like so many parents in 1987, they believed that it was difficult to keep children safe, and give them a good public education in city schools.

To paraphrase what many thought but few said, except to close friends and family, "the city schools are filled with blacks and Hispanics whose families either don't value education, or are too poor to move someplace else." The same kids were over-represented in crime, gangs, and the drop out rate.

These observations could not be discussed openly or rationally if it meant reflecting some of the root cause back onto the families, because those who monitored these discussions—including our own middle-class consciences—cried "racist." The guardians of righteousness called out parents who continued to take their children out of the city schools. These who were first to see racism as the prime motivator were either unable to or chose not to recognize that it was rational behavior to move children to safety.

By the time Leda finished mangling the blessing over the bread, her audience erupted in applause, as if she had just announced her engagement to a neurosurgeon. Leda clapped with glee as she looked around the table at the nurturing faces that beamed back at her.

"I can't wait until my Amy, the perennial student, gets married and gives me grandchildren." Aunt Marion omitted the fact that she already had grandchildren from her son Rob. But Rob's wife was Christian. She and Rob, like thousands of my generation, believed children could be raised to be of two faiths and of neither at the same time. Then, the notion continued, when the children grow to adulthood, without having had an education in either religion, or real role models for either, they could somehow wisely choose their own beliefs.

Rob felt that if they placed a Chanukah menorah alongside their Christmas tree, the children would somehow develop Jewish wisdom of the ages, and understand what it means to be a Jew. If they didn't, he didn't care. He considered himself a "cultural Jew," because he enjoyed lox and bagels on Sunday. Mom never criticized her brother and Aunt Marion directly, but I knew she didn't think much of their Jewish parenting skills. "They got out what they put in," she said when we first learned Rob would marry a Christian.

After one more generation, Rob's grandchildren might be only one-quarter Jewish. Beyond that, his progeny could be unaware of any Jewish ancestry, and they would never sit around a Shabbat dinner table debating ethics, laughing, and sharing in ancient traditions. They would not be given that particular form of a solid foundation to stand steady in an unstable world. There were and are handwringers among Jewish writers who believe American assimilation will painlessly accomplish what the Tsars and Hitler could not.

The assimilated families of Uncle Marty and Aunt Marion welcomed Rob's wife warmly, but Aunt Marion regretted not getting the daughter-in-law she had envisioned. Rob's wife had no interest in the traditions Aunt Marion had spared her own children, in her rush to make them successful American suburbanites. Now she tried unsuccessfully to share with her grandchildren the traditions she had ignored for a generation.

Rob and his wife never joined us for Shabbat dinner. Aunt Marion decided to pin her hopes for Jewish grandchildren on Amy, who was now on her third post-graduate degree, and, I believe, enjoying a lesbian relationship.

"You know who wanted to be here tonight for Glenny's birthday? Melva."

"You talked to Melva? How is she?" Nancy looked up from Leda for a moment.

Everyone wanted to hear about Melva. My mother told me earlier about Melva's visit of the previous day.

"Her son, Dion—remember him? He brought her here yesterday for lunch. Poor thing. She's so crippled with arthritis, and she coughs terribly from all those years of smoking.

"Anyhow, she couldn't come tonight, since she doesn't dare go out at night. She's terrified in her neighborhood. You know, Jerry and I often told her we would help her pay the rent somewhere around here, but she never wanted to live this far north when all her friends were on the South Side."

Grandma interjected. "Nowadays the colored are more afraid of their own than they are of whites."

"Pretty ironic, I'd say," Uncle Marty added.

Fearing the conversation would go somewhere awkward, Mom continued in a louder voice. "Even though she couldn't see Glen yesterday, she came to catch up on everyone. She asked about each of you."

"She was always such a dear soul. She doesn't work, does she?" The older she got, the more Aunt Marion found everyone to be "a dear soul."

"Are you kidding? She can barely walk. I hate to say it, but it was as if she were here to say her "good-byes." Before she left, she paused in the entry to survey the living room and dining room. She wanted to know who does the cleaning. When I told her about the Polish woman, she just shook her head. She said the floor looked like it had too much wax on it."

"That's so dear. She's protective of your house still."

"Marion, I have to tell you, I felt sad as she left. It was strange." Mom placed a platter of roasted chicken on the table, and stood with her arms akimbo, her face doubtful. "She was always like a family member, but she was an employee too, and while we adored each other, we weren't typical friends. I didn't know what to say or do, but I wanted to be helpful. We hugged for a long time, and told each other to take care."

When Mom told me about her meeting with Melva, I was saddened and felt remiss. I hadn't forgotten that I once promised Melva a big house with a rocking chair on the front porch, but I never came close. I'd still like to have a house like Twelve Oaks, with a big staircase to descend to greet my gentleman callers, but it was unlikely considering the trajectory of my income.

After Melva retired, poor health made her life more difficult. She was in and out of Cook County Hospital, because that was the only place to go without health insurance. I don't know what kind of care she received, because I never visited her. I was too involved in my early twenties with school, career, and the newly found joy of gay sex.

I knew she needed money, and that my parents sent her checks. I'd send her $25 or $50, two or three times a year. It was only recently that I started to have extra cash at the end of each month. I sent her cards on her birthday, Mother's Day, Valentine's Day, and Christmas, but I knew it wasn't enough. I told myself that things would get better for me, and there would be more time, and then I would send more. But of course there's never enough time.

I called Melva that morning, told her everything about work and my friends. I told her I missed her, and thought about her all the time. I asked if she'd like to go to a Cubs game with me sometime, and she just laughed and coughed, and told me I'd have to carry her on my back to get there. She sounded weak and tired.

My family and I attended Melva's funeral during the autumn of that year. When Mom called me with the news of Melva's passing, I thought of the lyrics of an old "Negro spiritual" I learned in grade school. It was about finally laying down one's burdens. At the funeral, her family treated us like dignitaries, and reminded me how much Melva loved me. My tears flowed freely as I listened to the cadence of the preacher; a cadence that brought me back to that Sabbath night long ago, when a South Side reverend spoke at our temple.

Melva had trudged through her life with quiet resignation and dignity, and I prayed she found her way to a peaceful eternity. She was among the souls most deserving of that peace.

"What's going on with her family?" Uncle Marty always liked Melva.

"Well, her husband is pretty much an invalid. Her son, Dion, is still a teacher. He's divorced and remarried. He has nine grandchildren—and he's about your age, Marty."

"Hey, Honey. How would you like to have nine grandchildren?" Uncle Marty patted Aunt Marion's hand.

"I'm only asking for one from my Amy."

"Oh, and Melva's sister, Dorsey, remember her? She worked for Lilly Roth all those years. Anyhow, last year she dropped dead of a heart attack right on the L. She was on her way to Lilly's and died. Remember Dorsey?"

My mother's recollection of Dorsey brought back my own memory. Around the time I was ten, I remember I picked up the phone to make a call; instead I overheard Melva talking to her sister Dorsey on the basement extension.

"Melva, you are too close to those kids. Don't forget your own family. Those Roth kids don't say a thing to me but, 'Hello, Dorsey,' and 'Good-bye, Dorsey,' and that's just how I like it. That Roth girl is giving her folks plenty of trouble. She has a boyfriend who wants to move to Canada, rather than go fight in Vietnam, and she says she's going to go with him. I tell her parents not to worry. Just hide that hair dryer she sits under all day and night, and she won't ever leave the house without it."

Dorsey was unaware of how clever she was, just like the black girls at school. She had a knack for nailing people with honest observations that cracked me up.

"Remember when everyone had a black housekeeper? Everyday on the Ls and trains it was like a mass migration of black women to the North Side by day, and back south at night. Now, I don't know anyone who has black help at home," Aunt Marion said.

"That's because nowadays, my dear, there's no shame in not working and collecting welfare, but apparently there is shame in being a cleaning woman. It's a good thing the Mexican and Polish women haven't heard the news, or they'd all stay home, and you ladies would have to find the next minority working its way up the ladder," Uncle Marty answered.

"Honey, did anyone tell you that this dinner is delicious?" Dad looked at Mom, who was now seated next to him, and smiled.

"Why thank you, Jerry. Now that you mention it, no one has."

"Well, it is."

Everyone jumped in. "Great." "Very good." "Terrific."

"I've had better."

"Oh, Marty, you never change. Just ignore him, Eileen."

"Listen Marion, after being his big sister for, how many years is it Marty? Fifty-seven years? I think I know to ignore ninety-nine percent of what he says."

"You mean you listen to one percent? I didn't think there was even that much worth listening to."

"Leda, do you hear how my beloved sister and my devoted wife talk to your great-uncle Marty? Isn't it terrible? I hope you'll be more respectful to me."

"Not if she repeats what we say about you in private, Uncle Marty."

"Et tu, Nancy? I'm cut to the quick."

"Uncle Marty, you know I'm only kidding. Everyone loves you—except Glen."

"Hey, don't get me involved. At least not until I cash my birthday checks."

So went another Shabbat dinner. Grandma, mostly quiet, watched Leda closely, eyes twinkling, and thinking I don't know what. Grandma was our last link to her generation.

Grandpa's legacy resided somewhere in each of us, reminding us to strive to be our best selves, and to lend a hand to anyone who might need one, without judgment. I struggled with that.

Uncle Marty was as unapologetic as ever for his opinions that we would come to call politically incorrect. In fact, the daily news fueled his belief that blacks were their own worst enemies, as a generation went on what appeared to be an orgy of drugs and violence, while children were left to fend for themselves, and the prisons filled with their absent fathers.

"It's a paradox," Mom would say. I see more and more middle class blacks everywhere, and at the same time, they remain invisible. Maybe it's a good sign that they've transitioned smoothly from second class to full citizenship."

"Well," said Uncle Marty, "the black women I see working at the post office seem to have no customer service work ethic at all. I defy anyone to deny they've had the experience of watching these indifferent automatons as they move like molasses in January. Holy hell, these women would never survive in the private sector with their lack of customer care. But you can't fire them. They're government employees."

"Marty, watch your language." Aunt Marion was probably the most unchanged over the years.

"Here is something to think about," I said. "For my whole life we've sat around this table talking about civil rights, social justice, and blacks. Why were these topics such a large part of our discussions?"

For a rare moment, no one said anything, each retreating into his or her own thoughts. Then Dad spoke up.

"Well, social justice and civil rights are tied together, and they are eternal topics, and central to our values. No doubt they've been in the forefront of American life during your lifetime."

Over in Hampden, gangs had found their way into the schools. The pushing and shoving we tolerated twenty years earlier now seemed quaint compared to the use of weapons and drugs. I no longer knew what the school board's attitude was toward that behavior, or if they ever recognized that they were complicit in its growth, in spite of their good intentions.

A few of the kids Nancy and I grew up with were raising their own children in Hampden. They believed the integrated experience, combined with outstanding educational programs, was an unparalleled combination for raising bright, productive adults. The majority of our friends, including Nancy's closest friend, Marla, and my friends Ken and Gary, chose to raise their kids in flagrantly homogenous suburbs beyond Hampden and Michigami.

I understood their decision not to return to Hampden, because I would never accept sending Leda to a school where she would likely suffer physical harm, and her education would be compromised to boost the self-esteem of bullies.

CHAPTER FORTY-EIGHT

Saturday, April 21, 2001

Ken called early that morning. "Hey, guess what I got in the mail?"

"Another subpoena from Cindy's lawyer?"

"No. Besides that."

"A letter from the ABA disbarring you after that last holiday party you threw with all those strippers?"

"No. Besides that."

"I give up. Tell me."

"There's going to be a thirty-year reunion for our junior high class next month. Isn't that a blast? Won't that be fun?"

"Ken, are you forgetting I didn't graduate from junior high school with you guys? I left on kind of a low note. There are maybe four of you that I still talk to, while perhaps a dozen want to lynch me."

"Oh, come on, Glen. It was 31 years ago. Who even cares? Besides, all the kids from grade school will be there. You haven't seen them since 1970."

"That's right, because I didn't go to Hampden High."

"Yeah, but now is your chance to see everyone. We never did a grade school or junior high thing. Come on Glen. I bet Ben Rubin will be there, and I hear he still looks hot."

I loved the way Ken comfortably teased me; but how did he know about the passion for Ben that I never revealed?

"I don't know. It would be funny to see how all those fifth graders look in their forties. I mean, look how funny you look now."

"Ha, ha. That's not what this twenty-five-year old paralegal said before she left here this morning."

"Straight men are pigs." I said.

"And you love that about us, don't you?"

"Never mind. Anyhow, I didn't get an invitation. I can't just crash the party."

"Oh please. You know how informal these things are. It's going to be in a bar in Hampden. I don't think anyone will be guarding a velvet rope."

"Well, I'll think about it."

"Glen, listen. Barbara Needleman will be there. She still wants you. I'm even jealous. She turned out to have the best tits at Hampden High."

"Gee. That's certainly going to make me want to go—NOT!"

"You're going. Gary and I already decided. Kevin McPherson and Curtis May are probably in prison. If they show up, we'll protect you."

"Just like you did back in seventh grade?"

"Yeah. Only this time, keep your mouth shut, you bigot."

"Okay Mr. N-double-A-C-P."

"So you'll go?"

"Get me the details. I'll go with you and Gary. Is Rachel going?"

"Spouses don't usually go to reunions, but knowing Gary and Rachel, she'll go, rather than be separated from him for even one evening. They're so lovey-dovey, I could puke."

"You're just jealous, because he has a perfect marriage and perfect kids. I've had Shabbat dinner at their house, and they remind me of my family when I was growing up. Thank God for families like Gary's or I'd end up the last Jew in America."

"I'm changing the subject. In fact, I'm hanging up. I've got the kids today. I'll get you the reunion details later. Bye, cocksucker."

"See you, carpet muncher."

CHAPTER FORTY-NINE

Saturday, May 19, 2001

I t was one of those warm May nights that enticed everyone to
do something somewhere around the city. I planned on drinking a few martinis at the reunion, so I left my car in the garage,
and took the L to the Hampden station. Ken, Gary, and Rachel
were there to meet me. The first thing I did was tell Rachel how
hot she looked. She was plain, but not unattractive, and her figure was full.

"What about me?" Ken demanded.

"Yes, Ken. You're pretty too. Of course, you'd never even get a
second look in Boystown."

The four of us walked to the bar from the L station. Illinois
was six years from a public smoking ban, so upon entering the
dark bar, we were assaulted with cigarette smoke. It mingled with
the scent of beer and the mothballs from the men's urinals. We
must've looked out of place, i.e. old, because the bartender silently pointed to a private room.

I hadn't decided how open I'd be about being gay. Some of my classmates must've heard through the grapevine. Others would pick up on that intangible gay vibe, and the more dense folks might divine I was "divine" by my lack of a wife, ex-wife, or kids.

If people were going to talk about me, I'd prefer they comment on my youthful appearance, or my recently acquired wealth. Neither being true, my sexuality was a more likely topic.

On top of the pressure of coming out directly to so many people, was the fear that the incident that drove me from school would be as big a story as it was in 1970. Which black kids would be there? Did my use of the "N" word loom as large in their minds as it did in mine?

There were about twenty-five animated people standing around the bar or tables of food. The center of the room was empty, begging for dancers to the Motown soundtrack. I was excited, zeroing in on faces I recognized. Debbie Spivey, the girl with whom I shared the Mace experience, ran over to us.

"Ken, Glen, and Gary, the studs of our seventh grade homeroom." We exchanged hugs, and Gary introduced her to Rachel.

Debbie had that healthy, North Shore, just-played-tennis-today look. She was divorced, and in touch with Ken since his divorce, so she knew my story. We had the "catch up" conversation that would be repeated several times that night. Debbie lived in one of the tonier suburbs just west of Sycamore Park, with her two kids. She must've had a good divorce attorney, because she spent her days volunteering at the Botanic Garden. Although she had gone to Yale, and majored in French, she quit her teaching job when her first child was born. Animated and perhaps tipsy, she waved the hand that wasn't holding the cosmopolitan back and forth as she talked about her kids.

As casually as if she were asking where I bought my Kenneth Cole shoes, Debbie asked if I had a boyfriend. Bless her. I was already glad I came, but I avoided eye contact with anyone else, until I ordered a very dry vodka martini, straight up.

The bartender was hot and gay, but I saved that thought for another time. At least I wasn't the only one in the room. I might even find an old classmate or two who I somehow missed at the bars over the years. Maybe Ben Rubin would come out to me, confessing his love after all these years.

That's when I saw him. He still had it. He was talking to two ruddy-faced, bloated jocks who hadn't held up as well as Ben. I heard bits and pieces about Ben from time to time. He had gone on to a successful college football career, quarterbacking his way into the local news. He made money, trading commodities on Chicago's exchanges. To frost his perfect cake, he married a model—Jewish yet—and his son was quarterback of Sycamore Park's football team.

I sauntered over to them, channeling early John Travolta. I reminded myself that Ben was my best friend before junior high school. The three jocks tensed up as I eased into their circle, but Ben's wife smiled warmly.

"Hi," I said to her. "I was Ben's best friend in grade school—before he became too cool for me." She laughed while Ben and the jocks smiled tightly. His wife's dark eyes twinkled, her skin flawless, and her smile dazzling. She radiated genuine kindness.

"Karen, this is Glen. He didn't go to high school with us, but we were good friends when we were younger. So what's up Glen?"

"Oh, just the usual. College, grad school, working, etc."

I got no response from Ben and the other two jocks. In fact, they closed their circle leaving me to talk to Karen. She was an active volunteer for the main Jewish charity in Chicago, helping to organize some of the more successful fund-raising events. Oh Ben. I can only imagine how you attracted such a wonder woman to be your wife. I liked her, and I was jealous of her—and of Ben—but for radically different reasons.

Realizing Ben was not going to be my next lover, I moved on and almost bumped into a black man who it seemed planted himself in front of me on purpose.

"Okay Glen, you have to guess who I am. I recognized you immediately. Now it's your turn."

I looked at the face, and as he began to smile, he took the form of an old friend.

"Cleon! Good to see you." We hugged warmly.

"How could I not recognize you?" I said. "You haven't changed at all. You still look like you did in third grade, except you aren't wearing a white shirt with a dickey underneath."

Cleon laughed. We stood close to each other, clinked glasses, and toasted to old friends. He was the happily married father of two children, and lived in Michigami, in the part that was part of the Hampden school district. His children were in the same elementary school where Cleon and I became friends.

"What do you do for a living?"

"I teach biology at Michigami High School," he answered with some detectable pride.

"Way to go, Cleon! A science teacher. Wow. And at my Alma Mater."

"That's right. I remember when you transferred out of Hampden. Just for the record, I didn't think it was fair that they pushed you out."

So there it was—the incident. It wasn't forgotten. But Cleon's comment was gracious, and left me freshly horrified that the "N" word once came out of my mouth.

"Oh God, I'm so sorry Cleon. It was a terrible day, an awful situation. My grandfather had just died, and Kevin and Curtis..."

Cleon interrupted me. "That's okay, honky," he said with a grin. "I was there. I said the same thing you said about them, only I was smart enough to say it under my breath."

I spontaneously hugged him again, and he reciprocated. I told him about my life and coming out. He never flinched.

"Well, it must've been tough for you. I hope things stay good, and no one ever calls *you* names." There was that grin again, and he winked at me.

We went through the formality of exchanging phone numbers, but we both knew we didn't have enough in common to build our friendship anew. The exchange of numbers was a sign to each other that we wished circumstances were otherwise. I took pride in the fact that our differences had nothing to do with race, but more with lifestyle.

"Cleon, one more thing. My parents still live in the house I grew up in. My mother and grandmother loved you. Grandma's gone now—she died in '95 at age 99 —but as long as you live and work in Michigami, stop by some day. My mother will freak out when you tell her who you are, and then she'll hug you to death. And bring your kids. She loves kids, and I haven't done her much good in that respect."

"I just might do that."

"Hey you. What are you doing here? I thought you'd be sheriff of Macon County Georgia by now." This was followed by uncontrollable laughter from the woman who said it— Pamela Blake. Tanya Wilkes, George Adams, and Charles Dawson were standing with Pamela, joining in the laughter. George looked as sexy as ever. Crowded in with them were Leslie, Debbie, Louis Gottfried (who was still good friends with George), and Ken, everyone a member of my seventh grade class.

I had a smile frozen on my face as I quickly ran a mental Geiger counter over Tanya, George, Charles, and particularly Pamela. I relaxed. The reading was zero.

"How you doing, boy?"

"That was pretty funny. You had me going for a minute." Everyone laughed again.

"Hey, when I called you a fag sometimes, you didn't have to take me so seriously. I hear you're living the life." That was George's attempt at humor. There was no chance I was staying in the closet that night.

"George, don't be so modest. You know about me from personal experience. Don't you remember?" More laughter, including from George, although I thought he suddenly looked less comfortable.

I looked around the room, and noted I was standing in the most integrated group. Whatever fears I harbored about the welcome I would receive from my former black classmates were replaced with a good dose of serotonin and other endorphins mixing nicely with the vodka. I was having a great time. The rest of the conversation was the same one repeated all evening as each person listed what she or he considered life's highlights. I was the lone exception to the marriage and children scenario. Each of us had at least one degree, and gone on to work in a managerial position or a profession. Tanya, George, Charles, Pamela, and Cleon: they were the nearly invisible middle-class blacks who represented what Grandpa and Mom believed was the future of all black America when given opportunity.

I took note of the fact that almost all of the blacks I spoke to, with the exception of Cleon and Tanya, still lived in Hampden. Tanya married a wealthy publisher, and lived in some downtown penthouse, and sent her kids to a private school. "I didn't want them exposed to any of those gang bangers." In 1970, I think her comment would have been considered heretical among black leaders. Was Tanya a black racist against blacks, or simply a mother who wanted the best for her children, not unlike my sister Nancy?

Gary was having a great time with some of the other geeks reminiscing about using slide rules in physics. These were the guys who didn't have sex until they had their first girlfriend in college; the girls they most likely stayed with through college, and then married, fearing lightening was unlikely to strike twice.

Adam Rivkin, Larry Kellman, and Jeff Fink were devoted family men. Initials abounded among these grandsons of poor immigrants: MD, JD, CPA. They lived in the suburbs that were the next step for the Jews who left Michigami, looking for bigger homes, and more isolated sub-divisions—the ones where they couldn't possibly walk to a grocery store or a drugstore like Sandberg's.

I spied tall George Turner, the guy I was supposed to lead around school when his group visited us in fourth grade, and who ended up leaving me in his wake. I remembered how he denied ever knowing me when asked by a co-worker of mine years earlier, so I decided I'd punish him by ignoring him—if only he would look my way. He was too busy flirting with Nancy Lefko and a gaggle of the mall girls.

Bruce, the kid who passed the sissy test on the school bus, and ended up with a bloody arm, now sported gold chains that protruded over his potbelly. He lived in Florida, and was evasive about his career.

Out of the corner of my eye I noticed two attractive women entering the room, laughing together. Ken was already rushing over to them, and I followed.

"Oh my God, Barbara, Sandy, you guys look great! You haven't changed since we all went to the movies together in seventh grade." I gushed a bit gayly about their appearance, but then I didn't care if either or both would sleep with me.

"I was going to say what Glen just said, but with a bit more testosterone in my voice."

Not to let Ken have the last word, I responded quickly. "Yes, now that he's divorced—it was infidelity on your part Ken, if I'm not mistaken—Ken is looking to hook up with…anyone."

We all laughed. Barbara and Sandy already knew I was gay, and that Ken was divorced. Sandy never married, and lived with some wealthy guy on a boat off Florida. I noticed she was looking wrinkly around the cleavage, but I resisted reminding her to avoid the sun. Barbara remained married to a guy she met in college, and lived a life much like my sister Nancy. I wanted to ask Barbara about her sexy brother, but decided against it. The other three graciously reminisced with me about junior high and grade school, since I hadn't shared their high school experiences. Ken never did get to see or touch Sandy's breasts.

The room had become crowded. I decided to look for Marybeth Mays and Donna Harding, the two black girls for whom I had the warmest feelings. Neither one attended. I returned to Tanya and George, and presented them with a verbal list of former black classmates to get whatever updates they could provide. Was it racist to only ask blacks about other blacks? They didn't seem to mind, so I continued.

Serena Gibson, who with her permanent scowl, eyes held like mere slits, hot temper, and formidable size, struck terror into anyone she approached, was a bailiff for Cook County—a perfect match. And now she was on the side of justice for all.

Michael Baker was on the Hampden police force. Like father, like son. I would like to have seen him. He and I were at the core of the incident on my last day in a Hampden school. I wondered how he remembered it.

Marybeth Mays was a nurse at Hampden Hospital. Tanya and George hadn't heard anything about Donna Harding since high school. Nor did they know anything about Derrick Dawson, who tried to steal my Fudgesicle, and squeezed an orange on Jeff Fink's head in shop class; or Everett Bryant, whose enormous cock was the talk of the locker room; or most importantly, Curtis May and Kevin McPherson. As the evening wore on, it became obvious that neither Curtis nor Kevin would attend. I'm not sure whether my joy at not being confronted by them was outweighed by my disappointment at not seeing them, and figuring out where I stood. We were now adults with over thirty years of civil rights behind us. Even if they hadn't forgotten me, and still harbored some animosity towards me, perhaps we could've worked out a truce. The feeling in the room was so light that I couldn't imagine another outcome. We might even hug and laugh about it, sort of like I did with Pamela, who had taken their side.

Darlene Fine, Ben Ruben's old girlfriend, played the only sad note of the evening, and it wasn't the fact that she put on forty pounds. She told us that Steve Tompkins, whose name was always followed with "the one whose parents are divorced," died of a drug overdose in Texas.

Norman Garfinkel looked embarrassed when I reminded him how he used to walk around the locker room with his cock pushed back between his legs, announcing that he couldn't find his dick. I should've been sensitive to the fact that his wife was standing next to him. Blame it on the vodka.

People began leaving. The initial excitement dissipated, and there was no one left to re-discover. I already had friendships with the people with whom I always had the most in common: Ken and Gary. I didn't strike up a new friendship with anyone who wasn't already a friend in junior high. No one changed much. The same thing that would've happened at a party thirty years ago happened again: after about ten minutes, we ran out of things to say.

CHAPTER FIFTY

Tuesday, November 4, 2008

As the election results came in on that wonderful, warm, magical night in Chicago, and it became clear that Barrack Obama would be our next president, my friends and I, were at first incredulous, and then overcome with joy, which lead to cheerful shouts. Illinois was no longer an island of blue in the middle of America. The co-opting of the Republican Party, and perhaps even the Supreme Court, by large corporations at the expense of the middle class, and by those who want America to become a theocracy, had driven the rest of us to give up any vestige of independence, and to rush into the arms of the Democratic Party. The fact that the face of the Party was now a black man was a bonus for me. It proved indisputably that millions of Americans could look beyond race, and judge a man by his character—and you should excuse me, Dr. King—by his *conduct*. I had proudly cast my ballot for Mr. Obama, proclaiming as I had for years that I do not judge on the basis of color. Grandpa would've been overcome with joy, and his pride in America uncontainable.

Obama *was* the better candidate, and I chose him over a white man. There could be no more blaming the honkys for keeping the black man down. Or so I naively hoped. (Admission: I came to regret my vote for Obama, but not because of his color, but rather his lack of the ability to lead. In my dislike for him as President, score another one for character over color).

There are some ill winds blowing over America's black citizens. Since 1970, there are generations raised by young parents in an atmosphere of unrelenting black on black crime, drugs, and thug worship. The violence is fueled by so much more than a simple hatred of whites. I overhear blacks on public transportation or calling out to each other in the street with a vocabulary and grammar that I can barely recognize as English. I can't foresee any successful integration into mainstream America. Instead, there is a growing chasm.

In one way, the world is becoming more color blind as technology and the global economy relentlessly call out for the brightest and the best no matter who they are. And judging by the faces in Silicon Valley, they are white, brown, and yellow, but not black.

Granted, I'm looking in from the outside, but it seems that for a number of blacks, life in 2008 is better than in 1970. I read that large numbers of the black population are leaving large cities for the suburbs. These are the growing number of middle-class blacks who don't want their children going to the crime ridden, city schools populated by other blacks. It used to be called "white flight," a sign of intolerance and bigotry. Does black flight make white flight look reasonable in hindsight?

The Asian American population, who came here asking for nothing, has increased, and continues to thrive and excel in every aspect of American life. Successful immigrants put demands on themselves, not on others.

My family knew instinctively that family, culture, and values that were modeled in real life—not just given lip service to— determined the success of the next generation. They demonstrated it around the Shabbat table, week after week, with lessons learned from thousands of years of teachings, and from two-thousand years of developing survival skills, as a tiny minority in mostly hostile lands.

Mom and Dad saw the flaw in assigning blame to others for any failure to raise moral children. I saw it when they returned frustrated from school board meetings, or in my mother's case, from her work at a school that was quickly becoming bi-lingual. But to verbalize critical observations in 1970 was unpopular and against the tide of America's flow—a movement that began righteously enough, with the struggle for civil rights.

CHAPTER FIFTY-ONE

Friday, June 24, 2011

It was the Friday after the "urban youth" attack on the woman on Michigan Avenue in front of Tiffany's. I waited on the L platform, on my weekly trek to Shabbat dinner. A group of black youths, wearing their pants pulled down almost to their knees posed boisterously nearby. One threw a crumpled potato chip bag onto the platform. This could have been the day back in 1970 when I witnessed the same thing on the way to the Cubs game. I seethed.

Among us were a smattering of black men and women in business attire, carrying briefcases, and listening to iPods through earphones. Other than their race, these professionals were indistinguishable from their white counterparts. When the train arrived, I waited to see which car the underwear brigade entered, so I could choose a different one.

When I entered the car, two seats were available, each next to a black man. The first man looked to be about forty. His casual clothes were disheveled, and in spite of announcements to not place items, "on the seat next to you, so that others may sit down," his canvas bag took up the seat to his left. His stony glare, dared me to ask him to move it, and reminded me of the time I'd looked into the eyes of Serena Gibson and Kevin McPherson in junior high. This man was living in 1970. The other black man, race not withstanding, looked like me. He stared out the window, a briefcase in his lap, and wires in his ears. I sat next to the guy most like me. Doesn't everyone?

Mom and Dad were well over eighty, but the weekly Shabbat dinner was sacrosanct. As I approached the house, I looked briefly at the dining room window to see if I could catch a glimpse of Grandma's ghost. Kugel, the Miniature Schnauzer who replaced Latke upon his death, peered excitedly out the window in my direction.

Mom, looking tinier each week, opened the door, and the familiar Friday night smells from the kitchen bathed me in comfort. Her menu was much the same as Grandma's. Nancy offered to take over the cooking, but Mom wasn't ready to relinquish her control. Mom's hair was neither its original dark brown, nor its natural white. She kept it light brown and continued her generation's habit of weekly trips to the beauty shop. On Friday nights, she wore dresses under her apron. Never pantsuits.

Dad also shrank, and the top of his head was completely bald, although around the Shabbat table it was covered by his yarmulke. The lenses on his glasses were much thicker than they used to be. Mom reminded us from time to time that when she married Dad he looked like Robert Alda. I came across Robert Alda in a movie from the 1930s, and based on old photos of Dad, she was right. Now he looked like Zadie.

At 6:00 we were seated, and I glanced at the faces around the table. Mom hovered near the door to the kitchen like Grandma used to. Dad sat at the head of the table. Nancy sat next to Dad. Seated between Nancy and her husband Ron were their two children: Leda, twenty-seven and a teacher, and Mica, a twenty-three-year-old law school student. Next around the table were my cousin Amy and her twelve-year-old son, Marty, named for Uncle Marty who died fourteen years earlier at age 67 of cardiac arrest.

Amy's life partner, Rose, sat on Marty's other side. Amy and Rose have been together for fifteen years. Rose, who is black, is a nurse. Amy, in spite of three post-graduate degrees, prefers life as a stay-at-home mom. Marty was the result of the in-vitro fertilization of one of Rose's eggs that was implanted in, and carried by Amy. The great-grandson of Leo and Mae Epstein; the grandson of Uncle Marty and Aunt Marion; and my cousin, Marty Epstein, is black. While growing up and listening to Grandpa and Uncle Marty, quiet Amy had come to her own conclusions about race and what mattered to her.

Aunt Marion, blond and lovely at eighty-something, sat between Rose and me. She never hid her favoritism for Marty over her other grandson. Rob's son was a bit older than Marty, but Aunt Marion hardly spoke about him. When Aunt Marion wasn't around, we debated if her favoritism for Marty was based on his bearing her late husband's name, or because he was a sweeter kid than Rob's, or because he was Jewish, while Rob's son was not. We all had our theories, but clearly Marty's race was immaterial to Aunt Marion. Another score for something over color.

Dad stood and asked Marty to stand next to him. He then placed one hand on Marty's head and blessed him, just as he had blessed Leda and Mica each week until they had graduated college, and as he had blessed Nancy and me a generation before. To Dad, the end of the childhood blessing came with a Bachelor's degree.

I recalled a conversation around this table forty years earlier when Uncle Marty elicited a few gasps after he asked Mom how she would feel if Nancy married a black man. Mom's response was she wouldn't care if he were a Jewish man of good character.

We affirmed Mom's words by discussing Marty's bar mitzvah date which was already set for the following April.

When the blessings were finished, Mom and Leda brought in the food. Aunt Marion paid Mom the same compliments she used to pay to Grandma. Ron asked for salt for his chicken soup, and Nancy told him he didn't need it. "Grandma Mae's recipe is perfect and doesn't need embellishment."

Mom laughed and handed a saltshaker to Ron. "Nancy, I'm not Grandma. If he wants salt, let him have salt. Of course, his blood pressure is another story."

"Ron, if you should smell Ben Gay in the middle of the night, you'll know Grandma Mae is around to haunt you." Dad joked.

Dad asked Marty about his interpretation of his Torah reading for his bar mitzvah, although it was ten months away. Coincidentally, Marty was given the same Torah portion for his bar mitzvah that I read and interpreted.

"Marty, you can use my bar mitzvah speech, and save yourself some time," I said, half joking. Marty quickly took to the idea. Dad saw my offer as an opportunity to give Marty a lesson in morality. Mom looked with admiration at Dad. It was the same look of admiration that she had for Grandpa and Dad when I was Marty's age, and they administered *The Ethics of The Fathers* to Nancy and me.

Amy and Rose gave me a ride home. Marty was staying with his Grandma Marion for the weekend. The car radio was turned to the news. A black man had walked up to an off duty black policeman, and shot him to death. I kept quiet. Rose felt free to comment. "Asshole. Fucking asshole." I silently agreed but didn't feel free to respond.

The next story was about a black alderman going to jail for corruption. This time I made a joke before Rose could say anything.

"Hey. It is good to see that blacks really are no different from the rest of us—especially the politicians." Amy and Rose both chuckled.

During the national news we endured a story about Republicans spending their energy to defend the "sacred institution of marriage" since it was "under assault from the President with support from the gay lobby."

"I think Newt Gingrich did enough damage to the 'sacred institution' without our help," Amy said. Rose and I grunted our agreement.

"In fact," Amy continued. "I'd like to see all those who think marriage is so sacred, work to make divorce illegal. Perhaps then they'd sound less hypocritical."

In International news, a report from the UN Human Rights Council—composed of such bastions of justice as China, Libya, Uganda, Iran, Cuba, Syria and Saudi Arabia—condemned Israel for defending its citizens from rockets fired by Hamas at Israeli civilian targets within Israel, thus completing the triple crown of subjects that tie my stomach in knots.

A vibration from my phone drew me out of the depths to the day-to-day. It was a text from Gary, asking me to call him when I got home.

CHAPTER FIFTY-TWO

Later That Night

"Hey, Glen. I thought you might be interested in this. Remember Mr. Wendell, our gym teacher?"

Remember him? He was my athletic mentor, my hero. From the day of the incident, after he rescued me from the mob, and carried me over his shoulder to the relative safety of his office, he became a continuous source of discomfort. He shamed me with his stony silence as I sat in his office waiting for Mom.

"Did he die?"

"No. Not yet. But he's terminally ill. He's at home in hospice care. His name was read from the list in our synagogue when they say the prayer for the sick. I know he wasn't Jewish, but how many Darnell Wendells could there be?"

Not many in a Michigami synagogue. Gary continued.

"Maybe one of his old students keeps in touch with him, and cares enough to put him on the list, or one of his kids or grand-kids married into the faith. Anyhow, I followed up, and found out the details, and I thought you might be interested. I remember you two had a sort of bond at one point."

Of all the blacks at school whom I offended back on that day, I felt the most angst about Mr. Wendell. I regretted not sitting down with him, and apologizing. If I'd just said, "I'm sorry, I'm ashamed of myself," and let him take it from there.

It would've been easy to locate Mr. Wendell. He lived in Michigami. But I was a lazy coward, and never made the effort. I made excuses: *I had been pushed to the limit. The insults I had received over the years in Hampden surely outweighed my one slip of the tongue. Some people deserved to hear what I said.*

But Mr. Wendell wasn't one of them, and he merited the chance to tell me what he thought of my "slip of the tongue," and to hear me say, "I'm sorry." If he wanted it, I was prepared to give him my explanation. But I wasn't willing to put all the control in his hands, with no guarantee of a favorable response. So for over forty years, whenever thoughts of Mr. Wendell came to mind, as they often did, I imprisoned them where thoughts survive by feeding off your conscience, until, and if, you're ready to free them, and face the consequences.

CHAPTER FIFTY-THREE

Saturday, June 25, 2011

I rang the doorbell on the street of modest houses, on the same block that Gary grew up. When I telephoned Mr. Wendell earlier that morning, I spoke to his wife, and introduced myself as Mr. Wendell's former student, and said I would like to pay him a visit. She immediately said "yes." I told her that I thought she should give him my name first, and ask if he would like to see me.

"Oh, don't worry. He loves to see all his former students—even the troublemakers."

"Well, I was a very specific troublemaker."

"Never you mind. Just come by. Saturdays are good. Anytime today. I won't say anything. We'll surprise him."

So, there I was. Was he up for this surprise? Maybe he wouldn't remember me, and it was my erratic ego that had caused me to think over all these years that he ever gave a damn about me, or what I said. That would give me an easy out, but not the resolution I sought.

Mrs. Wendell led me to the den where her husband sat on a recliner. It was hard to find the handsome, former football player residing within that small body, and behind the wizened face. He wore a silk bathrobe over pajamas and hospital socks that had holes cut out of the bottom. There was an I.V. pole behind him. I followed the tube from the hanging pack down to where it disappeared into the white tape on his left forearm. Mr. Wendell looked at me hard, and squinted. I hadn't said anything yet. Then his face broke into a wide smile, revealing a still impressive array of teeth.

"Why, it's you. Feigman. Glen Feigman. Holy Moses, boy. You're an old man now. You're making me feel old."

He reached out with his right arm.

"Hi, Mr. Wendell." I smiled back, and shook his hand. His grip, or lack thereof, matched his frail appearance.

"So you heard I was dying, huh? So you came to say 'good-bye' after, what is it, forty years of not saying 'hello'?"

"Not exactly. I've wanted to talk to you for a long time. Life got in the way, I guess."

"Feigman, I liked you. You weren't one for excuses. You were a hard worker. I figured you to be one who would go places. Catch me up. Married?"

"No." I thought I was comfortably out but I found myself hesitating.

"Are you gay, boy? I'm getting a vibe here. That's cool. I've got one of those. My boy Gerard likes the boys too. That's okay. Remember, I was always cool at school."

From the start he took control of our conversation. I let him continue.

"I know you went to college, probably graduate school, too. You got a good job? Are you making some decent cash?"

"Yes, yes, and I guess it's all relative, but I think so."

"Well, that's good."

"Are your folks still alive? I last saw your dad at your grandpa's funeral. Terrible day. And the last time I saw your mother was another terrible day in your life. You remember?"

So this is how it would begin.

"Yes. I remember. It was a lovely spring day, as I recall."

"I'll bet that's how you recall it. So tell me Glen, does your being here today have something to do with the events of that day back in, what year was it?"

"1970."

"1970. Damn, I wasn't even 40 years old. Now that I know what I know, I bet you noticed what a good looking guy I was." He smiled, again.

I blushed. I lowered my eyes like a shy maiden in front of Sir Lancelot. How right he was.

"1970. That was some time we were living in. Black power. Black pride. Black is beautiful. Say it loud. I'm black and I'm proud! I bet you were sick of hearing it."

"Not at all!" I lied.

"Yeah. Whatever. Listen, Glen. I met your family. I heard the things that they said about your grandfather at the funeral. You and a lot of those white kids—Jewish most of you—came from nice families that meant no harm to anyone. My granny from Mississippi used to call them 'genteel folk.' I knew that then, and I understand more now."

I wasn't sure where he was going, but I was certainly happy to have paid this visit.

"So you let that nut McPherson get to you. He got to you so bad, you crossed the line to say a naughty word. Nowadays, you can't say it even if you're seriously discussing the word itself. The "N" word, as we know it, is the only acceptable way for us non-thugs to say it. At least that's what I believe."

I emitted a closed mouth chuckle. Mr. Wendell's face reflected mischievous thoughts.

"Ooh! Glen Feigman said the "N" word. Oh my! That was not a cool thing to do in that school in 1970. It's not cool today either, under most circumstances. But even in 1970, I think we could have cut you some slack, considering what went on in that school every day, and what had happened to your family. But those were the early years of feeling out our new boundaries, when rational notions turned into irrational choices and behaviors. I'm not so sure we've come to the end of those times, or the new problems they've brought us."

I couldn't believe how keenly Mr. Wendell read the behaviors of our student body back then. Surely he spoke with wisdom that comes in hindsight. The changes that erupted in the years around 1970 were a relentless series of tremors, some mild, others violent. There was no time to analyze, diagnose, and prognosticate. We could only react, often in an attempt to ease the convulsions. Only the distance provided by the years could have provided the breathing room needed to notice the causal relationships Mr. Wendell now referenced.

"So tell me, Glen, does this have something to do with why you came to see me today? Did you have something to settle with me before I cross the finish line?"

Even at the end, straight guys cannot talk without employing sports analogies.

"Am I supposed to grant you some absolution for a sin that must've caused you guilt pains for forty years? Have you been wandering in the desert like Moses looking for the Promised Land? Ha! That's pretty good. I know you must feel guilty. Jews are always feeling guilty about something. Was saying the "N" word to a troubled boy like Kevin McPherson weighing you down all this time? Did it cause trouble for your family that also weighs on you? How can I help ease your suffering?" He grinned at me. I was speechless.

"You know, Feigman, it's true when they say some things take on more importance when you're at the end of your game, and others become trivial. The fact that you called Kevin McPherson something hurtful forty-odd years ago really doesn't matter much to me right now. I think even forty years ago it didn't matter too much, because I knew who you really were—except the gay thing, and now that doesn't matter."

"Aye, yi, yi. I feel so stupid. I don't know how to answer you. I know it might not mean a lot to you, but it still means a lot to me, because I respected you so much, and you were the only guy in my entire academic career who saw some athletic ability in me. You used to seek my input about the student council. The fact that you knew my family caused me to believe that what I said was a reflection on all of us. Yes, I felt guilty, and immediately wanted to apologize to you, to Kevin, and pretty much the whole black population of America. But things happened quickly, and everything got confused and tangled up and then…everyone went on with life. For me, it was unresolved, and I didn't have the courage or wisdom to fix it. I didn't seek the guidance I could've gotten from my parents, because I hated how it affected them."

Mr. Wendell didn't appear ready to jump in, so I continued.

"I learned at a recent class reunion that none of my black classmates from 1970, at least the ones that were at the reunion, remembered the incident with any animus. They made jokes about it. But it tore me up for a while, and it definitely created conflicts for my parents. The events of that time—Grandpa and then me—it confused my mother terribly."

I ran out of steam. He listened passively as I rambled. Now he looked at me, warmly.

"Okay, Feigman. If you're giving me the power to lay this heavy burden of yours to rest, then I thank you. I'm trying to rack up some good deeds, you know, just in case. Forgiveness is an important one. For both of us." He raised his right hand as if conferring a blessing upon me. "So, Glen Feigman, I forgive you. On behalf of the black people of the world, for whom

I am going to presume to speak, because I am sure they are all wrapped up in your concern and your welfare. I forgive you as well. You've done your forty year penance, and if you're the same kid I knew back then, you've done plenty of good in the world over the years."

"Well, I'd like to think so," I blushed a bit, and dammed up my natural urge to boast.

"I always saw that big-head side of you too. But that's okay. Nobody's perfect, eh, boy?"

We both laughed.

Mrs. Wendell entered the room, and asked I'd like some coffee and cake before I left. I sensed she was hoping I would decline; she looked at her husband in a way that told me he needed to rest.

"No, but thank you very much. I really should be going now."

She smiled, nodded, and disappeared.

Mr. Wendell and I looked at each other asymmetrically. My eyes were filled with their typical intense mix of sadness, joy, regret, guilt, and love. Mr. Wendell's eyes were only tired. Before I pulled my glance away, I saw one more instant of the twinkle that had charmed everyone who met him, including me.

I embraced him, carefully, and he patted my back with his right hand.

"You're a good man, Feigman. Be cool."

"You too, Sir." I don't know where the "Sir" came from. I never called anyone *Sir* in my life, unless I was trying to get some man's attention at a store or restaurant. But this time it seemed appropriate.

I thought quickly enough to spare him my usual, trite departing words, *be well*, since he was in hospice care. I felt his eyes follow me as I left the room. I heard a heavy sigh.

CHAPTER FIFTY-FOUR

A Few Minutes Later. We're here.

My route back to the city from Mr. Wendell's follows the canal that continues to separate Hampden from Michigami in so many ways. I'm in an upbeat, yet reflective mood. Maybe my exoneration from Mr. Wendell will finally exorcise my "N" word angst. It lay almost dormant for so long, but managed to give off a continuous low dose of radioactivity. I'll wait and see. I've been tricked before into thinking I put some thought or fear to rest, only later to find it was a temporary remission.

Perched near the bank of the Hampden side, I see my old junior high school, looking dated. A few years after my abrupt departure, they converted the junior high into an experimental school. I guess someone had his head out of his ass long enough to figure out that the population mix was untenable. The blacks and Jews were redistributed among three junior high schools in the district.

I'm glad for the exposure to integration I experienced during my years at the school. Many of the positive interactions I've had with blacks occurred at that school, although they coincided with so many negative ones.

Mr. Wendell, Cleon, Donna, et al were just people whose color became transparent to me, and knowing them gave me a glance at how good race relations could be. For better or worse, my junior high years informed my experiences with blacks, and formed a base for our future interactions. They started out so strong in elementary school, and started their slide with the black power movement.

My interracial experiences every day: in person, from the media, art, and popular entertainment, continue to affect my ability to go beyond first impressions based on skin color. I believe more than ever that I judge persons by the content of their character *and* their behavior, which so often is what you see right after color, and is often the visual representation of character. But the accumulated experiences such as the one I had in junior high, or standing on an L platform, or waiting in line at the post office, or the most recent experience walking down Michigan Avenue with my mother, make me cautious around blacks whom I don't know. I believe that is true for so many whites. I stand firm in my belief that personal experience is among the greatest factors in building race relations, and if those experiences tilt to the negative, then integration could drive the wedge between us even deeper, as it did for so many of us in 1970.

My hyperactive guilt gland thumps with talk of setting a higher bar for blacks to prove their character based on my experiences. I preach that until we can talk openly about race—I mean really openly—we will never reach a level of racial harmony in America that I truly would love to see. But I've been conditioned to shudder from any audible words or thoughts that disparage blacks in America. I know I'm not the only one, and that's going to continue to be an impediment to progress in race relations.

If the truth can set us free, then we're in trouble if we can't even think it, let alone say it.

The ups and downs of the intermingling of peoples of different races, religions, sexual orientations, and any other way we slice and dice ourselves plays out on everyone, and in all directions. If Louis Farrakhan took a moment to get to know my family, perhaps he wouldn't have his all-encompassing, knee-jerk hatred of Jews. Having known Melva stopped me in my tracks many times from making a sweeping generalization.

I'm more than halfway home now from Mr. Wendell's, and I have no tidy summary to make. Race relations are complicated in America, thanks to our unfortunate history. *Everyone's A Little Bit Racist*, a song from the Broadway musical *Avenue Q*, inevitably brings the laughter of recognition from the audience when it's performed.

Should we beat ourselves up? Do we acknowledge it, and do nothing, because maybe we feel justified in our personal beliefs? Or do we find ways to heal? "Repair the world," *Tikkun Olam*, is a tenant of Judaism. Applying that concept to my Hampden years through to today, I find as it says in our High Holiday liturgy, that the work is difficult, and the job isn't finished. It may never be.

There is no denying the guilt I carried with me from using the "N" word, and from the subsequent torment it brought to Mom. I'm not sure that the fallout from my incident was solely responsible for her troubled descent (or was it an ascent?) from a world of certainty to one shaded in gray. My outburst that lead to changing the school I attended; the circumstances around Grandpa's death; our run-ins with thieves, Mace sprayers, and rock throwers that year; followed by Mom's disappointing and frightening attempt to teach at an all black school, coalesced, and shook her to her foundation, loosening what had been life-long convictions.

Last night is when I dreamed I was standing alongside Dr. King as he made his "I have a dream" speech, and I fruitlessly attempted to get him to add, "conduct" to the alliteration of content of character. What, if anything, would be different today in race relations, and in the condition of the black community, if Dr. King took my humble advice, and included *conduct* as a part of the basis for how we should judge one another? Could it have created another guidepost for black America, and modified some of the extreme behaviors and conditions I witness and read about almost daily? In turn, would there have been more successes than failures at integration?

I can't believe that the talking heads of the Hampden school board and the angry black parents are correct in their assertion that the large, growing, and possibly permanent black underclass world of violence, crime, drugs, un-employability, and prison lie solely at the feet of some systematic effort to keep blacks down.

No matter who you are or when you read this, our struggles in 1970 through to this very day are likely your struggles too, although they might've morphed a bit. In 1970 we still believed, at least in America, that everything would continue to get better, and that our trajectory on all issues was positive. I can't say that has been the case. I want to believe that from wherever you might be looking back, you can say we were right—but I'm skeptical.

Like me, you probably gravitate to people who are most like yourself. Folks who are different can be threatening—at least until we get to know them.

I'm a few minutes from home, and my thoughts no longer linger in the troubled hallways of junior high or the intractable subject of race relations. Instead, I imagine our dining room table in Michigami set for Shabbat dinner. The ancient brass candlesticks and silver Kiddush cup my ancestors carried with them as they escaped misery toward the dream that America was for them, gleam from the reflected light of the chandelier. Like the wife of a Nantucket sailor, Grandma stands her watch at the front window, scrutinizing the horizon for a sign of Grandpa.

Matzah leaps with joy at the arrivals of Grandpa, Bubbie and Zadie, Mom and Dad, Uncle Marty, and Aunt Marion, my cousins, my great aunts, and other guests who join us from time to time on Friday nights. Grandma goes to the stove and lifts the lids on the pots, and opens the oven door, allowing the scents of Shabbat eve to merge with the sounds of my family. It's 1970, and the world outside the dining room window, the one facing our mysterious Catholic neighbors across the street, is in upheaval. We can't keep the world out, but we try to manage the changes without losing our way.

At the table, Dad blesses Nancy, my cousins, and me as our grandparents and Mom look on with love and pride. I feel safe with Dad's hand on my head. The other blessings are said, and we begin another Shabbat dinner replete with questions, discussions, arguments, opinions, reflections, and laughter, and all with an emphasis on ethics. This was the school that most effectively taught me, and challenged me to be my best self. I was blessed to have those Shabbat dinners, with a family that took responsibility for the man I was to become. I wish something like it for everyone else. It could only lead to a healed world.

Later, on those Shabbat nights, as my guilt and I would fall into sleep, the house would fall silent except for the hum of the dishwasher.

ABOUT THE AUTHOR

Glen Shuld is a graduate of Northwestern University and the Kellogg Graduate School of Management where he earned his master's degree. After growing up in a progressive home in Evanston, Illinois, he went on to work in marketing management at a Fortune 500 company for many years, and taught as an adjunct professor for the University of Chicago's Graham School of Continuing Education.

Currently, Shuld resides with his life-partner in Chicago, and is an owner of a commercial real estate investment company. He actively supports a number of social justice organizations, as well as animal and environmental protection agencies.

GLOSSARY OF YIDDISH TERMS
IN THE BOOK

(*Ch* is given the guttural pronunciation such as in the German *ach*)

A Gut a danke – Thanks to God.

Bar/Bat Mitzvah – Son or daughter of the commandment. At 13 a Jewish boy or girl is called to read from the Torah for the first time symbolizing his/her taking on the responsibility of living by God's Commandments. There are 613 spelled out in the Torah. Their specific relevance varies from Orthodox to Reform beliefs.

Bima – The altar from where the Torah is read.

Bubbie – Grandmother.

Challah – The braided egg bread used for Sabbath dinners and special occasions.

Drek – Crap.

Farshtunkinah – Stinking.

Goyim – Non-Jews. Other nations.

Goyisha – A non-Jewish type of person, object, or style.

Gut in himmel – God in heaven!

Guta nashuma – Good soul.

Haggadah – The book read at Passover Seders (see Seder) containing the biblical story of the Exodus from Egypt.

Hernuch – Listen to this. Listen again.

Hora – A group dance done in a circle, often with embellishments.

Kaluki – A type of gin rummy best played with four people, each with a hand of 13 cards.

Kazatsky – The dance usually done by men in a squatting position with their arms folded as they kick one leg out and back, and then the other, requiring physical strength, stamina, and healthy knees.

Kiddush cup – Literally, sanctification cup. The Kiddush refers to the blessing said over wine before the Sabbath dinner.

Kinder – Children

Kugle – Pudding. Often a noodle pudding: Lukshun Kugle.

Latke – A potato pancake, fried in oil and eaten to celebrate Hanukkah.

L'chayim – To life, used as a toast.

Machitenista (f), Machiteniste (m), Machitunim (pl) – The term for the direct relationship between the two sets of parents of a married couple. There is no English word for this relationship.

Mamela – Literally little mama, used as a term of endearment.

Matzah – The unleavened bread used at Passover.

Mensch – Literally a person, but signifies a person who is good down to their very core, and who does the right thing.

Mishpacha - Family

Mishugah. Mishuganeh. Mishagoyim. – Crazy. A crazy person. Crazy people. Mishigoss is craziness.

Mitzvah. Mitzvot (pl). – One of Gods 613 Commandments in the Torah, hence a good deed. See Bar mitzvah.

Mumzer – Bastard.

Oneg Shabbat – A small repast after Shabbat services.

Oy vey iz meer – Oh, woe is me.

Pipik – Belly button. Sometimes pronounced *puhpik*

Pish – To pee

Pushky – Small box used to collect money for charity or a rainy day.

Shmuck – A person who is a dick.

Shmutz – Dirt. Shmutzadik is dirty.

Shvartze(s) –The color black and black people.

Seder – Literally "order." Used to describe the ritual meal eaten on Passover, with foods symbolizing the Exodus from Egypt, and when the *Haggadah* (see Haggadah) is read.

Shabbat – Sabbath

Shanda – A shame

Shanda fer de shlaynim – A shame in front of the neighbors. Used if someone airs private matters publicly. Something one Jew might do that causes anti-Semites to judge all Jews accordingly.

Sheyna punim – Pretty face.

Shivah – The Hebrew word for seven, used for the seven days of mourning after a Jewish funeral.

Shtetl – A small village. Think of Anatevkah in *Fiddler on the Roof.*

Tallit – Prayer shawl with 613 pieces of fringe to serve as a constant reminder of the 613 Commandments or *mitzvot* (plural of *mitzvah*) in the Torah.

Tatala – Literally, little papa, used as a term of endearment.

Tuches – Your butt, your backside, your behind, etc.

Ver Vesach Vos – Go know from such things.

Vey iz meer – Woe is me!

Vilde chaya(s) – Wildlife, wild animal(s).

Zadie – Grandfather.

ACKNOWLEDGEMENTS

I would like to acknowledge the contributions of the following people to help me realize *The Color of Character*. Their assistance came in many ways, including, but not limited to: editorial skills, encouragement, example, friendship, love, patience, and wisdom.

Dr. Barry Bikshorn
Diane Briere de L'Isle
Patricia Bruhn
Dr. Eric and Heather Corndorf
Henry Engelhardt
Justine Knizeski
Amy Kolen
Randee Sable
Shirley Shechtman
Rabbi Victor Weissberg
Howard Weissman
Douglas Wood
Stephen Wright

A special acknowledgement to the late Ms. Ora Lee Bennett. She was the embodiment of the noblest characteristics of the human spirit: humble, compassionate, kind, and loving.